Lauralee

Linda Lael Miller

PUBLISHED BY POCKET BOOKS NEW YORK

This novel is a work of historical fiction. Names, characters, places and incidents relating to non-historical figures are either the product of the author's imagination or are used fictitiously. Any resemblance of such non-historical incidents, places or figures to actual events or locales or persons, living or dead, is entirely coincidental.

Another *Original* publication of POCKET BOOKS

POCKET BOOKS, a division of Simon & Schuster, Inc.
1230 Avenue of the Americas, New York, N.Y. 10020

ISBN: 0-671-60049-4

First Pocket Books printing December, 1986

10 9 8 7 6 5 4 3 2 1

POCKET and colophon are registered trademarks
of Simon & Schuster, Inc.

Printed in the U.S.A.

The Courtship of Jay McCallum, Esq.

"Mr. McCallum!" Lauralee hissed in the darkness of the saloon. A match was struck; the glass on a kerosene lamp clinked.

"I brought you some supper," she said, in a small voice.

"Thank you," he said, taking the plate from her.

"Aren't you going to ask me what I'm doing here?" Lauralee prodded, minutes later.

"I don't need to. I already know."

Lauralee was mortified. "You do?"

"Yep."

Lauralee moved to flee, but Jay caught her wrist.

"Lauralee," he said in a throaty rasp, and then he kissed her.

It was devastating, that kiss, crumbling things that had always stood strong inside Lauralee. Passion pounded in her ears. . . .

Somehow, the lamp was extinguished. . . .

Books by Linda Lael Miller

Banner O'Brien
Corbin's Fancy
Desire and Destiny
Fletcher's Woman
Lauralee
Memory's Embrace
Willow

Published by POCKET BOOKS

In loving memory of
Guy and Florence Wiley,
gentle spirits and true pioneers

CHAPTER
ONE

Halpern's Ferry, Washington
August, 1901

The scream was high-pitched and keening, carrying across the narrow stretch of the meadow and over the creek to the orchard. Lauralee Parker stiffened on her ladder for a split second, every sense laid bare to the sound, and then dropped the unwieldy apparatus with which she had been spraying the high branches of an apple tree. Clad for work in a divided bloomer skirt and one of Virgil's old shirts, she shinnied down the rungs and raced off toward the house.

A slender woman used to the rigors of farm life, Lauralee was a fleet runner, but not so fleet as Joe Little Eagle, her hired man. He passed her easily, taking the creek in one bounding leap, hardly slowing down at all for the steep embankment on the opposite side. His bare back dissolved into a shimmering coppery streak as he crossed the meadow beyond.

As Lauralee splashed through the stream, she lost her broad-brimmed straw hat scrambling up the grassy

1

bank. Her silver-saffron hair threw off its pins and tumbled down her back as she ran, and her aquamarine eyes opened wide at the ringing sound of a pistol shot. Fear almost stopped her, but she bolted on after only the briefest hesitation, perspiring now, her heart flailing painfully against her rib cage.

At last, at last, the weathered two-story house came into full view. Joe was already there, standing Indian-still in the bright summer sun, and so was Tim McCallum, owner of the Mud Bucket Saloon. Fighting the weight of her sodden shoes every step of the way, Lauralee lunged on.

McCallum, a tall young man with light hair and a bony look about him, was slipping his pistol back into its holster, a smug grin curving his lips.

Lauralee's fear was displaced by a pounding rage. It had finally happened! Carousers from that pit of sin and vice on the other side of the road had dared to venture onto her property! By all that was holy, if they'd dared to hurt Clarie or Alexander—

But Alexander, Lauralee's ten-month-old son, sat in silence upon his blanket on the shady side of the vegetable garden, while Clarie stood between two rows of red onions, the hoe handle clasped in her hands, trembling visibly. Lauralee looked around for the midday revelers and saw only Joe Little Eagle and Mr. McCallum.

"What happened?" she gasped, falling to her knees on Alexander's blanket and, after giving him a swift inspection, clasping him close. He felt wriggly and plump in her arms, and he broke the silence that had followed his mother's question with a throaty wail.

"Snake," Clarie said, her voice trancelike. "There was a snake."

A chill danced up and down Lauralee's spine as she

2

cast her eyes from Joe Little Eagle's round, impassive face to Tim McCallum's arrogant one. And then she saw the gruesome fragments of a rattler, lying within inches of the blanket's edge. Lauralee's throat burned, and she swayed, holding her baby that much more tightly. "God in heaven," she breathed.

Joe gathered the scattered pieces of the snake and flung them into the line of lilac bushes, with their sun-wilted purple flowers, that hid the outhouse from plain view. Lauralee made herself meet McCallum's steady, challenging gaze.

"You heard Clarie scream," she said, reconstructing the unwitnessed incident in her mind as she spoke. "You shot the snake."

"That's right, Mrs. Parker," came the expressionless reply.

Lauralee hated having to thank this man for anything. He was her enemy and she was his, but he had saved Alexander's life and that was all that mattered. She rose resolutely to her aching, stream-soaked feet, her child squalling in her arms. "Mr. McCallum," she said evenly, her chin high. "I'm most grateful to you."

Now mockery danced in Mr. McCallum's blue-gray eyes. "I never thought I'd hear that from the leader of the Prayer Raiders."

The reminder that Mr. McCallum's infamous Mud Bucket Saloon—how galling that the awful place had to be just across the road from her farmhouse—was the last to stand before the local temperance campaign was a deliberate one, and it made Lauralee's blood rise to her head and pound beneath her temples and behind her eyes. "One thing has little enough to do with the other," she remarked.

Joe chose that moment to return to his work in the orchards, and Clarie, still trembling, set her hoe against the side of the house. She stumbled over to Lauralee, reached out for Alexander, and carried him inside.

Pausing at the back door, twelve-year-old Clarie gave her stepmother one defiant glance, and then, face so pale that every freckle was visible, she spoke directly to Mr. McCallum. "Thank you."

Tim answered with a nod, his eyes never leaving Lauralee's flushed face. "It wasn't my fault, you know. What happened to Virgil, I mean."

The softness in his tone shamed Lauralee for a moment, but she had only to remember that horrible night just eleven months past to overcome the weakness. Virgil Parker had died—because of drink and a hand of cards—leaving his heavily pregnant wife and his young daughter to fend for themselves.

Lauralee permitted herself to remember the pain and the shock. Men from the Mud Bucket Saloon, Tim McCallum among them, had carried Virgil home on a slab of splintered wood. His shirtfront had been soaked with blood . . .

Lauralee lifted her chin, brought herself sternly back into the difficult and grinding present. "If my husband hadn't been in your saloon—"

"That," McCallum interrupted, "was Virgil's own choice. I didn't come over here and drag him to the Mud Bucket, Mrs. Parker."

"You be sure and mention that, Mr. McCallum, when you face the Lord on Judgment Day!"

The saloonkeeper rolled his eyes toward the sky and shook his head. "There's just no reasoning with you, is there? You gotta blame somebody for what Virgil did, what he was. Well, why don't you just march into that fine mortgaged house of yours, Mrs. Parker, and look into the first mirror you come across!"

Lauralee flushed beneath the suntan her hat hadn't

4

prevented, praying that this despoiler would never know what a raw place he'd touched inside her. Had some lack in her, as a woman and as a wife, driven her husband to drink and thus to ruin?

"Get off my land, Mr. McCallum."

The shameless libertine stood stock-still. What an evil irony it was that for all he sold ardent spirits to corrupt other men, he had no apparent weakness for liquor himself. "You know what you need most, Mrs. Parker?" he dared to ask. "Another husband, a good blistering, and a tumble in bed. In that order."

Lauralee seethed, nearly choking on the screaming rage she was holding back. "If you don't get off my land this instant, I swear I'll shoot you dead!"

McCallum chuckled and shook his head again, but he did leave, his strides long as he disappeared around the tall unpainted house she and Virgil had built together with their own hands. They'd been happy in those early days, full of dreams for the forty acres that stretched from the winding, rutted road out front all the way down to the banks of the fierce Columbia River.

Tears stung Lauralee's eyes, but she was, as always, quick to force them back. Stepping high to reach the raised threshold of the back door, she entered the kitchen.

Clarie was there, sniffling and still pale, resolutely spooning cold stew into Alexander's mouth. Overdue for his nap, he spewed most of the food back at her, covering his bib and the loosely tied dishtowel that had held him in his chair.

Lauralee hesitated, watching the girl, wondering whether to keep her distance or enfold Clarie in a reassuring embrace. Since Virgil's death, there had been an odd, indefinable strain between them.

"Are you all right?"

Clarie, so like her father with her bright brown hair and coffee-colored eyes, lifted her chin and nodded once. "I'm sorry I didn't kill that snake myself, that's all," she said. "I was too scared. All I could do was scream."

"The important thing is that you and Alexander are both safe," Lauralee answered softly.

Clarie shifted in her chair. Her small back went rigid and then relaxed again, and she did not meet Lauralee's eyes when she spoke. "Maybe folks are right about us. Maybe we can't look after a place like this without a man to help us."

Lauralee swallowed hard. Today, patience seemed elusive. "That's pure nonsense, Clarinda Parker, and you know it. Besides, Joe helps us, doesn't he?"

Clarie whirled about suddenly, the plate of stew clenched in her hands, her face streaked with garden dirt and tears. "What if Mr. McCallum hadn't heard me scream, Lauralee?!" she cried. "What if he hadn't been here to shoot that snake?!"

Lauralee sighed, then closed her eyes for a moment. "Let's imagine that there had been a man on the place other than Joe. Do you really think things would have turned out any differently?"

Clarie considered, sniffled again. "Maybe not. But we're still all alone in this house except when Jenny French comes to board or Mr. Neggers passes through and rents the spare room. Mr. McCallum's saloon is right across the road, and it would be easy for . . . for drunken men to break in here and hurt us."

Lauralee had lain awake on more than one night listening to the sounds of sodden revelry flowing across the dark road, wondering what she would do if someone did try the door, but she couldn't let Clarie suspect that she had ever even entertained such a notion. "We're safe, Clarie," she insisted quietly.

"We were safe when Papa was here." Clarie set the plate aside with a thump, untied the dishtowel that kept Alexander from falling, and wiped his face with a corner of it. Her shoulders, narrow beneath the worn calico of her dress, were stiff again.

Clarie's statement could have been debated, for once Virgil had begun to drink in earnest, he had developed the ability to change, in the space of a moment, from a gentle man to a glowering sot with an evil, unpredictable temper. During those times, both Lauralee and Clarie had had to be excruciatingly careful not to irk him in any way.

"I have work to do in the orchard," Lauralee said, having put down the urge to remind Clarie of her father's shortcomings. "After you eat, please get back to your gardening."

Clarie made a face, but she was, as always, obedient. Lauralee wished she could indulge the girl just once, wished they could both put on pretty dresses and go into nearby Halpern's Ferry for a strawberry ice or perhaps a few pretty hair ribbons. But she could spare neither the time nor the money.

The trees, some of them due to bear in the fall but many still just seedlings, required every moment of her time and every cent she could scrape together. As Mr. Timothy McCallum had so ungraciously pointed out, the property was mortgaged and that left precious little margin for error.

Driven by these thoughts, Lauralee turned to leave the house, though she would have loved to stay and chat with Clarie or play the melodeon or read. She was stopped by a grumbled, "What do I tell Prissy Priscilla when she gets here?"

Matter-of-factly, Lauralee went back, kissed Clarie's forehead and Alexander's. "I'll be back in plenty of time for Priscilla's lesson," she promised. "But if

7

she should get here before I'm through, tell her to sit down at that melodeon and practice."

"She won't pay me any mind, the saucy thing," muttered Clarie. "I hate her. I hate every ruffle and ribbon of her, even if she is my cousin."

Priscilla Yates, the much-indulged only child of Lauralee's widowed brother, Ellery, was not actually Clarie's cousin, but Lauralee didn't remind the girl of that. To do so would only make Clarie feel more the outsider.

Lauralee shook her head and hurried out, steeling herself for the long hours of work still ahead. As she crossed the yard, she could hear the tinny music of a piano and swells of raucous laughter coming from the Mud Bucket Saloon. The sounds seemed to mock her for the calluses on her hands, the sunburn on her nose, the tumbledown state of her hair.

She took another route back to the orchard, skirting the meadow and the broadest part of the creek for the quiet little clearing where she and Virgil had lived when they'd first come to this land, six years before. Lauralee had been so young and so innocent then—only seventeen, and full of dreams.

The cabin was still there, and so was the blackened circle of stones where there had been so many fires to heat soap kettles and pots of laundry. She stepped through the open doorway of the cabin; the one-room interior was dusty and ripe with the smell of rats and mice. Massive cobwebs glittered in the sunshine that streamed through broad holes in the roof, and weeds thrived on the dirt floor. Lauralee smiled sadly, remembering, seeing herself as a young and diligent bride. Many the morning she'd awakened to find toadstools growing in front of her hearth and beneath her table, and she'd swept them away with her broom.

Lauralee touched the wooden crate Virgil had nailed

to one of the log walls to serve as her cupboard. There had been no mortgaged house in those days, no Alexander, no Clarie—for Virgil hadn't admitted to having a daughter until he was forced to—and certainly no Mud Bucket Saloon across the way. That place had been nothing more than a cow barn then, and to Lauralee's mind, it had come down in the world since.

She turned away from the makeshift cupboard that had so pleased her in its time and went outside, her throat tight. Mindful that she should not be dallying here, tormenting herself with memories when there was so much to do, Lauralee nonetheless lingered. Nonetheless remembered.

It seemed that she could hear Virgil's laughter on the balmy wind blowing up from the direction of the river. Most everything had been funny to Virgil then, as though life were some rousing game and the two of them were children, allowed to play out late.

Ellery, Lauralee's brother and guardian, had not approved of Virgil Parker. He'd called Virgil a drifter and a no-account and said that Lauralee would come to no good if she married the man. One day, however, Ellery's wife, Margaret, had caught her young sister-in-law and the handsome Mr. Parker in a situation that could only be described as compromising. Margaret, convinced that it was better to marry than to burn, had seen to it that the wedding took place immediately. Ellery, the owner of a prosperous freight line, had loaned the newlyweds the money to buy the land, but until after Margaret's death, he'd expressed his disapproval of Lauralee's marriage by withholding his love.

The memory still stung, and Lauralee forced it out of her mind. Standing in the flower-speckled clearing between the cabin and the stream, she caught the sides of her bloomer skirt in roughened hands and turned around and around, pretending she and Virgil were dancing again, waltzing in the grass as they had done in those faraway fairy-tale days.

Lauralee finally halted herself, dropped her gaze to the soft, loamy ground. She and Virgil had lain together here when the weather was warm, alone in the world but happy. So happy. Virgil had held her, kissed her in places that still ached for the touch of his lips or his hands; sometimes the pleasure had been so great that she'd feared to die of it. But that had been another Virgil, dead to Lauralee long before an angry gambler had plunged a knife into his chest.

Despairing, dashing at tears with the back of one grubby hand, Lauralee made her way back toward the orchard, leaving the laughing, passionate ghosts of herself and Virgil behind. By the time she had passed through the acre of seedling trees that reached no higher than her waist—they seemed to implore heaven, with their bare and spindly branches, for rain—she had set the past firmly behind her. She found the metal spraying device where she had dropped it and climbed back up the ladder among the green leaves of the apple tree.

"Think it will rain anytime soon?" she called out, not because she thought Joe Little Eagle could see into the future, but because she needed the sound of another human voice.

Branches rustled in a nearby tree; Joe was hidden from view, but he was there. "Sky's gray at the edges, Mrs. Parker," he answered presently. "We'll have rain tomorrow."

Pressing repeatedly at the long handle that pumped a noxious concoction she and Joe had brewed in the barn a few days before, Lauralee tried not to mind the smell of the stuff, the way it burned her eyes and her throat. When the rain came, it would nurture the seedlings, of course, but it would also wash away the chemical that protected the older trees. Seemed like a person couldn't have a good thing without suffering a bad one in payment.

God knew, the place wasn't much. It listed to the right, all weathered boards and ugliness. As if to bring the structure back into balance with the earth, a sign had been hung over the swinging doors with rusty, uneven links of chain. The words MUD BUCKET SA-LOON slanted upward from the left.

Grinning, Jay McCallum swept off his hat, ran a hand through his dark hair, and then swung one leg over the saddle horn and slipped to the ground. A man would have to be thirsty as hell to drink in a place like this, he observed to himself as he tethered the horse he'd ridden upriver from Colville to a rickety hitching post. There were a half dozen other geldings tied to the same rail, and if they had a mind to, they could pull the whole thing out of the ground and head south.

The inside of the saloon was worse, if possible, than the outside. The floors were nothing but spit-strewn sawdust, the tables were giant spools that had once held cable, and the women—well, Jay decided it might be better not to notice them at all.

He scanned the faces at the tables, looking for Tim, and then approached the bar, which consisted of two long boards, balanced at each end by wooden barrels.

The bartender gave a pint fruit jar a cursory wipe with a rag and dragged rheumy eyes from Jay's mid-section to his face. "What'll it be, mister? We got whiskey. We got beer."

Jay preferred imported brandy, but he wasn't fool enough to say so. He declined refreshment politely and asked, "Tim McCallum around?"

11

The barkeep bent as far forward as his enormous belly would allow, and the whole bar teetered. "Who's askin'?" he countered, squinting.

"His brother."

"His brother!" crowed the old man, suddenly delighted. "Hey, Mabel! Sheba! This here's Tim's brother!"

Mabel and Sheba were closing in from opposite sides, and their reputation preceded them so pungently that Jay's eyes watered. Holding his breath, he looked up and saw Tim hurrying down a stairway on the far side of the room. Even in the bad light making its way through broad cracks in the wall, Jay could see that his brother was worried about something. But then, considering the wording of Tim's telegraph message, that figured.

Catching sight of Jay, Tim brightened. The relief in his face was touching, but it was disconcerting, too. "We can talk upstairs," he said, skipping the boisterous greeting that would have been typical of him.

Jay followed his youngest brother up the ramshackle stairs to a second floor, which no doubt served as a brothel as well as housing the small corner room where Tim slept and kept an office of sorts.

"You've got a room in town, I suppose," Tim remarked, standing at a grime-streaked window now, his back to Jay.

Jay thought gratefully of the hotel room he had taken, with its wide, clean bed and its stationary bathtub. "Yes," he answered, folding his arms across his chest, his hat in one hand. Because it never did any good to prod Tim, he simply waited.

"How's everybody in Spokane?"

Jay rolled his eyes. "Fine. But you didn't ask me to come all the way up here just so you could hear a report on the family, did you?"

12

Tim lowered his head, still rigidly intent on something beyond that window. "I'm in trouble, Jay."

Jay felt weary. He felt a need for a bath and clean clothes and a drink. But he didn't feel surprised. "I'd guessed that," he said.

"See that house across the road?"

Jay approached the window and stood beside Tim, giving the bare-lumber farmhouse a cursory glance. He'd seen it from outside and felt no need to scrutinize it now. "Yes," he said with a sigh. He was saddlesore and he was hungry and he was wondering if Tim had brought him all the way up here to show him a house.

"The woman who lives there is going to ruin me, Jay. She's—"

"Wait a minute," Jay broke in calmly, for soothing Tim was an old, old habit. "How can one woman ruin you?"

"She's the one I wrote you about a few months ago. The one who got the Pearl Handle and the Pig and Dog closed down."

Jay bit back a grin. "Single-handedly?"

Tim bridled, sensing his brother's amusement and resenting it. "Not by half. She must have a hundred women behind her, and they all carry hymnals and hatchets!"

"That's a combination for you—hymnals and hatchets, I mean. Exactly what did they do, Tim, to close the Pearl Pig, or whatever it was?"

"The Pig and Dog," Tim insisted, reddening. "And the Pearl Handle."

"I stand corrected. Now, will you please answer my question?"

Tim's fist knotted, then relaxed again. "They started by singing hymns, that's all. Just standing outside singing hymns. When that didn't work, they started kneeling on the sidewalk, saying prayers. That got rid

13

of a few customers, I can tell you—but not enough to suit Mrs. Parker. Oh, no—she and her raiders came into the Pig and Dog one Sunday morning and they reduced it to kindling!"

Jay bit his lower lip. "And the other place?"

"Hell, they didn't have to go near it. Bill Whitman just nailed it shut and left town. The Mud Bucket is the last place within forty miles where a man can get a drink."

Brandy could be had at the hotel in town, but Jay didn't bother to mention that. It was obvious that Tim was talking about places to be patronized by men with more thirst than money. "So this is Mrs. Parker's next target."

Tim nodded and ran a hand through his fair hair. "Yeah. And they've already sung the hymns and said the prayers, too. Do you know what three choruses of 'Onward, Christian Soldiers' can do to a man, Jay?"

Jay could well imagine, particularly if that man happened to have a shot of rotgut whiskey in his hand and a trollop on his knee. "Exactly what is it you want me to do, Tim?"

"You could stop Lauralee. You could reason with her, threaten her with jail, something! After all, you're a lawyer!"

Lauralee. Jay liked the sound and taste of the name. Too bad it was tacked to a wart-faced bluestocking with a penchant for wrecking saloons. "Have you tried to talk to her yourself?"

"Yes, and it was no damn use at all! Just this morning, I shot a snake that would have killed her little boy, and do you know what she said, Jay? She said, 'I'm grateful to you.' "

"What should she have said, Tim?"

"It wasn't that she should have said anything different. In practically her next breath, she told me that her husband wouldn't be dead if he hadn't been in my saloon. I'm telling you, she's going to tear down this place just for spite!"

Again, Jay sighed. To his way of thinking, it wouldn't be much of a loss. A good rainstorm could reduce the Mud Bucket to an even better approximation of its name, and it wasn't as though there weren't any other avenues of livelihood open to Tim. After all, he came from one of the wealthiest families in the state. A little fence-mending on his part, and he could be back where he belonged. "Why is this place so important to you?"

Tim met his level gaze with a glare. "Because it's mine, damnit! Maybe the Mud Bucket doesn't look like much, but it's mine!"

Jay shook his head. "I'll talk to Mrs. Parker," he conceded. Without even meeting the woman, he had serious doubts that he would be able to make any real headway with her—these temperance types tended to be fanatical—but he owed it to Tim to try. "If I can get this woman to leave you alone, I want something in return for my effort, Tim."

Tim looked wary. "What?"

"You'll have to agree to come back to Spokane with me, just for a few days, and try to work things out with the family."

"That would be impossible!"

Jay knew better, knew how much his father and mother wanted to come to some kind of peace with the youngest of their four sons. "All I'm asking is that you try."

Tim sighed and let his forehead rest against the window frame. "All right."

Jay crossed the room and opened the door, hat in

hand. "I'm going back to town for the night. If you want to talk things over a little more, you're welcome to come along."

Tim was peering out through the window again, his profile taut with a look of sheer hatred. "Damn that son-of-a-bitching Virgil Parker anyway," he breathed.

Jay took that for an answer and went out into the hall, down the shaky stairs. Mabel and Sheba were lying in wait, but he managed to get past them and out into the fresh air.

Tim McCallum stood at the window for a long time, watching the shadows fall over the road. Night took forever to come, but come it did. He saw lights burning in Lauralee Parker's front parlor, and finally turned away.

He could hear music, laughter, the clink of bottles against the rims of glasses, coming from downstairs. Tim was making money, money of his own, money that he wasn't beholden to his father for, or to anyone else. He thought about his brothers, one by one.

Tim had never been a solid citizen like Brice, or smart like Jay. Chance, the youngest except for Tim himself, was a notorious waster, but he was good-looking and women chased after him. Those qualities, like Brice's unshakable nature and Jay's forbidding intelligence, were traits that Tim didn't feel he could claim.

Normally, he would have gone downstairs and enjoyed a few hands of cards with his customers, but he wasn't in the mood tonight. No, tonight he felt bereft and very far from home.

He should have gone with Jay, he supposed, gotten himself a good dinner at the hotel in Halpern's Ferry. But he was too worried, too much on edge. Something really terrible was about to happen—he knew it—and Lauralee Parker was going to be behind it.

The rattle of wheels in the road out front sent Tim back to the window. He spat on the forefingers of his right hand and wiped clean a part of the glass, trying to see.

There were at least a dozen buggies and wagons, lamps swinging golden in the darkness, turning one by one onto the Parker property.

He'd been right. The raid would take place tonight. Lauralee's crinoline-clad army was gathering! How long would it be before they marched on the one thing he'd ever built on his own and destroyed it?

Tim tried to stay calm. The first thing to do was send somebody to town for Jay. Jay would know what to do. He went to the top of the stairs and called out, and by some miracle, the bartender heard him over the din.

Charlie huffed up the stairs, and the two men stood, talking in whispers, in the shadowy hallway.

"I don't want the customers to know yet, do you understand me?" Tim hissed. "If they find out that Mrs. Parker is fixing to raid us, they'll hightail it out of here. Just send somebody to fetch my brother, and make it fast!"

"I reckon that scrawny weasel what's been livin' out back in the shed could go," Charlie mused.

Tim swore and half shoved the hulking man toward the stairs, impatient. He paced for a while, then went back to the window, trying to keep an eye on the forces rallying across the road.

He couldn't see much of anything now, it was too dark, but he watched anyway.

The splintering pain at the nape of his neck came as a brutal surprise to Tim. His knees gave out, and he fell face first onto the dirty floor, his blood flowing out of him, pooling around him, drowning him. He couldn't cry out, though he tried, and the cold languor in his muscles made it impossible to move.

His assailant crouched beside him, tangled a hand in his hair, and wrenched his head around. "That's for what you did to Virgil," a distorted voice said.

The pain, exploding white-hot in Tim's head and his middle, was too great to be borne. He closed his eyes.

It was a relief to die.

CHAPTER
TWO

Lauralee had mistakenly thought the hectic day was over and done. She had planned to have a bath and perhaps look through her pattern books for a table-cloth to crochet over the coming winter. Now, as the first wagons and buggies jolted into the dooryard, she gasped. "Good heavens, Clarie! I forget all about the temperance meeting!"

Clarie looked patently unsympathetic. "There isn't any pie left, either," she said.

Still wearing her bloomer skirt and Virgil's ancient cambric shirt, Lauralee panicked. She raced up the back stairs, down the hallway, into the front bedroom. There, she frantically brushed out her tangled hair and pinned it up. She put on her best skirt, a black sateen that had seen far too many wearings, along with a white shirtwaist.

Through the open window, she could hear the horses and buggies below, her friends greeting one another in the darkness. Over this, in an oppressive layer, was the constant hubbub coming from the Mud Bucket Saloon. Lauralee cast one look at the empty, neatly made bed and felt a wave of inexplicable loneliness sweep over her. She closed the window with a thump, blew out the lamp, and left the room as hastily as she had entered it.

Clarie had set coffee on to perk, but that was all the help she was willing to lend the temperance cause, it appeared. She collected Alexander and, without a word to Lauralee or any of the dozen women gathered in the kitchen, went upstairs.

"Odd child," remarked Adrienne Burch. Like Lauralee, Adrienne was a widow, but there the similarities ended. Adrienne was very tall, with dark hair and eyes, and her clothes were elegantly fashioned of the best silk, satin, and lawn. There was no mortgage on her house—surely the grandest structure within miles of Halpern's Ferry—and Lauralee couldn't even imagine her with calluses on her hands or a sunburned nose.

"Clarie has had a very difficult day," said Lauralee in a crisply polite voice.

Adrienne, not really liked by any of the members of the group but tolerated because every hatchet and hymnal was needed for the cause, smiled in a rather condescending way and said, "None of us have really been ourselves since Virgil died, have we?"

Lauralee frowned, but before she could ask what had prompted the woman to make such an odd remark, Elmira Doobermeyer insisted that the meeting be called to order.

Once the assemblage had gathered around the large round table and a prayer for guidance had been offered, Lauralee forget what Adrienne had said and concentrated on the business at hand. Certain members of the group came out in favor of marching on the Mud Bucket Saloon that very night. The hymns and prayers had been ignored, they argued, and now it was time for real action.

Lauralee felt an inward hesitation, resembling guilt. Was it right, no matter how just the cause, to destroy another person's property? And what if someone was hurt?

Adrienne, sitting at Lauralee's immediate right, was quick to notice her hostess's reticence. "Virgil would be alive today," she said, in an undertone, "if it weren't for that place."

Lauralee was once again jarred. She searched Adrienne's face, saw nothing but a sort of calm innocence. "We cannot march in the darkness," she said firmly after a moment of indefinable despair. "That is underhanded, and I won't have a part in it."

A lively debate ensued; there were those, of course, who wanted action. They were quick to present the case for battling evil when and where it arose. Hadn't Jesus Himself driven the moneylenders from the temple in a splendid, holy rage? Could those called to wage war upon the demon rum do any less, be it night or day?

There were also those who wished to achieve their end by peaceful means. "Lauralee is right," insisted shy Susan Clark, who seldom spoke her mind. "The Lord's work is not done in darkness but in the broad light of day."

"Mr. McCallum has repeatedly resisted our attempts to right this wickedness!" countered Marion Wilson. "I say we go over there right now and show those drunken wasters that we will not have our decent community fouled—"

Lauralee held up both hands. "We will approach Mr. McCallum in the morning," she said. "We will sing and pray again."

One of the more militant members looked disappointed. "No hatchets?"

A soft, niggling shame brushed against Lauralee's spirit. If it hadn't been for Tim McCallum and his quick action, Alexander would be dead of snakebite. Didn't she owe the man something for saving her son's life? At the same time she was wondering these things, however, reality seemed to dissolve, and instead of her friends gathered around that table, she saw Virgil laid out upon it, his eyes weighted with pennies. She saw herself trying to wash the blood and the smell of liquor from his flesh. She saw his terrible wounds.

"Tomorrow we will march and sing and pray. There will be no hatchets," she said in a choked voice, and with reluctant mutterings, the company of women turned the conversation to other matters. Would Jenny French, the schoolteacher, be boarding with Lauralee through the summer? Poor Jenny. It was a real pity about her father, wasn't it? Little wonder she'd arrived for the temperance meeting late and retired early. Shouldn't the Methodist church be painted again? Did anyone have a new and interesting pattern for a tea cozy?

Adrienne was the last to depart. "Have you seen my gloves?" she asked, glancing distractedly about Lauralee's humble kitchen. "I was sure I brought them along."

Lauralee could not wait to be alone, though at the same time, she dreaded the prospect. She didn't want to think, didn't want to come to terms with the possibilities that were nibbling at the corners of her mind. "Do you suppose it's wrong, Adrienne—what we're doing, I mean?"

"Wrong?" Adrienne echoed brightly, giving up on her vanished gloves with a pretty shrug. "Why, Lauralee, I'm surprised at you! You, of all people—"

22

Lauralee looked in the direction of the Mud Bucket Saloon, and though she couldn't actually see it, of course, it was as clear in her mind as if she'd been standing in front of it at midday. Would destroying that last bastion of sin and degradation really change things? Would it bring Virgil back or even avenge his death?

"Lauralee?"

Adrienne's query made her start. And for some reason it gave her the courage to form the question that had been chafing her throughout the meeting. "What did you mean when you said that none of us have been ourselves since Virgil died?"

The dark eyes were averted, though they sparkled oddly. "Nothing," Adrienne finally answered in a small voice.

Lauralee stiffened, certain that Adrienne was lying, that there was some vital truth still to be told. A truth that would bring terrible pain and yet was necessary to know—or to admit to knowing already. Lauralee had not been entirely free of the suspicions any troubled marriage would engender. "All those nights when I thought Virgil was drinking—"

Suddenly Adrienne's beautiful eyes were brimming with tears. She made an incoherent sound, like a cry of grief, and then fled the kitchen for the muggy summer darkness outside.

Lauralee did not go after Adrienne; there was no need to ask further questions. She sank into a chair, covered her face with both hands, and uttered a soft, broken cry of her own.

"I hate that woman," Clarie announced, startling her stepmother. Sometimes the girl moved with the stealth of an Indian.

Lauralee lowered her hands and drew a deep breath, determined not to break down in front of a child who had pain enough of her own. "That is the second time today, Clarinda, that you've told me you hate someone."

Wearing a nightgown and slippers, her hair brushed and hanging loose, Clarie sank into a chair near Lauralee's. "I didn't mean it about Priscilla," she muttered, her head down. "She's nasty and spoiled, but I don't really hate her."

"What about Mrs. Burch?" Lauralee asked, her throat tight because she knew the answer already, knew that it would be hurtful to say and hurtful to hear.

Clarie looked absolutely miserable. "Papa went to her house lots of times. Everybody knew it."

Lauralee fought down a screaming rage. Lord in heaven, she was losing her mind! She wanted to march out to Virgil's grave on the grassy knoll overlooking the river and—and what? Shout at him? Cry and curse? Demand an explanation?

"Not everyone knew, Clarie," she said, rising out of her chair with a despondent, high-chinned sort of dignity. "Not everyone."

"Lauralee—"

The world seemed dark to Lauralee; she groped her way to the stairs. "Good night, Clarinda," she said, and mounted one step and then another. In the room where Virgil had vowed that he loved her, where he had fathered their child, she undressed by rote, put on a nightdress and a robe, and unpinned her hair. She went into Alexander's room and then Clarie's. Jenny French, the young schoolteacher, was curled up on one side of the bed, huddled beneath the quilt in a forlorn heap.

Though the school term would not begin for several weeks, Lauralee had not been surprised by the girl's unexpected arrival. Her house was something of a refuge to Jenny, and she came and went as the spirit moved her.

"Jenny?"

The girl stirred beneath her covers, and the moonlight outlined her form and caught on the tangle of red-brown hair fanned out over the pillow casing. "It's Pa again," she said thickly, and there was a tremor in her voice that touched Lauralee and enlisted her ready sympathies.

"We'll talk in the morning," she said quietly as Clarie slipped past her in the doorway.

"I'm sorry I didn't stay downstairs for the meeting," Jenny offered as Lauralee turned to go. "I couldn't pay any mind to it, what with all that happened up home."

"It's all right," Lauralee replied, remembering how wan and pinched Jenny's face had been. She'd seemed unable to endure the company of women gathered in the kitchen and fled upstairs at the first opportunity.

No one who knew Jenny's father, Isaiah French, would have wondered at her behavior. Dismissing the entire matter from her mind, Lauralee went back to her lonely room.

Tears slid down her cheeks as she curled up in the cushioned rocking chair. She tried not to think about Virgil and his betrayal, and yet the two became one and filled her whole being.

As he climbed those slapdash stairs, something gripped Jay McCallum's spirit and shook it within him. "Tim?"

No answer weaved its way through the cacophony coming up from the first floor. The door was slightly ajar and lamplight flickered within, and Jay, not normally a superstitious man, sensed an evil so profound as to be almost palpable.

He pushed the door open with the toe of one freshly polished boot. "Tim?" he repeated, and there was a raspy urgency in his voice this time.

Tim lay sprawled on the floorboards, a hatchet imbedded in the back of his neck, his arms spread out, his face a staring crimson mask.

Jay swayed slightly, closed his eyes. With the deep breath he drew came the battleground smells of blood and death, and his stomach turned painfully, forcing acid into the back of his throat. "Oh, Jesus," he groaned, and he did not take the name in vain. It was a prayer of desperation, of disbelief.

One of the soiled doves from downstairs had followed Jay, and he was grateful, for her scream broke the strange inertia that had restrained him at the threshold. He crossed the room and dropped to one knee beside his brother.

There was so much blood, so much, and Tim—God, in heaven, he looked so young and so pale—was dead. "No," Jay muttered. "Oh no—"

Mabel—or was it Sheba?—continued to shriek, and that eventually brought a stampede of booted feet up the stairs. Men filled the room, muttering, swearing, smelling to high heaven of rotgut whiskey.

"Get out of here," Jay rasped. "All of you, get out."

The bartender and the jumpy, pockmarked little man who had come to the hotel to fetch Jay remained. "Tim was the only friend I had," observed the latter. "I ain't goin' noplace."

"Who would do somethin' like this?" blubbered the fat barkeeper. "You tell me who!"

No one, of course, could do that. Except the murderer. And Jay McCallum would have to get to the other side of his grief before he could turn his mind to finding and punishing Tim's killer.

Gently, Jay removed the hatchet and turned his

brother onto his back. He lifted him into his arms and carried him to the narrow cot on the far side of the room. He sent the bartender for water and cloth, and when those things were brought to him, he bent over Tim's body and washed away as much of the blood as he could.

In the flickering, weak light of the lantern he could almost believe that Tim was only sleeping. He wanted so much to believe that, but Jay did not permit himself the false comfort. Tim was dead; that was reality.

He drew up the one chair in sight and sat down to keep his vigil. All during the long night he was flung back and forth between the past, when Tim had been a little boy constantly at his heels, and the future, when he would have to tell his family what had befallen their black sheep.

By morning, word of the crime had filtered into every corner of Halpern's Ferry; the news brought the marshal, the doctor, and the undertaker in a dense little pack, all of them horrified.

Jay rose, muscles and spirit intertwined in a single pulsing ache, to greet them. The inevitable questions were asked and Jay told what he knew. There was no need to point out where the body had been; the spot was stained crimson. The hatchet lay on the floor, hideously smeared.

The marshal was in his mid-thirties, like Jay, a tall man with fair hair and a substantial look about him. The horror in his eyes protested that things of this sort just didn't happen around his town. "See anybody?"

"No," Jay replied flatly. If he had seen the murderer, there would have been another body for the undertaker to carry away.

The doctor and the undertaker were both bent over the waxen shell that had been Tim, but the marshal stooped and took up the bloody hatchet, his mouth curved in disgust. He muttered an oath and then ventured, "Any trouble between you and your brother, Mr. McCallum?"

Jay had been expecting that question—after all, he'd been the first person on the scene, and his clothes and hands were stained with Tim's blood—but it filled him with a raw, twisting fury all the same. The succinctness of his answer cost him dearly. "No."

"Mr. McCallum didn't kill Tim," put in a feminine voice from the open doorway. Jay turned to see Sheba—or Mabel—standing there in a short, shabby purple dress. The kohl from her eyes ran down her swollen cheeks in two black streaks, mingling with smeared lip rouge and dirt. "I was right behind him when he opened the door."

The marshal exchanged a look with the doctor, who had drawn a bedraggled blanket up over Tim's face.

"I was only doing my job," the lawman stated defensively.

"See that you do," Jay warned, and then, after a last look in the direction of the cot, he turned on one heel, pressed past the sniffling woman at the door, and went down the stairs and outside. There, he could breathe.

"Lauralee!" Clarie's voice was a horrified squeal, jolting Lauralee awake. She started and then stretched painfully, her muscles cramped from a night spent curled up in the rocking chair. Her eyes felt swollen and itchy, and she was ashamed that all the vestiges of her suffering should be so plainly seen.

"What now?" she snapped.

Clarie was carrying a cooing Alexander on one hip. Her brown eyes, so like Virgil's, darted from the undisturbed bed to Lauralee's face, and she swallowed hard before blurting out, "The undertaker's wagon is over at the Mud Bucket!"

Lauralee hurried to the window. Sure enough, Mr. Everett's grim wagon was there, and so was Doc Jameson's buggy. Alarm squeezed her stomach into a knot. "What do you suppose—"

"Somebody's dead, of course," replied Clarie with the morbid levity of the very young. "I bet it's Tim McCallum."

Lauralee shuddered. There was no love lost between herself and Mr. McCallum, that was certain, but she would never, ever have wished him dead. "Wake up Jenny and get breakfast started," she told the girl, taking a prim calico dress from the wardrobe. "What goes on at the Mud Bucket Saloon is no concern of ours."

"That isn't what you and the others were saying last night at the meeting," Clarie pointed out, flinching as Alexander knotted one plump hand in her hair and gave it a cheerful wrench. "And I can't wake Jenny up because she isn't here."

Lauralee sighed. "That girl," she muttered. "Here one moment, gone the next—"

Clarie pried Alexander's fingers from her hair. "Are you still going to raid the Mud Bucket?"

A blush rose to Lauralee's face, and she averted her eyes. "That wouldn't be Christian."

Clarie drew in a quick breath, as though she might say something, and then thought better of it and left the room, taking Alexander with her.

Lauralee washed and dressed, braided her pale hair, and wound it into a coronet atop her head. Once downstairs, she couldn't bring herself to eat breakfast. She kept wondering what had taken place across the road, and when she wasn't brooding over the gruesome possibilities, she was imagining Virgil and Adrienne together.

The rain Joe Little Eagle had foretold the day before was imminent. Dark clouds collided in the sky and the atmosphere was muggy, charged with some fury yet to come.

Feeling nervous, Lauralee fed the cows and searched the sky. She watched the road for the buggies and wagons of her fellow temperance crusaders, even though she knew they weren't going to come. Word of the death at the Mud Bucket would have reached them long before this; they would know every last detail, while Lauralee, living a stone's throw from the place, had no idea what had happened.

If she could have found Joe, she would have sent him over to make discreet inquiries, but a search of the barn and orchards turned up no sign of him. He was as bad as Jenny, Lauralee thought, a will-o'-the-wisp, coming and going like the breeze.

Finally, when she could bear the oppressive curiosity no longer, Lauralee went inside the house and put on her hooded cloak. The first heavy drops of rain were just beginning to hit the windowsills.

Clarie, having fed the chickens and washed the breakfast dishes, was sitting at the table, reading, while Alexander played nearby on the floor. She looked up at Lauralee with wide, questioning eyes. "You're not going over there, are you?" she asked, awe in her voice.

Lauralee nodded and went out without speaking. The wind was high, flinging tepid summer raindrops into her face. Staunchly, she made her way down to the gate, across the road. It was among the hardest things she had ever done—after all, Virgil had died violently in that very place—but she felt compelled somehow to go there.

30

A tall, muscular man with rumpled dark hair and pewter-gray eyes was standing on the saloon's sloping porch, seemingly unaware of the rain that was turning his white shirt transparent.

Lauralee noticed the blood stains then—they were all over his clothes and his hands—and she stopped cold, a few feet from the hitching rail, afraid to go farther, yet unable to go back.

The man didn't seem to notice her any more than he noticed the rain. The muscles of one thick shoulder flexed as he lifted a chipped enamel mug to his mouth. Steam curled up from the cup, wafting around his straight and slightly arrogant nose and causing him to squint. She saw a flash of white, white teeth as he lowered the mug from his lips. That, in point of fact, was the moment when he saw Lauralee.

His eyes slid up and down her slender cloaked figure and then dismissed her. His disinterest carried an odd and shaming sting.

"Excuse me," Lauralee said firmly, though inwardly she quavered because this man had blood on his person and he didn't seem to mind it at all.

"What the devil do you want?" The words were hard-bitten and sharp, and they caused Lauralee to retreat a step. The rain was pounding at the ground now, making haphazard honeycombs in the dirt and raising an acrid, earthy smell.

"I—I live across the road. My name is Lauralee Parker—"

He set the coffee mug aside with a thunderous thump on the rail against which he'd been leaning only a moment before. Lauralee had no chance to blink, let alone flee, because within the space of an instant he was standing before her, clasping her upper arms in his hands.

Lauralee was struck dumb with terror; she could

only stare up into those ferocious gray eyes, her breath trapped in her throat.

Something fearsome moved in the stranger's face, but then, as suddenly as she had been grabbed, Lauralee was released. She quite nearly fell, and before she could turn and run away, as good sense dictated, Marshal Townsend came out of the Mud Bucket, followed by the doctor and the undertaker. Between them, Doc Jameson and Mr. Everett carried a long pinewood box.

Lauralee's worst suspicions were confirmed. "Tim?" she asked of no one in particular, and Pete Townsend nodded as he approached her. The star-shaped badge pinned to his long canvas raincoat looked uncommonly heavy.

The stranger was glowering at Lauralee again, still oblivious to the rain, as though he would enjoy tearing her apart. "You got what you wanted, Mrs. Parker," he said. And then he spread his hands wide and smiled a vicious, soul-chilling smile. "No more Mud Bucket Saloon. Your prayers have been answered."

Pete Townsend, who had been courting Lauralee in a somewhat shy fashion for several months, flashed a look of mingled fury and compassion at the dark-haired man and said, "Go on home, Lauralee. There's nothing you can do here."

"It's all been done for her, hasn't it?" demanded the blood-stained giant. The flintlike eyes turned toward Lauralee and pinioned her like a lance flung in battle. "Or were you wielding your legendary hatchet, Mrs. Parker?"

Lauralee felt the color seep from her face, and her knees weakened. "Are you accusing me of—"

Pete spoke more forcefully now: "Lauralee, go home!"

She wanted to stay, she wanted to point out that *she*

wasn't the one whose clothes were covered with a dead man's blood, she wanted, conversely, to offer comfort. But the rain was drenching her cloak and the calico dress beneath it, and Pete Townsend looked as though he might fling her over one shoulder and carry her home if she didn't go of her own volition.

She turned away blindly, navigating the deep, rain-filled ruts in the road by some unconscious instinct.

Inside her house, Lauralee took off her cloak and hung it on its peg beside the back door, avoiding Clarie's eyes. "Tim McCallum is dead," she said. "He was murdered."

"Murdered!"

Lauralee went to the stove and poured herself a cup of coffee. Rain lashed at the windows—working in the orchard would be impossible, of course. She took no pleasure in the day of rare leisure ahead, because there was one man in the world who believed her capable of taking a human life.

"Who did it?" Clarie wanted to know.

Lauralee set her coffee aside and went to the break-front squeezed behind the kitchen table. She opened one drawer and then another, rummaging distractedly for her pattern books. She would choose the most difficult project she could find—perhaps that table-cloth with a version of the Last Supper worked in the center. "Merciful heavens," she snapped, in belated answer. "How should I know?"

"You didn't like Tim McCallum," challenged Clarie.

Lauralee met her stepdaughter's gaze. "I didn't want him dead, either."

"Some folks might say you killed him."

Lauralee could bear no more innuendo. "Well, I didn't!" she yelled.

Alexander jumped in fear and then squalled, while Clarie's eyes brimmed with tears. Lauralee was shamed; the child was sensitive, perceiving every rebuff as a lack of love. Little wonder when her own mother had dropped her off on Virgil's doorstep, promising to return for her when "things looked up." Five years had passed since then, but Clarie was still waiting.

Lauralee fell into a chair, her pattern books in her lap. "I'm sorry," she said.

Alexander scrambled to her, clutching at her skirt with his strong, plump little hands. She lifted him onto her lap and held him close.

Clarie was watching the rain sheeting against the windowpanes. "It's only right, you know," she mused, in a faraway voice.

"What is only right?" Lauralee asked, Alexander's fair hair soft against her cheek.

"That Mr. McCallum died."

"Clarie!"

"Well, it was because of him that we lost Papa, wasn't it?"

Lauralee shivered even though there was a good fire snapping in the cookstove warming the kitchen. "That was a dreadful thing to say, Clarinda Parker."

Clarie scraped her chair back, closed the book she had been reading, and clasped it against her chest. "I don't care," she said lightly, and then she turned in a swirl of long brown hair and adolescent defiance, and left the room.

Lauralee could not, in good conscience, reprimand the girl further. Clarie's attitude stemmed from things she had heard under this very roof, from Lauralee's own lips. Shamed, she put Alexander back on his blanket on the floor, where he played happily with the blocks Joe Little Eagle had carved for him.

She got out her crochet hook and a spool of delicate thread and worked the foundation chain for the tablecloth. In the parlor, the melodeon made a few wheezing sounds of protest as random keys were touched.

Lauralee stiffened and bit her lower lip as Clarie began to play a funeral dirge.

In the end, Jay McCallum couldn't bring himself to send a wire to his family. A thing like this had to be told in person, face to face, no matter how much harder and more painful it would be for himself.

He paid off Mabel and Sheba, the bartender, and the squirrely character who lived in the shed behind the saloon and sent them all packing. There didn't seem to be any point in boarding up the doors and windows: How could a shack like that be damaged?

In Halpern's Ferry, a busy little town with a shrieking sawmill but no railroad, Jay hired a wagon and team at the livery stable and drove as far as Colville, hauling Tim's casket with him. There, he boarded a train.

Two days had passed, the wagon trip from Halpern's Ferry to Colville having taken longer than he had anticipated, when Jay reached Spokane. After hiring another wagon at the train terminal, he took his brother home.

The family reacted as Jay expected: His father shut himself away in his study at the back of the house and would talk to no one; his mother, who had always believed that Tim would one day come home, refused to accept his death; his brothers, Chance and Brice, wanted to find Tim's killer and lynch him, and their wives wept.

Amidst all this, Tim was buried in the family plot.

Jay grieved in his own way, throwing himself into his law practice, reading briefs and depositions far into the night. By telegraph, he stayed in constant contact with the marshal in Halpern's Ferry, knowing that the tempest in his spirit would not subside until Tim's murderer—or murderess—had been found, tried, convicted, and punished.

Summer slipped into fall and fall into winter and winter into spring.

Marshal Townsend had decided by then that the killer had been a transient, long gone. Jay's theory was quite different. It had been simmering in his mind throughout the endless, dismal winter.

Over the objections of his mother and father, Jay closed his offices in Spokane and set out for Halpern's Ferry.

It was time to go into the saloon business and see who took serious exception.

CHAPTER
THREE

As spring spilled wildflowers over the meadow in bright tangles of red and yellow, blue and purple, the trees in the orchard sprouted gossamer pink blossoms on every branch. Lauralee Parker put aside her Last Supper tablecloth—she'd gotten all the way up to Judas Iscariot and still had not been able to resolve the quandaries that plagued her—and turned to such tasks as putting in the garden and pruning the seedling trees in the newer part of the orchard.

Joe Little Eagle worked, in his customary silence, beside her. Sometimes Lauralee watched him out of the corner of one eye and wondered where he'd gotten to after Tim McCallum's death. He'd been gone well over a month; then, when it was time to harvest the first crop of apples, he had returned. Joe hadn't explained his absence, and Lauralee hadn't asked. At the time, she had only been concerned with getting the fruit picked and sold and meeting the payment due at the bank.

Now, though, as things came to life around her, she often asked herself who had killed Mr. McCallum and why. Joe's curious disappearance didn't seem to cast any suspicion in his direction—Pete Townsend had questioned him only briefly—but Lauralee couldn't help remembering why she and Virgil had been able to buy this land in the first place. They'd purchased it from Joe Little Eagle; he'd killed another member of the Colville tribe in a fight and needed money to pay for his defense in court. In the end, he'd been acquitted because twelve disinterested jurors had decided that if one "injun" killed another, it was no great loss.

Lauralee heard wagons on the road and stopped her pruning to listen, squinting beneath the broad brim of her straw hat, curiously unsettled by what should have been a sound so ordinary as to go entirely unnoticed.

"They stopped," she mused aloud, frowning.

Joe Little Eagle went right on pruning, but he nodded. "They aren't here for us, Mrs. Parker. They're at the Mud Bucket."

Lauralee bit her lower lip. Why would anyone want to go to that haunted, cobwebby place? Everybody, former patrons and temperance crusaders alike, knew that the saloon had been closed. "Maybe they're going to tear it down."

The muscles in Joe's shoulders glistened as he worked the pruning shears. "Maybe," he said, but he sounded doubtful and not a little secretive in the bargain.

Lauralee looked at him curiously. "Do you know something that you aren't telling me, Joe Little Eagle?" she demanded.

"Only that if we don't keep these trees pruned, they won't bear fruit when the time comes."

Shamed, Lauralee went back to work. She clipped and clipped, her hands burning with new calluses, the small of her back knotting painfully as winter-dormant muscles were brought into play.

After an hour, the steady, purposeful *thwack-thwack-thwack* sound of hammers began to drift across the Parker property. Lauralee set down her shears and put her hands to her hips in exasperation. There was nothing for it. She wasn't going to get anything done if she didn't find out what was happening over there.

Joe gave her a look of mingled repect and amusement, but he didn't so much as break his stride. With a toss of her head—who was boss around here, anyway?—Lauralee marched out of the orchard.

Halfway to the house, she met Clarie and Jenny French. Now that the term was over, Jenny was helping with the housework, gardening, and Alexander's care in return for her board and room. Teacher or not, the girl's education left much to be desired, in Lauralee's opinion, for she could barely read and write herself, let alone teach those skills to others. Consequently, during the quiet evenings, after the work was done, Jenny studied subjects assigned and monitored by Lauralee.

"Mrs. Parker!" the young woman gasped hurriedly, trying to beat Clarie to some momentous announcement. "They're tearing down the Mud Bucket Saloon!"

Lauralee let out a long breath. "That is good news," she said, at the same time asking herself if she had been expecting bad news instead.

"Yeah, but it looks to me," Clarie preened, Alexander perched, as always, on her hip, "like they're going to build something else there. Why else would they have all that new lumber?"

Lauralee's curiosity, already rampant, grew to unbearable proportions. "This bears looking into," she said.

"Can we go with you?" pleaded Jenny, who had the

lovely face and voluptuous body of a woman and the temperament of a child. Her lush red-brown hair was always falling from its pins, and her wide blue eyes gave her a tousled-angel look that Lauralee sometimes suspected was wholly misleading.

"It is 'may we,' Jenny," Lauralee imparted, already on her way again. "I see no harm in your coming along."

The two young girls hurried after her, chattering, speculating on who might be building what, just as Lauralee herself was speculating, though not out loud, of course.

He was there—the gray-eyed man who had all but accused Lauralee of murdering Tim McCallum with her own hands. Shirtless in the sunshine, he sat astraddle a high beam, a hammer in one hand.

Lauralee stopped so suddenly that Clarie and Jenny almost collided with her. There were workmen everywhere, some of them in the same scandalous state of near undress as their leader.

Looking down at her, Tim McCallum's brother grinned, showing those perfect white teeth of his, and executed a mocking salute with the hammer. "Hello, Mrs. Parker," he called out, pleasantly enough. "I hope you brought your hatchet—we could use the help."

Lauralee simmered, color flowing up over her neck into her face. She hoped that the brim of her hat would hide that. It was only by the most monumental effort that she allowed his blatant slur on her character to pass. "I demand to know what you're doing," she said.

He laughed, tossing back his head. His muscular neck moved with his loud amusement. Dark hair covered his broad chest in a V shape, and his legs looked uncommonly powerful as they gripped the beam that supported him. "That isn't any of your business, is it?" he challenged when his mirth had passed. "This property belongs to me."

The workmen weren't even pretending to go about their tasks; their hammers and saws and crowbars were still, and their eyes were fixed on Lauralee.

"This property," the widow Parker persisted evenly, "borders mine. Therefore I have every right to know what use you plan to make of it."

Thick, sun-browned shoulders moved in an insolent shrug. "Fair enough," came the affable response, but Mr. McCallum's slate-gray eyes snapped with annoyance. "We're tearing this eyesore down."

"Good!" Satisfied, Lauralee turned to go.

Mr. McCallum stopped her with "In order to put up a bigger and better saloon, of course."

Slowly, Lauralee turned back. "I beg your pardon?"

He was shinnying down a support beam, striding toward her, dusting his hands against the entirely too tight fabric of his trousers. "We can't call it the Mud Bucket, though, can we? Too inelegant for the kind of place I have in mind. Maybe you could suggest a better name, Mrs. Parker."

Lauralee trembled with fury as he neared her. "I will not allow you to build a saloon here," she said, hoping he wouldn't notice the slight quiver in her voice.

One dark eyebrow quirked, and challenging amusement flashed in the gray eyes. "How do you intend to stop me, Mrs. Parker?"

She lifted her chin. "There are means, I assure you."

"Ah, yes. Hatchets. Hymnals." He stopped, put his

hands on his hips, and assessed Lauralee's work clothes with a frank sweep of his eyes. "You can sing and pray all you want, Mrs. Parker, but if you step on to my land with a hatchet, I'll personally tan your self-righteous hide."

Had Clarie and Jenny not been standing so close on her heels, Lauralee would have retreated a step. Cornered, she could only jut out her chin and snap, "Self-righteous?!"

"What would you call it, Mrs. Parker?"

Lauralee was too angry to speak for a moment, too angry to move. How dare this man threaten her with physical violence? How dare he call her self-righteous? She found her voice. "If you ever touch me, Mr. McCallum, I will—"

"You'll what, Mrs. Parker? Kill me?"

Lauralee's fingers clenched; she longed to slap this dreadful man across the face, but she didn't dare.

Again, he took in her shabby clothes, her work-roughened hands, her floppy hat, though this time his assessment was leisurely. "Don't confuse me with my brother, Mrs. Parker," he warned. "My name is Jay, not Tim, and no frustrated bluestocking is going to cost me so much as a wink of sleep. Do I make myself clear?"

Lauralee longed to spit in his face, but she could not indulge that yearning in front of the girls and the workmen, of course. "I would rather be a bluestocking," she said with chilly dignity, "than a dirty, rotten rumsucker!"

At this, Jay McCallum flung back his head and howled with laughter, his workers quickly joining in. The humiliation was insufferable, and Lauralee turned, back rigid, to walk away. Wide-eyed, Jenny and Clarie parted for her, like a human Red Sea.

"Maybe this place doesn't need a fancy name after all," McCallum called after her. "We'll call it the Rumsucker."

A jolt of pure fury went through Lauralee, but she kept on walking, not once looking back.

As the days passed, Lauralee's outrage did not. It grew with every thump of Mr. Jay McCallum's hammers, with every curse word that rose on the fresh spring breeze to traverse her property line and turn her ears to crimson.

Lauralee was loath to call the temperance committee back to duty—any association with them meant automatic association with Adrienne Burch—but the day the sign reading RUMSUCKER SALOON was hung, she knew she had to put her personal qualms aside and summon her forces.

The delicate warriors arrived on a bright Thursday afternoon, in wagons, in buggies, in surreys, and even on foot. They carried Bibles and hymnals but, by Lauralee's order, none of the hatchets Mr. McCallum was so fond of mentioning, and crossed the road in a dignified stream of dark sateen and righteous wrath.

The new saloon was nothing but framework and floors as yet, but it stood three stories high and promised unlimited corruption. Mr. McCallum, wearing a dark broadcloth suit and a round-brimmed hat banded with hammered silver, stood waiting on the porch, his arms folded across his chest, an insolent grin on his face. The ever-present workmen didn't look quite so confident, however; many of them had wives, sisters, or mothers among the crusaders.

At Lauralee's command, the women began to march around the towering structure, heads high, Bibles clutched to bosoms, voices raised in conquering song. Seven times they would encircle the building, just as

Joshua had seven times circled the impregnable walls of Jericho.

The strains of "Onward, Christian Soldiers" rang in the air. Behind his grin, Jay McCallum seethed.

He watched Lauralee Parker pass, her face flushed to a fetching pink, her eyes—they were the damnedest blue-green color he'd ever seen—bright with conviction. Mrs. Parker was taller than most women, and her shape was trim and womanly, somber sateen dress notwithstanding. Jay didn't have to wonder what she would look like without clothes—he could imagine all too well.

When Lauralee came by the second time, he fell into step beside her, holding his hat respectfully in his hand. He remembered what Tim had said about the effect of this song on the average man as, one by one, his workers laid down their tools and drifted away.

"Is this your worst?" Jay asked over the rousing rendition of the hymn that had become the temperance movement's anthem. "I'm a little disappointed, Mrs. Parker."

Lauralee gave him a look but went right on singing. She was no Jenny Lind, and Jay was developing a headache. Quiet rage smoldered within him, and he considered making an example of the widow Parker, turning her over his knee and blistering her right in front of that corset-bound army of hers, but he knew he'd never be able to bring himself to strike her, his earlier threat notwithstanding. It was, he observed to himself, a pity that a man couldn't turn his conscience off and on at will.

For all that, Jay was not a passive man and he had to do something. "Damnit!" he roared. "You've made your point!"

Lauralee stopped cold, held up one hand as a signal

to her Christian Soldiers. They came to an obedient halt behind her and fell into a very welcome silence.

"Have I indeed made my point, Mr. McCallum?"

She was asking if Jay meant to give up, go away with his tail between his legs! "We open for business in less than a month," he replied coldly, evenly, barely suppressing his fury.

Lauralee flushed and her intriguing bosom rose on a deep breath. The innocent motion stirred something unexpected and infuriating in Jay McCallum, a wanting that would make his nights miserable for a month of Sundays.

She opened her mouth to speak and then closed it again. Pete Townsend, the marshal, had just ridden up, and he was striding through the assemblage, his jawline hard, his eyes fixed on Lauralee.

"So you're at it again," the lawman rasped in quiet annoyance.

Lauralee's beautiful eyes widened, and she swallowed visibly. "Yes. Have you any objection, Marshal Townsend?"

"You're damn right I have an objection. You get this flock of hens out of here before there's trouble!"

Lauralee glared at Townsend and then at Jay and began to sing and march again. Her loyal followers sang and marched, too.

"I'll arrest you, Lauralee!" raged the marshal, double-stepping along beside the delectable troublemaker. "Don't you think for one minute that just because I bought your basket at the Christmas social, I won't arrest you!"

Jay, keeping pace as best he could, felt a surge of jealousy. So the marshal was courting Mrs. Parker, was he? The idea was flat-out irritating!

Lauralee sang louder and Townsend was beside himself, turning red and stumbling to keep up.

"I'll be happy to press charges," Jay put in, partly to keep things interesting and partly because he felt left out. Damnit, this was his saloon, wasn't it? Wasn't Mrs. Parker's campaign supposed to be directed at him?

"Did you hear that, Lauralee?" Townsend bellowed. "Mr. McCallum here is ready to press charges! Are you going to make me throw you in jail?"

Lauralee gazed straight ahead, and Jay found himself half admiring her boneheaded courage. " '. . . marching as to war,' " she sang, at the top of her lungs, " 'with the Cross of Jesus, going on before . . .' "

Townsend swept off his battered hat and beat at one leg with it. "All right, then!" he shouted. "Lauralee Parker, you are under arrest!"

She stopped and extended both hands, wrists together, for the cuffs.

Jay was furious again. Damnit all to hell, the arrogant little chit was actually going to let herself be jailed! This was taking martyrdom a step too far.

Red to his ears, the marshal took handcuffs from a loop on his belt and snapped them into place. "The egg money isn't going to cover your bail, Lauralee," he warned.

The egg money. Jay wanted to call a halt to this farce before it could go any further, but something within him would not allow him to give ground. Besides, he remembered with a jolt, Lauralee Parker might very well be Tim's murderess. He had gotten so caught up in the drama of it all that he'd let that all-important fact slip his mind.

It was humiliating to be bailed out of jail by Virgil's mistress, but Adrienne Burch, having inherited her

46

late husband's sawmill, was the only one in Lauralee's circle of acquaintances who had the money. She had considered sending word of her plight to Ellery, asking his assistance, but her brother was not sympathetic to the temperance cause and he would certainly have subjected her to a long and very dull discourse on the responsibilities of womanhood. Lauralee felt certain that righting public wrongs, however peaceably, would not be among them.

"You had no right to do this," Adrienne told a glaring Pete Townsend as Lauralee left the town's one jail cell, a musty cubicle with a sawdust floor and one barred window.

"I had every right!" Pete shouted back.

"It was a peaceful assembly!" Adrienne retorted.

"You were on private property!"

"What's done is done," Lauralee interceded, wondering what she would tell Alexander when he grew up and inquired as to why his mother had a history of criminal behavior.

Marshal Townsend was clearly not willing to let the subject drop. Clasping the edges of his heavy oak desk, he leaned forward, his eyes a heated, angry blue as he looked at Lauralee. "You leave Mr. McCallum alone," he warned.

Lauralee squared her shoulders and held her head high. "I make no promises to do that, Mr. Townsend," she responded coldly. "No promises at all."

Pete started to round the desk. "Lauralee—"

At Adrienne's dramatic lead, Lauralee whirled and swept out of the jailhouse without a backward glance. She was hurt that Pete would take Jay McCallum's side against her.

Adrienne's fancy surrey was waiting in the street, a wicker picnic basket sitting prominently on the rear seat. Somehow, the woman managed to look elegant even as she climbed into the vehicle, swathed in full skirts, and took up the reins.

"Of course I'll drive you home," she said, and her eyes challenged Lauralee to refuse the offer.

Inwardly, Lauralee sighed. Adrienne had spent good money to meet her bail. How could she turn down the offered ride without seeming petulant and small-minded?

She got into the seat beside Adrienne, folded her work-roughened hands in her lap, and spoke softly. "Thank you for paying my bail. I—I don't know when I can reimburse you."

Adrienne brought down the reins with a snapping motion of her gloved hands, and the team of expensive sorrel horses jolted into motion. "We have a great deal in common, you and I," she said, giving Lauralee a sidelong glance from behind the veil of her hat.

The statement was an ambiguous one and Lauralee wasn't about to pursue it. Smiling despite the hard core of pain that scraped the inside of her throat as surely as if she'd swallowed a pine cone whole, she looked back at the picnic basket in silent question.

Adrienne noticed the motion and make a startling reply to it. "Mr. McCallum is new in our community, after all. We don't want him to get the impression that Halpern's Ferry is an unfriendly town, do we?"

Lauralee's mouth dropped open. "You're inviting Mr. McCallum—that libertine—on a picnic? What about temperance, Adrienne?"

Again, Adrienne shrugged, and her lush mouth quirked just a bit, though she kept her dark eyes on the road. "Perhaps," she said in a sultry voice that Laura-lee had never heard her use before, "we can catch more flies with honey. . . ."

Lauralee folded her arms across her chest now, in

an effort to keep from grabbing Adrienne Burch by the throat and throttling her. The gall of the woman! Pretending to identify with the cause of temperance, marching and singing right along with the rest, and then inviting the very object of their campaign on a picnic! After a long moment, she managed to ask, "Why did you pay my bail, Adrienne?"

They were passing the sawmill, with its smell of machine oil and freshly sawed lumber, that was making Adrienne Burch richer with every passing second, and she acknowledged it with a brief smile. "I did it for Virgil. Whatever your deficiencies as a wife, Lauralee, he wouldn't have wanted the mother of his son languishing in a jail cell."

Though it was agony, Lauralee waited until the surrey was well out into the countryside before she reached out and closed strong hands over Adrienne's, forcing her to stop the team.

"You were in love with Virgil," she said.

Adrienne sighed and pursed her lips as though reluctant to discuss Lauralee's statement. Her eyes, however, revealed her eagerness. "Virgil loved you, Lauralee. He loved you very much. But he had needs you failed to meet."

Lauralee knew what "needs" Adrienne was referring to, of course. Pain and fury mingled within her, creating a third emotion too awesome to bear a name. "That's a lie," she struggled to say, remembering the ecstasy she and Virgil had shared. "I'll have you know—"

Adrienne interrupted with a desultory wave of one hand. "Yes, yes—I know you pleased Virgil. I'm talking about other things."

Lauralee's eyes widened, and the raw lump in her throat ached. "What things?" she whispered.

"Respect, for one. Lauralee, you treated Virgil like

49

a child, incapable of making the smallest decision—"

"Respect!" Lauralee trembled. "How could I respect Virgil, Adrienne? He was a drunk!"

Adrienne turned in the surrey seat to face Lauralee, her dark eyes shining with tears. "He was a man, Lauralee, driven by more pain than you and I can even imagine. I could respect Virgil because I didn't expect anything of him. I just wanted to be with him. I didn't criticize him, and I didn't try to change him. I loved Virgil just the way he was."

Lauralee's hands fell away from Adrienne's, and she looked away to hide the tears that were stinging her eyes.

The surrey began to move again, and not another word was spoken. Adrienne dropped Lauralee off at her front gate and then casually drove across the road to the saloon.

Lauralee heard Adrienne call out a sunny, musical greeting to Jay McCallum, heard his cheerful response. And she was wounded to the very core of her being.

Jay sat on the grass, watching Mrs. Adrienne Burch as she poured wine into elegant glasses and wondering what the hell she was up to. She was a beautiful woman, impossible to overlook, and she had been part of the hymnal brigade; he remembered her clearly. So why the wine, the dainty watercress sandwiches, and the come-hither smiles?

"I presume your devoted leader is out of the hoosegow?" Jay ventured, though he had, of course, seen Mrs. Burch let Lauralee off at her gate just minutes before.

She laughed; it was a throaty sound that left Jay totally unmoved, much to his regret. After all, it had been some considerable time since he had had a woman, and he suspected that this one would be particularly entertaining, not to mention inventive. "Our Lauralee," she said, and whatever emotion she bore toward Mrs. Parker was not a fond one for all her gentle, indulgent tone. "She is forever in trouble. I'd like to shake her sometimes."

Jay remembered how straight Lauralee's back had been as she'd marched up the road toward her un-painted house, a crusader just back from the dungeons. He grinned and shook his head. Oh, there were a great many things he wanted to do to Mrs. Parker, but shaking her wasn't among them.

Abruptly, his theories about Tim's murder rolled back into his mind. Undeniable as Lauralee Parker's charms were, he couldn't afford to forget his suspicions. "Why are you here, Mrs. Burch?" he asked, in order to divert his thoughts.

"Adrienne," she corrected, pouting prettily. "I wanted to welcome you to our community."

Jay arched an eyebrow. "Is that why you were here earlier, marching around my building with the rest of them?"

Adrienne winced, but mischief danced in her eyes. "You must understand, Mr. McCallum, that entertainment of any sort is at a premium in Halpern's Ferry. This is particularly trying to a woman of my . . . sophistication."

There it was, beneath those heavy, batting eye-lashes. An invitation too direct to go unnoticed. How he wished Lauralee Parker would look at him that way. Or did he? And if so, why? He swore under his breath and plucked a blade of quack grass from the ground.

"You look distracted, Mr. McCallum," Adrienne put in sweetly. "Am I keeping you from your work?"

Jay stood up like a sleepwalker, gazing across the

road. He was going about this in the wrong way. He would ask Mrs. Lauralee Parker outright whether or not she had killed Tim. If she was guilty, she would lie, of course, but he was good at detecting fabrications, thanks to years of experience in the courtroom.

"Yes," he answered belatedly. "I mean, no. Mrs. Burch, if you'll excuse me—"

"Adrienne!" she complained, and he heard the rustling of her skirts as she rose to protest his going.

But Jay's course was set. He crossed the road, climbed over the tumbledown rail fence, and sprinted into Lauralee's yard. A young girl was halfheartedly flinging kernels of dried corn to a flock of noisy chickens, and she looked at Jay as though he were the devil's best friend.

"Where is Mrs. Parker?" he asked gently, hoping to put the child at ease.

Her brown eyes widened. "Why do you want to know?"

Jay smiled. "I want to talk with her, that's all."

"You wouldn't hurt Lauralee, would you?"

The question surprised Jay, though he supposed it shouldn't have. He and Lauralee were known to be at cross purposes, after all. "Of course not," he answered, somewhat testily.

The child believed him and gestured toward a line of trees atop a hillside. "She's up there."

Jay's strides were long as he covered the distance, all the while arguing with himself. He should go back to his own property, mind his own business, arrange a tryst with Adrienne Burch. Instead, he was drawn toward Lauralee.

When he reached the top of the hill, he found her beside a grave, marked with a humble stone, her head down, her shoulders moving convulsively. The wind rising from the river beyond lifted a tendril of pale hair at the nape of her neck, and Jay McCallum ached inside.

He was intruding, but he could not turn away and he could not call out to her. He could only watch, spellbound.

Suddenly, so suddenly that Jay was nearly startled into revealing himself, Lauralee made a wailing sound, a sound of anguished fury. She drew back one ugly, practical little shoe and kicked Virgil Parker's headstone as hard as she could.

"Damn you, Virgil!" she screamed. "I swear, if you weren't already dead, I'd kill you myself!"

Jay stared, stunned as Lauralee hauled off and kicked the stone again, this time hurting her foot. She howled in furious pain and hopped around in a fitful circle. On the third round, she saw Jay.

She froze, her aquamarine eyes flashing behind a diamond-bright sheen of tears. "You!" she hissed. The tears flowed down her cheeks, leaving streaks, and Jay noticed that her hair had tumbled down to rest in untidy loops upon her shoulders. "Haven't you caused me enough trouble for one day? Aren't you satisfied that I was arrested, that that awful woman had to bail me out of jail?"

Before Jay could even begin to think of an answer, Lauralee dropped to her knees, covered her face with both hands, and sobbed.

Jay McCallum was not a man to be swayed by tears—he knew too many women who could produce them at will—but he was moved by this woman's pain because he sensed that she rarely gave in to it. He also sensed—perhaps it was wishful thinking—that Lauralee had not killed Tim. Something deep within him maintained that while this woman might well do mur-

53

der to defend herself or a loved one, she was simply not capable of creeping up behind someone and lodging a hatchet in the back of his neck.

The river sang its chortling, distant song, the bees buzzed, the sweet-scented grasses swayed in the spring breeze. Jay went to Lauralee, knelt down, and drew her gently into his arms.

CHAPTER
FOUR

Lauralee allowed her forehead to rest against Jay's warm, solid chest as she wept. That he, of all people, should be the one to lend strength in this moment of weakness was a supreme irony.

In good time, Lauralee's tears subsided, for although weeping was certainly a welcome release, it was also boring. The desire to go on being held by this man remained, despite all reason; Jay's arms encircled her waist with a power that protected but did not crush. Alas, with this feeling of safety came other feelings, other needs. There was a warm stirring in Lauralee, and because of that, she tried to draw away.

Jay held her fast. Instead of being alarmed, Lauralee responded to the scent and substance of him, the pressure of his muscled thighs against her own softer ones, the steady beat of his heart beneath her cheek. Tilting her head back, she searched the strong planes and angles of his face and saw there a bafflement as great as her own.

Lauralee raised her hands tentatively to his shoulders, wanting at once to clasp and to push away. With a strangled groan, Jay bent his head and touched his lips to hers, cautiously at first, and then with a boldness that threatened to sear away all propriety and restraint.

Even after telling herself that this man was not her husband, that he was indeed an enemy, that he had believed her capable of murder, Lauralee found it all but impossible to withdraw.

"No," she pleaded, into the warmth of his shoulder. "Please. No."

Jay sighed, then got slowly to his feet, pulling a mortified Lauralee along with him, catching her chin in one hand and forcing her to meet his eyes. "That was most enlightening," he said after a long interval of just holding her that way, his touch causing the blood to rise into Lauralee's face.

"What was enlightening?" she snapped when she'd caught her breath, hoping that Jay couldn't see or sense the confounding, painful needs he'd stirred in her.

"I've misjudged you, Mrs. Parker. I would have sworn you were the type to scorn the sins of the flesh."

Lauralee reeled under the verbal blow and then rallied on the very strength of her anger. She moved to stomp on Jay's instep and instead found herself wrenched against the iron wall of his midsection and held there, a squirming captive. Of course, the motion made things infinitely worse, not only for Lauralee, but quite obviously for Jay, too. She took a wicked satisfaction in his discomfort and managed to sputter, "Why, you reprehensible, ignominious deviant! How can you stand here, not six feet from my husband's grave, and say such things?!"

Jay was philosophical. "Such big words. Too bad

they're not big enough to hide the fact that you want me as badly as I want you."

"I most certainly do not 'want' you—I *hate* you! Let me go this instant!"

Jay cupped his hands, bold as you please, beneath Lauralee's bottom, thrusting her closer yet. She gave a soft wail of despair at what his body promised to hers and saw tender amusement in his gray eyes.

"I should have guessed," he mused to himself, his strong hands still holding Lauralee deliciously, unbearably, close. "I should have guessed."

Only the force of will kept Lauralee from lifting her fingers to Jay McCallum's dark, rumpled hair to learn the texture and weight of it. "Let me go!" she hissed.

He released her so suddenly that Lauralee toppled backward, landing on her tingling backside on the soft grass. For all the abruptness of the motion, there was no rancor in Jay's face or in his bearing. "I can wait," he said, rubbing his chin, where a new beard was beginning to show. "The question is, can you?"

Fury throbbed in Lauralee, an aching, searing fury all the more intense for her sensing of the truth underlying Jay McCallum's outrageous remark. "I can wait forever," she blustered, all bravado and ruffled dignity. "And I assure you, I will!"

Jay McCallum grinned and gestured idly toward his nasty saloon, just visible through the trees. "I'll be right across the road," he said, and Lauralee clasped bunches of quack grass in each hand to keep from flinging herself at him in a violence of pounding fists, flying feet, and clawing fingernails.

Jay assessed her once more. A grin curved his lips, and he shook his head at some private wonder, then turned to walk away.

"Enjoy your picnic with Mrs. Burch," Lauralee

challenged, the words slipping out before she could catch them.

Jay stopped and turned to face her again, steel-gray mischief bright in his eyes. "Jealous, Mrs. Parker?"

Lauralee scrambled awkwardly to her feet. In the presence of this man, all grace seemed to flee her. The grass she had been gripping in her right hand came with her, complete with roots and a clod of dense dirt. Stung, she hurled the whole of it at Jay and felt profound gratification when it struck his shoulder and left a stain on his white linen shirt.

Jay's reaction was somewhat disappointing. He folded his arms and went right on grinning. "Oh, you do tempt me, Mrs. Parker, to forget that this is hallowed ground. You do tempt me."

This was not, of course, the first time Jay had addressed Lauralee as Mrs. Parker, but somehow, in that place and that moment, after all that had gone before, she was shamed by it. The fact that Virgil had not been the best of husbands in no way justified the wicked things Lauralee had felt when Jay McCallum had kissed and held her. Her shoulders slumped a little and a lump formed in her throat. "Go back to your picnic," she said dispiritedly. "You'll find Adrienne most delicious, I'm sure."

Jay paused, and Lauralee saw by the look in his eyes that she had revealed something better kept secret. He was clearly savoring his small triumph, but mercifully he made no comment. An emotion Lauralee didn't dare put a name to crackled between them for a moment, and then Jay was striding away.

After an interval spent grappling with her slippery composure, Lauralee put all the wounding events of the day to the back of her mind—her arrest, the things Adrienne had told her during the surrey ride home from town, her own scandalous exchange with a man

58

who posed a singular threat to every value and belief she possessed.

Lauralee went resolutely to the orchard, where there was, as always, work to do.

Jay crossed Lauralee's property and then the road without any conscious memory of the walk. Those workmen who had dared to drift back after the hymn-singing incident were hammering and sawing industri-ously. Adrienne Burch sat upon her inviting blanket, sipping wine and watching Jay's approach with win-some interest. The sky was above and the earth was below and yet the world, as far as Jay McCallum was concerned, had been wholly and irrevocably altered. It was as though he had been a paperboard figure living among paperboard figures until Lauralee. Now every-thing in and around him was coming to life, taking on depth and vividness and substance.

For the first time, he noticed the color of Adrienne's dress—it was the same deep burgundy as the wine she had poured for him, and trimmed with braided cord and ruched in strategic places. "You were Virgil Parker's mistress," he said bluntly, standing over the plaid blanket she had spread out on the ground earlier, casting a shadow over Adrienne that must have seemed, from her viewpoint, slightly ominous. For the life of him, he couldn't figure out why he gave a damn what her answer might be, but he did.

"I was his . . . friend," Adrienne admitted coyly after delicately clearing her throat. And then she pouted. Jay hated when women pouted; it was theatri-cal, superficial. "Has Lauralee been crying on your shoulder, Mr. McCallum?"

For a moment, Jay wondered if this woman pos-sessed some sixth sense; he even glanced down at his shirtfront to see if the marks of Lauralee's tears lingered there. Instead, he saw the smudges left by the clod of dirt she had thrown at him, and that made him smile. "I don't think Mrs. Parker cries on anybody's shoulder," he said, because all at once Lauralee's pride was as precious to him as his own.

"Something must have given you the idea that Virgil and I were close," Adrienne persisted, tilting her head to one side and deliberately widening her eyes. Her expression, for all its cultivated innocence, made promises that at any other time in the history of creation Jay would have found impossible to resist.

"I think you'd better go home, Mrs. Burch," he said distractedly, his mind back on that quiet, tree-sheltered knoll, with Lauralee. "A building site can be dangerous." Jay extended one hand to help Adrienne to her feet, and she took, it seemed to him, an inordinate amount of time to do such a simple thing, even considering the ridiculous yardage in her skirt.

"Won't you come to supper?" she said, her dark gaze gliding, like a caress, from Jay's midsection to his face.

If this woman ever met with financial reverses, Jay reflected to himself, she could make a fortune selling anything from hatpins to clipper ships. Her tenacious nature would assure success. "I don't think so," he said.

Adrienne cast a knowing glance toward the Parker property. "You'll find Lauralee lacking, Mr. McCallum. Just as Virgil did."

Jay smiled an acid smile, usually reserved for purposes of intimidating the opposition in court. "It would be my guess that whatever was lacking, Mrs. Burch, was lacking in Virgil."

Adrienne flushed slightly but recovered her aplomb with admirable ease. "Dinner will be served at eight," she retorted, "in case you change your mind."

"I'm sure I won't."

Adrienne arched one perfect featherlike eyebrow, as if to ask, "Are you?" and then walked to her surrey and stood there waiting until Jay was forced to go and help her into the seat.

Mrs. Burch was plump in all the right places. She was perfumed and soft.

Jay McCallum cursed himself for every kind of fool. Thanks to that uncanny interlude with Lauralee, he was going to be in anguish all night. Why couldn't he bring himself to accept this opportunity for what it was? Adrienne Burch was a perfect proxy for passion, wasn't she? She could assuage the sweet pain Lauralee had aroused and yet she was worldly enough to expect nothing in return, beyond the satisfaction of her own needs, of course.

"Eight o'clock," she repeated, taking the reins into her hands. The tip of her tongue came out to moisten her lips with a studied languor. Jay's desire grew within him, but it was all directed at Lauralee, and he knew with a certain sweet horror that no other woman could appease it, however accommodating and beautiful she might be.

Adrienne was certainly both, and Jay swore under his breath as he watched her drive away.

Lauralee stood quietly at the bedroom window, the day's work done, the pale purple of twilight settling over the road and the towering skeleton of a building beyond in long, velvety shadows. The workers were long gone, but Jay remained, somewhere out of sight. His horse, tethered to the front wheel of an empty lumber wagon, was proof of that.

Lauralee sighed. It was getting dark. Did the man intend to sleep over there? Had he had any supper? There were no signs of a campfire.

Downstairs, Clarie and Jenny were preparing the evening meal amidst a clatter of kettles and pots, their youthful voices rising, songlike. Lauralee knew she should be helping with the work, not standing there mooning over a man she couldn't have and didn't want.

Very much.

Mr. McCallum was a waster, Lauralee told herself staunchly. In her imagination, she consulted with Ellery, whom she seldom saw, and he agreed without reservation.

Indeed, Mr. McCallum was a rum-seller in the bargain, or he meant to become one in the near future. And yet he drew Lauralee, seemingly without effort, as Virgil never had. She wanted Jay to kiss her again, wanted to lie pliant and soft and womanly beneath the hard length of him . . .

Lauralee ached, not only in her body but in her spirit. What kind of woman was she, thinking such wicked thoughts? Come to that, if she had to feel this passion, why couldn't she have felt it toward Pete Townsend, who was a decent, steady man and handsome, too? If she gave Pete the least encouragement, she knew he would marry her, and that was a gesture she couldn't expect from Jay.

Against her better judgment, Lauralee fancied being gathered into a man's arms again, perhaps in this very room. She imagined being caressed and kissed and then thoroughly taken. Her blood heated and those parts of her that were uniquely feminine throbbed with hopeless, hurtful need. The man in her fantasy was not Pete Townsend, or even Virgil. God forgive her, it was Jay McCallum.

Despondently, Lauralee crossed her arms over calico-covered breasts that yearned to be bared, nipples that craved to give suckle, not to an infant but to a man. It had been so long, so very long.

Supper, for all the youthful merriment generated by Jenny, Alexander, and Clarie, was a trial to Lauralee, something to be survived, gotten through, so that she could go to bed and sleep. Sleep! As if she could expect to rest with an unconscionable, burning riot going on inside her.

Once the meal had ended and the dishes had been washed and put away, Lauralee put Alexander to bed in the tiny room adjoining her own. The task took too little time, too little thought, and she soon found herself standing at the window again.

In the bright light of summer stars and a full moon, Lauralee could see Jay McCallum sitting on the first floor of his building, his back resting against a sturdy beam, his long, powerful legs stretched out in front of him. The light of a cheroot glowed crimson, rising and falling like a firefly trying to decide which way to go.

Lauralee was patently annoyed. Everyone knew Jay had a room at the hotel in Halpern's Ferry—the best one the whole place had to offer, in fact. Why didn't he go and sleep there, for pity's sake?

She flounced away from the window after a considerable interval, undressing and wrenching on a prim flannel nightgown. She took down her hair and brushed it with vicious strokes, and when Clarie and Jenny called out good night from the hallway, she practically growled in response.

In bed, Lauralee tried to read. She tried to pray. Finally she blew out the lamp and settled back against the pillows and her mind carried her back to that spot near Virgil's grave—oh, Lord in heaven, his *grave*— where Jay McCallum had so cavalierly awakened desires that should have slept. She felt the kiss again as surely as if Jay were here beside her, in this wide and lonely bed.

The thoughts and feelings that followed made her unbearably restless. "Damn!" she hissed, flinging back the covers, sitting up, running both hands through the tangle of silver-gold hair that fell to her waist. She went, against her will, to the window.

A cloud had covered the moon, and the Rumsucker Saloon was only a shadow with sharp corners. There wasn't even the light of a cheroot, but Jay was there, Lauralee could sense that. Oh, the pull of him was strong, like some invisible rope stretching across the road, winding itself around her, tugging.

It all came to Lauralee then, in an infuriating moment of illumination. This was a game Jay was playing, and she was losing. She grabbed for her wrapper and rammed her feet into her slippers. She didn't pause to consider what she was doing, what she was risking, for she didn't dare. She could be certain of only one thing: Should she lose this strange battle, she would not lose graciously!

Downstairs in the dark kitchen, Lauralee lit the lamp suspended over the table, wrenched a plate from the cupboard, pulled open the wooden ice box in the corner. She dumped a glob of mashed potatoes onto the plate, adding congealed gravy for sheer spite. Two pieces of cold, crusty fried chicken, left over from supper like the other things, were plopped on top of the entire mess.

The wind outside was surprisingly cool. Lauralee clutched her wrapper closed with one hand and stormed down the starlit path, through the gate, and across the road.

"Mr. McCallum!" she whispered fiercely in the direction of the specterlike building rising out of all things sinful.

A match was struck; the glass globe of a lantern clinked. There was Mr. McCallum, stretched out on the first floor of the Rumsucker Saloon, looking sleep-rumpled, testy, and not the least bit surprised. Lauralee silently damned him for not having the civility to pretend to a measure of wonderment. It would have been a small concession on his part, considering the way he had mesmerized her into paying a call.

There was a striped wool blanket covering Jay; he tossed that aside, probably hoping to startle Lauralee and without question succeeding. He was, however, fully dressed.

Lauralee didn't know what to say or do. Drat it all, her ire had swept her up and carried her over there, and now it was ebbing away. She felt foolish and forward, standing there in her nightclothes, a plate of leftovers shaking in her hands.

"Come here and sit down," Jay said softly.

Lauralee obeyed, to her own surprise. He took the plate from her and set it aside, then draped the blanket around her shoulders, giving her its warmth and a bit of dignity.

"I brought you some supper," she said after much time had passed. The remark had been witless, and Lauralee would have given next year's apple crop to take it back.

Jay might have made reference to the humiliating similarities between Lauralee's visit and the picnic he had been treated to earlier by Adrienne Burch, but he did not indulge. "Thank you," he said, and he took up the plate, loosed a chicken thigh from the small mountain of cold potatoes, and began to eat.

"Aren't you going to ask what I'm doing here?" Lauralee prodded minutes later, when she could bear his seeming lack of curiosity no longer.

Jay flung the denuded thigh bone into the darkness

65

and addressed himself to the other piece of chicken. "I don't need to ask. I already know."

Lauralee was wildly embarrassed even though a part of her reasoned that of course Jay would know why she was there because he had somehow drawn her. "You do?"

"Yes."

"You do not!"

"Oh, but I do."

Lauralee swallowed, glad of the semi-darkness that would hide her flushed face, at least until the moon came out again. For now, there was only the flickering glow of the lantern, and that was quickly diffused by the night. "Why, then?" she challenged. "Why am I here, Mr. Oh-So-Smart?"

Jay rolled his eyes in mocking reply and went right on chewing.

Lauralee moved to throw off the blanket and flee; just as quickly, Jay caught her wrist in his free hand and forestalled her escape. He tossed away the chicken piece and put aside the plate with a thump that seemed to echo all the way to Judgment Day and back again.

Inelegantly, he wiped his hands on the legs of his rough-spun work trousers, and then his fingers were enmeshed in Lauralee's hair, his thumbs caressing the valleys beneath her ears. "Lauralee," he said in a throaty, savoring rasp, and then he kissed her.

Again.

It was devastating, that kiss, crumbling things that had stood strong within Lauralee for as long as she could remember. Passion howled through her like some internal storm, pounding inside her ears and shrieking around the corners of her heart. Just as the moon shone bright again, the kerosene lantern mysteriously flickered out.

Jay lowered Lauralee gently to the fragrant new floorboards, covered her trembling body partially with his own and partially with the blanket that bore his scent and intoxicated her. Still Jay kissed her, consuming her, and her soft cries echoed against the inner walls of his mouth.

He was a wizard, he was. He had drawn her here by mystic means and by that same secret knowledge he divined all the places where Lauralee craved to be touched. He dispensed with her wrapper, slowly drew up her nightgown, his hand paying brief, searing visits to her thighs, the curve of her waist, her breasts.

Presently, the kiss ended. Jay drew back, his fingers working loose the buttons of Lauralee's nightdress, baring her breasts to the moonlight and the slicing silver hunger of his gaze. Her nipples puckered into taut buds, like exotic flowers on a jungle night, and Jay groaned as he bent to touch them, each in turn, with the tip of his tongue.

Lauralee gasped with a pleasure long craved and long denied, her back arching. Jay chuckled hoarsely as she knotted frantic fingers in his hair and pressed him to plunder.

After what was to Lauralee an agony of deliberation, he chose one nipple to favor, to circle with his tongue, to graze with his teeth, and when the gentle torment became unbearable, causing her to toss and fret, he suckled. Lauralee cried out, but the cry became a crooning that flowed ceaselessly from some shameless place deep within her.

She writhed as he turned to the other breast, enjoyed it at his leisure, her hands moving beneath his shirt to course frantically up and down the corded warmth of his back.

At Lauralee's urging, Jay poised himself above her. He moaned and closed his eyes as she opened the buttons of his trousers and displaced them, gasped as she greeted his magnificence with her hands, at once taming and paying homage. A primitive shudder moved the length of his frame as she caressed him, but he submitted to her attentions, his head thrust far back, the muscles in his neck and upper chest flexing over words of sweet despair.

"Take me," Lauralee whispered. "Take me now."

Instead, Jay held back, his breath loud over the chorus of night creatures, his chest and shoulders heaving with an effort to recover himself. He trembled as Lauralee opened his shirt and tangled her fingers in the rich matting of ebony hair she found beneath. "We can't," he despaired when he could speak. "You're not yourself, Lauralee—you're not thinking straight—"

He was wrong. Lauralee was herself as she had not been in a very long time. She was a woman in the fullest, grandest sense of the word, and as such she knew how to override his protests. She caught him in both hands and shaped him to a straining, fearsome splendor.

Jay gave in with a raw cry and sought her warmth with a fierce thrust that Lauralee welcomed, lifting her hips, enclosing him eagerly.

For several brief and glorious moments, Lauralee wielded a power too awesome to grasp, but then this was taken from her. Jay held his hands beneath her bottom and delved deep within her, mastering and molding her. She was worshiped and reprimanded, made to purr and made to plead. Finally, on a tide of passion, she was made to rise, weeping, her body in delicious, incessant spasm.

The power was Lauralee's again as she fell, sated, into the tender rhythm that demanded all these same things of Jay. It was he who begged, he who was reformed, tantalized, exalted, he who stiffened, again and again, as the needs of his body overrode the restraints of his mind and demanded appeasement.

One lover was the chalice and one the wine and neither, in that moment, was more nor less than the other.

They lay still for a long time, entwined, the night sounds muffled by the heavy rasp of their breathing. Spiritually as well as physically, they were as yet one person and neither wanted to spoil the singular splendor of that. The time of separation was inevitable, of course. Lauralee accepted that, and still, she nearly wept as she felt her soul break its bond with his and stand apart, tremulous but strong.

She wound her fingers in Jay's dark hair as his lips moved against the moist skin of her neck. I love you, she wanted to say, for there was no explaining the fact, no justifying it: It was simply true. For Lauralee, the fierce joining of Jay's body to her own had been a time of enlightenment; she knew now that she could not have given herself to him so fully if she had not loved him first.

She wept, because loving Jay was hopeless.

At the sound of her grief, Jay lifted his head, searched her face. "I told you you were going to feel this way," he ventured hoarsely. "Damnit, Lauralee, I told you."

He mistook her heartache for shame, then. Well, that only went to show what Jay McCallum knew about anything. Lauralee could never have been ashamed of such soaring joy, such fullness, not if she lived a thousand and one years. "Do you think I regret what we did?" she whispered.

Jay realigned himself, stroked away her tears with his thumbs. "If not, why are you crying?"

"Men!"

Jay shrugged. "It was an honest question, wasn't it?"

Lauralee tried to sit up, but Jay wouldn't allow it. Rather than lash her injured pride by trying to escape, she pretended resignation to her circumstances. "I behaved exactly the same way with Virgil, you know," she said, meaning to hurt Jay.

It was immediately evident that she had succeeded. His jaw tightened and his eyes narrowed and his voice had a mocking quality designed to field pain. "Thank you for sharing that. It's good to know that you're consistent, Mrs. Parker."

Jay's words cut, just as he had intended them to do. Lauralee struggled to slip from beneath him, but he clasped her hands together at the wrists and held them high above her head.

"Let me go," she breathed, furious beyond all measure.

Jay sat up, but the pressure of his hand, still imprisoning her wrists, did not relax. With his other hand, he stroked the curve of her hips, traced her rib cage, captured one plump breast and dallied with the nipple until Lauralee had to bite her lip to keep from crying out some wanton encouragement. She arched her neck and closed her eyes in angry ecstasy as he relearned each separate part of her body, lay obediently still when he released her, shivered as he moved away from her, and rejoiced when he returned. Submitted mutely as he cleansed her with a bit of wet cloth.

When Jay set the cloth aside, he tangled a gentle finger in the curls at the meeting of her thighs. "I can put up with a lot from you, Lauralee—your marches, your hymns—" his mouth formed a mocking grin "—your stretch in the poky. But there is one thing I will not tolerate, and that is being compared with your dear, departed husband. Do I make myself clear?"

The grin was gone and his last words had been spoken in deadly earnest. Lauralee did understand and she nodded, unable to speak because his finger had strayed deeper, stroking the core of her femininity into a tight knot of wanting. Pleasure forced her to rise in welcome to each caress. As Jay parted her, baring the tiny nubbin of flesh to the night air and some mastery she could not anticipate, she called his name.

He bent and partook of her and Lauralee was lost. Each pass of his tongue, each nibble, each gentle nip, drove her further and further outside herself. He was taming her, and there was no way she could defy him.

Come the morning, Lauralee could almost believe she had dreamed the events of the night before. She was back in her own room, after all, dressing for another day of work.

Something was different, though. She was alive in every fiber and bit of her body, and her senses still pulsed with the singular delights of being a woman.

She smiled as she pulled on a bloomer skirt and one of Virgil's shirts to work in the orchard, feeling beautiful even in those shabby garments. There was something to be said for the occasional brazen act, she reflected as she brushed her hair and then pinned it into place. Not, of course, that she intended to go creeping across the road again in the near future to engage in another tryst with Mr. Jay McCallum.

Her cheeks colored as she considered the embarrassment that would have resulted if she'd fallen asleep over there, on the floor of the Rumsucker Saloon, and then awakened to find half the male population of Halpern's Ferry staring down at her. What a tale they'd have to carry home at the end of the workday!

Lauralee laughed as she went downstairs to the kitchen. It would almost be worth the scandal to see Adrienne Burch's face when she heard the story.

Downstairs, Clarie was humming as she set the table while Jenny patiently urged Alexander to eat his oatmeal. He was almost two now, talking in phrases if not sentences, but he had not fully mastered the spoon.

"Mama!" he crowed at the sight of Lauralee, arms waving as though he might rise into the air and fly about the kitchen like a bird.

Feeling a bit like flying herself, Lauralee bent and kissed him soundly on the forehead. His skin felt warm, and she frowned.

"Stay with Sander!" he crowed, his plump cheeks flushed. "Mama, stay with Sander!"

Lauralee felt a familiar twinge of guilt. She always had to go to the orchard, leaving Alexander with Clarie or Jenny, but what else could she do? She'd tried taking him along once, and he'd not only been stung by a bee, he'd toddled off and nearly drowned in the creek. "Clarie needs you to help her tend the chickens and weed the garden," she reasoned weakly.

Alexander's face puckered and turned bright red. "Stay with Sander!" he bellowed.

Gone was Lauralee's bright, shimmering mood. She had to go to the orchard; Joe Little Eagle could not be expected to do the work alone. Resolutely, she turned and left the kitchen, unable to eat, Alexander's cries of dismay following after her, each one landing on her spirit with the force of a prizefighter's fist.

Two hours later, Jenny came to fetch her, looking frightened. Alexander was sick, she said. He was running a fever and there were spots on his stomach.

As Lauralee raced home, she kept hearing his pleas. *Mama, stay. Stay with Sander . . .*

CHAPTER
FIVE

"Are you out of your mind?" demanded Brice McCallum, assessing the framework of the Rumsucker Saloon with a scowl.

Jay had not expected his elder brother, especially at this early hour, and he was caught off guard. In that moment, he knew how Tim must have felt that long-ago day when he himself had arrived in Halpern's Ferry and asked much the same question, though not in those exact words. He was struck by a pang of grief and regret.

Tim, he thought, I'm sorry.

"Well?" pressed Brice, every inch the impatient older brother. Brice was not tall, but he was as solidly built as the proverbial brick outhouse. He was a quiet, single-minded man and only those who knew him well, as Jay did, ever suspected the formidable measure of his intelligence.

Jay sighed. "Leave it alone, Brice," he said.

Brice's nostrils flared and he ran one hand through

his thick chestnut-colored hair, which showed no gray despite the fact that he was nearing forty. He'd arrived in Halpern's Ferry the day before by stagecoach and passed the night at the hotel, so his carefully tailored tweed coat and fitted breeches betrayed nothing of the rigors of the trip from Spokane. Jay, still clad in yesterday's dark trousers and loose linen shirt, felt seedy by comparison.

"Dad isn't well, you know."

Jay leaned back against a support beam and folded his arms. "I'm aware of that, Brice," he answered quietly. "Did the senator send you here?"

"No," came the exasperated response. There was a short, unsettling silence, and then Brice's ice-blue eyes came squarely to Jay's face. "I know you came here to find Tim's killer, Jay, and I understand your need to do that. We'd all like to see the bastard hanged, whoever he is, but I fail to see how rebuilding one mistake over the top of another is going to accomplish anything."

Jay felt more the little brother than the man, and that, at thirty-five years of age, was galling. "I know what I'm doing."

"Do you?" One of Brice's eyebrows arched. "I wonder."

Truth to tell, Jay wondered too. He was normally a methodical man, not given to rash decisions, yet here he was, building the Rumsucker Saloon in the middle of nowhere. Here he was, neglecting his family and his legal practice and the political ambitions he had cherished for years. And for what?

Oh, at first he'd believed that Lauralee Parker could have killed Tim, but now he knew differently. He'd been inside her soul and he knew.

"What about the Senate?" Brice threw out in that calm, challenging way of his, his hands clasped to-

74

gether behind his back. "Dad wants to retire, let you finish out his term. That would give you two full years to prove yourself, Jay. In '04, you would be elected in your own right."

Until just the day before, Jay had wanted nothing more than a seat in the United States Senate; he had been groomed for it, trained for it, most of his life. Now, thanks to a hellion with aquamarine eyes and calluses on her hands, the dream lacked something vital. It lacked Lauralee.

Jay turned away from Brice, from the farmhouse across the road, but he could not quite turn away from the challenge. Nor could he bring himself to suggest that Brice or Chance, their remaining brother, complete their father's term. Damnit, the job was his. His.

Brice saw his advantage and pressed it. "If you don't come back, Jay, and take hold, Dad will send Chance in your place. He'll have no other choice. His health isn't what it used to be, and Tim's death nearly finished him. Dad simply isn't up to traveling back and forth to Washington anymore, let alone representing his constituents the way they deserve to be represented."

Jay rounded on his brother suddenly. Chance, born just a year before Tim, was now the youngest. He was an affable hothead and, despite his marriage, an inveterate lady's man. "Chance can't even be faithful to his wife! How the hell can he be expected to look after the interests of an entire state?"

Brice, fighting back a grin of triumph, shrugged. "Very frankly, I have no idea. I do know this: The legislature convenes in just over a month, Jay. If you don't come back to Spokane, square away your practice, and work out some kind of agreement with Dad, Chance is as good as on his way to Washington."

The very thought was galling. "A month?" Jay

echoed, despairing, his gaze slicing involuntarily to the farm across the road.

Brice, a powerful man in his own right but lacking any leaning whatsoever toward political matters, was perceptive. "A woman," he guessed aloud. "I should have suspected."

Jay could not deny Lauralee, though he would have liked to. To keep from spilling out all the crazy things he felt, he bit down hard on his lower lip and folded his arms across his chest, as if to hold it all inside.

Brice chuckled, able to read his brother as easily as he read soil conditions or estimated the number of bushels to be reaped from a field of wheat. "So it's finally happened, has it? Well, I don't mind telling you that we despaired of it. Thought you were going to go on keeping mistresses from here to doomsday."

"I can't marry her," Jay mourned, aware of how much he was revealing but unable to help himself. He'd always been close to Brice, and confiding in him was a habit. "She would never leave that land." Because that would mean giving up her independence, he added to himself. It would mean giving up Virgil.

Brice leaned against a beam and smiled. "Being a farmer myself, I can understand an attachment to the land. Real love is the best thing that can happen in this life, though, and a woman generally has the good sense to know that."

Jay rubbed his chin with one hand, thinking that he needed a shave and a hot bath. He gave his brother a sidelong glance and grinned. "You've got everything, Brice—Lucy, land of your own, happiness. You know, I hope, how lucky you are."

Brice had never been given to excessive humility, though his pride was, like the rest of his nature, carefully controlled. At the mention of his beautiful wife and the waving acres of wheat surrounding his grand house, he beamed. The only thing he and Lucy lacked was children, and they seemed to be resigned to that disappointment, happy with each other. "Yes, as a matter of fact, I do." He paused, and a deep fondness passed silently between the two brothers. "I'm taking the afternoon stage as far as Colville. Are you going with me?"

Jay's entire body ached, protesting a night spent making love on a hard wooden floor. With one hand, he worked the knotted muscles at the back of his neck. "I don't know," he answered honestly. "I've got some things to do in Halpern's Ferry, so I'll ride that far with you, anyway."

Wisely, Brice pressed the question no further.

Alexander was fretful, and his cheeks burned the palms of Lauralee's hands when she touched him. There were, just as Jenny had said, spots breaking out all over his body. Perhaps, she thought frantically as she lifted the whimpering little boy into her arms, this was her punishment for what she had done the night before with Jay McCallum.

"Shall I fetch the doc?" Clarie asked, her brown eyes wide and worried. In that hazy, distracted moment, the girl so resembled Virgil that Lauralee felt a stinging pang of guilt.

She had no time to examine the notion, however; Alexander was ill, and something had to be done. "Yes. And please hurry, Clarie." Lauralee moved to lay Alexander on the nearest flat surface, the kitchen table, then remembered his father lying there and carried him into the front parlor instead. Sitting down on the settee, she began removing the child's clothes.

"What should I do?" implored Jenny, wringing her hands and hovering so close that Lauralee had to overcome an un-Christian urge to slap her away.

"Bring me a basin of cool water and some cloth," she snapped, but a moment later she added a sighed "Please."

Lauralee bathed Alexander again and again, talking to him in a soft voice, trying to comfort him. His fever grew worse and the spots spread first to his arms and legs, then to his face and back.

"We should have sent for Mr. Ellery, too," Jenny put in, anxious to be helpful.

Again, Lauralee bridled. Her brother was all the family she had left—Lauralee barely remembered her mother and father, who had died when she was just about Alexander's age—but Ellery might as well have been a stranger for all the love he bore his younger sister. "He's probably away on business or something," she said evenly. "Besides, what could he do for Alexander that we can't?"

Jenny looked bewildered; like many women, she believed that the presence of a man somehow nullified any sort of danger. "I just thought—"

Alexander gave a fitful squall, and Lauralee wrapped the child in a blanket and began to pace the floor with him. His flesh was so hot that she could feel it through her cambric work shirt. How high would his temperature climb by nightfall, when fevers invariably worsened?

Outwardly, for her child's sake, Lauralee was calm. Inwardly, she wept in despair and barely controlled panic. What if her baby died? God in heaven, what if he died?

After nearly two hours, Clarie returned with Doc Jameson. "I was on my way to town," the girl spouted, her voice a high-pitched irritant. "Guess who stopped and gave me a ride? Guess who helped me find the doc?"

Lauralee didn't care who had given Clarie a ride or

helped her track down the doctor; she cared only that he was finally there. "Do something," she implored the elderly man. "Alexander is so sick—do something."

Doc Jameson took the half-conscious child from his mother's arms with a look of wary resignation and carried him into the small spare bedroom that Mr. Neggers, the peddler, sometimes rented.

"Mr. Jay McCallum gave me a ride, that's who," Clarie went on with bright desperation. "I rode on the back of his horse, just like an Indian squaw—"

The door of the spare room was closed against Lauralee; she considered flinging herself at it until it collapsed. "Oh, Clarie, be quiet!" she cried.

Clarie retreated a step, hugging herself with both arms, and Lauralee instantly regretted her sharpness. The girl was frightened, just as frightened as Lauralee herself maybe, and if prattling helped her deal with her fear, what harm could it do?

"I'm sorry," Lauralee said.

The apology had been offered too late; Clarie's face hardened into a mask and she turned away.

"Don't mind her," Jenny fretted, staying too close to Lauralee. "She's just a-feared, that's all. She don't mean—"

"How did you ever get through Normal School?" Lauralee snapped by reflex. She regretted that, too. Being cruel to Jenny would not make Alexander better.

For the briefest moment, Jenny's pretty face contorted with a look of hatred so intense that Lauralee could not credit it. She put it down to imagination when, in the next instant, the young woman wilted like a delicate spring flower beneath an August sun and muttered, "I studied as hard as I could, Lauralee."

Lauralee patted the girl's arm. "I know you did,

Jenny. I'm sorry I spoke unkindly—I'm just so afraid."

Jenny's arm stiffened, then relaxed again. "I studied real hard. Virgil—Mr. Parker—he said that was the way to do—"

Lauralee was impatient again, but this time she held her tongue. Jenny was only trying to distract her from her worry, to help her get through the waiting. "Not now, Jenny, please," she said quietly. And then, because she could bear the suspense no longer, she went to the spare room door and opened it.

Doc Jameson had just completed his examination, and the sad resignation in his eyes as he looked down at the fever-ridden little boy lying on the bed was shattering to Lauralee. A shiver went through her, and she clasped the cool iron footboard in both hands, trying to steady herself.

"Doc?" she prompted shakily when the old man didn't speak.

"Measles," he said. The disease was a dreaded one; some children were blinded or rendered deaf by it, others died.

Lauralee closed her eyes for a moment, swayed, and took a firmer grip, a desperate grip, on the footboard. The angry red spots covering Alexander's body had been proof enough that he had the measles; she had hoped, by some miracle, to be mistaken. She had wanted Doc Jameson to say that Alexander was suffering from heat rash or a case of poison ivy, but not measles. Please, God, not measles.

She'd lost her parents to typhoid fever; she'd lost Virgil. And now it appeared that she might lose Alexander, too. "No," she choked out. "Oh, God in heaven, no—"

The doctor caught her hands in his and held them tightly. "Lauralee."

She drew in a deep breath, forced herself to be calm, to think. "What can we do for him?" she asked reasonably, knowing even as she spoke that there was no medicine, no treatment, no way to help Alexander beyond making him as comfortable as possible.

"Well, we can try to bring the fever down—"

Suddenly, Lauralee was filled with rage, rage directed at the hapless doctor, at the world in general and, most of all, at herself. "That isn't enough!"

Doc Jameson was used to frantic parents; no doubt he had encountered many. He patted Lauralee's shoulder and replied gently, "You'll want to pray for him, of course."

"Pray!" mocked Lauralee, who had believed in God all her life. She had endured much, her faith unshaken, but now, in the face of Alexander's peril, she doubted. What good did it do to pray? Had prayer saved Virgil? Had it protected her son from harm or brought real love, long a deep and driving hunger within her, into her life? "I have no confidence in prayer."

"That is a pity," Doc Jameson replied, writing out brief and, to Lauralee, inadequate instructions for Alexander's care. Having done this, he closed his familiar black bag and reached for his hat. In the doorway of the tiny room, he paused. "You'll let me know if you need anything?"

Lauralee swallowed hard, the paper Doc Jameson had given her crumpled between her fingers. Only by the greatest of effort did she keep from lashing out at the doctor, demanding to know what good he could do in the future when he was so very useless now. "Yes," she managed to say.

The doctor came out of Lauralee's house by the rear door, head down, hat in hand.

Jay, who had been waiting beside Doc Jameson's

81

buggy, tensed at the sight of him. From the moment he'd encountered Clarie on the road and heard about the boy's illness, he'd wanted to be at Lauralee's side, helping her in any way he could, but some instinct deep within had warned him to keep his distance until the time was right. He cleared his throat as the physician approached and tossed his bag into the seat of the buggy.

"Well?" Jay demanded when Doc Jameson didn't volunteer any information.

"Measles. The boy's mighty sick—won't last the night the way he's going."

Jay closed his eyes briefly, then opened them again. In the space of that instant the doctor had somehow hefted his heavy body into the buggy seat and taken up the reins.

A desperate idea took shape in Jay's mind. "If I could get him to Spokane, to the hospital there—"

The elderly doctor shook his head. "Alexander couldn't bear up under a stagecoach ride. He's too small and too weak."

Jay had never been good at giving up; now he found it impossible. "What about a steamboat?" he pressed. "What if we took Lauralee's little boy as far as Colville on a steamer and then caught the late train to Spokane?"

Doc Jameson sighed despondently. He was sweating in his dark suit, from his helplessness. "I don't reckon you'd have anything to lose by trying," he responded. "Or much to gain, either."

Jay realized that he had been holding the doctor's horse and now let go, turning to stride toward the house and knock at the back door. He was admitted to the tidy kitchen by Clarie.

"Lauralee's with the baby, Mr. McCallum," she said stiffly. She was pale and it was clear that the full weight of the situation had settled into her mind; earlier, when Jay and Brice had seen her running along the road to Halpern's Ferry and stopped for her, she had nearly talked them to death.

Jay wondered what to do. After all, this wasn't his house, Lauralee wasn't his wife, the baby wasn't his son. He couldn't just seize control of things; he didn't have the right.

"I'll tell her you're here," Clarie conceded unexpectedly, and her brown hair swung around her shoulders as she turned on one heel to leave the kitchen.

Moments later, she was back, followed by the lady who boarded with Lauralee. Clarie had told Jay all about Jenny, how she had a teaching certificate but could barely read or write, how her father lived in the hills and was a drinking man, sometimes violent and sometimes too affectionate.

"Lauralee says you're to go away and never come back," Clarie announced, chin high but trembling. "She says you've done quite enough as it is, thank you."

Jay had feared just this, that Lauralee would believe the boy's illness was some sort of divine punishment for the unbridled passion of the night before. Couldn't she see how irrational such a viewpoint was? She wasn't a stupid woman.

"The hell!" Jay muttered, passing Clarie and the voluptuous little schoolteacher, seeking Lauralee and finding her by instinct.

She stood beside a narrow bed in a room just off the parlor, staring down at her half-conscious child with tear-bright aquamarine eyes.

"Lauralee."

Her shoulders stiffened beneath an ugly blue shirt made for a man, and Jay could see that her throat worked spasmodically. When Lauralee looked at Jay, she wounded him. "Are you satisfied?" she whispered brokenly.

The words struck Jay like blows, but he drew nearer, folded his arms across his chest. Not an hour ago, he'd dreamed of courting this woman properly, of marrying her, of taking her with him to Washington. It seemed incredible that a hope of that magnitude could be dashed so quickly.

He allowed his eyes to rest on the child, who fretted in his discomfort. "This is not the wrath of God, Lauralee," Jay said as reasonably as he could

Crystal tears streaked down Lauralee's cheeks, spilled onto the ragged shirt to shimmer there and lend the garment an odd elegance. "Isn't it?" Lauralee breathed, and her gaze, too, was fixed on the little boy. "I came to you in my nightgown, like some kind of strumpet. I gave myself to you and I didn't even have the decency to be ashamed!"

"What does that have to do with Alexander being sick?"

Lauralee's chin trembled; Jay ached to draw her into his arms, comfort her, but he didn't dare.

"God is angry with me," she insisted.

Jay was terribly afraid—afraid that Lauralee truly believed what she was saying. Afraid that the fallacy would be borne out by the death of her child. "Listen to yourself, Lauralee. Think of all you've been taught about God, all you've believed. Do you really think He would strike down an innocent child—"

" 'The sins of the fathers,' " quoted Lauralee in a soft, faraway voice more frightening to Jay than a scream would have been. "Virgil sinned. I've sinned—"

"And God is wrathful." Jay deliberately made the words contemptuous, and their bite jolted Lauralee

84

out of her reverie. Her eyes wide, she stared at Jay. Clearly, she did not know how to answer.

"I can't lose Alexander," she said after a very long time. "Oh, Jay, I can't lose him."

Even then Jay did not dare to touch Lauralee. He spoke softly, caressing her with his voice, instead of his hands, sheltering her in reason instead of in his arms. "There is a hospital in Spokane. We can take Alexander there, Lauralee, if you agree to it."

Jay saw then what he had prayed for: hope rising in Lauralee's eyes, color returning to her face. He found himself imploring heaven that this hope would not be in vain.

All this, and he wasn't even religious.

"How could we take Alexander so far? The stage-coach—"

"The stagecoach is out of the question. The doctor said the ride would be too long and too rough. We'll hire one of the steamboats at Burch's Mill to take us as far as Colville, then we'll catch the train."

Lauralee's face brightened and she burst out of her inertia in a frenzy of activity, gathering clothes for the child, dressing him, spouting orders for Jenny and Clarie, who were to remain behind and help someone called Joe Little Eagle look after the orchards.

Jay went outside at a sprint, found a battered buggy in the barn but no horse. Undaunted, he hitched his own gelding to the dusty vehicle, and ten minutes later, he and Lauralee were on their way to Halpern's Ferry.

Brice, bless the benevolent fates, was just boarding the stagecoach when they arrived in town. At Jay's shout, he gestured for the driver to toss down the carpetbag he'd stowed atop the coach and strode toward the buggy.

Jay got down from the buggy seat and drew his brother aside to explain. It was agreed that since the situation was so delicate, Brice would be the one to ask Adrienne Burch for the use of one of her steamboats.

The request was granted, but with one glaring hitch. Adrienne decided to come along.

"I'll handle the lady," Brice assured Jay in a comforting undertone as the small riverboat chugged away from the dock on its unscheduled journey. "You take Lauralee and the little one into the wheelhouse, out of the sun, and look after them."

Jay complied instantly, glad to leave the charming Mrs. Burch to his brother.

Lauralee sat huddled in a corner of the wheelhouse, out of the captain's way, Alexander stirring against her shoulder. She prayed, despite her earlier words, promising God all manner of outlandish things if only He would spare her baby. She was conscious of Jay's presence, but she could not look at him.

"Why did that woman insist on coming with us?" Lauralee murmured to herself. "She doesn't care about Alexander—"

"Don't worry about Adrienne," Jay responded, making Lauralee aware that she had spoken out loud. "Brice will see to her."

"Brice?"

"My brother."

Lauralee still did not look at Jay; she was playing a desperate game. If she did not look at him, the rule went, Alexander would not die. "What a strange name," she said. "Brice, I mean."

"It was my grandmother's maiden name." Jay seemed intent on talking. Maybe he was like Clarie. Maybe talking made a crisis easier for him to bear.

Distractedly, Lauralee hoped that Clarie would remember to give the chickens water as well as feed.

"There were four of us until Tim died," Jay went on. "Brice is the oldest, I was born next, and then Chance came along. Chance is short for Chancelor, another family name."

Who cares? thought Lauralee, but the sound of Jay's voice offered a strange sort of comfort, so she listened, eyes carefully averted, as Jay told her all about his father, the senator, and his mother, the senator's wife. He seemed to possess an inexhaustible supply of relatives.

Both of his brothers were married, the elder happily, the younger unhappily. Lauralee wondered which brother was outside, on deck, keeping Adrienne Burch at bay. She supposed, given the woman's charms, that it was probably the younger one, with the faltering marriage.

Lauralee rocked Alexander in her arms, all the while clinging to Jay's voice as though it were a rope strung through a dark cave, to be followed, hand over hand, until the light was reached. She was aware, too, of the sawdust-speckled floor of the wheelhouse and the smells of machine oil and human sweat.

Finally, at long last, they reached Colville. They hired a wagon and drove to the train depot on the main street.

"Whatever you do, don't mention that the baby has measles," Brice cautioned in a low voice as Jay went to buy the tickets. Adrienne was still hovering nearby, her eyes moving up and down her conscripted escort's frame as though he were a poem to be committed to memory.

At the word *measles*, Adrienne flinched and retreated a step. "I do have shopping to do," she said in a faltering voice.

"Don't let us detain you," Lauralee responded, checking the blanket that covered Alexander's face. Brice was right; it wouldn't do to have anyone see the spots. If word got out that the baby was suffering from measles, they would not be allowed to ride the train.

In the end, Jay managed to obtain seats in an otherwise empty car. This was the only concession they dared make to the contagious nature of Alexander's illness.

Soon after they were settled in their seats, the train plummeted into noisy motion. Jay wanted to hold Alexander for a while, but Lauralee could not give him up, even though he was heavy and her arms ached.

"Lauralee, why won't you look at me?" Jay asked minutes later as they clattered toward Spokane.

Lauralee couldn't answer his question. A new rule had been added to her mental game: Not only must she avoid looking at Jay, she must not speak to him, either.

Jay was persistent. "Will you at least have something to eat? There must be a dining car—"

"I'm not hungry," she broke in.

"You are hungry," Jay insisted. "And you need to eat. What good will you be to Alexander if you don't stay strong?"

Lauralee agreed to eat, though she tasted none of the food Jay brought her from the dining car. Feeding herself was an awkward process, since she refused to let go of Alexander even to do that, but she managed to chew and swallow, chew and swallow, until Jay was satisfied with her efforts and took away the plate.

No sooner had he done that and returned when he wanted her to lie down and rest. Lauralee shook her head, and Jay became annoyed.

"Damnit, woman, you need—"

For the first time, Brice interceded. "Leave Lauralee alone, Jay. There's such a thing as too much concern, you know."

Lauralee could not look at Jay to gauge his reaction to this. He made an exasperated sound, but he subsided.

It was dark by the time they reached Spokane. Lauralee took no note of the city, beyond its clamorous railroad yard. She cared only about reaching the hospital.

When they arrived there, Alexander was immediately taken from her. The shock was complete. The man she had refused to look at came into clear focus, Lauralee's insulation was gone, and reality was everywhere.

Lauralee could not bear it. Her knees buckled beneath her, the gas-lit hospital went dark, and Jay's hands caught her under the arms just as she would have slipped straight into hell.

CHAPTER
SIX

The room was sumptuous, filled with silk and sunlight and good smells. Lauralee sat up in bed with a jolt, disoriented and anxious.

A maid, wearing a sedate black sateen uniform, was fussing with a service cart, and Jay McCallum slept soundly, snoring just a little, in a nearby chair. His clothes were hopelessly rumpled and his face unshaven.

Looking at him, Lauralee remembered everything— Alexander's condition, the hectic trip to Spokane, the grim brick hospital in the center of town. She had no business lying about in this shamefully luxurious room; she had to go to her son!

"Where are my clothes?" she demanded of the maid, who had seemed to be unaware of Lauralee's presence until that moment.

Jay awakened with a start and dismissed the young servant with a yawning nod of his head before she could answer Lauralee's question. "Relax," he said, shifting in his chair and then rising to stretch. "Alexander is all right. The hospital would have telephoned if anything bad had happened."

Lauralee was comforted by his logic, but she looked about for her clothes all the same. "I must go to him. He'll be frightened—"

Jay's voice remained even, quiet. "I know you need to be near Alexander now, and that's understandable." He glanced at the service cart, where steam was seeping around the edges of silver plate covers. "Eat. While you're doing that, I'll see if my mother can't scare up something for you to wear."

Lauralee clutched at her blankets. She longed to fling them aside and bolt out of bed, but she was wearing only a thin satin nightgown. She knew the gown could not be her own and dared not so much as wonder how it had come to be on her body. "Just give me my own things, please!"

The service cart rattled as Jay rolled it to within reach of the bed. "A man's shirt and a pair of bloomers? Do you want to be thrown out of the hospital for a derelict? Just eat, and I'll get you something decent to put on—"

"Decent!" Lauralee hissed.

Jay shook his head in bewilderment. "Just eat," he said, and then he was gone and Lauralee ate because the food smelled so good and she was hungry and what use could she be to Alexander if she was faint with starvation?

There was a tap at her door just as she was growing wild with renewed impatience, and at her call, a lovely young woman with rich brown hair and sad gray eyes swept into the room. Though it was still early, the visitor was beautifully dressed in a froth of pink lawn and white lace. In her arms she carried a summery gown of white cambric embroidered with tiny yellow flowers and sprigs of green.

"Good morning, Mrs. Parker," she said shyly, approaching the bed and laying out the gown, along with

91

underthings and stockings and even a pair of slippers. "I'm Kate, Kate McCallum. Jay thought some of my things might fit you, so he asked me to—"

Lauralee dived for the dress and the lingerie so suddenly that Kate stepped back and raised one hand to her throat. "Thank you!" Lauralee cried, darting around one end of an elaborately painted dressing screen. There, she peeled off the lovely satin nightgown and struggled into the clothes that had been provided for her, nearly toppling over several times in her effort to be quick. Alexander would be scared to death—she just knew it—finding himself in a strange place, surrounded by people he didn't know . . .

"Jay telephoned the hospital," the lingering Kate ventured from the other side of the screen. "Your little boy is still very ill, of course, but his fever is down slightly."

Thank you, God, Lauralee thought as she whisked around the screen at last, fully clad. Kate buttoned the back of the borrowed dress for her and then pointed toward a door on the other side of the room. "The wash room is in there."

Lauralee blushed. In her haste to dress and go to Alexander, she had forgotten all about her ablutions and brushing her hair. She dashed toward the indicated door and found a marble basin, a bathtub, and a commode, all of which appeared to be connected to an indoor plumbing system. Had she had the time, Lauralee would have been impressed; as it was, she simply made herself presentable and hurried out.

Kate led the way out of the room, down a wide hallway with beautifully carved woodwork around its doors and deep carpeting on the floor. There were paintings on the walls fit to hang in a museum.

The stairs were broad and sweeping and the floor of the entryway at their base, as large as Lauralee's whole house, was of glistening marble. A cherrywood clock stood beside the door, and sunlight spilled through a large fanlight window above it. In this light stood Jay McCallum, neatly dressed and shaven.

"Ready?" he asked, and his eyes touched Lauralee warmly. Gently.

Had Lauralee not been so concerned about her son, she would probably have remarked to herself that it was an odd thing, the owner of the Rumsucker Saloon coming from such luxurious surroundings as these. She did wonder how she could have been brought to such a place and still have no conscious memory of arriving. "Yes, I'm ready," she said quickly, sparing a glance and a muttered, "Thank you so much," for Kate, who stood behind her.

As he opened the door, Jay too looked at Kate, and Lauralee thought she read an angry sympathy in his gaze. As he ushered her down a flower-edged brick walk, he frowned.

"Is Kate your sister?" Lauralee asked as a coachman came forward to open the gate for them. The door of an immaculate carriage stood ajar.

"Kate is my brother's wife," Jay answered, helping Lauralee into the carriage and then following to settle into the seat opposite hers. "She did tell you that I spoke with someone at the hospital earlier, didn't she?"

Lauralee nodded. "You have a telephone," she said, cheered to know that in just a few minutes she would be with Alexander again. "I should like to use it sometime. There's only one in Halpern's Ferry, you know. It's in the grocery, and though I've looked at it, I've never had occasion to telephone anyone."

The look of quiet annoyance in Jay's eyes, there since he'd encountered Kate in the entryway, suddenly faded away, replaced by a twinkle. Oddly enough, he chuckled as though he found her simple remark infinitely amusing.

Pete Townsend could not have said why he felt drawn to the site of McCallum's saloon or what he hoped to find there. Maybe he just wanted to be close to that farm across the road, and thus, however indirectly, to Lauralee.

He walked around the incomplete building once, twice, a third time. The place was quiet except for the buzzing of bees and the insistent chirps of birds; work on it had been suspended until further notice, owing to Mr. McCallum's taking Lauralee and her baby to Spokane in such a hurry.

Pete sighed. He hoped those fancy city doctors could succeed where Doc Jameson had failed; Lauralee had lost plenty in her lifetime, and she couldn't spare that boy. She'd stood against so many things—Virgil's slide into drunkenness and then his death, the daily rigors of keeping a forty-acre place on the right side of bankruptcy, the orneriness of that Burch woman—but there were limits to what a body could hold up under.

He sat on what had been the south wall of the Mud Bucket Saloon, a platform lying weathered and sun-scented in the grass. There was talk about Lauralee and Jay McCallum; folks were wondering why those two would be thick enough to head off somewhere in such a rush, sick baby or no sick baby.

Pete wondered, too. He loved Lauralee Parker and he supposed she knew it, but she hadn't encouraged him in any way. No, she'd been polite and friendly, but she was like that with most everybody.

He sighed again, plucked a piece of grass from the ground, and split it into two parts just for something to do with his hands. If Lauralee never spoke to him

94

again, it was his own fault—he'd been the one to arrest her, like a damn fool, and put her in the position of having to be bailed out by a woman she had every cause to hate.

Pete leaned back, feeling the warmth of the old boards through his shirt, the brim of his battered hat shielding his eyes from the sun. His mind went back to the murder of Tim McCallum and all that bothered him about it.

For one thing, it reminded him of the way Virgil Parker had died. That had happened here, too, and there were other similarities; Pete sensed those, even if he couldn't quite put his finger on what they were.

Parker had been playing cards, drinking, and bragging about what he had waiting for him across the road. Remembering, Pete wrenched off his hat and then put it on again, pulling down hard on the brim. Damnit, he'd wanted to kill Parker himself at the time, for talking that way about Lauralee, for shaming her by carrying on with Adrienne Burch the way he had.

There had been an argument over a hand of cards and Virgil had staggered outside. Nobody, except for Pete himself, had paid much attention, and he'd been too heartsick over Lauralee to notice that the gambler Parker had been quibbling with followed. Nobody had seen that gambler since, but Virgil had been found on the ground, around to one side of the building, dead of a knife wound to the chest. The weapon itself had never turned up.

Pete would never forget—and God knew, he'd tried—the look on Lauralee's face when he and some of the men from the Mud Bucket had carried Virgil home on an old door that had been part of Tim McCallum's bar. She'd thanked them, then asked them all to leave. And she'd sent Clarie and Jenny French back upstairs; they hadn't wanted to go, but

Lauralee's tone of voice would have frightened Genghis Khan into obedience.

Wearing her nightgown and a wrapper, her silver-blond hair draped over one shoulder in a thick braid, she'd gone to the stove to stoke up the fire and put water on to heat.

Pete had hesitated in the doorway, hurting for her. "Mrs. Parker, if there's anything—"

She'd cut him off with a sweep of those incredible blue-green eyes and a firm, "Leave me be to look after my husband now, Pete. I've got to do that for it to be over."

I've got to do that for it to be over. The words echoed across time to nag at Pete Townsend. A lot of women would have screamed and cried, but there had been a stillness in Lauralee, a certain quiet resignation, as though she'd been expecting the remains of her man to be brought home in just that way.

Had she come across that road, met Virgil outside the Mud Bucket Saloon, and stabbed him to death, maybe with a kitchen knife? She could have done it, even though she'd been far along with her baby at the time. Lauralee was taller than most women, and she was strong. She had had reason enough to be fed up with Virgil Parker.

Pete thrust himself to his feet, exasperated. It was crazy to be sitting here, thinking thoughts like those, when he knew Lauralee didn't have it in her to kill anybody. Not Virgil, not Tim McCallum, not anybody.

And it was getting him nowhere. Pete Townsend was a thorough soul, and it galled him that two murderers, Virgil's and Tim McCallum's, were going scot-free.

The doctor looked optimistic, though in a guarded sort of way. He was young, terse, and, judging by his manner and his way of speaking, very well educated.

96

Lauralee stood a little closer to Jay, there beside Alexander's railed bed, waiting.

"There is every chance that your little boy will live, Mrs. Parker," announced the physician, his eyes meeting and holding hers. "His fever is down."

Lauralee swayed, clasped the iron rails before her for support. Thank God, she thought, thank God.

"However," the doctor went on, and at that word, Jay's arm slid around her waist, firm and strong. "There appears to be damage to the child's hearing."

"Damage?" Lauralee echoed, looking down at Alexander now. He was only half awake, his plump little face still covered with red spots.

Unexpectedly, Dr. Kerrigan clapped his hands over the crib. Both Lauralee and Jay reacted by reflex, but Alexander, looking up at his mother, didn't move.

"Is this temporary?" Jay asked in a low voice when Lauralee could not speak.

Dr. Kerrigan shrugged. "We have no way of knowing that. A measure of the boy's hearing may return; then again, it may not."

Lauralee's fingers knotted on the cold railing. "I don't care," she said to Jay and the doctor and all of creation. "I don't care. Alexander is alive and that is all that matters."

Dr. Kerrigan smiled wearily. "Indeed, that is a miracle in itself. You'll be wise to take each day as it comes, Mrs. Parker—some of them will be difficult, of course—but even if your son's hearing loss is permanent, there is hope. There are ways to teach the deaf, options that have not been open to us before."

Lauralee tried not to think about the inevitable struggles and heartaches that lay ahead. "What can I do to help him now?"

"Alexander will need to remain here for a time, until he regains his strength, and you'll want to sit with him,

97

I suppose." The doctor's handsome face sobered again, and keenly intelligent blue eyes carried a warning. "Don't exhaust yourself, Mrs. Parker. Don't deprive yourself of the rest you need. Take time for regular meals and even the occasional entertainment. You'll be a hindrance to this child rather than a help if you don't look after your own well-being."

Something new occurred to Lauralee. "The cost of Alexander's care—"

Dr. Kerrigan, no doubt a very busy man, was turning away. There were other patients who needed him. "The people downstairs can tell you about that," he said.

Lauralee glanced at Jay and thought he looked a mite uncomfortable. For one thing, he seemed to be having trouble meeting her eyes.

"Don't worry about the money," he said.

Don't worry about the money. That was certainly easy for a man who lived as Jay McCallum did to say! For a woman who could barely meet her yearly mortgage payments and keep food on the table, it was a considerable challenge.

Jay's gaze sliced to hers and read her thoughts there. "I've already made financial arrangements," he announced somewhat defensively.

Lauralee was at once shaken and grateful. She had no money to speak of, and Alexander probably wouldn't be alive if it weren't for the care he'd gotten in this place. Still, to be obligated to Jay McCallum for hundreds or even thousands of dollars was not a happy prospect. "Why, Jay? Why did you do it?"

"Because I can afford to, among other reasons," he snapped. "Besides, it was my idea to bring Alexander here in the first place, wasn't it?"

Lauralee lifted her chin. "It was, and I'm grateful, of course," she conceded. "But Alexander is my son, my responsibility. I confess to wondering what you hope to gain in return."

Jay's jaw hardened and his gray eyes darkened until they resembled a tornado sky. "Sometimes, Mrs. Parker, people do things for other people without any kind of ulterior motive," he said, his voice quiet and cutting. And then he was striding angrily out of the hospital ward.

Lauralee closed her eyes for a moment, despairing, and then turned her thoughts back to a course of firm good cheer. She spent the morning with Alexander, holding his hand, telling him stories that he couldn't hear, praying that the broth she patiently spooned into his mouth would sustain him, give him strength.

Exactly at noon, Kate McCallum appeared, elegantly dressed in a dark gray dress corded with black trim, her hands gloved, her stylish hat at just the right angle on her perfectly coiffed copper-brown hair.

"How is he?" she asked, and there was pain in her eyes as she looked down at Alexander.

Lauralee put aside the peevish comparisons she'd been making between herself and this oddly downhearted young woman and worked up a smile. "Better."

Kate smiled back, though with an effort that was just as obvious as Lauralee's had probably been. "Jay wants me to see that you eat some lunch. I thought we could go over to the Columbia Hotel; it's just across the street, and they have good food there."

Secretly, Lauralee was injured that Jay had sent an emissary instead of coming back in person, but she quickly overcame that self-indulgence. Jay had done enough, and he was, no doubt, busy with all the matters left untended during his time in Halpern's Ferry. After bending to kiss Alexander's forehead—he was just nodding off to sleep—she followed Kate out of the ward, down a flight of foot-worn stairs, past a crop of wooden desks, and out into the sunshine.

The streets, mostly brick, were busy. Trolley cars clanged past, gathering power from metal rods that attached them to electrical wires overhead. People dashed in every direction, all in a hurry, and Lauralee, despite her hunger, felt a childish desire to rush back inside the relative quiet of the hospital and hide from it all.

Kate firmly took her arm. "Spokane is very different from the country, isn't it?" she asked, and then she stepped off the curb, and Lauralee, of course, was compelled to accompany her.

Lauralee wondered about the sadness that was always in this woman's eyes, even when she smiled. Kate was young and beautiful and she lived in almost boundless luxury. What was it that grieved her so when she should be happy? "Yes," she answered as they crossed the hazardous street and were admitted to the lobby of the hotel by a liveried doorman. "It's very different."

"I hope you'll come to the theater with me," Kate said as they entered an enormous, bustling dining room and were led to a table by a moustachioed waiter. "I simply love the theater, and Chance will never go with me."

They were seated at a table covered in white linen; a yellow rosebud in a silver vase stood in the center. "Chance?" Lauralee asked. The name sounded familiar.

Kate sighed. "My husband, Chancelor. He's Jay's younger brother."

"Oh," said Lauralee, sensing the need to say much more, but not knowing, of course, what it was that should be said.

Jay's sister-in-law had taken up a menu and was

pondering its offerings thoughtfully. "If you're with us long enough, you'll probably encounter him. He passes through occasionally to visit." Though the words were spoken lightly, almost distractedly, they resounded with pain.

"Visit?" Lauralee asked over the top of her own menu. "Doesn't he live where you do?"

Kate's shoulders slumped just a little, though she was still intent, or so it appeared, on what she would choose for her luncheon. "Officially, yes," she said.

Ordinarily, Lauralee would not have questioned that alarming and cryptic statement, but her instincts told her that Kate wanted, even needed, to talk. "A lot of men are kept away from home on business," she threw out after a few moments of mental groping.

Kate's lush mouth curved in an ironic smile. "Chance's only business is taking up where Tim left off. He's a rounder and a rascal, and if I had any courage at all, I would leave him."

The waiter came; Kate ordered stuffed peppers and Lauralee did, too, because it spared her the task of deciding among a full two dozen choices. When the moustachioed man had gone away, Lauralee leaned forward in her velvet-upholstered chair.

"Do you love your husband?" she asked, in a low and forthright voice.

The question was instantly regretted, for tears gathered in Kate's thickly lashed eyes and shimmered there. "Yes. More's the pity. I love Chance very much."

"Then you mustn't leave him," said Lauralee resolutely.

"I have my pride, you know," argued Kate. "Chance keeps at least one mistress—the wanton thing actually had the gall to present herself to me in Filbert's Department Store just the other day."

Lauralee drew in a scandalized breath, and her eyes widened. "What did she say?"

"She just wanted to let me know that she had a line of credit in that store—thanks to my husband. Lauralee, I was mortified."

Lauralee thought of Virgil and Adrienne Burch. "Does Chance drink?"

One tear slipped down Kate's cheek, and she dashed it away with a gloved hand. "No more than other men do, I suppose." She paused, drew a deep breath. "I shouldn't be telling you this, Lauralee, burdening you with my troubles when you have so many of your own—it's just that I have no one to talk to. My parents are both gone, and Chance's mother thinks that if I'd only be a better wife—"

Lauralee reached out, closed her hand over one of Kate's. "I'm sure you're a very good wife," she said.

Kate sniffled and held her head at a brave angle. "That's what Lucy says—she's Brice's wife, you know, and she understands, but she lives miles from the city and I don't see her often."

The stuffed peppers arrived and the two women began to eat, neither with remarkable appetite. Lauralee was remembering the last days with Virgil and how hard it was to bear up, with no one to talk to, no one to confide in.

"Perhaps you should take a trip," she suggested quite impulsively.

Kate brightened, set down her fork, her luncheon barely touched. "You know, Lucy says that, too. She says it would be good for me to get away from things for a while."

Lauralee thought that she would probably like Lucy McCallum should she ever have the good fortune to meet her. "I have no doubt that it would."

"And I'd love to have Chance wondering where *I*

am, for a change. As it is, he takes me very much for granted. But where would I go, Lauralee? I'm not brave enough to travel to New York or San Francisco alone, and if I went to visit Lucy, why, that would be the same to Chance as if I were safe in the old family home."

"You could come to my house," Lauralee suggested, once again speaking on impulse. What was happening to her? She was not a person given to flighty thoughts, and here she was, interfering in a marriage, for heaven's sake!

Kate looked so grateful and so intrigued that Lauralee couldn't bring herself to withdraw the invitation. She already had Clarie and Jenny to think about, not to mention the orchard and Alexander's health and myriad other things.

"Of course, we have to work very hard," Lauralee said. "And there aren't any servants or marble floors or carriages to ride in."

"I would like to work," said Kate, with bright and guileless resolution. "I've never done it before."

There was nothing for it. Lauralee was going to have another chick under her wing. Act in haste, repent at leisure. Still, she liked Kate, and she did want to help her. "It might be some time before we can leave, of course. Alexander has to be stronger."

Kate nodded, picked up her fork, and ate with the appetite of a millhand. Her hopeful attitude was heartening to Lauralee, who smiled when, as they were about to part in front of the hospital, Kate said, "I'm going to buy myself some calico dresses and some bonnets and some good sturdy shoes. I don't even care if I encounter that awful woman again!"

It was portentous that Kate should speak of awful women, for when Lauralee reached the ward where Alexander was recovering, Adrienne Burch was there, standing at the foot of his criblike bed, looking for all the world as though she had the right to be anywhere near him.

"How is Alexander, Lauralee?" she asked, and the question was so tenderly phrased that Lauralee's simmering annoyance cooled.

She replied with polite dignity. "It seems that the worst is past. Thank you, Adrienne, for the use of your boat—we probably wouldn't have gotten here in time if it hadn't been for that."

Adrienne gave a distracted nod and resumed staring at Alexander. Perhaps it was his resemblance to Virgil that interested her so; Lauralee had no way of knowing.

"I hoped to have a child once," Mrs. Burch imparted presently, and she lifted her eyes from Alexander to the wall behind his bed, seeming to see through that and all eternity besides.

Lauralee approached her son, adjusted his covers, touched his soft, lustrous hair. She remembered Frank Burch, Adrienne's late husband; he had been an older man, in ill health, not the sort one would expect to father children. All the same, that was one thing most men could do, old or young, sick or well.

When Lauralee didn't speak, Adrienne came back from the distances where she had been wandering and her eyes betrayed a pain as deep as any Lauralee had ever seen.

"You have everything, Lauralee Parker," she said with a bitterness that was stunning for all its quietness. "Everything."

Coming from a woman who lived in the largest and best house in Halpern's Ferry, from a woman who could afford to buy virtually anything she wanted, that was, to Lauralee's mind, an odd statement. But as Adrienne turned to leave and Alexander made a tiny sound in his sleep, the idea didn't seem quite so peculiar after all.

Jay's mother was obviously disappointed that Lauralee Parker, the mystery woman, had chosen to have dinner in her room. "You'd think she'd want to meet her hostess, at least," Mrs. McCallum sniffed. "And where, may I ask, is Kate?"

Jay smiled into a spoonful of soup. "Kate is with Lauralee," he said, though he would have liked to keep that bit of information from his younger brother, who had deigned to put in an appearance this evening.

Chance, sitting directly across the table from Jay, was sulking, not even pretending to eat. "Damnit, when a man comes home, he expects to find his wife waiting for him," he complained.

Jay suppressed an urge to drag his brother out into the garden and beat hell out of him. Before he could voice this desire, his mother broke in.

"Don't use profanity, Chancelor dear," she whined. "It is most unbecoming."

Jay and his father exchanged long-suffering looks and went on eating without comment. How could the senator even consider sending this spoiled whelp to Washington, for God's sake?

Chance startled everybody by sliding back his chair, standing up, and bellowing, "Kate!"

"Sit down and shut up," said the senator.

"Albert, don't speak to Chancelor that way," puled Eleanor. "He has a right—"

The senator broke in crisply. "You shut up too, Eleanor."

Jay hid a grin behind a biscuit. Chance dropped back into his chair, his brown eyes snapping with rage. He ran one hand through his rumpled, dark blond hair and then took up his fork.

Eleanor began to cry, dabbing at her face with a lace-edged napkin.

I don't like my own mother, Jay marveled to himself. I love her, but I don't like her. Isn't that a hell of a thing?

"Eleanor," said the senator with an indulgent sort of sternness. "Go to your room."

Chance's eyes met Jay's, and despite all that was between them, they each burst out laughing.

Eleanor wailed at this humiliation and fled, taking the lacy napkin with her.

"I'll say one thing for you, Dad," Chance remarked affably. "You sure know how to handle a woman."

Senator McCallum, a tall, robust-looking man with gray hair and deep lines in his face, did not smile. "Too bad I never knew how to handle you," he retorted.

Chance reddened, obviously insulted. "Now, I suppose, you're going to start comparing me to Jay and Brice."

The senator pondered as he chewed. "I wouldn't even know how to begin," he finally answered.

Chance shoved away his plate, glaring. "What the hell do you mean by that?"

No answer was forthcoming. The senator simply watched his youngest son, as though challenging him to figure the matter out for himself.

After biting off one swear word, roughly in the middle, Chance left the table, storming out of the dining room. "Kate!" he roared, no doubt bounding, cavalier fashion, up the stairs.

Jay took a sip from his wine and then cleared his throat. "So you really plan to unleash that on the United States Senate? Haven't they got enough problems, since McKinley's assassination, without Chance?"

Senator McCallum sighed. "This house would be a peaceful place with Chance away," he observed. "But I suppose palming him off on my colleagues wouldn't be very patriotic."

"It would be downright seditious," Jay remarked, only half in jest.

The senator arched a steel-gray eyebrow. "Do I have another choice, Jay?"

Jay lowered his head for a moment. "I want to go—"

"But?" prompted his father.

"There are . . . other considerations."

"Such as that pretty little thing upstairs?"

Jay smiled. "You don't miss much, do you, Dad?"

"As little as possible. What was her name again?"

"Lauralee. Lauralee Parker."

"Eleanor tells me that her boy is desperately ill."

Jay nodded. "He's going to live, but according to the doctor, he might be deaf."

"I'm sorry."

There was a short, comforting silence, which Jay broke. "I think I'm in love with Lauralee."

"More in love with her than with politics?"

Jay didn't know how to answer that question. He had always enjoyed women, but he'd never met one who meant more to him than the complex inner workings of democracy.

The senator spoke with quiet reason. "The solution seems simple to me, Jay. Marry your Lauralee, and take her to Washington with you. She'd be an asset to you. And her boy would benefit—I know of a very good school there where they're making tremendous progress with deaf children."

Jay lifted his eyes to the ceiling. Alexander's well-being was the one thing that might persuade Lauralee to leave that wretched orchard of hers. He made up his mind to approach her with the idea at the first opportunity.

Kate flinched and closed her eyes, simultaneously setting down her fork. The door of Lauralee's bedroom burst open and a tall, well-built man wearing riding boots, tailored breeches, and a shirt more befitting a pirate than the son of a senator appeared in the opening.

"My husband," Kate confided in a nervous whisper.

"I'd guessed that much," said Lauralee, giving Chancelor McCallum an objective assessment. He was handsome, indeed, with his boastful brown eyes and his butternut hair and his dashing manner.

When he saw Lauralee, Chance's fury faded away, leaving a deliberately endearing grin in its wake. He bowed a sweeping bow.

"Arrogant ass," muttered Lauralee under her breath. "How do you do?" she added aloud, smiling.

The brazen eyes took her measure and the grin broadened. "Introduce me," he said out of one side of his mouth to Kate.

Kate flushed, humiliated and angry, and before she could speak and get herself into trouble, Lauralee stood up and offered her hand.

"My name is Lauralee Parker," she said cheerfully. "I am Jay's friend."

That took a bit of the wind from Chance's sails, much to Lauralee's delight. Let him wonder what was meant, in this instance, by the word *friend*.

"Oh," said Chance, looking as disappointed as he sounded. For her part, Lauralee was relieved that he had enough honor to be daunted, at least a little, by the possibilities implied.

He was obviously at a loss, a problem Lauralee

would have guessed he rarely suffered. Finally, he bent, kissed Kate on the cheek, and left the room.

Had Chance McCallum been her husband, Lauralee would have followed after him and slapped his face, but Kate simply gazed at the door with a wounded yet adoring look in her eyes.

These McCallum men, Lauralee decided, bore watching. She smiled to herself. It was a dirty job, but somebody had to do it.

CHAPTER
SEVEN

Jay was sitting at a massive roll-top in a small, cluttered study, his back to Lauralee, his booted feet propped up on the desk's surface, reading. Every few seconds, he would pause and make odd, tentative motions with his hands, sometimes using both, sometimes just one.

Lauralee had no idea what he was doing, but she was strangely moved by the determined set of his shoulders, the tilt of his head. Feeling the force of his concentration, she was filled with an almost incomprehensible tenderness, and she longed to cross that little room and tangle her fingers in the ebony richness of his hair. "Jay?"

He closed the heavy book with a resolute thump and set it on the desk, his swivel chair creaking as he turned. Smiling, he extended one hand to Lauralee, and unable to resist, she went to him and allowed herself to be pulled onto his lap.

It had been a long time since she had been held with this sort of undemanding gentleness, and despite the scandalous impropriety of it all, Lauralee felt no compunction whatsoever.

Jay's thighs were long and hard beneath her, his chest a strong wall against her back. His hands, clasped innocuously in front of her, were in no way touching Lauralee and yet she was achingly conscious of them. Suppose they were to begin stroking her, those strong, sun-browned hands? Suppose they were to close, with tender boldness, over her breasts?

She shivered and Jay chuckled, the sound brushing the sensitive nape of her neck like a caress. "What is it, little one?"

Lauralee sighed. She could not answer that question and still call herself a decent woman, now, could she? But then, considering what she and Jay had done that night at the Rumsucker Saloon, she probably couldn't lay claim to decency anyway. "I—I need to send a wire to Clarie," she managed to say. "They'll all be worrying about Alexander—"

Jay's lips, warm and firm, grazed her nape, sending an involuntary shudder through her. "I took care of that after we talked to the doctor this morning," he said.

Lauralee knew she would behave in an untoward manner if he dallied with the back of her neck for so much as another moment. She turned on his lap and looked into his eyes, which was a daring enough proposition in itself.

"Do you take care of everything, Mr. McCallum?"

Jay's grin was slow, imperiously smug, and very magnetic. Lauralee felt her whole self, not just her mouth, being pulled toward it. "I try," he said, in a rumbling whisper.

If he were to kiss her, Lauralee would be lost. She knew that, and she didn't want to be lost, but she couldn't seem to pull away. Exerting some primal magic, Jay summoned her closer and closer until their mouths were touching. One of his hands—how she craved it and yet yearned to twist away—slid up from her waist to her breast.

Jay's fingertips were tracing this fullness, barely touching, and yet Lauralee's nipple leaped to pulsing attention beneath the dress and camisole borrowed from Kate. And all the while, he was kissing her, shaping her mouth with his, his tongue sparring gently with hers and then conquering.

Lauralee trembled—how was it possible that her need could be greater than it had been when she had gone to him in the night that other time, throwing herself at him like some brazen wanton?

In response to her trembling, Jay cupped her breast full in his hand, his thumb skillfully attending the hidden nipple, and his kiss deepened.

Thrusting herself away from him took almost super-human effort, but Lauralee managed it. She bounded out of his lap and stood staring down at him, her breath a gasping sound in the quiet, her face hot.

Grinning, Jay rose from his chair. The heavy door shutting the room off from the rest of the house closed with one push of the palm of his hand.

Lauralee's heart was pounding against her rib cage, and she pressed one hand to her breast in an effort to calm it. Even through the sleeve of his shirt, she could see the muscles work in Jay's upper arm as he reached up to dim the one light in the room.

She retreated a step, though her every instinct urged her forward, into his arms, and felt the edge of a couch or chair against the back of her legs. Lauralee cast a wild look over her shoulder; as luck would have it, it was a couch.

Jay kept his distance for the moment, folding his arms across his chest, his eyes sparkling with an insolent sort of affection. "All you have to do, Laura-lee, is tell me that you don't want me to make love to you, and that will be the end of it. Can you tell me that?"

For the life of her, she couldn't. Her throat ached over the words any good woman would surely say under the circumstances, but Lauralee could not get them out.

"That's what I thought," Jay said with soft gruffness, coming toward her then, reaching up to unpin her hair. As his fingers worked in that tangle of silk, shivers went through Lauralee in waves. She closed her eyes and swayed slightly.

The falling of her hair was strangely sensuous, seeming to take minutes rather than moments. Jay combed it with his splayed fingers, the palms of his hands passing over her temples, soothing her and yet arousing her, too.

"You are so beautiful," he marveled, and then his hands were on her shoulderblades, making circles there, and he was kissing her.

Lauralee felt as though she'd just been wrapped in folds of molten velvet. When her dress slid away from her shoulders, the soft heat became a sweet torment. When the camisole came away too, baring her breasts, she whimpered, the sound instantly lost in the depths of his mouth.

The kiss ended. Jay stepped back, his eyes dark with tender ferocity as they assessed the plump, pink-crested bounty so proudly displayed for him. With a desolate moan, he bent to taste one straining morsel with just the tip of his tongue and was overcome by a greed as old as sunsets and stars.

Glorying in what she could give him, overcome by the tender misery he engendered with his lips and teeth and tongue, Lauralee let her head fall backward and entangled her fingertips in Jay's hair as he took suckle. She had no sense of time or space. It was as though she had become a shimmering silver mirage, like the ones sometimes seen in the far distance on a hot summer day.

Presently, she felt her dress and camisole sliding away, along with her drawers. Jay was kneeling before her—that in itself seemed too incredible to believe—his hands rolling down her stockings, removing them and the little slippers.

Jay did not rise, but lifted his hands to her hips, kneading the flesh there until it tingled, and his lips made a tracery of passion on her bare stomach. Lauralee was beyond thought; she wound her fingers in his hair, letting them transmit messages of their own.

The first daring, darting touch of his tongue brought her fully alive; she made an earthy sound in the depths of her throat and tensed, her head flung back, her eyes sightless. Passion jolted, deliciously fierce, between the tender, hidden place where he nipped and kissed and lapped at her and the inescapable clasp of his hands at her buttocks, then spread into every part of her.

She would die if he stopped, die if he didn't, and she gave a soft, throaty wail in her frustration. The sensation was a brutally pleasing one, warm and piercing, and the only thing more unendurable than its presence would be its absence.

Lauralee's release began with a trembling that went soul deep, destroying her from the core of her being, reconstructing her into a clawing, desperate creature who would be appeased no matter what the cost. She was sobbing softly, too weak to stand, when Jay lowered her to the couch and began removing his own clothes.

Finally, he stood naked before her, every muscle etched with the dim light of the gas lamp, and she was stunned by the majesty of him, by her own yearning need for him.

Jay chuckled as he came to her and poised himself above her. "Woman," he rasped. "Will I never have you in a bed?"

He could have had her anywhere, but Lauralee didn't say that, of course. Instead of answering him, she clasped her strong hands, despairing that they were so work-roughened, over the muscled tautness of his buttocks. Jay groaned brokenly at her urging, trying to withhold what she demanded from him, the effort almost too much, even for him.

He closed his eyes, his face taut. "Lauralee—my God—if you don't marry me—"

Marry him? Lauralee felt a bursting hope and, at the same time, fathomless despair. The passion that had roiled within her drained away, but it was too late. Suddenly, forcefully, Jay lunged within her, possessing her completely, driving, with each long thrust, all coherent thought from her mind.

Lauralee became a wild thing, seeking more of him and then still more, finally flinging her legs around him and crushing him to her. A noisy delirium swept around them both, his cries tangling with hers, as their joining culminated in its inevitable, sweet violence.

It left them shuddering, their flesh bonded by perspiration. Lauralee wriggled and Jay moaned and convulsed upon her, again and then once more. When the spasms had passed, he fell to her, and she welcomed his weight, welcomed the warmth of his breath against her neck.

"I can't leave without you," he said after a very long time. "God help me, I can't."

Lauralee was filled with an instant, icy alarm. "Leave? Where would you go?"

"Washington," came the husky response.

"We're in Washington!" cried Lauralee, afraid.

"D.C.," he clarified.

Washington, D.C.! Why, that was on the other side of the country, so far away that Lauralee could hardly grasp the distance! "Why would you want to go there?" she wailed in panic.

He laughed, a low and wholly masculine sound, as he slid downward and began toying with her breasts again. "I'm supposed to take over my father's seat in the United States Senate—"

Lauralee arched involuntarily as he circled her right nipple with the tip of his tongue. "The—United States—"

"Senate," he finished for her, busy with his prize.

Lauralee's thoughts were not rational; they skittered about in her head like marbles in the bottom of a lard tin. "You can't go!"

Jay lifted his head and looked into her eyes. "Not without you," he said.

The tension within Lauralee drained away, though the quivering need Jay had so easily renewed did not. "You want me to go? Wh—what about Alexander? What about Clarie and my trees—"

Jay rolled his eyes. "Damn your trees. Alexander and Clarie can go with us, of course."

Lauralee loved this man wholeheartedly, without reservation or shame. But he had not said he cared for her, not once. "Damn my trees!" she blustered. "Jay McCallum, those trees are important to me! I've worked—"

He found one of her hands and his fingers caressed the callused places. "I know how hard you've worked. But think what this would mean for Clarie. There are schools in Washington where she could study music,

116

history, literature. What is she learning now, Laura-lee?"

Lauralee thought with despair of the one-room schoolhouse Clarie attended. The few textbooks there were dog-eared and outdated, and poor Jenny could offer very little as a teacher, because she knew so little herself. And what would become of Alexander? Suppose his hearing never returned? How could he be expected to grasp any knowledge at all under circumstances like that?

Jay went on, reading her thoughts clearly in her eyes. "My father knows of a special school in Washington, where Alexander could learn to communicate and to read and write and figure too, when he's ready."

"A school?" Lauralee was suspicious. If Jay thought for one moment that she was going to leave her son in some institution, he could think again. "Would he live there?"

"Of course not," Jay answered easily. "He would live with us. Think what a difference a special education could make to him, Lauralee."

To imagine Alexander facing a lifetime of silence was crushing, and so was the guilt that attended it. Her newfound hopes for the future floated away. Some mother she was, doing these unspeakable things with Jay McCallum when her baby was lying in a hospital . . .

"Stop it!" Jay ordered sternly, still in tune with her mind, it seemed. "I know exactly what you're thinking, and damnit all to hell, I won't have it! Our making love has nothing whatsoever to do with Alexander's being ill!"

"Then why are you yelling?"

"I am not yelling!"

117

His voice echoed off the walls, and Lauralee burst out laughing. In retaliation, Jay tickled her until she shrieked.

"Now who's yelling? Say you'll marry me, and I'll stop."

Tears were slipping down Lauralee's cheeks. "Coercion—extortion—"

"Yes or no, woman?" Jay bellowed, tickling her again.

"Yes!" she wailed.

Jay released her and bounded up off the couch where he had possessed her so thoroughly. "All right, then," he ordered triumphantly. "Get yourself dressed. I know a judge—"

Lauralee's enthusiasm was waning. What had she agreed to? She hardly knew this man. What she felt for him might just be animal lust rather than love. It might be . . .

Jay pulled her up and gave her bare bottom an innocuous swat with one hand. "Hurry up, I can see your mind changing even as we speak."

She began to dress, but not fast enough to suit Jay. He donned his own clothes in a wink and then proceeded to shuffle Lauralee into hers. "Why are you in such a hurry?" she hissed, angry and scared and at the same time eager to be Jay's wife.

"How can you ask me that," he countered mischievously, "after what just occurred in this very room?"

Lauralee stiffened as he buttoned up the back of her crumpled dress. "I want to know, Jay McCallum. I'm not going anywhere until you tell me."

"All right, then, I'll tell you: I am not going to kiss you good night at the door of your room and trot off to my own, which would be the only proper thing to do if we weren't married to each other."

118

"Propriety didn't bother you very much a few minutes ago, Jay McCallum!"

"I couldn't help myself. I was overcome with passion, seduced in environs I had every reason to believe were sacrosanct." He draped one hand across his forehead, the very picture of shattered virtue. "How will I live with myself if you don't do the honorable thing?"

Lauralee laughed and shoved him with both hands, but when he opened the door for her, she went through it. "Don't you talk to me about honor, you rascal!" she whispered. "You were closer to the truth when you said you wanted me in your bed tonight instead of my own."

He smiled, shrugging into a suitcoat snatched from a coat-tree.

The judge Jay had spoken of lived within walking distance of the house. A tall, slender fellow with bright red hair, he was surprisingly young to hold such an office, to Lauralee's mind.

After only the briefest greetings had been exchanged between the two men, an introduction was made. The amusement in the judge's dark green eyes was embarrassing.

Jay stated his desire to marry Lauralee with typical bluntness. "There is the matter of the license, of course."

"You haven't one, I presume," guessed Judge Ryan, looking officious now. "You do need one, you know, if you want this marriage to be legal."

"Of course I know," Jay snapped, annoyed now. "I'm a lawyer, damnit. You've got the power to issue a special license, so do it!"

"My friend has always been persuasive," Judge

Ryan confided to Lauralee as an aside. "It's his charm, I think."

"It's nothing of the sort," Lauralee retorted in all seriousness, and both men laughed.

"We'd best get this over with before the lady comes to her senses," the judge said with a sigh, but the mischievous twinkle was still dancing in his eyes. He looked as though he might still be laughing inside.

After that, everything happened so fast that if Lauralee had wanted to come to her senses, which she didn't, she wouldn't have had the chance. A license was issued, the judge's spinster sister and a maid were called in to act as witnesses, and the ceremony was performed.

Judge Ryan sent the maid for brandy so a toast might be offered, and inwardly, Lauralee braced herself for a quarrel with Jay. If he insisted that she take liquor when he knew her position—

When the brandy was brought, however, and Lauralee quietly declined her portion, Jay said nothing at all. A toast was made and Jay thanked his friend and then they left, hurrying home in the light of gas-powered streetlamps.

Lauralee felt oddly light-headed, even though she had not taken spirits with the others. Happiness welled up inside her from some hidden spring and her heart pounded against the base of her throat as though it sought to fly away like a bird.

A disturbing thought came to her. "Is it possible for one to become intoxicated by inhaling the fumes of alcohol?" she asked.

Jay threw back his head and laughed and lights came up in the houses around them. He didn't seem to care that they were being observed from behind curtains and draperies. Catching Lauralee up in his arms, he spun her round and round. She was so dizzy by the time he set her down that she stumbled and had to grasp Jay's lapels to keep from falling.

"Jay McCallum, I asked you a simple question—"

He chuckled and bent to kiss her gently on the lips. "I'm sorry, Temperance. I shouldn't have laughed. But for the record, no, it isn't possible to get drunk by breathing fumes."

Lauralee was relieved. A fine thing if she, the leader of the Halpern's Ferry Temperance Movement, had made such an error. "I do wonder why I feel so strange," she mused. "I declare, I'm quite tipsy."

Jay smiled at her, caught her arm in his, and began hurrying along the sidewalk again, toward his father's house. "And quite beautiful," he said gently.

And if Jay knew why Lauralee felt tipsy, he didn't explain.

Inside the shadowy, night-quiet house, Jay swept Lauralee up into his arms and carried her up the broad stairway, suppressing her giggles with a long, consuming kiss.

They were on the second floor and moving along a hallway before that ended. Jay groped with a doorknob and then they were in a dark room that carried his distinctive scent.

Lauralee had expected to be tossed onto a bed; she was disappointed when she was set firmly on her feet instead. Jay gave her bottom an affectionate swat and turned up the lights, revealing the room.

It was spacious and littered with books, papers, and discarded clothes. There was a fireplace in one corner, fronted by two masculine-looking leather chairs, and the bed was unmade.

"Not very romantic, is it?" Jay muttered ruefully, looking about and then sighing and shedding his coat in a philosophical fashion.

Lauralee had been swept into this on the tide of their

121

furious lovemaking downstairs, in the study. She was married now, and it wasn't a game, and she was scared all over again. This man had all sorts of legal and moral power over her, and she could blame no one but herself for the dangerous position she was in. Her lower lip trembled, and Jay, noticing immediately, stilled it with a gentle index finger.

"Don't be afraid, Mrs. McCallum. Our political differences aside, you haven't married a monster. Just a man."

Lauralee's mind was whirling with devastating possibilities. Jay could take her land and sell it. He could force her to send Clarie away. He could even put Alexander into an orphanage if he so chose! All these dastardly privileges were his under the law, and who knew the law better than he did, as an attorney and a future senator? God in heaven, if only he would say he loved her!

He caught her hand in his and led her into an adjoining room. Lauralee's eyes widened, for here was a massive marble bathtub, set right into the floor, its spigots of glistening brass! There was a commode, a sink, and shelves full of snow-white damask towels.

Lauralee was frowning at the tank, with its dangling brass chain, hanging high above the commode. "It seems to me that it wouldn't be safe to sit under that," she observed, and Jay roared with laughter.

"Taking you to Washington ought to be a real adventure," he said when his crude amusement had subsided to some degree, bending to put a plug into the bottom of the tub and turn on the spigots.

Lauralee blushed, feeling like a hayseed. At the moment, benefits to Clarie and Alexander notwithstanding, the idea of going to live in the capital of the United States was a terrifying prospect. What did she know of that sort of life? Indoor conveniences were still new to her, and so were telephones and gas lights.

She turned her hands palms up and stared at the calluses there, tears making the rough places shift and shimmer. "Oh Lord," she wailed.

Jay was closer than she'd realized; he kissed her forehead. "They'll heal," he said gently. "Besides, you'll be wearing gloves most of the time anyway."

Gloves! Was that meant to comfort her? Lauralee was wild with despair. With gloves would come the elegant clothes Jay would expect her to wear, and she knew nothing of choosing such things! She would be the gauche, inept Westerner and everyone in Washington would laugh at her.

Jay turned her with a wrench and began unbuttoning her dress, briskly this time. "If you don't stop worrying over every little thing, woman, I swear I'll turn you across my knee. Now, get into that tub!"

Lauralee's hands trembled as she took off the dress, her camisole, her drawers and stockings and slippers. She couldn't look back at Jay, so she stepped into the hot, deep bathwater and sat down.

Jay knelt beside the tub and reached to turn off the spigots. "Lauralee," he ordered quietly. "Look at me."

She looked, her eyes bright with tears. "I can't go to Washington. My trees—"

Jay was reaching for a washcloth and a bar of buttermilk soap. "Are they more important than your son, Lauralee? Are they more important than Clarie?" He grinned, lifted one of her legs, and began to lather it with tender industry, as though he bathed women every day of the week. "Exactly who is Clarie, anyway?"

123

Lauralee settled back against the tub, soothed by the hot water, comforted by Jay's washing. "She's Virgil's daughter. Her mother dropped her off one day, after we'd been married a while, and she hasn't been back since."

"You say that as though Virgil's having a daughter came as something of a surprise."

"It did. He hadn't bothered to mention Clarie to me, or her mother, for that matter." Lauralee lowered her voice. "They weren't ever married, Virgil and Clarie's mother. You'd think she'd be a strumpet, wouldn't you? But Louise was very nice. She was a schoolteacher, and leaving her little girl was so hard for her . . ."

Jay lowered Lauralee's leg into the water and took up the other. "I suppose Clarie looks for her to come back."

"She does. It breaks my heart sometimes. I—I love Clarie, and I wouldn't want to give her up, but I wish she and Louise could be together."

"Maybe we can arrange something," Jay said. "What was Virgil like?"

It was inevitable, Lauralee supposed, that the second husband should wonder about the first. "He was wonderful before he began to drink—always laughing. We worked hard, but Virgil made it seem like a game."

Jay's eyes were fixed upon his unlikely work. "You loved him," he said, without apparent emotion.

Lauralee ached. "Yes."

"Did he always drink?"

She closed her eyes, remembering. "Now that I think about it, yes. But it was a long time before it became a problem—that happened gradually, so slowly that I didn't really notice it."

124

A silence, oddly comfortable in view of what they had been discussing, settled over the newlyweds as Jay continued to bathe Lauralee. He washed her face, her arms, her stomach, her breasts, her back, and then the most private part of her. It was a sensuous, lulling thing, submitting to that, and by the time Jay lifted her from the water to dry her with a soft towel, she sagged against him, sleepy and trusting, and there might never have been a Virgil Parker.

Jay chuckled and lifted her into his arms, and her head bobbed against his shoulder as he carried her back into the cluttered bedroom and set her on the bed. She fell to one side, eyes just barely open, damp hair coming down from its pins, and he left her there while he rummaged through a heavy mahogany wardrobe.

When he returned to the bed, he was carrying a soft white shirt. He pulled Lauralee back into a sitting position and patiently put the garment on her, buttoning it as high as her breasts.

Then he drew back the covers, settled her between them, tucked her in, and bent to kiss her. Nearly asleep, Lauralee reached up and clasped her arms around his neck.

Again, Jay chuckled. But he removed her arms and stood up straight, undoing his string tie with one hand and flinging it aside. She was going to have to break him of his slovenly habits, she thought as she snuggled down into the sheets.

He left her, and she sensed his going and despaired of it. As tired as Lauralee was, she wanted to be held, wanted a sweet tender joining before she gave herself up to sleep.

There was water running. Lauralee heard Jay splashing in the bathtub, knew he was naked, wanted to go to him and bathe him just as he had bathed her, but her muscles were leaden and unresponsive to the orders issued by her mind.

When Jay came to bed and stretched out beside Lauralee, she reached out automatically to caress him, tangling her fingers in the thick, dark fur swirling on his chest. He smelled so good, so clean. So Jay.

Lauralee yawned loudly. "I—want you. This is—our wedding night—"

"You want to sleep," he countered in a low voice, but his body tensed beneath the slow explorations of her hand.

She snuggled closer; soft, sleepy thrills rippled through her body as she fitted her curves to the hard planes of his hip, his rib cage, his thigh.

In some deep, wide-awake part of her brain, Lauralee remembered something long forgotten. She raised herself onto one elbow, yawning again, and began kissing Jay's broad chest. He moaned involuntarily and tried to thrust her away, but she remained, growing bolder now, tasting his nipples with the tip of her tongue, each in turn, and then kissing her way down over his granite belly.

"Lauralee," he groaned as she captured him in one sure, strong hand. "Oh—God—Lauralee—"

She kissed him and he arched his back, giving a gasping cry that both warned and pleaded. His fingers fumbled in her hair, removing the pins that had held it up out of the bathwater, flinging them away, fanning the silken curtain out to cover him.

Lauralee bit him in soft mischief and teased. "It won't help to hide from me."

Jay's hips gave an eager upward thrust at the nip, and he made a strangled, helpless sound that echoed inside his chest. He writhed as she pleasured him, his

126

thighs quivering beneath her hands. "You—little witch—" he choked out.

Lauralee laughed and tormented him further, until, with a cry, he caught her at the waist and lifted her to sit astraddle of him. His strong, straining shaft filled her; his hands clasped the shirt she wore and pulled, sending buttons flying.

Lauralee was no longer laughing; the fierce strokes of his manhood had rendered her mindless. His hands closed over her breasts, caressing them, kneading them, working nipples that seemed connected to the molten ache roaring at her center.

"Jay," she begged. "Jay, Jay—"

He took her waist in strong hands and began to raise and lower her in a rhythmic torment the like of which she had never felt before. Frantic, she trust her legs straight out, toward the pillows, and settled full upon him, shivering.

The bedsprings creaked and Jay's throaty cries of lust were louder still as he lifted her with the force of his passion, reaching deep inside her.

Lauralee knotted her fingers in the dense hair covering his chest as he drove her to climax and then joined her in that place of blinding, whirlwind glory, his body shuddering beneath hers.

It was a very long time before either of them could speak; Jay, as usual, recovered himself more quickly. Still within her, grinning in the moonlight streaming in through a window, he massaged her breasts, her back, her bottom.

"Damn," he said. "I wanted our marriage to be a surprise."

Lauralee blushed, wildly embarrassed. No doubt, everyone in the household had heard them howling in their scandalous abandon. She moved to free herself, planning to turn away and pout, but Jay held her fast.

"Oh no you don't," he said, his voice a low rumble. "You started this, remember. And I have plans for you, Mrs. McCallum."

He did indeed have plans. Wicked, delicious plans. And he executed every last one of them before the night was over.

CHAPTER
EIGHT

Jay had certainly gotten his wish. His marriage to Lauralee, announced as the family gathered for breakfast, came as a complete surprise to everyone. To some, the shock was pleasant: Kate squealed with delight and clapped her hands, and Jay's father smiled over the gold-edged rim of his coffee cup. Chance, dressed for swashbuckling rather than any adult pursuit, leaned back against a sideboard, folded his arms, and assessed his new sister-in-law with amused, appreciative eyes.

Mrs. Eleanor McCallum fainted dead away.

Lauralee was alarmed, watching with wide eyes as Jay and the senator went immediately to the woman's aid.

"Don't worry," Chance whispered from close beside Lauralee. "She didn't like Kate or Lucy, either."

The elder Mrs. McCallum was coming around, her eyelashes fluttering on her papery cheeks, a small, desolate moan rattling in her throat. Lauralee, wearing another of Kate's dresses because she had none of her own, looked down at the dotted swiss and wondered what it was about her that had given her new mother-in-law such an awful turn.

"Ragamuffin—" the woman muttered as Jay and his father hauled her to her feet. "Fortune-hunter—"

Ragamuffin. Fortune-hunter. It took Lauralee several moments to realize that Jay's mother was talking about her. She flushed, barely able to keep from protesting that she hadn't known the McCallums had money—to her, Jay had been the owner of the Rumsucker Saloon! Besides that, it hadn't been her idea to get married in the middle of the night. . . .

The senator settled his disoriented wife into a chair at the long dining table, with its linen cloth and ivory napkin rings, speaking firmly as he held a glass of water out to her. "Eleanor, I will hear no more of that. Lauralee is a part of our family now, and she will be treated as such."

"God help her," muttered Chance.

Kate was looking anxiously in Lauralee's direction, biting her lower lip.

Eleanor McCallum sniffed. Lauralee had not laid eyes on Jay's mother until she had walked into the dining room minutes before—there had not been time for formal introductions.

Now, studying the small, delicately boned woman, with her gray-streaked fair hair and wide brown eyes, her bejeweled fingers and her costly clothes, Lauralee felt out of her depth. And this was just a taste of what would happen in Washington, D.C.

Lauralee's throat squeezed into a knot and panic dizzied her; she might have turned and fled if Jay hadn't caught her eye and stayed her, sustained her, with a look of overwhelming tenderness.

When his gaze shifted to his mother, however, it became sharp, and a muscle pulsed at the base of his jawline. "Lauralee and I have to get to the hospital," he said evenly. "We'll have breakfast downtown."

Kate had edged to Lauralee's side and draped one encouraging arm around her waist.

Eleanor assessed the unexpected addition to her family with naked contempt. "Look at her. A country wench, without a decent stitch to wear. And what has she brought us? An heir with the right to bear our name? No—she's brought us another man's crippled brat."

There was a stunned silence, then a wild stirring, like the rousing of angry bees, only without sound.

Lauralee forced herself to stand still where she was. She didn't care what Mrs. McCallum thought of her person or her clothes, but the words *crippled brat* were like the cutting lashes of a whip, biting into her spirit. What could Alexander, an innocent child, have done to inspire such vicious loathing?

Jay looked as though he'd been struck; he paled, the muscles in the side of his neck stood out, but he was either incapable of speech or unable to trust himself to utter a word. The senator, equally appalled, was no more articulate.

No, it was Chance who burst out, "Good God, Mother, even for you, that was a viperous thing to say!"

Jay, standing within strangling distance of his mother, turned from his post beside her chair with visible effort, strode across the room without a word to anyone, and caught Lauralee's elbow in one hand. He propelled her from the dining room, into the entry-way, out through the front door.

Eleanor shrieked something, Lauralee closed her eyes against it, and Jay slammed the door.

They were settled in the carriage and well away

131

from the house before he spoke. "I'm sorry, Lauralee. I should have known how she would react—I should have spared you the grief."

In all her life, Lauralee had never experienced such hatred. "Why would your mother talk about Alexander that way?" she asked. "I didn't mind what she said about me so much, but how could she despise a child—"

"*I* mind what she said about you," Jay broke in angrily. "I mind very much." He paused, making a visible effort to regain his composure. "If it's any comfort—and I doubt that it will be—Mother treated Kate and Brice's Lucy just that way."

Lauralee shuddered. Lucy lived at a distance, but poor Kate! Between her errant husband and his odious, snarling mother, her life must have been hell. "Has she always been so unhappy, your mother, I mean?" she asked after a very long time.

Jay gaped at Lauralee, obviously surprised at her question. "Unhappy? Frankly, I've always thought of her as cruel, at least where new daughters-in-law are concerned."

The carriage jostled over brick-cobbled streets, winding among other grand houses. "Happy people are rarely cruel, Jay," Lauralee observed, wishing she had not come into this marriage, this strange family, quite so rashly.

He took her hand and held it in his own. When Lauralee looked back at him, his gray eyes were distant, fixed on some point in his past. "When we were kids, things were different. Dad was only a small-town lawyer, making very little money and taking all the cases nobody else wanted. Mother was happy then, and she was beautiful, too. I think she changed when Sarah died."

"Sarah?"

"My sister. She was Chance's twin. They were about six years old when it happened, always together and always in trouble. One day, they found an old rowboat and decided to sail it across the millpond."

Lauralee tensed. She could guess the rest of the story, but she listened in silence, sensing that Jay needed to tell it.

His face was bleak as he went on. "The boat over-turned. Neither Chance nor Sarah could swim, but Chance managed to hold on to the hull until a couple of millworkers saw what had happened and came to help. Sarah drowned."

"Your mother's only daughter," Lauralee reflected sadly, feeling Eleanor McCallum's despair.

"Yes. I guess it explains some other things, too—Mother has been smothering Chance with her 'devotion' ever since. Brice and I were both closer to Dad, anyway, and we were a little older, so that didn't have much effect on us, but it drove Tim out of the house."

Tim. The mention of him jarred Lauralee and reminded her of the problems she had left behind at Halpern's Ferry. Problems that were bound to catch up. Something reckless inside Lauralee made her say, "You thought I murdered Tim, didn't you? You made those remarks about hatchets—"

Jay met his wife's eyes squarely. "I admit that I entertained the notion until I came to know you."

Lauralee flushed with quiet outrage and memories of that night they had shared, on the bare wooden floor of an open, half-constructed building. "Are you speaking biblically, Mr. McCallum?"

Jay frowned. "Do you seriously think I could have touched you if I'd really believed you were a murder-ess?" he countered. "I loved Tim, Lauralee, and I had to blame somebody to get through losing him."

Lauralee remembered Virgil's death and understood. She had had few weapons against her despair, but one had come readily to hand: laying the fault at Tim McCallum's feet. In thinking about that, she had been able to hold well-founded fears at bay until she'd gained the strength to deal with them. "I can hardly criticize you," she said quietly, "when I accused your brother of destroying Virgil. The plain fact of the matter is that Virgil destroyed himself."

Jay squeezed Lauralee's hand but said nothing further until they had reached the hospital. "Before we go and see Alexander," he suggested, "let's have some breakfast."

Lauralee stared at her husband as he lifted her down from the carriage. "How can you think of eating after the things your mother said?"

He gave her a look of indulgent exasperation. "I choose not to let my mother ruin my day—or my appetite. And I'm hungry."

Lauralee's stomach selected that moment to grumble inelegantly. "But Alexander—"

"If Alexander needed us, someone from the hospital would have telephoned. Remember what the doctor said, Lauralee, about missing meals?"

Lauralee's dominant instinct was to rush to Alexander's side, with no thought of her own needs, but she knew that Jay was right. To be of use to Alexander, she must look after herself, remain strong.

Jay nodded to the carriage driver and, as the vehicle clattered away, offered his arm to Lauralee. She took it, and they enjoyed a lively breakfast in the hotel dining room across the street, where she and Kate had had luncheon the day before.

Thus, a pattern was set. Mr. and Mrs. Jay McCallum left the august residence on Spokane's South Hill at the same time every morning, avoiding Eleanor entirely. They ate breakfast at the hotel and visited

Alexander, Jay staying only minutes before going off to his law office, where he was tying up all sorts of loose ends in preparation for the imminent move to Washington.

Lauralee gave little thought to the adventure herself, perhaps because it frightened her so much. She devoted her days to Alexander, who was rapidly recovering although still unable to hear, and at night she became another person altogether. Behind the door of the room she shared with Jay, she was a temptress and an innocent, a queen and a slave. Each night, it seemed, they reached a new level of passion, discovered yet another way to pleasure each other.

It was all too easy to forget that there was a very large, very dangerous world beyond the walls of that comfortable room.

One day, when Lauralee had been in Spokane for two weeks, the fact was brought home to her in a surprising way. She had returned from the hospital early, feeling quite exhausted, and Kate was in her room, sitting forlornly on the edge of the bed.

Behind her, in colorful billows of satin and silk, lawn and velvet, were dozens of gowns, brimming from their fancy white boxes like bits of fallen rainbow.

Lauralee's curiosity was surpassed only by her concern for her sister-in-law, who looked to be on the verge of tears. "Kate? What is it?"

Kate's lower lip trembled as she lifted her head and met Lauralee's gaze, her lovely eyes glistening with tears. "I had such fun this morning, choosing all these clothes for you to take to Washington," she said. "I was taking them out of their boxes, wondering if they would fit you and if you'd like them, when it finally dawned on me that you really are going away!"

At this, Kate sobbed, covering her face with both hands. Lauralee hurried across the room, sat down on the bed, and drew Kate into her arms. And, seeing those beautiful dresses, the fact of leaving came home to her as well.

"I'll be all alone!" Kate cried.

Lauralee, always wanting to fix things, make them better, had to bite her lower lip to keep from inviting Kate to go to Washington, too. "Everything will be all right," she promised, though she couldn't think how that would be true. She wanted to find Chance McCallum and kick him square in the shin.

"I bought calico dresses and everything!" wailed Kate.

An idea struck Lauralee, and she gave Kate a little shake to catch her attention. "I have to go back to Halpern's Ferry at least for a few days, to see to things there. Why don't you come along? Perhaps on the way back you could visit Brice and Lucy."

"I'll still have to come back here to Chance's love affairs and the Dragon Woman!" she sniffled, but her small body was no longer racked with sobs and there was hope in her eyes.

Lauralee could offer a light at the end of the tunnel, at least where their mother-in-law was concerned. "The senator is taking Mrs. McCallum away, Kate. They're sailing to the Orient."

"She'll never agree to that!"

Lauralee grinned. "She wasn't given a choice, as far as I know. For all practical intents and purposes, Kate, this house will be yours. You'll be its mistress. And I think it might be a very good thing if you and Chance were here by yourselves for a while."

"Chance is never around!"

"Perhaps it isn't you he's trying to avoid," Lauralee reflected, remembering what Jay had said that morning in the carriage about the influence Mrs. McCallum's misguided adoration had had on Chance. "Perhaps it's his mother."

Kate brightened. "Do you really think so?"

Lauralee regretted bringing up the possibility; after all, that was all it was. And if Chance continued to live the rounder's life after his parents sailed for the Far East, which he well might, Kate's hopes would be shattered. The thought of her wandering, alone and in despair, in this vast house was heartbreaking. "We can never be certain how anything is going to turn out, Kate. I want you to promise me that you'll go to Lucy if your marriage doesn't work out."

Kate bounded up off the bed, all tearful smiles and certainty, grasping a crimson velvet ballgown in her hands and holding it up in front of her. "It will work out! I know it will!"

Lauralee wished she could be so sure. What had she done, offering a hope that might turn out to be false? "You were sweet," she said softly, "to shop for all these pretty things."

"I knew you wouldn't get a chance," Kate sang. "The stores are all closed by the time you leave the hospital, you know."

The remainder of the afternoon—Lauralee had intended to devote it to a badly needed nap—was given over to the trying on and altering of the beautiful clothes Kate had chosen. The stunning gowns, some for travel, some for daywear, some for the glamorous social functions a senator's wife no doubt attended, needed only a stitch here and there, work Kate was eager to do. It struck Lauralee that the younger Mrs. McCallum had a distinct flair for color and line; every dress she had chosen was becoming, perfectly suited to Lauralee's coloring and figure.

By the time Jay entered the room, looking tired and

carrying a familiar book beneath his arm—he studied the volume often, it seemed to Lauralee, though she had never bothered to read its title—Kate was gathering up dresses by the armload, all of them pinned and marked with tailor's chalk in strategic places. She gave Jay a dimpled smile, winked at Lauralee, and waltzed out.

"Kate has taken it upon herself," Lauralee said with a somewhat sad smile, "to see that I do not disgrace the McCallum name when I burst upon the Washington social scene."

Jay tossed aside the book and pulled Lauralee into his arms. "Disgrace the McCallum name, is it? I think a more realistic approach would be to wonder if the lot of us can measure up to you, my love."

Lauralee let her forehead rest against his solid chest, drawing strength from the scent and texture and substance of him. My love, he'd said. It was the closest he'd ever come to declaring any deep affection for her. Considering the wild and lovely moments they had shared, that was quite something.

"Alexander will be able to leave the hospital tomorrow," she said without looking up. "And I need to go back to Halpern's Ferry, Jay, to get Clarie and make arrangements for Jenny and for my land and—"

Jay caught his hand under her chin and lifted it. "You're still a little scared of going to Washington, aren't you?" he said gently.

Lauralee could not lie to him. "Scared? I'm terrified, Jay McCallum. What do I know about parties and dances and formal receptions? What do I know about—"

He smothered her fretting with a kiss, his strong hands cupping her bottom and pressing her close against him. How brazenly, totally masculine he was, Lauralee thought as all ideas of Washington and her orchards and even Alexander spun away from her, all flung madly from a vortex created by this one incredible, wonderful, confusing man.

They missed dinner completely.

Jay awakened in the deep quiet of the night, Lauralee's curves warm and soft against his flesh, and smiled. It took all the forebearance he possessed to not reach out and squeeze that shapely backside of hers, but he did manage to resist. She needed her sleep.

Jay, on the other hand, was wide awake and ravenous. He got out of bed carefully, groped around until he found his clothes and boots, and dressed, after a fashion. It wasn't likely that he would meet anyone on the way to the kitchen or on the way back at this hour of the night, but there was always the factor of the unexpected.

Grinning, he left the bedroom, made his way down the rear staircase and into the kitchen. There, he turned up the lights and found cheese, bread, and cold meat for a sandwich. He was about to go back to the second floor when he heard the distinctive click of pool balls coming from his father's study.

Jay grinned again. In another week, his mother and father would be sailing for the Orient; the trip would be good for them and everyone else in the family, too. He decided to go into the study and ask his father what had prompted such an undertaking.

"Dad?"

Chance, bent over the pool table, cue stick in hand, chuckled somewhat bitterly and shook his head. The balls clicked, breaking in a random pattern of numbers and bright colors. "Dad's been in bed for hours," he said. "If you're looking for company, I'm all there is."

Jay was about to turn away, but something held him in the doorway, some note in Chance's voice. He leaned against the doorframe and watched in silence as his brother executed a skillful shot.

Chance's hair was rumpled, as was his loose-fitting shirt. Jay wondered where the hell he got shirts like that, anyway; they made him look like a pirate captain, ready to rob, rape, and plunder. Irreverent brown eyes lifted and met with questioning gray ones.

"What is it about me that puzzles you so much, Jay?" Chance asked with unexpected, although typical, directness. "Every time you look at me, you're asking yourself questions."

Jay remained in the doorway while his brother hung up his cue stick and went to a side table to pour himself a drink. "You don't puzzle me at all, Chance. If anything, I understand you too well."

Chance turned, lifted his glass in a mocking toast. "Bullshit," he said. "You look at me and you say to yourself, 'What makes old Chance such a waste of time?'"

"I'm not that concerned, actually, but you're partly right—I do ask myself questions."

Chance grinned, as though some lofty theory, which he had held all along, had just been proven correct. "Such as?"

"Such as this: How can you hurt Kate the way you do when you know how much she loves you?"

"Have a drink," Chance responded buoyantly. He was a master at avoiding subjects he did not wish to discuss.

Jay was still eating his sandwich; he declined the drink, but came into the study and fell into the cushioned leather chair behind his father's desk. "Do you love Kate?" he asked as Chance left the liquor cabinet to sit on the edge of the pool table.

"Yes," Chance answered without hesitation, frowning, as though surprised by the question.

"Then why do you treat her the way you do?"

"What way do I treat her?"

It was all Jay could do not to shout with frustration. "Damnit all to hell," he bit out. "You know what I'm talking about. The women, the nights away from home—Chance, one of these days, Kate's going to leave you."

Chance was incensed; his color heightened and his knuckles turned white where he grasped the side of the pool table. His drink, set aside with a thump, threatened to topple over and spill all over the felt. "By God, if she tries anything like that, I'll drag her back here by the hair!"

Jay lost his appetite and tossed the sandwich into the wastebasket beside the desk. "You're incredible!" he said.

Chance only shrugged, and there was a modest air about him that made Jay want to lunge over the desk and stuff his brother's head into a corner pocket. What the hell did he have to be modest about?

"Kate is unhappy, Chance. That's all I'm going to say on the subject, so take warning and do something about it."

"After two weeks of marriage, you're an expert, Jay?"

"I don't claim to be anything of the sort."

"Then why are you giving me advice? Because you're my big brother?"

"Because I care about you, Chance."

Chance made a beckoning gesture with both hands, a motion so exaggerated that it would have been comical had it not been for the snapping annoyance in his eyes. "So advise me, since you know so much!"

"I told you that I wouldn't elaborate beyond what I said before, Chance, and I meant it." Jay got up from the desk chair and started out of the room. He had reached the doorway before his brother stopped him again.

"Jay?"

Jay did not turn; he simply waited. "What?"

"I wanted that seat in the Senate. I could have handled it, despite what you and Dad and Brice think."

Jay sighed. This, then, was what Chance had been getting at all along, what had kept him up until this ungodly hour of the night. Resigned, Jay went back into the room, poured himself a double shot of brandy, and returned to the chair behind his father's desk. This time, he kicked his booted feet up onto the surface, settling in to listen to whatever else his brother might have to say.

When Chance was sullenly silent, Jay urged him on with a lift of his glass. "I'm here and I'm listening. Let's hear it. All of it."

"I'm not a child, damnit!" Chance hissed, bending over the desk to glare into Jay's face.

Jay took a leisurely sip from his glass. "You're thirty-three years old, so I should hope not," he said. Then, after considering his brother for a few moments, he added, "You do realize, don't you, that you're not qualified to serve in the Senate?"

"Why? Because I don't have a law degree, like you and Brice? I've been to college!"

"I wasn't making comparisons, Chance. I'm telling you that the legislature is not a party. It's not a game."

"You don't think I'm capable—"

Jay broke in quietly. "I didn't say that. You're capable of anything, Chance. But being capable and actually living up to your responsibilities are two very different things. You don't seem to know how to give your best effort to any one thing, your marriage being

142

the most notable example. And then there's the fact that you don't work."

"Why should I work? I'm rich!"

Jay took another sip of his brandy. This conversation was getting him nowhere, just what he might have expected of a dialogue with Chance. "You said you wanted to talk. If you can't handle even that, then why did you call me back here?"

Chance lowered his head. "All I want is for Dad to trust me the way he trusts you. The way he trusts Brice."

"You've got to earn that. Dad's not going to sit up in bed one bright, sunny morning and say, 'Today I'll trust Chance.' Can you honestly say that you've given him any reason to feel that he can rely on you for anything other than scandal?"

There was a silence, one that had the makings of a shouting match or even an out-and-out fight. Either of those things would have been better, in Jay's opinion, than what actually happened. Chance thrust himself off the pool table and stormed out of the study; moments later, he heard the front door slam.

Jay got up, went to the liquor cabinet, and brought the entire decanter of brandy back to the desk with him. He refilled his glass, spilled most of that down his shirtfront, and refilled it again.

He should go after Chance, he knew that. Chance was his brother and he loved him. But trying to talk to the man was a study in futility; Chance always managed to turn everything back to the comparisons he imagined his father was making between him and his older sons.

Frustrated, Jay downed the contents of his glass and poured more brandy into it. He yawned, frowned at the glass, and set it aside. Chance would have to work

143

things out for himself, he decided. As for him, well, he was going to go back up those stairs, back to his bed and his wife. Just another second or so, and he'd have the energy.

Lauralee found Jay in his father's study, reeking of spirits and passed-out drunk. Instantly, her bright mood faded, replaced by a quiet, wounding rage.

All of the terrible experiences alcohol had wrought in her life came to the fore, real enough to see, to touch. They were all full of pain and shame.

Oh yes, Lauralee had been through all this before with Virgil, and she wasn't about to go through it again. Swallowing the sobs of despair that burned in her throat, she turned and left the room as quietly as she could.

The possibility that she might be overreacting to an innocent situation occurred to Lauralee as she hurried up the main staircase, but she refused to examine it. If her life with Virgil had taught her one truth, it was that where a drunkard is concerned, things are generally every bit as bad as they look. More often, worse.

The pretty dream was over; it was time to fetch her son, go back to her own life and her own land, and once more try to rebuild.

It was going to be more difficult than before, for by the time Virgil had died, Lauralee had lost all the love she'd once felt for him. Oh, she had grieved for him, suffered over his death, but a part of her had been glad—God help her, *glad*—to be free of the problems, the worries, the embarrassments.

Her love for Jay would not be so easily forgotten, unfortunately, for it was much stronger than any emotion she'd ever felt for her first husband. It was all-consuming and therefore dangerous.

In the bedroom she had shared so happily and so

briefly with Jay, Lauralee clasped her palms to her face to cool her flaming cheeks and paced, trying to think. It was hard to reason, hard to plan, but she knew that she must do both. She must escape while she could, for if she stayed, if she gave Jay a chance to cajole her into forgiving him, she would find herself back in the same trap. Jay's position in life would ensure that the tragedy took place on a grander scale, but it would be the same nightmare, with the same excuses, the same promises destined to be broken the same lies and the same pain.

Lauralee stopped pacing. It wouldn't be the same pain—not at all. It would be infinitely worse.

CHAPTER
NINE

Alexander was discharged from the hospital that very morning, as Lauralee had hoped. She bathed him, dressed him in fresh clothes from the little satchel she had packed at home that frantic day when she had thought her son was surely lost.

"We'll go home now," she said into Alexander's soft hair. "We'll go home where we belong."

Alexander could not hear her, of course; Lauralee was beginning to accept the fact that he might never hear. It was another problem, a tragic one at that, but she would deal with it somehow. For a moment, she mourned because now there would be no special schooling for her son, nothing to fit him for functioning successfully in a hearing world.

She carried Alexander down the hospital stairs and out into the morning, wondering what to do now. It wouldn't be fair, would it, to simply disappear, without a word to Jay; she knew she should tell him that their marriage was over, that it had been a mistake. Could she face him, though? And what of Kate? It would be unkind to abandon her. Plans and promises had been made.

The driver who had brought Lauralee to the hospital was waiting at the curb. He opened the lacquered door and held Alexander until Lauralee was settled inside.

"Home, Mrs. McCallum?"

Mrs. McCallum. It was the first time anyone other than Jay had addressed Lauralee by her new name. Under the circumstances, hearing it was painful, as was the word *home*. "Please," she said, and soon the carriage was moving up the hill, toward the grand house where she had lived as a pampered princess.

Lauralee sighed. She could not be married to a drunken man again, never mind that she loved Jay as she had never known how to love Virgil. Not even for palaces, velvet dresses, carriages, like this one, awaiting her bidding, not for the glorious nights in Jay's arms, not even for the undeniable benefits this marriage could have provided for Alexander and Clarie. The apple trees, the forty acres of land along the river at Halpern's Ferry—those were the things set aside, by God's hand, to be hers.

Upon reaching the McCallum house, Lauralee searched high and low for Jay, Alexander held safely in her arms the whole while, but she failed to find him. She was standing in the entry hall, wondering how to proceed, when Kate came down the stairs, took one look at her face, and demanded, "Lauralee, what's wrong?"

It all spilled out of Lauralee, though she had meant to maintain her dignity no matter what happened. She told Kate of finding Jay in the study that morning in a drunken stupor.

Kate looked puzzled but concerned, too. "Why, Lauralee, Jay isn't a drunkard. He—"

Lauralee would listen to none of that. The people nearest and dearest to an inebriate often had trouble accepting reality, denying the situation no matter what evidence there might be to the contrary. At first, with Virgil, she had done that herself, making excuses, stretching things, coloring the truth to cover his lapses.

She drew a deep breath. "I'm leaving, Kate. Now, today. If you wish, you are welcome to come with me."

"Of course I'm coming—I didn't buy all that calico for nothing. But aren't you going to say anything to Jay, anything at all?"

Lauralee lifted her chin. "Are you going to say anything to Chance?" she countered. "Anything at all?"

Kate saw the point her friend was making and, with hasty reluctance, turned and hurried up the stairs to pack. In a surprisingly short time, she was back, ready to go, summoning the carriage.

"They'll know exactly where we've gone, you know," Kate said as they traveled toward the railroad depot beside the Spokane River. "The driver will tell Jay or Chance that he brought us here, and they'll guess the rest."

Lauralee had no reason to hide—she wasn't the one with a fatal moral weakness, after all. Jay was. But she could understand Kate's concern; her entire plan hinged on unsettling Chance, making him wonder where his docile little wife had gotten off to. "We'll let the driver overhear us talking about visiting Brice's farm," Lauralee suggested. "That will give you the advantage of time, since it might be days or even weeks before Chance becomes concerned and goes there to look for you."

Kate did not look pleased. "Days or even weeks?" she echoed. "He'd better miss me before then!"

"He will. But you said yourself that Chance would

regard your being with Lucy and Brice as the next best thing to having you at home."

Kate settled back against the rich, pliant leather of the carriage seat, frowning. "I wonder, now that I think of it, if my being gone will matter to Chance at all. Why, he might not even notice!"

"He'll notice," Lauralee said, for if she had confidence in one thing in all the world, it was the power of the masculine ego. "Still, if you have doubts, Kate, you should go home."

"I'm going with you," Kate replied determinedly, and the subject was closed. After the carriage had come to a stop and the driver was unloading the two heavy trunks she had brought along, she sang out, "Oh, Lauralee, just wait until you meet our Lucy! She's such a treasure!"

Lauralee was trying to manage both Alexander and the satchel that contained his clothes. The driver had certainly heard Kate's remarks, and so had half the other travelers gathered in the depot. "Don't you think you're overdoing it just a bit?" she whispered.

Before Kate could answer, a masculine voice interceded. Jay's voice.

"Put Alexander down. He can walk."

Lauralee stiffened, not so brave about the confrontation now that it had been thrust upon her so suddenly. She turned and looked up into Jay McCallum's wan face, conscious of him in every part of her.

"Put him down," Jay repeated.

Torn between flinging herself at Jay and screaming at him, Lauralee set Alexander on his feet and lifted her chin. "I'm leaving you," she said.

"I had guessed that much, since you didn't bother to say good-bye. And where is Kate going?"

"With me. And we will thank you, Jay McCallum, to let Chance find her for himself. You'll spoil everything if you tell him where she's gone."

Jay's arrogant nose was within inches of Lauralee's, his voice low and raspy. No trace of his drinking spree showed in his features or fouled his breath. "What makes you think I'm going to let you get on that train?" he drawled.

Lauralee knew that he could stop her if he chose, for his physical strength was, of course, superior to her own. Not only that, but he had the power of the law behind him. "Marrying you was a mistake," she said bravely. "For both our sakes, it's better if we part now."

"Why was marrying me a mistake?"

Alexander was clutching at Lauralee's skirts, whimpering to be lifted into her arms. She was about to reach for him when Jay spoke again.

"Don't give in to him, Lauralee. He's big enough to walk, and if you coddle Alexander now, he'll be helpless before you know it."

Jay was right, of course. The tendency to smooth Alexander's way, natural as it was to a mother, was one to be governed carefully.

Steam whistles were sounding, conductors were shouting; it was time to buy tickets and go. "It is very difficult for me to do this," Lauralee said with dignity, meeting Jay's eyes. "Please don't make it harder."

"I think I deserve a word of explanation, don't you?"

Lauralee had rehearsed what she would say ever since finding Jay in the study that morning, sodden with liquor, but now that the time was here, she couldn't come up with one sensible word. She simply turned, Alexander toddling at her side, to leave.

Jay caught her arm in his hand and stayed her. It

was then that Kate spoke, interceding gently. "Laura-lee things that you drink too much," she said. "She saw you in the study this morning."

Jay released Lauralee's arm, and the silence that followed was dreadful. Evidently, he was not going to deny overimbibing or expend further effort to make her stay with him.

Lauralee squared her shoulders and gripped Alexander's small hand, then marched resolutely toward the ticket counter. Kate joined her there, paying the fare, watching her sister-in-law with a sidelong, worried expression all during the transaction.

"Jay's gone, Lauralee," she said as they made their way toward a train bound for Colville. Lauralee lifted her chin. "That is just as well," she lied.

As he left the railroad station, hurting as he had never hurt before in the whole of his life, Jay McCallum struggled against an almost incomprehensible need to go back, fetch Lauralee, haul her home over one shoulder, if it came to that. But he knew he couldn't.

Outside, in the clatter of the railroad yard, he paused, drew a deep breath. The scents of sawdust and grease and soot filled his nostrils while the essence of what Lauralee must have felt when she found him asleep in his father's study that morning filled his mind. His soul.

Jay had no compulsion to drink, and he never had, but explaining that to Lauralee, in her current state, would have been the most futile of enterprises. She would not be able to understand, not yet; her experiences with Virgil Parker would prevent that. As painful as it was, he was going to have to let her go for now, allow her to work the matter out in her own mind.

151

And what was he to do in the meantime? Go insane? Swearing under his breath, Jay thrust his hands into the pockets of his trousers and tried to think rationally. He could not go home to that enormous, empty house on the hill, not without Lauralee, not with his mother there. She would be entirely too pleased that the "country wench" was gone.

There were other places, of course, where Jay could take refuge. He could go to his latest mistress, who still resided in the small house he had bought for her. Marietta had cried and raged when he had gone to her, that first day back in Spokane, and told her that he could no longer visit her, but she would take him back. He had only to ask, flowers or a trinket in hand, and things would be the same as before.

Jay brought himself up short. Things were never going to be the same as before, and he might as well face that uncomfortable truth. Lauralee had changed everything. And even though she was leaving him at this very moment, Jay knew that he could not turn to Marietta for solace.

He had to think.

He was supposed to leave for Washington in exactly fourteen days. His father was depending on him, had booked passage for a long sea journey because Jay had promised to take over his duties in the Senate. What was he supposed to do now, go back to that echoing, empty place on the South Hill and tell his father that the agreement was off? That he wouldn't be able to think a coherent thought until he'd resolved the situation with Lauralee?

Jay had given his word; he could not, would not, go back on it. He went into the depot again, careful not to look for Lauralee, and bought a ticket for a train headed in the opposite direction.

Two hours later, he had reached his destination,

obtained a horse at the livery stable, and ridden up to the gracious brick house tht stood in the center of acres of wind-waved, rippling wheat.

Lucy came out of the house and bounded toward him, her arms outspread, her face alight. Despite his despondent state of mind, Jay couldn't help smiling as he dismounted.

Lucy was nearly as tall as he was, a sturdy woman with long dark hair always worn in a braid. She flung herself into Jay's hug. "What are you doing here? Why didn't you let us know you were coming? Is it true that you're married now?"

Jay laughed. "One question at a time, if you please. I came on the spur of the moment, because I wanted to see you and Brice. And, yes, I guess you could say that I'm married."

Lucy's bright hazel eyes peered around his shoulder, as though she thought he might be hiding a wife in his hip pocket or under his saddle blanket. "Well, for heaven's sake, where is she?"

A boy came from the barn and collected Jay's horse. Lucy took her brother-in-law's arm and ushered him toward the house. "Don't tell me—" she fretted.

"She's already left me," Jay admitted, and though he smiled, he knew that Lucy sensed his pain and confusion all the same. He sighed and let the awkward smile fall away. "It's a day of reckoning for the McCallum men, it seems. Lauralee took Kate with her."

They had reached the door, which Lucy had left standing open in her haste to greet the unexpected visitor. She paused there, looking up at Jay, her tender heart in her eyes. "Oh my," she said. "Chance will have a thing or two to say about that!"

Jay shrugged as Lucy preceded him into the house, led the way into her spacious, well-lit country parlor,

153

with its bay windows, brass fittings, and colorful hand-made pillows and coverlets. She sat down, her hands together in her lap, and Jay took a seat facing her.

He watched the struggle in her gentle, earthy face; she was trying not to pry, and because of her nature, which insisted on spilling into everything and filling it with love and life, that was an impossible task.

"Jay," she finally wailed. "What happened?"

A young girl shuffled in, questioning and diffident, and Lucy sent her off to the kitchen for coffee and "those cookies we made yesterday."

Jay felt at home in this house as he never did in Spokane, and for a few moments, he just sat there, absorbing the quiet, orderly atmosphere. When he sensed that Lucy could not bear the suspense for another moment, he explained how he had met Laura-lee, how Alexander's illness had brought them to Spokane, how he had married her. He told Lucy about Virgil Parker and what little he knew of the man's drinking habits and finished with the misunderstanding that had occurred that morning, when Lauralee had found him in the senator's study and jumped to the conclusion that he was sleeping off a binge.

"Oh, Jay!" Lucy cried when the story was over. "Didn't you try to explain?"

"That would have been a waste of time, given what Lauralee went through with Virgil. Anything I might have said would have come across as the empty excuse of a remorseful souse."

Lucy sighed. "I see what you mean." Her eyes swept over the riotous reds, greens, blues, and yellows in the hooked rug at her feet, then returned to Jay's face. "Surely you're not going to let Lauralee go because of something so silly!"

"I love her too much to do that," Jay replied with gruff honesty.

154

The girl came back, carrying a tray set with two cups of steaming coffee and a platter of oatmeal cookies. When she was gone again, Lucy handed one cup to Jay and took up the other for herself.

Because knowing when to change a subject was one of her many graces, she bent forward slightly and confided, "I wish I could see Chance McCallum's face when he finds out there's a rebellion afoot!"

Jay grinned wearily. "That is where we differ, Lucy love. I wouldn't want to be within five miles of the place."

"Of course it may be days before he notices," Lucy observed in an annoyed tone, setting down her cup.

Before Jay could respond to that, Brice came striding into the room, wearing the clothes of a field hand and a broad, surprised smile.

Jay was obliged to repeat the whole grim story, though he did manage, with help from Lucy, to put the task off until the midday meal.

Brice, who had always believed—naively, in Jay's opinion—that the affairs of men flowed, riverlike, into some pool of ultimate good, was undisturbed. "Go and get her," he said, chewing. "Tell her, plain and simple, that you're no drunk and you won't have any more of this running away business."

Jay and Lucy exchanged long-suffering looks, but neither commented.

Brice glanced at his wife and quipped, "I hope you aren't planning to jump the matrimonial ship, my love. I don't think I'm up to all the following and wooing that would be required of me."

Jay smiled, until he caught the expression of sadness on Lucy's face. There barely a moment, it was nonetheless frightening.

"Lucy?" he ventured softly when Brice had left the dining room momentarily to fetch sugar for his coffee.

155

Lucy was sitting rigid in her chair, her head down, her eyes carefully averted. "Don't ask me, Jay," she pleaded, "because I can't bear to tell you."

A cold sort of horror settled over Jay, but he did not press Lucy to say more. He knew she couldn't abandon Brice—the love the two of them shared was so fierce as to be almost an entity in itself—but something was very, very wrong.

Throughout the rest of the meal, Jay's precise legal mind sorted through the possibilities, which sifted down to just one: Brice—or Lucy herself—was sick. He shuddered to think of what either would suffer if left without the other.

Lauralee had been in a state during the trip to Spokane from Halpern's Ferry, able to think only of what might happen to Alexander. Now, on the return leg of the journey, which required the three travelers to spend one night in a Colville hotel because they had missed the stagecoach, she was wondering how her life could have been so irrevocably altered in such a short time.

Lauralee had a dreadful headache, and when Kate decided to explore the town of Colville, taking Alexander with her, she sank gratefully onto her bed in the hotel room, a cool cloth draped over her forehead.

In retrospect, she realized she had been rash in deciding that Virgil and Jay were cut from the same yard of goods. Wasn't it possible that Jay had simply fallen asleep in that chair in his father's study? Of course he'd smelled to high heaven of liquor, but lots of men took spirits now and then with no apparent harm done. Some men could get thoroughly drunk on occasion and not make a habit of indulging.

Not that Lauralee approved of liquor. She had seen it do too much damage, not only to Virgil but to other people, too—most notably the husbands, fathers, and sons of the women in her temperance group.

Why did it seem that some were compelled to consume the stuff while others could take the Demon or leave it alone? It was a mystery that had tormented Lauralee for a long time, one she would probably never be able to solve. And the whole question made her headache worse.

She began to cry, ascribing that to physical pain and not the tearing emptiness in her heart. It was Lauralee's experience that tears usually expended themselves quickly, but in this case they were renewed again and again, and she was in a pitiable state when Kate came back into the room and put Alexander onto the floor with a toy she had bought for him.

She sat down on the edge of the bed and placed a sisterly hand on Lauralee's back. "I feel the same way," she confided softly. "All broken and scared inside. Lauralee, do you think we should go home?"

If Lauralee Parker McCallum had one glaring fault, it was her stubborn, rigid pride. She sat up and tossed the now-tepid cloth aside, dashing away her tears. "You may do what you want, of course. For me, home is at Halpern's Ferry, not in Spokane." *Home,* countered a voice in the depths of her soul, *is where Jay McCallum is. And you know it.*

Kate was watching Alexander, who was trying to spin the top she had bought for him and grumbling because it kept falling over. "I love Chance so much, Lauralee. I always have."

Lauralee took Kate's hand and held it in her own. "I know," she answered. "I know."

"Maybe I was wrong to leave, but I just had to make him notice me, Lauralee. He treats me like a child, always ruffling my hair or swatting my bottom. Then he goes off to one of his women. . . ."

Lauralee felt Kate's sorrow, and shared it. "Chance must care for you," she offered, "or he wouldn't have married you in the first place. How did you meet him, Kate?"

"I was only twelve the first time I saw Chance—he came to a garden party that our neighbors held. He was so handsome, always laughing—I fell in love with him that very day, Lauralee, but he didn't notice me, of course. He was absolutely besotted with my friend Susan's older sister, Victoria, and he spent the next five years courting her."

"What happened?"

Kate's shoulders moved in a childlike shrug. "Victoria was killed in a carriage accident—it was dreadful. Chance, of course, was devastated, and he drank until it became a positive scandal. One night he asked me to marry him—I suppose it was some kind of joke to him, but I said yes, and to my surprise, he actually followed through. He put a ladder to my window, just like they do in stories, and I climbed down it and we ran away.

"My parents were furious, of course. They threatened to annul the marriage. I don't know why Chance fought that the way he did—he'd sobered up by then and he must have had regrets."

Lauralee found herself smiling, for the story was so romantic despite all its tragic overtones. Sensing that there was more, she waited quietly for Kate to go on, which she did, blushing copiously as she talked.

"The first time we made—made love was awful, Lauralee. I was scared—it hurt so—and I cried. Ever since then, Chance rarely comes to our bed. It's my fault that he turns to other women, Lauralee."

Lauralee couldn't help it. She giggled. "Nonsense! It's Chance's fault, at least in part."

Kate was staring at her, her eyes wide. "Why are you laughing?"

Lauralee didn't know the answer to that question; perhaps she was overtired or hysterical or just plain addlepated. "What do you do, Kate, when Chance does come to your bed?"

Color glowed in Kate's cheeks. "Do? What is there to do? Chance does everything!"

Lauralee clapped one hand to her mouth, but that was of no help. She howled with amusement. She laughed so hard that she fell backward on the lumpy bed and held her stomach with both hands.

Kate bounded to her feet, horrified. "Lauralee McCallum, this is not funny!"

"Chance—does—everything!" wailed Lauralee, her mirth coming in gales now, tears rolling down her face.

Kate was peering down at her as though she feared that Lauralee had gone quite around the bend. "Isn't Chance supposed to do everything?" she whispered, her eyes so round and serious that Lauralee laughed that much harder.

"For pity's sake, no!"

Alexander, sensing the merriment he could not hear, came to his mother, clasped her skirts in his hands, and bounced up and down, chortling in the throaty way of small children. Lauralee scooped him into her arms and held him tight, thinking that if she loved him another smidgen, she would not be able to bear it.

Kate was pacing the room, and the look of one who has just made a great and troublesome discovery was upon her. "What could I do," she muttered distractedly as she moved, "besides lay there?"

Lauralee bit down on her lower lip, lest she be overcome by another spate of uncontrollable mirth. When she could trust herself to speak, she said, "Sit down here beside me, Kate McCallum. I have a few things to tell you."

The poor, sweet innocent sat down, all ears. As Lauralee explained, choosing the most delicate words that she could, Kate's eyes grew wider and wider until they seemed to fill her whole face.

"Well, why didn't somebody tell me?!" she flared when it was over, shooting to her feet. "Why didn't Chance or Lucy or *somebody* tell me?!"

Lauralee shrugged. "I'd guess that you never ventured to ask Lucy, and the idea may never have occurred to Chance—men are not noted for heartfelt explorations of the subject, you know. They are creatures of comfort and they don't often take the time to consider the whys of lovemaking. It's only the whens that concern them."

Kate clasped herself with her arms, as if to stay herself from rash action of some sort. Like racing back to Spokane, perhaps, and assaulting Chance McCallum with all she'd learned in the past few minutes.

Just imagining that scenario started Lauralee laughing all over again.

Kate blushed furiously. "Lauralee McCallum, you stop that! This situation is serious!"

Alexander looked puzzled, his eyes moving from Kate's angry face to his mother's laughing one. For his sake, Lauralee did her best to compose herself.

"I won't go back to him," Kate suddenly decided, pacing again, thoughtful. "No, I won't hold him that way. Either Chance McCallum loves me, or he doesn't."

"Here, here," said Lauralee, getting into the spirit of things.

"I'll not pander to his baser desires just to keep him at home of a night!"

Giggles threatened again, rising rich and wide into Lauralee's throat, and she gulped them down. "I should say not," she agreed.

160

Kate paused again, one finger to her chin. "There is, of course, the matter of your theory." A sparkle leaped into the beautiful gray eyes, always so sad before. "I really would like to prove it."

"You'll have your chance, I'm sure," Lauralee said, and then she and Kate both burst out laughing at the unintended double entendre.

Lauralee's headache was gone, as if by magic. Somehow, laughter always lightened a person's troubles, it seemed to her. It took the edge off even the bleakest despair.

Lauralee went to the mirror, unpinned her hair, brushed it thoroughly, and swept it back into place again. She straightened her dress and splashed cold water over her face. There had been enough crying for one day: now it was time to square her shoulders and get on with the business of living.

"This hotel was an excellent restaurant," she announced, her eyes still laughing as she looked at Kate. "Let's go and get some supper. Since you're the rich one, Mrs. McCallum, you can pay."

Kate's lovely gray eyes twinkled. "Hardly. I'm having everything billed to Chance."

"In that case," Lauralee replied, "I am uncommonly hungry."

Kate opened the door with a flourish. "Only the best will do," she said.

CHAPTER
TEN

Lucy McCallum sat at the tiny desk in the sewing room, pen in hand, brow furrowed. How did one ask what she was about to ask of Mary? How?

A breeze lifted the curtains at the open window, bringing in the good scents of growing things and of summer, carrying Lucy far away, to Boston and her girlhood.

Even then, Lucy's younger sister had been unconventional. Mothers had warned their daughters against behaving the way Mary Cornell did, and for the most part, those daughters heeded the advice. But inside, Lucy suspected, they longed to be as daring, as bright, as funny as Mary.

Mary had driven her teachers mad with her antics, constantly amazing a more retiring Lucy with the sheer scope of her imagination. Oh yes, mischief had danced in those round brown eyes—she'd smoked cheroots, Mary had, and practiced swearing like a man. One day, in the glimmering heat of a city summer, she had gone so far as to crop off her lovely dark hair, leaving it in a raven pile on the parlor floor, saying that she rather liked the bouncy curls around her face and didn't Lucy like them, too?

Lucy smiled as she reflected on those days in Boston. How agitated Papa, a stern Presbyterian minister, had been, certain that his younger daughter was bound for Dante's nightmare. Mama, on the other hand, had simply smiled into her teacup and said, Never you mind, Mary would be all right.

And Mary was all right. She made speeches, she wrote books and articles, for she had a cause: the welfare of children, especially as it applied to their schooling and their working in factories, fields, and mills.

Mary had never been married, but it wasn't as though she hadn't had the opportunity. Lucy wondered if her sister had sensed her destiny all along.

But that was silly, of course. There was every chance that Mary wouldn't even recall the promise Lucy had extracted from her long ago, when they had sat together on a garden wall, discussing the future. Lucy had just married Brice McCallum and was about to leave for the faraway, mysterious West, to live on his farm there.

Perhaps because their first real parting was fast approaching, Mary and Lucy had spoken from their hearts.

"If anything should happen to me," Lucy had ventured quietly, "will you promise to look after Brice?"

Mary had smiled. "Nothing will happen to you, goose," she had replied, the heels of her high-button shoes making a clatter as she tapped them against the stones in the old wall. "Not anything bad, anyway. You'll have lots of babies and plenty of money and that big farmhouse Brice talks so much about. You'll be happy, Lucy Cornell McCallum, or I'll know the reason why!"

163

Brice's voice, raised in boisterous farewell to a departing Jay, came in through the sewing room window. Dear heaven, had there ever been a better man than Brice, a gentler man? Lucy doubted it, and her heart filled her throat to think of leaving him.

Mary's predictions had been right, for the most part. Lucy had been happy, gloriously happy. There had been money—something in short supply during Lucy's childhood. Only the babies had been lacking, and while she despaired of that sometimes, Brice McCallum so filled Lucy's life that she was more than content.

She had been, anyway, until the pain had started. Until she had seen the doctor, just a few weeks before, in Spokane.

Resolutely, Lucy put pen to paper. "Dear Mary," she wrote, her eyes scalding with tears. "Remember that day when we sat on Papa's garden wall and talked about babies and farms? You made me a solemn promise and I pray that you recall it, for the time has come, my dear sister, when I must prevail upon your honor. Please come, as soon as you can."

The letter went on for several pages, and it was difficult, of course, to write. More than once, Lucy McCallum had to stop and weep a while, not for herself but for Brice, before going on.

It was nearly nightfall when the stagecoach finally rattled into the town of Halpern's Ferry, and Lauralee was weary, not only of body, but of spirit. Pete Townsend was there—it seemed he always was when he was needed—and she gratefully accepted his offer to drive her and Kate and Alexander to the farm in a borrowed buckboard.

Pete did not know, of course, that Lauralee was

married, and she did not have the heart to tell him just then, though she did, of course, introduce Kate. Naturally, the name McCallum registered with him immediately.

After helping the two women into the wagon and hoisting their trunks into the back, he climbed up himself and took the reins in sure, competent hands, permitting a delighted Alexander to sit on his lap and pretend to drive the team.

Clarie and Jenny had apparently heard the team and wagon long before it rounded the last bend in the road, for they were there at the gate, beaming, all but jumping up and down in their delight.

Clarie immediately reached for Alexander and held him close in a hug. She followed along behind the wagon as it lumbered toward the house, still carrying the little boy, her eyes closed, her lips moving. Jenny, on the other hand, scrambled alongside, obviously in an agony of curiosity over Kate, the fine clothes that Lauralee was wearing, and what had gone on in faraway Spokane. No doubt, the place seemed, to a girl of Jenny's limited experience, as distant and mysterious as Mars.

Lauralee did not look forward to explaining her impulsive marriage.

Pete stopped the wagon beside the house, pressed the brake lever into place with one booted foot, and swept off his hat, then put it back on again. He always did that when he was nervous, and knowing that made Lauralee nervous in turn.

She knew that Pete loved her. What would she say if he declared himself, asked her to marry him? How could she explain the situation without hurting him?

It was impossible, of course. After a full day inside

that infernal, cramped stagecoach, everything seemed impossible. Lauralee wished she could march up to her room, close and lock the door behind her, and sleep for a week, but that luxury was not to be. Alexander needed to be bathed and given his supper and tucked into bed. Clarie must be told about his deafness and about Lauralee's confusing new status as a married woman. The spare room would have to be done up for Kate, and her things needed unpacking. And when all that had been taken care of, the trees in both orchards must be inspected. Lauralee knew she wouldn't be able to sleep if she didn't do that, gathering twilight or not.

Pete unloaded the trunks from the wagon and carried them inside without complaint. It was then that Lauralee noticed how Jenny watched him, her eyes sweeping over his body with every move he made and acknowledging each as splendid.

"Alexander doesn't hear me!" Clarie cried, catching up, holding her charge so tightly that he squirmed to be free. "What's the matter with him, Lauralee?"

Kate, who looked as exhausted as Lauralee felt, patted her sister-in-law's arm and then reached out for Alexander, who went to her with an eagerness that tightened Clarie's features. "Why don't you and Clarie take a walk?" she suggested softly.

Jenny dragged her eyes from Pete, who was already disappearing into the house with the second trunk. "I'll get supper on," she volunteered.

Lauralee hooked her arm through Clarie's. "Let's go and have a look at the orchards before it gets dark," she said, feeling the tremor of alarm that went through the girl's slender body. "Has Joe been pruning the trees and carrying water when it was needed?"

Clarie cast one look back at Kate, whose presence no doubt puzzled her almost as much as Alexander's lack of response when she'd spoken to him. "Who is that woman?"

"I told you, her name is Kate McCallum," Lauralee responded.

"Why did you bring her here? I don't like the way she was so quick to take Alexander—"

"Kate is very nice, Clarie," Lauralee broke in as they walked swiftly through the high grass, toward the creek and the orchards beyond. "You'll like her very much once you get to know her."

Clarie considered that, and if she made a decision one way or the other, it wasn't revealed in her face.

They reached the part of the orchard where the young trees, still seedlings, grew. The ground around them was parched, and Lauralee wished distractedly that she could irrigate them somehow. It didn't look like there would be rain anytime in the near future, and carrying water to them would be a backbreaking job.

Clarie stood a little apart, her arms folded, paying no attention to the state of the trees Lauralee was worrying over. "Alexander can't hear anymore, can he?"

Lauralee straightened, bracing herself, making herself meet Clarie's frightened brown eyes. "No, Clarie. He can't hear. He might someday, but we mustn't place our hopes on that. We have to look to God and ourselves for ways to help him."

Clarie's face was wan, her lower lip set in an attitude of defiance. "First Papa dies. Now Alexander can't hear. I don't believe in God anymore!"

"Clarie—"

"I don't! If there is a God, he's mean and spiteful!"

Lauralee folded her arms across her chest. "Mean and spiteful, Clarie? God allowed Alexander to live. Was that mean and spiteful?"

"What good is living if you can't be like everybody else? If you can't hear—"

"If you think about that question for a while, Clarie, you'll have your answer."

Clarie, as could be expected, was in no state to ponder such weighty matters as life and death. She loved Alexander, she had cared for him, and in many ways, he was hers as much as Lauralee's. "There's something else, isn't there? Something you're not telling me?"

"Yes," Lauralee sighed. "There is. But I'm not sure you're ready to hear it."

The sun was setting, and the mosquitoes were coming out. Clarie swatted at one with a fury all out of proportion to the affront. "If you don't tell me, I'll wonder something fierce, Lauralee! And I hate to wonder!"

Lauralee permitted herself a smile. Clarie was a bright, spirited girl, and one day she would be a beauty in the bargain. The smile faded. What sort of woman might Clarie have become if she'd been able to go to school in Washington, D.C., and stretch her horizons far beyond the borders of this forty-acre farm? What might Alexander have become, despite his deafness?

"While I was in Spokane, Clarie, I married Mr. Jay McCallum."

Clarie's mouth dropped open; her red-rimmed eyes widened. One of her arms rose in a spasmodic reference to the half-finished saloon across the road. "That Mr. Jay McCallum?!"

Lauralee sighed. "Yes."

"Why in the world would you marry him, of all people?"

"Because I love Jay, Clarie. I love him very, very much."

Clarie's quick mind worked over all the implications of that for some seconds. "I thought you loved Papa."

"I did. But your papa is dead, Clarie."

Another long silence ensued while this matter was mentally sorted and shelved as the others had been. It was so much for Clarie to absorb all at once, and Lauralee ached for her.

"Where is Mr. Jay McCallum, then? If he's your husband, why isn't he here?"

For the first time since her arrival, Lauralee allowed her own eyes to stray toward the towering Rumsucker Saloon. A crushing loneliness pummeled her, threatening, quite literally, to force her to her knees. "There was a problem, Clarie. A serious problem. I can't talk about it now."

Lauralee went about examining her trees. Clarie followed along behind her in silence, angry and confused but wanting to be close, too.

Pete Townsend, blessedly, was gone by the time Lauralee and Clarie reached the house. Kate, having already tended to Alexander and put him to bed, was pulling down and lighting the suspended lamp that hung over the kitchen table, while Jenny turned sizzling fried potatoes in a skillet. On a griddle, eggs were cooking alongside thick strips of salt pork.

Not much was said during supper, nor while Jenny and Lauralee did the dishes. Kate sat at the table, staring out at the country darkness, which must have seemed dense and unfamiliar to her, and Clarie had already gone upstairs.

Lauralee suspected that she was not in bed, but sitting in Alexander's room, watching him sleep and wondering what would become of him when he grew up to be a man and couldn't hear. That same gnawing dread lurked at the edges of Lauralee's mind too, but she put it away, too tired to deal with it.

Jenny went off to bed soon after the dishtowel was hung up to dry, and Lauralee carried the two basins of water out to dump them in the yard. There, she saw Joe Little Eagle in the light of the barn doorway; he waved in greeting and she knew that he had tended the cows, a task that had completely escaped her.

She went back inside the house, set the enameled basins in their place, wiped her hands on her cotton apron. Kate was still gazing out at the night, and she looked as small and uncertain as Clarie.

"If you want to go home to Chance," Lauralee ventured softly, "just do it. No one could blame you."

Kate's shoulders were slumped beneath one of the calico dresses she had been so eager to wear, but her eyes snapped with gray fire when they met Lauralee's. "I'll not brood for that man! Why, I'll wager that he isn't even at home. He's probably out—out womanizing!"

There was every likelihood that Chance was doing just that, but Lauralee didn't say so, of course. She took off her apron and hung it on a peg, where coats and cloaks and mufflers were kept during the snowy winters. "I'll take you to your room, Kate. You're tired; it's time you rested."

"Jenny already showed me where it is, and she made up the bed, too." Kate's lower lip protruded slightly. "How could I be twenty-two years old and not know how to make a bed, Lauralee?"

"You'll learn soon enough," Lauralee said, imagining Kate not only making beds, but churning butter, milking cows, and weeding the onion patch, too. She turned away to hide her smile. "Good night, Kate," she said, and then she went up the stairs and into the darkened hallway.

She stopped briefly to look in on Jenny and Clarie and found them both sleeping. Alexander, too, was resting soundly, in his small bed. All the same, Lauralee left the door that connected his room with her own just a bit ajar.

The bed she had shared with Virgil and then slept in alone for such a long time looked as wide as a desert and as cold as the North Pole, but Lauralee was too weary to consider such things in depth. She sat down on the edge of the mattress and began the arduous task of unhooking the buttons on her shoes.

When that had been done, she took off her dress—really, it was another of Kate's, for the alterations on her new clothes had not been finished—and put on a flannel nightgown taken from her bureau. She washed her face and cleaned her teeth and, yawning, went to stand at the window, looking out, as she had done one eventful night only a few weeks before.

There was no moon on this night to reveal the skeleton of the Rumsucker Saloon, and no crimson cheroot tip glowed in the darkness. Jay wasn't there, wasn't anywhere near, and the weight of that knowledge was almost more than Lauralee could stand up under.

There was every chance that she would never see Jay McCallum again; no doubt, he would divorce her and go on as planned, traveling to Washington, taking over his father's seat in the Senate, and eventually marrying some gracious woman whose gloves would not constantly be snagging on the calluses on her hands.

A jealousy so heated that it singed away her despair surged through Lauralee. She stomped over to the bed, flung back the covers, and muttered as she kicked and squirmed her way into the bedding and squeezed her eyes shut.

Within minutes, she was sleeping. And dreaming.

It was raining in Lauralee's dream, a hard, slashing rain that bent the young trees in the orchards to the ground and battered at the windows of the house. There was wind, too, and it howled around the corners of the house and whooshed beneath the windowsills and the spaces under the doors.

Lauralee saw herself going outside, in a nightgown, the fierce wind blowing her hair back in straight golden lines. The cellar doors were clattering in the storm, threatening to come unfastened.

That was why she was there, to fasten the doors. But before she could make her way to them—it was a struggle to move against the wind and the icy, tearing bite of the rain—they were flung open and a man came up out of the cellar.

Virgil. It was Virgil, though he was barely recognizable for the blood that saturated his clothes and covered his face in a hideous scarlet mask.

In her dream, Lauralee recoiled, retreating as he advanced, terrified. She knew that Virgil was angry, and she knew why: She had lain with Jay McCallum. She had become another man's wife.

Virgil's strides were long, and he did not seem to be held to a slow pace as Lauralee was. He reached her, grasped her shoulders, his hands leaving ugly stains on her rain-drenched nightgown.

"Murder," he said. "Murder."

Lauralee awakened with a start, thrust out of her dream by the impetus of horror. She sat in the tangled blankets, her hands clasped to her mouth, her breath ragged and hurting as it hastened in and out of her lungs, sawing at them and at her constricted throat.

"Who murdered you, Virgil?" she whispered when she had the breath to speak. "It wasn't that gambler,

172

was it? It didn't happen the way we all believed it did."

There was no answer, of course, and there was no storm outside. If there had been, Lauralee would not have been able to regain her composure at all, for then the nightmare would have seemed real. And it wasn't real—it wasn't!

Lauralee did not sleep well that night; all through it, she was half awake, listening for the wind and the *thump-thump* of unlatched cellar doors. Listening for Virgil's voice saying, "Murder. Murder."

She was relieved when the hectic, harried brightness of the morning came.

Encountering Adrienne Burch in Colville was either the best of luck or the worst, Jay couldn't be sure which. She invited him to travel on to Halpern's Ferry aboard her lumber boat, which would be leaving within the hour, and he accepted because refusing would have meant spending another night where he was and then enduring a bone-jarring stagecoach ride the following day.

Jay was troubled about Lucy and half mad with the need of Lauralee; hoping that Adrienne would leave him in peace to stare at the churning gray-green river water and grapple with all the quandaries that plagued him, he went immediately to the railing on the port side.

It was a vain hope, as he had half expected it would be. Adrienne was not by nature a kind or accommodating person; she wanted something in return for this trip, and probably for the one several weeks before, too. Jay kept his eyes on the chips of lumber and bark swirling in the water as she joined him at the railing, her hip deliberately brushing his thigh.

"Are you planning to open your saloon after all?" she asked, her voice piping over the sound of the craft's steam-powered engines. "You'll have a great deal of trouble with Lauralee Parker if you do."

Jay cleared his throat. If he hadn't been in the presence of a lady—if, indeed, he was in the presence of a lady—he would have spat over the side. "Lauralee McCallum," he said, half to himself. "Her name is Lauralee McCallum now."

Even over all the noise, he heard Adrienne's indrawn breath. He turned, the wind dancing in his hair as it was in hers, and met her gaze, waiting.

"You married her?" she asked with quiet dignity. Lumbermen were clamoring all over the boat—it had been unloaded in Colville—but Adrienne didn't seem to be aware of them. Possessing a certain regal distance as she did, she might have been Cleopatra, traveling the Nile aboard her barge.

"Yes," Jay replied. The fact that he was Lauralee's husband would probably deepen his appeal to this woman rather than quell it, but one never knew.

"Then you've brought more trouble on yourself than I thought," she said, chin high, flowery hat at a fashionable angle. Then she turned and indicated the wheelhouse with a gracious gesture of one gloved hand. "Shall we?"

Jay would have preferred to remain on deck, in the fresh air, where he could alternately peer into the river and watch the scenery go by, but he was curious about this woman and he wanted to talk to her in private.

It soon became apparent that Adrienne Burch did not have talking in mind. While Jay leaned against the wheelhouse door, she reached up, her mouth quirking because she knew that the gesture uplifted her fine breasts, and unpinned her hat.

The captain stepped away from the wheel without

174

being asked, and Jay had to move aside so the man could go out on deck.

"Take the wheel," Adrienne urged in a sultry voice.

"If I don't?"

"We'll wind up aground," Adrienne said. "Or worse."

Jay took the wheel. What the hell; he'd never piloted a steamer before.

Adrienne kept her distance for a time, though she was making him conscious of her in other ways. Jay grinned, thinking that even though her subtle attempts at seduction were hopeless, they were damn interesting.

She came to stand beside him at the wheel, after making a sensuous show of removing the braid-trimmed capelet she had worn over her dress, her thigh again touching his. Jay almost wished he didn't love his wife so much; he knew exactly what Adrienne had in mind and it would have been satisfying to be attended in that way in a wheelhouse. Alas, he did love Lauralee, and the woman who could make him betray her had not drawn breath.

Sure enough, Adrienne's hand ventured out to caress him and then her fingers were on the first button of his trousers.

Jay removed her hand, gently but firmly, with one of his own, the other still on the huge wooden wheel.

Her eyes widened, questioning and deep brown. And she smelled good, like lilies of the valley after a gentle rain. Damnit all to hell, why couldn't this have happened before he'd met Lauralee?

"I want you, Jay McCallum," Adrienne said forthrightly, "and I'll have you."

"Why?" Jay asked evenly, turning his attention back to the broad, temperamental river. "Because I'm Lauralee's husband?"

She didn't answer that, but then, she didn't have to. Her feelings about Lauralee were evident in the stiffening of her beautiful, lush body. "I could pleasure you until you wanted to die of it," she snapped.

"I know," Jay replied ruefully. Some perverse part of his mind wondered if letting Adrienne have her way would really constitute cheating; it was a moot question.

She touched him again, and again he dislodged her hand, though not so gently this time. And not soon enough, either. He was so hard that he hurt, and all he needed was for Lauralee to see him getting off Adrienne Burch's lumber boat in that condition.

Jay was grateful when the captain returned and took over the wheel again; he went back out on deck and stood at the railing once more, gulping fresh, mist-laden air.

Adrienne seemed determined to torment him. She stood close again, and if he could stop her from touching him, he could not, without throwing her overboard at least, stop her from talking.

She told him, without so much as a blush or a catch of shame in her voice, all the ways that she could please him. Was he sure he wouldn't like to go back into the wheelhouse, she asked, just for a few glorious minutes?

Jay had no reason to doubt that those "few minutes" would be glorious, and while he had no intention of indulging Adrienne, he was a man and part of him wanted to do just that.

His stony silence only seemed to make Adrienne more determined. She was aware, of course, of his discomfort—that was embarrassingly obvious.

Finally, the steamer docked at Halpern's Ferry and Jay was on the small, shifting peer before the vessel had even been secured.

"I'll be happy to drive you out to Lauralee's place!" Adrienne sang out from the deck.

Jay did not turn, did not stop walking, even though it hurt like all hell to walk. It was several miles to Lauralee's farm; maybe by the time he reached it, he would be presentable.

CHAPTER
ELEVEN

The sky was a brassy, glaring blue. After emptying a bucket of creek water at the base of yet another young apple tree, Lauralee offered a silent prayer for rain. Failing that, might she just have the strength and patience to go on carrying water from the stream to the orchard?

The buckets were heavy and their narrow handles seemed to cut into Lauralee's fingers. The small of her back ached and she longed to collapse somewhere and sleep, but it was still early afternoon and there were hours of this drudgery ahead.

Lauralee was used to hard work, of course, but she was worried about Kate, who had insisted on helping. It would have been better for her to start with easier tasks, such as separating the milk from the cream, churning the cream to butter, pressing the butter into the special wooden molds that made it attractive enough to bring a good price from the owner of the general store in town. But Kate, raised to be a lady, had wanted instead to do "real farm work."

She was doing that now, and Lauralee had to admire

the way she struggled back and forth from the creek, lugging the heavy buckets, never complaining.

Of course, Joe Little Eagle should have been there in her place, but he had not returned from town yet. That was strange all in itself, for he always came back as soon as he'd delivered the dairy goods to Mr. Wallerman at the mercantile. By now, he should have been in the orchards.

"If it doesn't rain," Kate asked bravely as she and Lauralee started back toward the creek with their buckets, "will we have to keep this up all summer?"

Lauralee hadn't the heart to answer honestly, so she pretended not to hear the question. The younger trees were not as strong as the older ones, which grew in the moist ground along the creek; their leaves were limp and withering, and even though the two women had worked since breakfast, taking only a short time out to eat sandwiches brought by Clarie, fully half of the newer orchard still needed to be watered.

They reached the creek and bent to fill their buckets; the hot sun pounded at the back of Lauralee's neck and burned through the fabric of her oldest work clothes to draw sticky sweat from her flesh. And if she felt this way, all achy and raw, what must the uninitiated Kate be feeling?

"Lord in heaven," Lauralee muttered as they straightened, ready to make the arduous return journey to the thirsty trees. "Kate McCallum, you are as gray as a dirty sheet! You go back to the house and rest this minute."

Kate's chin jutted out, but her shoulders were sagging under the weight of the two brimming pails she carried. No doubt her fingers felt as though they had been severed from her hands. "I won't," she said stubbornly. "Not unless you go with me."

Lauralee considered the situation. She was going to

be carrying water as long as there was light to see by, and maybe after that; some of the trees would surely die if she didn't continue working. But Kate, from the looks of her, might perish as well if she didn't sit down for a while. And she clearly wasn't going to return to the house alone. "All right," Lauralee conceded. "I want to see if Joe is back, anyway."

Joe was not back. Sitting at the kitchen table, sipping the lemonade that Jenny had been just about to carry out to the orchards, Lauralee wondered what could be keeping him. Had he absconded with the small amount of money Mr. Wallerman would have given him for that day's delivery?

Lauralee couldn't believe he had. If Joe had had a mind to steal, he'd let plenty of opportunities go by. It would have been easy, for example, to empty out the cocoa tin in which Lauralee kept the dairy money and the pittances she received for renting out the spare room from time to time and teaching the occasional lesson at the melodeon.

She set down her lemonade glass with a thoughtful frown. "Jenny, you and Clarie did send the milk and butter to town every day while I was gone, didn't you?"

Jenny beamed, proud, and with reason, of a job well done. "Every day except Sunday," she confirmed. "And we took what was in the cocoa tin to the bank every few days, just like you told us to." She went to the sideboard, where tablecloths and other linens were stored, and brought out both the cocoa tin and Lauralee's bankbook.

The tin contained a dollar bill and some change. The bankbook was in order, too, though the amount penned at the bottom of the column fell far short of the mortgage payment that would come due in late October, just when the apples had been harvested. Please God, Lauralee thought, let there be apples to harvest.

Kate was reading Lauralee's frown with her usual uncanny perception. "I could give you the money, Lauralee, if you need it."

Lauralee refused the offer with a sharpness that stung Kate visibly. She didn't apologize because she hoped that her friend—Lauralee could not seem to think of herself as a McCallum and thus as Kate's sister-in-law—would take umbrage and remain here at the house instead of going back to the orchards.

"Where are Clarie and Alexander?" she asked Jenny, avoiding Kate's eyes.

"Clarie's in the garden, I think," came the immediate answer. "And Alexander is napping."

"I'd like you and Clarie to walk to town and try to find out what's happened to Joe. I need his help." Now Lauralee could look at Kate. "Would you mind staying here and taking care of Alexander while the girls are gone?"

Kate knew that she had been maneuvered by a sort of deliberate mercy, but she could not refuse any request that concerned Alexander. She nodded and, with a ladylike sniff, turned her head.

That was good; it prevented her from seeing Lauralee's smile.

The walk out from town, under the broiling sun, was longer than Jay expected. He had not had any real rest in days, and even as his building and Lauralee's farmhouse came into view, he began to yawn.

He wondered how he would be received, but only briefly. If the woman meant to throw him out, she would damn well have to do it tomorrow.

Jay climbed over Lauralee's broad, splintery

fence—the thing ought to be painted—and moved slowly toward the house. Now that he was near and wanted to hurry, it seemed that he couldn't; his muscles wouldn't cooperate.

He rounded the weatherbeaten house, tapped at the kitchen door, which stood partially open, and then went inside.

Kate was sitting at the table, sipping lemonade and looking as though she'd just finished building a Western version of China's Great Wall. Single-handedly. Her eyes widened at the sight of Jay and then slipped to one side, only briefly but long enough to reveal that she had hoped to see Chance coming in behind him.

"Jay McCallum," she said after a moment of heroic recovery, "you look dreadful."

Jay took in her mud-speckled calico dress, her tumbledown hair, the salve glistening on her hands. "You aren't exactly a page from *Godey's Ladies Book* yourself," he replied, gravitating to a bucket of water and lifting the dipper to his mouth. When he had quenched his thirst, he turned back to his sister-in-law. "Where the devil did you manage to find mud in weather like this?"

Kate blushed, or Jay thought she did. It was hard to tell, what with the sunburn that glowed on her face. "Lauralee and I were watering the trees. She's still at it, and if you were any kind of husband, you would go right out there and make her come inside!"

Jay was too tired to go anywhere. "I assume the bedrooms are upstairs?"

Kate averted her eyes for a moment and bit her lower lip. "Aren't you even going to tell Lauralee you're here?"

"No," replied Jay, yawning. "And don't you do it,

either. I'm in no mood to be ravaged by my adoring wife."

Kate did blush then; sunburn or no, there was no mistaking it. "Men!" she sputtered, but then she directed him to Lauralee's room.

Jay climbed the stairs, went into the room in question, and sat down on the edge of a neatly made bed. He pulled off his boots and the rest of his clothes, except for his underwear, and stretched out on top of the covers. Time enough to shave and bathe and make love to his wife later. For now, he only wanted to sleep.

As he was drifting off, he remembered that his horse was stabled in Halpern's Ferry; he'd left the animal at the livery stable the day he and Lauralee had rushed off to Spokane in such haste. The walk to the farm, under the hot summer sun, had been unnecessary.

Perhaps because the bedding carried the distinctive scent of her, Jay dreamed of Lauralee. The breeze coming in through the open window, wafting over his bare skin, became her caresses, her bold, exploring kisses.

The need of her half awakened him; he felt something damp against one side of his chest and opened his eyes to see what it was. Alexander was curled up against him, wearing only a diaper, one tiny hand resting on Jay's stomach. Jay grinned and went back to sleep.

When Joe Little Eagle came to the orchards offering no explanation for his late return from town, Lauralee didn't question him. She was too grateful for his help.

Almost on his heels, Kate appeared, bringing a berry bowl containing a paste of vinegar and salt and water and looking oddly secretive. "Clarie said you'd want this," she announced, offering the bowl. "Does it really keep away mosquitoes?"

Lauralee nodded, took the bowl, and smeared some of the paste on her arms and over her face. Kate was intrigued and followed suit, and the two women laughed at each other.

After that, the work went faster. Kate carried one of Lauralee's buckets, while Joe was able to manage two. The dry ground around the trees became moist circles of mud.

As the afternoon waned and evening approached, the mosquitoes came too, whirring out of their nests by the creek and along the river, buzzing at the grainy paste that had dried on the women's skin. Lauralee had expected Kate to be driven back to the house by this assault, but she went right on working, humming as she watered the trees and trudged back and forth to the creek, casting the occasional mysterious glance in Lauralee's direction.

Lauralee was too tired to ask what her friend was thinking, too intent on getting each tree watered before the sun went down.

Her determination was destroyed, however, when Jenny came bounding into the orchard, wide-eyed and breathless, and blurted out, "Oh, Lauralee, Mr. McCallum is sleeping in your bed! I didn't believe it when Clarie told me, so I went to see for myself. Thunderation, he's there all right, and he's near naked, too!"

Lauralee's brimming water bucket fell to the ground and spilled. She glared at Kate and accused, "You knew! You knew and you didn't tell me!"

"Jay asked me not to," Kate replied brightly, her eyes full of mischief and weariness. "He said you would ravage him, and he wanted to sleep—"

"Ravage him?!" yelled Lauralee, abandoning her

bucket and her trees and her friends to stomp toward the house. "I'll *kill* him!"

As she hurried homeward, Lauralee wondered how the soaring, sweet joy she was feeling could coexist with the fury that was also within her. The gall of that man, lying "near naked" in a house that contained young girls! And helping himself to her bed as though he were master of the manor!

Lauralee reached the yard, her hands clenched at her sides in anger while her heart tripped with happiness, her hair falling from beneath her straw hat, the hem of her patched calico dress muddy.

Adrienne Burch was just drawing her fancy surrey to a stop beside the house, looking cool and unruffled in a pink lawn dress and a broad-brimmed straw hat decorated with pastel flowers. In her hand she carried a sizable leather satchel.

"Oh, Lauralee," she trilled, starting a bit and putting her free hand, which, of course, was immaculately gloved, to her alabaster throat. "You gave me quite a turn." Adrienne bent forward slightly from the waist, squinting. "What is that—that stuff on your face?"

Jolts of electrified humiliation went through Lauralee's body, but she managed to appear calm on the outside. "I'm wearing vinegar and salt, Adrienne," she explained evenly. "It keeps the mosquitoes away."

Adrienne's discerning eyes swept over Lauralee, from the top of her head to the toes of her muddy shoes. "Dear me, I should think they would be afraid to come near you even without the vinegar."

Kate had appeared at Lauralee's side, a staunch supporter wearing her own vinegar-and-salt without shame, as though it were the latest fashion. "Do you want something?" she asked of Adrienne.

Adrienne resembled a coy little girl as she fluttered her lashes in a parody of innocence and held out the satchel. "I only came to bring this. Jay left it on my boat, you see, and I knew he would need his clothes."

I'm going to kill her, Lauralee thought. I'm going to jerk that satchel out of Adrienne Burch's milk-white hands and bludgeon her to death with it. And when I'm finished with her, I'll proceed to murder Jay!

Kate caught Lauralee's arm subtly, just as she would have plunged headlong into savagery, and smiled broadly at Adrienne. "How thoughtful of you. We're all so grateful!"

Adrienne set the satchel down in the grass, moving gingerly, casting the occasional hungry look toward the house. Except for the sound of young girls' laughter and the faint strains of the melodeon, the place was quiet.

"Aren't you even going to invite me in for a lemonade or a cup of tea?" Mrs. Burch asked at length.

"Actually, no," Lauralee said with dignity absorbed from Kate's manner. "I'm not a lady of leisure, Adrienne. I have work to do."

With decorum, Adrienne went back to her surrey and drove away, leaving a cloud of dry dust behind her.

Lauralee stood stock-still, arms folded, until Adrienne's surrey had gone through the gate—she didn't even have the courtesy to stop and close it after herself, that woman—still very much inclined toward wholesale slaughter.

Kate was brightly philosophical. "Well, whoever she was, she's gone," she chimed, smiling as though that settled everything.

Lauralee glowered at her friend, strode over to Jay's satchel—he'd forgotten it on Adrienne's boat, had he—and kicked the expensive leather bag as hard as

186

she could. It stood staunch and heavy in the dust, so she kicked it again.

A window on the second floor slid open, and Jay appeared in the chasm, shirtless, unshaven, his dark hair rumpled. "Do you mind?" he shouted. "That valise is valuable!"

"What are you doing in my room?" Lauralee screamed. "What, for that matter, are you doing in my house?"

Jay rested his elbows on the windowsill and grinned insufferably, his teeth flashing white. "I live here," he replied.

Lauralee rested sore hands on her hips. "So you've decided where you live, then? I wasn't sure, considering that it was Adrienne who had your baggage. On her boat!"

His bare shoulders moved with suppressed laughter. "I think we've got this turned around. I'm supposed to stand on the ground and you should be in the window, saying, 'Jay, Jay, wherefore art thou, Jay?' "

"Don't you dare drag Shakespeare into this!" Lauralee shouted. "And put your clothes on!"

He leered at her, gave a raucous shout of laughter, and turned away from the window.

"That man," Lauralee muttered, kicking at the ground with the toe of one shoe, torn between her considerable pride and a devastating need to go upstairs and make love to Jay McCallum.

Kate was smiling sadly, a faraway look in her eyes. "He's wonderful, isn't he?" she said, and then she went into the house. Lauralee followed, leaving the satchel in the yard, and washed away the mosquito paste, busying herself, as best she could, in the kitchen. She had forgotten all about the thirsty trees in the orchard; all her thoughts were upstairs, traipsing after Jay.

"Could I have my satchel, please?" he called lamely from the top of the stairs. "Right now, I'm not wearing much more than Alexander is."

There were young girls present. For that reason and that reason alone, or so she told herself, Lauralee marched outside, got the satchel, and carried it half-way up the stairs.

If Jay wanted the bag, he could just come the rest of the way to fetch it.

Alexander, clad in a diaper that was probably sodden, was inching his way backward down the stairs, just as he had always done. Lauralee forgot his proficiency, though, and bounded up, prepared to catch him if he fell.

"Leave him alone," Jay said quietly. "He's doing just fine."

Alexander was doing fine. He flung one bright, aren't-I-wonderful smile up at his mother and neatly skirted the barrier of the satchel. Lauralee was glad that she hadn't "rescued" him, thus spoiling his obvious pride in doing for himself.

She sank against the wall with a sigh. "I'll never get used to this," she mourned.

Jay came nearer and bent to catch the handle of the satchel in his hand. "I don't suppose you have indoor plumbing?" he ventured, his voice gruff with an emotion Lauralee suspected might be similar to her own.

"This isn't Spokane," she said tightly, not daring to look at him. "If you want to bathe, you'll have to do that in the creek. We haven't time to heat water for you."

That was telling him. That was laying down the law. The rounder! If Jay McCallum thought he was going to be waited on in this house, he was sadly mistaken!

Lauralee told Jay all this with the set of her chin and the flash of her eyes and went back down the stairs.

And Clarie and Jenny happily made a liar of her by heating water for Jay to bathe in, maneuvering the steaming kettles around the meal they were cooking.

Stewing, Lauralee paced. How had Jay happened to be on Adrienne Burch's boat? And exactly what had so absorbed him that he'd left his satchel behind? She could well imagine! She would avoid that rounder, that's all. Pretend he didn't exist.

Only Alexander was wet and all his diapers were upstairs. How could she get up there and down again without encountering Jay?

She considered sending one of the girls, then dismissed the idea. They were busy setting the table, making supper. Preparing bathwater.

Kate might have gone, but she was in the parlor, playing a melancholy tune on the melodeon. Probably mooning for Chance. Lauralee couldn't bring herself to bother her friend, especially when the poor dear had had such a long, difficult day.

Resigned, Lauralee marched up the stairs, along the hallway, and into Alexander's room. The door of her own was slightly ajar, and through it she could see part of the bed, part of a long, muscled, hairy leg.

Again, she was angry. It was indecent, that's what it was, a full-grown man lying about like that, exposed.

Lauralee went to the door, meaning to close it, and wound up peering around its edge. Jay was sprawled out on the bed, wearing only a pair of boxer shorts, and he was, incredibly, sound asleep.

A feeling of tenderness was Lauralee's undoing, for all that he'd cavorted with Adrienne Burch aboard her boat, for all that he'd made himself at home in this house as though it were his own, she was drawn to him. She went to the side of the bed and gently brushed a lock of hair back from his brow. He stirred.

For the sake of modesty, she went to the door,

closed it quietly. What was she doing lingering in this room, watching Jay McCallum sleep when Alexander needed his diaper changed?

But Lauralee couldn't pull herself away. She loved the sight of Jay's long, muscled legs, his broad furred chest, his arms. Unable to help herself, Lauralee went to him and ran one hand, her touch as light as the breeze from outside, up and down his thigh.

A shudder went through him and his eyes opened with an apparent start, but they were clear and un-clouded—a fact that made Lauralee wonder if he had really been sleeping at all. He caught her around the waist before she could move away from the bed and hurled her down beside him with a facetious growl.

Jay kissed Lauralee only briefly, but that was enough to kill all her anger and all her good intentions. She crooned softly, despairingly, as he opened her dress, revealing her muslin camisole but not displacing it. No, he simply bent his head to dampen straining nipples with his tongue, causing them to chafe against the muslin. At the same time, he drew Lauralee's skirt up and up, and the breeze followed, raising goose-bumps along her legs as they were bared to her knees and then to her thighs. He undid the tie of her drawers, grappled with them for a moment, and then ripped them away, laying her most tender treasure bare.

He began to nip at the rosebud peaks of her breasts—how they throbbed against that thin, moist layer of muslin—while his fingers found another bud and urged it to bloom.

Lauralee writhed, delirious with pleasure. Instinct forced her legs wide apart, permitting Jay to plunder with piratelike freedom. And plunder he did, massaging her, plucking at her, finally venturing inside her.

"Oh," she groaned. "Oh, oh—"

190

He was still teasing her breasts, kissing them, scraping them gently with his teeth—would he never bare them and suckle? Frantic, Lauralee brought one hand up, clasped her worn camisole, and ripped it away. Her breasts bounced free in glorious rebellion, only to be captured by Jay. A long, shuddering groan moved through his length as he closed his mouth over one yearning morsel and then, greedily, over the other.

Lauralee's hips began to move, rising higher and higher, searching, and the bedsprings squeaked. Chuckling, Jay withdrew his hand and swatted her bottom. "This is a household of innocents, remember?" he teased.

Lauralee's disappointment was fathomless. She ached for fulfillment, she groped for his hand, trying to draw it back to her. "Take me," she pleaded softly, shameless in her desperation.

Jay rose from the bed and pulled her after him, removing her dress and what remained of her underthings. "I'll take you all right," he answered, admiring her curves, stroking them with his hands until she shivered, "but not on that bed. The damn thing sounds like a threshing machine."

His hands were cupped over her breasts. The passion was building again and it possessed such force that Lauralee swayed on her feet. Jay caught her by the waist and they drifted toward the floor, or so it seemed to her.

Jay was on his knees, only a hooked rug separating him from the bare wooden floor, and Lauralee knelt facing him. She soared on the throaty moan he gave as she drew his shorts down and revealed his manhood.

She moved to stroke him, but he caught her hand and would not allow it. She was watching him with wanton, questioning eyes when he suddenly grasped her hips, lifted her, and brought her down upon the full, reaching hardness of his shaft.

"Ooooh," Lauralee gasped, her head falling back in submission to glory as he lifted her, lowered her, lifted her. Just as that glory would have enfolded her completely, Jay stopped and made her lean back a way, still filled with him, so that he could tongue the peak of one breast, suckle at the other.

She became wild with her need and instinctively thrust her legs out wide, and when she did, sweet, scalding spasms of release were her reward. She trembled and quaked with them, and she would have cried out, too, had Jay not muffled the sound by claiming her mouth with his own.

He gave a great shudder as they kissed, and then his cries battled her own and his powerful hips would have flung her through the ceiling had he not held her in place while he thrust, withdrew, thrust again. He was bent backward, nearly to the floor, when the wild sheathing and unsheathing culminated in glorious, reverent surrender.

Lauralee was moved, not only by the power of her own releases, but by the beauty of his. She sat upon him, smoothing his heaving, hair-roughed chest with her hands.

Finally, he had recovered enough to speak. "Oh, woman," was all Jay said, but it conveyed volumes to Lauralee.

Fear compelled her to ask. "Jay, did you and Adrienne—on the boat—did you . . ."

His eyes laughed at her question, but it was a gentle mirth. "No," he answered. "We didn't."

Lauralee believed him, and the force of her relief flung her forward, to bury her face in Jay's shoulder, to dampen the flesh there with her tears. Gently, speaking softly, he removed the few pins that remained in her hair and spread it with his fingers, and even when he met with a tangle, there was no pain.

After a time, he went to the washstand, returned with a basin of tepid water and a cloth. Kneeling beside Lauralee, who was now lying prone on the hooked rug, he began to bathe her.

The bath cooled Lauralee's flaming skin, but at the same time, the motions of the cloth fanned the pounding heat within her. She groaned as it coursed over the flesh of her inner thighs, arched her back as Jay urged her legs to part.

"I couldn't stay away," he muttered hoarsely as he laid aside the cloth. His fingers burrowed into the warm curls at the joining of her thighs, claiming her with a swiftness that made her hips strain upward. His thumb worked a wicked, simultaneous magic.

Lauralee whimpered. "Supper—Alexander's diaper—oh, God—"

Jay laughed with a gentle gruffness. "I couldn't agree more," he teased, his fingers delving deeper.

Lauralee's breath came in a series of fevered gasps and the room, Jay with it, became a colorful blur. Though she willed her hips to still themselves, they rose and fell in frantic pleasure. Finally, a great shudder moved through Lauralee, and her entire body convulsed with release. Jay's free hand covered her mouth to muffle the wail of satisfaction she gave, and when her body had ceased its sweet spasms, Lauralee bit that hand as hard as she could.

Jay hissed an exclamation and scowled down at her. After a moment, a wicked light danced in his eyes and he stretched out above her, his magnificent frame brushing against her breasts, her hips, her thighs and stomach. "I see you haven't been brought entirely to heel," he said in a voice so low that Lauralee might have imagined it.

193

On the chance that she hadn't, she stiffened. "To heel—?" she sputtered breathlessly.

Her legs were parting again. Lauralee didn't know if she was moving them herself or if Jay was, and after another moment or so, she didn't care. She made a soft, crooning sound as he entered her.

CHAPTER
TWELVE

"Mama!" Alexander called from outside the bedroom door. "Mama, Sander in! Sander in!"

Lauralee disentangled herself from Jay, rose from the floor, and pulled on a wrapper. She hesitated at the door, her hand on the knob, glowering at her husband over one shoulder. Waiting for him to do the decent thing.

"Wedded bliss," said Jay in a wry tone as he moved from the floor to the bed and covered himself, at least to the waist, with the brightly colored quilt.

Lauralee opened the door and Alexander was standing there, in his soggy diaper, looking forlorn. "Sander wet," he said.

Guilt swept through Lauralee, brushing away the warm ache of being so thoroughly loved only moments before. Alexander's deafness had a way of coming home to her at the most wounding times; suppose he could never say any words but those few he had learned before he lost his hearing? How could he ever learn to speak properly when the ability to listen to others had been taken from him?

"He's too old to be wearing diapers," Jay observed, finding a cheroot and a match somewhere among his discarded clothes. The very clothes, in fact, that he had worn to ride on Adrienne Burch's lumber boat.

Angry all over again, Lauralee stomped into Alexander's room to fetch the diaper she had come upstairs for in the first place. It hurt a little that her son did not toddle after her as he usually did; instead, he climbed up onto the bed, and when Lauralee returned, the little boy was nestled as close to Jay as he could get, chirping happily and grasping at the illusive clouds of blue-gray smoke swirling from the cheroot.

The use of tobacco, as far as Lauralee was concerned, was not only foolish, but sinful. Still, at that moment, the aroma of the stuff was strangely reassuring. To hide this softening in her principles, she snatched Alexander away from Jay and began unpinning his diaper. "When it comes to Alexander, you don't approve of anything I do," she complained. "I hold him too much. I rescue him too often. And now he should be in long pants, I suppose!"

"Alexander is growing up, Lauralee. It's time he was housebroken."

"Housebroken! Alexander is a child, not a dog! And furthermore—"

The job was finished; Alexander's wet diaper had been exchanged for a dry one. Lauralee took the other into his room, dropped it into a pail set aside for the purpose, and came back to pour water into the basin on the bureau top and wash her hands.

"Furthermore, what?" Jay prompted, as though there had been no interruption in the conversation at all.

Lauralee's shoulders sagged. There were so many things to do, so many things to think about. The trees. Jenny and Clarie. Kate. The cows and the scant amount of money in the cocoa tin. Adrienne Burch and this handsome husband she had not for one moment planned to acquire.

And Jay was right, damn his hide, about Alexander. The child was too big to be wearing diapers, but when had there been time for proper toilet training?

"Come here," Jay said with gentle gruffness, and when Lauralee could bring herself to look at him, she saw that he was extending one arm to enfold her against him. Alexander sat on his belly, chattering and bouncing up and down.

Lauralee hesitated and then went to lie on the bed, to be held close and secure against the side of Jay McCallum's hard, hairy chest.

Through the tangle of her hair, Jay kissed Lauralee's temple. "You're a fine mother," he said. "This boy is lucky to have you."

Except for Alexander's energetic gyrations on Jay's stomach, the room was silent. Finally, Lauralee broke the quiet with a tearful giggle. "And you were worried about the bed squeaking," she said.

Jay laughed. Evidently, he was comfortable as he was, for he made no move to dislodge Alexander. Though Lauralee waited, he said nothing at all.

"What about Washington?" she finally ventured. The issue could no longer be avoided.

"What about it?" Jay returned presently, moving to fling his cheroot over his head and out the open window.

Lauralee's throat was tight. "Are you going?"

Jay sighed, tickling Alexander under the chin, making him laugh and squirm all the more. "That depends on you, Lauralee. I promised my father I would, but I can't go without you and Alexander."

Lauralee was silent, absorbing that. Never before had her thoughts and opinions mattered so much to anyone; even Virgil, who had loved her, in the early days of their marriage at least, had never consulted her in even the most minor decisions. Now here was this man, apparently willing to forego the opportunity of a lifetime if she would not share in it. "I thought you would be angry over—over the way I left."

"I am. Remind me to beat you soundly sometime in the next twenty or thirty years. I have my faults, woman, but being a drunk isn't one of them." He paused, sighed philosophically. "You looked at me in the study that morning and you saw Virgil, didn't you?"

Lauralee gulped, ashamed. She had done just that. Furthermore, she had panicked and run away like a child. "Yes. I'm sorry, Jay."

He shifted silently to kiss her forehead. It was a mere touch of his lips, that kiss, and yet it sent sleepy shards of need all the way to the tips of Lauralee McCallum's toes. "I'm sorry too, love. I should have passed up the brandy and gone back to our bed, where I belonged."

"What were you doing downstairs at that hour anyway?" Lauralee asked, frowning.

He saw her frown, considered it for a moment, then smoothed it away with one index finger. "If you will remember, Mrs. McCallum, we missed dinner that night. I woke up and I was hungry. I went downstairs to scare up something to eat, and I saw Chance was in the study. Like a fool, I tried to talk to him."

"About Kate?"

Jay said nothing; he was winding a finger in one wheat-gold curl at the side of Alexander's head.

Lauralee respected Jay's reluctance to divulge a confidence, if that was what his reticence represented, especially one that concerned his brother. Still, Kate's feelings and well-being mattered too, didn't they?

"Kate told me how she met Chance, and all about their marriage. Jay, is he still mourning Victoria? Is that the problem?"

Alexander finally became bored with bouncing on Jay's middle and crawled down off the bed to waddle out of the room. Always aware of the steep stairs, Lauralee moved to stop him, found herself restrained, held firmly against that impervious chest.

She closed her eyes and prayed that her son would not go tumbling down the steps. Apparently, he navigated them without incident, for there was no outcry, and the happy hubbub going on downstairs continued without noticeable interruption.

With his free hand, Jay soothed the tension from Lauralee's body, probably well aware that he was creating unease of entirely another sort. "Chance loves Kate," he said. "He told me so himself. Just stay out of their business, Lauralee, and they'll work everything out themselves."

"You seem awfully confident of that."

"I know Chance. He's not pining for Victoria, believe me. He was upset when she was killed—we all were—but he never loved her."

"Kate told me that Chance courted Victoria for years!"

"Courted is hardly the word I would choose to describe what Chance did. He and Victoria would never have married. They were playmates."

Lauralee didn't care to pursue that statement. "Do you think I was wrong to invite Kate to stay here?"

"No," Jay replied without hesitation. "Kate is a grown woman; she could have refused if she'd wanted to."

"Chance will come looking for her, won't he?" Good heavens, if he didn't, what was Kate going to do?

Jay's shoulder moved, beneath Lauralee's cheek, in a sturdy shrug. "With Chance, you never know. He did tell me—on the very night of my moral downfall, in fact—that if Kate ran away, he would drag her back home by the hair."

Lauralee was horrified; she stiffened and again Jay soothed her until all her taut muscles relaxed. "He'd better not try to hurt her in my presence," she said, but she was yawning.

"Chance would never hurt any woman."

Jay spoke with much conviction; honesty compelled Lauralee to contradict him. "That isn't true, Jay. He's been hurting Kate since he married her."

Before Jay could offer any reply to that statement, the sound of an arriving wagon, going at breakneck speed, jarred them both out of their sleepy state and into full alertness. Lauralee, still wearing her wrapper, scrambled to the window while Jay got hastily into a pair of trousers and a shirt wrenched from his satchel.

Jenny's father, clearly drunk, came careening up from the gate, standing up in the wagon box, lashing the two pitiful horses and shouting his daughter's name.

"My God," Lauralee whispered, alarmed. "It's Isaiah French—"

"Who the hell is Isaiah French?" Jay bit out, struggling to button his trousers.

The door burst open and Jenny was there, looking wild-eyed and sick. "Pa's here! Oh, Lauralee, Pa's here and he's been drinking! Don't let him take me away—I'm sorry for all the bad things I did—please, Lauralee, don't let him take me—"

The wagon clattered to a noisy stop outside, the horses nickering and flinging back their heads in pain and confusion. "Jenny!" The drunken bellow rose, ugly and coarse, on the still summer air. "Jenny French!"

"I won't let him take you," Lauralee promised, clasping Jenny's hands. She might have said more, except for the quick look of warning Jay gave her.

"How old are you, Jenny?" he asked.

Jenny's lower lip quivered and tears rolled out of her thickly lashed eyes. Lauralee had not, until that moment, realized what a beauty the girl was coming to be, with her deep blue eyes and her lush auburn hair. "S-Seventeen, Mr. McCallum," she answered respectfully. "Does—does Pa have say-so over me?"

Jay was already out of the bedroom, striding down the hallway, ready to confront Mr. Isaiah French. "Unfortunately," he answered, "yes. He does."

After that, Lauralee practically had to force Jenny to come down the stairs with her, to go out into the yard and face up to Isaiah, who was already looking down his bulbous, red-veined nose at Jay.

"All I want is my girl, mister," the wavering sot whined. "No trouble. Just my own dear sweetie-girl."

Jay looked back at Jenny. "Do you want to go with your father, Jenny?" he asked. It was a hollow question; though he knew the answer, it had to be presented.

Jenny huddled closer under Lauralee's arm and shook her head. "No, sir, Mr. McCallum. I don't want to go with him. I won't go with him!"

His maudlin attempt to engage sympathy having failed, Isaiah tried to look dangerous. Had Jay not been there, he might well have succeeded, but as it was, Mr. French was revealed as his true self, a swaggering buffoon, pretending to courage but possessing none. "Now, Jenny, I'm your pa—"

Jenny's chin rose and she stiffened with determina-

201

tion. "You put your hands on me when you're drinking! You got no right to put your hands on me, Pa!"

Isaiah belched. "I only touch you the way a pa will, sweetie-girl—"

"No!" Jenny blurted. "It's wrong the way you touch me. You go away, Pa. I don't want to be with you. I want to stay here with Lauralee."

Mr. French looked murderous for a moment, and his glazed eyes touched on Lauralee with hatred and some secret contempt that seemed to amuse him in spite of all his fury. "She's taken you in, missus," he muttered. "She's done taken you in, fine and dandy-like." In turn, French assessed Jay McCallum, as if to weigh him as an opponent. His own superior size and bull-like strength notwithstanding, his decision to avoid physical confrontation was an obvious one. He cleared his throat and swaggered a bit, in the way of those who are afraid but will not have it known. "I'll just go and get Marshal Townsend, then. The law's on my side. Oh, yes indeedy, he'll take my part."

With that, Isaiah French spat an ugly stream of brown juice into the grass, turned, and got back into his wagon. Sure enough, he headed toward Halpern's Ferry instead of his hardscrabble, high-in-the-hills farm.

"He'll be back," Jay said quietly and with resignation. "He's right about the law. It's squarely behind him."

"It can't be!" Lauralee cried. "It can't! You heard what Jenny said—"

"I heard," Jay broke in, his voice still low, though there was an undercurrent of fury in it. "That's considered a family matter."

"A family matter!"

"We have to do something," Kate said calmly. Until that moment, Lauralee had not been aware of her or of

Clarie, who stood beside her, Alexander balanced on one hip.

"Put him down," Lauralee said distractedly. "He's big enough to walk."

A sad grin crossed Jay's face, and his eyes shifted from Lauralee to Kate. "If you have an idea, Katie, this is the time to share it."

"Why, we'll just hide Jenny until that awful man gives up and goes away!"

Jay was skeptical. "Where? In the cellar? The barn, perhaps?"

"We'll send her to Lucy and Brice. I've been meaning to visit them anyway—I could go along. That dreadful tosspot would never know to look for Jenny there!"

"You're probably right," Jay said, but he sounded reluctant and Lauralee saw his soul rise into his eyes. He looked away, in a belated attempt to hide whatever it was that pained him. "Lucy and Brice have problems of their own right now."

"You know what Lucy would say if she were here, Jay," Kate insisted quietly. "She'd want to help."

Jay sighed and nodded, and for just a moment Lauralee was jealous of the stock he seemed to place in Lucy McCallum. "I know," he said at length. "But there are other places where Jenny could hide. With Adrienne Burch, for instance."

Almost imperceptibly, Jenny stiffened again, and Lauralee had an odd feeling that the girl was holding her breath.

Suddenly, Lauralee was red-hot, foot-stomping mad, and in the space of an instant, too. "Of all the harebrained ideas I've ever heard, Jay McCallum, that's the worst!"

Jay silenced her with one uplifted hand and a reasonably modulated, "Adrienne has a big house. She has a certain standing in the community. I don't believe Isaiah would ever think to look for Jenny there."

How do you know that Adrienne Burch has a big house? Lauralee wanted to scream, but she bit down hard on her lower lip and kept her peace, difficult as it was. A cool wind was blowing down from the mountains, but it did nothing to ease her temper. The clouds gathering overhead, clouds she should have been glad to see because the trees in the orchard needed rain so desperately, darkened not only the sky but Lauralee's spirit.

Kate frowned pensively. "Adrienne Burch. Is that the woman who was here this afternoon, bringing your satchel?"

Jay nodded, his eyes back on Lauralee, teasing her.

"Would she be willing to go along with a plan like this?" Kate went on. "After all, it is dangerous, isn't it?"

"Adrienne will do anything I ask her to," Jay said, with such confident arrogance that it was all Lauralee could do not to fling herself at him and tear him apart. "Jenny, go inside and pack what you need. You can stay at Adrienne's until we can get you on a stagecoach without your father knowing about it."

Reluctantly, Lauralee released Jenny so that the girl could go off to do as she had been bidden. The poor creature was desperate; why else would she want to take shelter in a viper's pit, even temporarily?

Kate and Clarie went inside to help Jenny pack, Alexander with them. The last shadows of twilight were falling over the yard and the pink blossoms in the orchard; within minutes, it would be dark.

"How do you know what kind of house Adrienne Burch has?" Lauralee demanded, her voice quiet. Soft.

Jay grinned, shrugged. "She told me, of course.

204

And don't make the same mistake you made the day you left me, Lauralee—I'm not Virgil."

"What's that supposed to mean?"

"It means that I'm sober and in full possession of my senses. Why would I risk losing you for a woman like that?"

Lauralee bit her lower lip. She wanted to trust Jay, she needed to, but she wasn't sure she could. "I suppose you mean to see Jenny safely to Adrienne's house as soon as it's dark?"

"Unless you'd rather do it," Jay countered, damnably compliant. "Keep in mind, though, that you might meet old Isaiah along the road."

Just the prospect of that made Lauralee shiver. She had plenty of things she'd like to say to Isaiah French, to be sure, but what good was reason against a madman?

Of course, she could go along with Jay and Jenny, but Lauralee found that idea almost as unappealing as the thought of encountering Mr. French along a dark road. She did, after all, have some pride, and if she tagged along, Adrienne would know exactly why she was there—to make sure that the second husband didn't go the way of the first.

"You go," she finally conceded. "But don't you stay late, Jay McCallum."

He laughed as he approached her, pulled her close to the hard, heated strength of him. The cool breeze billowed around them, carrying the sounds and scents of approaching night. "I'll be home early. Oil the bedsprings, Mrs. McCallum," he teased, his lips on her forehead. "I've got plans for you."

Lauralee trembled. How could she love this man so much, need him so much, when he did and said such outlandish things? Drat it all, he was going off to Adrienne Burch's house, where all manner of irresistible perils probably awaited him, and here she was wondering just where she'd last seen that oil Virgil had used for creaking door hinges.

The marshal came after supper, accompanied by Isaiah French. Lauralee had a hard time meeting Pete Townsend's honest gaze, and not just because she was going to have to lie to him about Jenny, either.

Kate and Clarie were in the parlor, one playing the melodeon, both singing. It was a sweet, homey sound; it made Lauralee think distractedly of how she would miss this place when she left it, for leave it she would. She'd managed to come to terms with that much, at least.

"Mr. French here says you won't give him his daughter, Lauralee," Pete said, hanging up his hat and, at his hostess's gestured invitation, taking a seat at the table. "You can't keep a man's daughter from him, you know."

Lauralee had brushed her hair and pinned it up. She wore one of the dresses that Kate had bought for her and altered just since Mr. French's last visit and over this was a lacy white apron. She poured coffee for the two men and then sliced pie for them, dried apple made from her special Christmas recipe. "I'm afraid Jenny just isn't under this roof anywhere," she said pleasantly. That wasn't a lie, now was it?

"She was right here today!" protested Isaiah French through a mouthful of pie, thumping at the clean tablecloth with one grubby forefinger. "This evenin', in fact!"

"She isn't here now," said Lauralee, her smile unwavering.

Pete's gaze was level, and something in it jarred Lauralee. He knew she was hiding Jenny French, maybe he even knew where, and yet, for reasons of his own, he was pretending to carry out a search for her.

"Drat that girl," muttered Mr. French, chewing industriously on his pie and making a noxious slurping sound as he attacked his coffee. "I just want her to help her ma, that's all I want. Susannah ain't well, you know."

Susannah. What a lovely name for a woman saddled to such an odious man. Lauralee had been introduced to Jenny's mother once, at a church picnic, but she barely remembered her. She did recall a sense of hopelessness and defeat, however, and a meek manner.

"Could be that Jenny's run off," Pete put in, his eyes fixed on Lauralee's, warning her. "Might have got herself a beau or something."

"Better not be that murderin' Joe Little Eagle," French grumbled. "I don't want no war-whoop in my family, no sir."

Lauralee simmered, though her smile remained fixedly in place. This was a man who let pigs and chickens wander in and out of his cabin at will, according to Jenny, a man who didn't bathe for months at a time, a man who would "put his hands on" his own daughter. And he looked down on Joe Little Eagle?

"Now, Isaiah," Pete began quickly, to keep the peace. "Joe was acquitted of killing that other Indian. We all know that."

"I ain't talkin' about his doin' in Charlie Red Pony. I'm talkin' about Mr. Tim McCallum." Rheumy eyes moved, smarmy and speculative, over Lauralee, but she hid her revulsion. "Maybe I'm even talkin' about Virgil Parker. Some folks say that gambler didn't do that murder, you know."

"Why on earth would you accuse Joe?" Lauralee asked. She was still smiling, but she was shaken inside and a little sick at the reminder. "He didn't have anything against Virgil or Mr. McCallum."

207

"McCallum was killed with a tommy-hawk, weren't he? And Virgil was knifed. Everybody knows them Injuns like to whittle on a white man."

Pete flashed Lauralee another warning look. "We're not doing much good here, Isaiah," he said with a sigh, his pie and coffee hardly touched. "It's pretty dark for you to try driving up that mountain road. Why don't you spend the night at my office?"

Isaiah wasn't offended at the invitation to sleep in a jail cell; in a town the size of Halpern's Ferry, the bed just went to waste most of the time anyway. Pete Townsend often allowed a drifter or a man far from home to sleep there. "Reckon I might do that. No good to Susannah if I'm lying at the bottom of the ridge, now, am I?"

Lauralee could hardly restrain herself from unkind comment.

In the parlor, Clarie and Kate sang boisterously. *"Oh, Susannah, oh don't you cry for me . . ."*

Lauralee and Pete looked at each other and laughed in silence. When Isaiah pushed his plate away and went outside, Pete lingered a moment, looking hesitant and embarrassed.

"Adrienne Burch has told half the county that you and Jay McCallum are married. Is it true, Lauralee?"

Lauralee wanted to cry because the price of her happiness was hurting Pete, and Pete didn't deserve hurting. "Yes, it's true."

The marshal took his hat from the peg beside the door, turned it by the brim. "You know I wish you the best, Mrs. McCallum. And I was right sorry to hear about the little boy. I hope he's better now."

Moments before, she had been Lauralee. Now she was Mrs. McCallum—it was Pete's way of letting go gracefully, of saying that he didn't want to make the situation any more awkward than it already was. "Alexander will be fine," she said. "I thank you for your good wishes, Pete. And for everything you've done."

He hesitated, red to his ears. "There's something else I wanted to tell you, Mrs. McCallum. I got a wire today from the marshal down in the Dalles—that's in Oregon—he says he might have that gambler that killed Virgil. I'm going down there tomorrow to have a look; if it's the same man, I'll fetch him back here to be tried."

Lauralee felt a chill slither up and down her spine. She wanted Virgil's killer brought to justice, of course. So why did she feel so uneasy at what should have been good news? "There weren't any witnesses, were there?"

Pete looked at her sharply for a moment, as though seeing her for the first time, but then he recovered himself. "Nobody actually saw the murder, as far as we know, but I'd sure like to hear what that gambling man has to say for himself. If he didn't do the killing, he might have seen who did."

"Wouldn't he have told you that?"

Again, Pete was watching Lauralee with that closeness that made her uneasy. "The gambler? I reckon he was too scared, if he did see something. He was a stranger here, and folks are always more inclined to suspect a stranger. Besides, we'd all heard him bickering with Virgil inside the Mud Bucket."

Lauralee clasped the back of a chair, her knuckles turning white with the force of her grip. Pete noticed and she relaxed her hands in shame, as though she'd done something terribly wrong. Her stomach did a painful flip and then roiled as she met Pete's eyes and realized what he was thinking. "Pete Townsend," she breathed, "you can't possibly believe that I would murder my own husband?"

Pete made no comment, no comment at all. He

simply put on his hat, gave Lauralee one despairing look, and went out into the night. Moments later, Lauralee heard a wagon leaving.

She sank into a chair, feeling faint, dropping her head to her knees until the lightness in her brain passed away.

Lauralee was already in bed when Jay got home, and she didn't ask about his visit to Adrienne's house. She didn't ask about Jenny or whether or not he'd met Pete Townsend and Mr. French along the road from town.

Jay undressed in the darkness, gave a pleased chuckle when he knelt on the bed and it didn't squeak—at least, not much—under his weight. "You're not asleep," he said, "so stop trying to pretend you are."

Lauralee turned to him; she hadn't been trying to pretend anything. "Jay," she began softly, "Pete Townsend was here tonight."

He got under the covers, stretched out beside her. "We expected that, didn't we?"

"He said they might have found that gambler who was supposed to have killed Virgil outside the Mud Bucket. Pete's going down to Oregon to see if it's the same man."

Jay slid one arm under her, pulled her close, his hand gently kneading the flesh on her bottom. "I wish they'd find whoever killed Tim," he said.

Suddenly, Lauralee burst into tears. She couldn't restrain herself. "Pete actually implied that I might have murdered Virgil myself!" she wailed.

Jay held her very close. "Shhh. That's crazy. Townsend's no ball of fire, but he's smarter than that."

"I asked him outright," sniffled Lauralee, "if that was what he thought, that I'd been the one to kill Virgil, I mean. And he didn't deny it, Jay!"

"As Clarie put it, Pete Townsend is sweet on you. Word is all over that we're married. Don't you think it's possible that he was just striking back at you for choosing me instead of him?"

"Pete Townsend hasn't a vindictive bone in his body! He truly thinks—"

Jay silenced her with a kiss. The kiss deepened, and after a time, he eased Lauralee's nightgown upward with gentle, unerring hands. Long, delicious minutes later, Lauralee was soaring, her cries of fierce release muted by her husband's mouth as he moved upon her.

CHAPTER THIRTEEN

Lauralee was dreaming again. Perhaps it was the rain that brought it on, for a part of her mind was wide awake and knew that a summer storm was pounding at the windows and the roof, that Jay was sleeping beside her, that the young trees in the orchard needed what the skies poured down upon them.

But in the dream she was alone, not outside as before, but still in bed. And yet she could see the gray movements of the storm, lifting the cellar doors, rattling them. They opened and a man rose out of the dank place below.

Lauralee was frightened but, as dreamers so often are, powerless to move or even cry out. Caught between two separate realities, she watched in growing horror as the specter-man laid aside the cellar doors, stepped out, came around the house to the door. He opened it easily. He was crossing the kitchen, soundlessly climbing the stairs, moving along the hallway.

He was covered in blood. It stained his clothes,

colored his hands and face, dried in his hair. And he was coming closer.

Lauralee was paralyzed with fear, her throat dry and shut tight, so that she couldn't cry out. He reached the door, came through it, stood at the foot of the bed.

Lauralee could not see his face, but she knew that this was not Virgil. She tried to awaken herself, end the nightmare, but the surface of consciousness seemed so far away. So hopelessly far away.

"Oh no," she managed to croak, "no!" Or was she screaming?

The hideous nightmare figure left the foot of the bed to stand beside Lauralee, over her. The visitor was Tim McCallum and he was staring sightlessly down into her face. One of his stained hands rose, slowly, so slowly, dripping blood—he meant to touch her!

Lauralee screamed at last, twisting to avoid the cold hand of a dead man, frantic in her fear.

"Lauralee!" Hands were gripping her shoulders, holding her still. Vital hands, strong with life. Jay's hands. "Lauralee!"

She gave a gasping sob of relief, opened her eyes, and, in the same moment, flung her arms around Jay's neck.

"Just a dream—" he was saying, only some of his words reaching her, "—all right—over—"

Lauralee wept into his warm, sturdy neck, clinging, sure that if she let go, she would be back in the depths of her nightmare, caught there, powerless and afraid. "It was awful—he came out of the cellar—he was covered in blood—"

"Shhh."

Lauralee gave a great shudder even as the warmth of Jay's body began seeping into her own cold one. "Why are they haunting me? First Virgil, now Tim— why?"

Jay sat up rather suddenly, struck a match, and lit the lamp on the bedside table. "Virgil? Tim? Lauralee, what are you talking about?"

The light, dim and flickering as it was, was comforting. The wan, wary look on Jay's face was not.

How could she tell him about the nightmares? If she did, Jay would think that she had indeed killed Virgil, and perhaps Tim, too. He would think that her conscience was punishing her for the crimes.

"Lauralee?"

"I'm tired," she lied. "I want to go back to sleep." In truth, Lauralee was afraid to close her eyes; she knew that she would still be staring at the ceiling when the sun came up.

"Tell me what you meant about Virgil and Tim, about them haunting you." Jay spoke quietly, evenly. And he was keeping his distance, no longer touching Lauralee, no longer offering comfort.

She was afraid. "It's nothing, Jay—"

"I don't believe you," he responded flatly. He struck another match, lit a cheroot, and the acrid smells of sulfur and smoke, so comforting before, called to mind all that Lauralee had ever been taught about hellfire. The match made an ominous clinking sound as it fell into the dish Jay had appropriated earlier to serve as an ashtray.

Lauralee put one hand to her throat, not only afraid, but injured, too. How could Jay be so cold and hard now when he had held her, comforted her, only moments before? When he had made love to her earlier, with a sort of ferocious tenderness? "Do you love me, Jay McCallum?" she asked, and then she slapped her hand over her mouth, unable to believe she had asked such a question.

"Don't, Lauralee," he said. "Don't try to confuse the issue."

Confuse the issue? Lauralee trembled. Jay had removed her nightgown earlier, and now she bent and tried to recover it from the floor. Her fingers touched the fabric, then she was wrenched back, forced to lie flat, Jay's face suspended above hers.

"Tell me about your dream, Mrs. McCallum," he said.

That form of address had been an endearment since their hasty marriage; now it sounded contemptuous and vaguely threatening. Lauralee didn't know which was more horrifying: the prospect of telling Jay about the dreams she'd had or the knowledge that for all his following her here, for all his getting Alexander the care he'd needed, for all his plans to take her to Washington, he didn't love her.

She was too proud to cry, though she wanted to. Lord in heaven, she wanted to weep and weep and then weep some more. "Let go of me," she said.

The release was a thrusting motion, as though he did not want her near him. Jay took his still smoldering cheroot from the dish and began to smoke again, staring up at the ceiling. Waiting.

Lauralee reached for her nightgown once more, caught hold of it, pulled it on as much for a barrier between herself and this stranger as for modesty and warmth. "I had a dream—a nightmare, really—about your brother Tim. A few days ago I had a similar one about Virgil. Are you satisfied?"

There was a softening in Jay that Lauralee sensed even though she could see no outward evidence of it. Or was she only hoping, wishing?

"What happened in these dreams?"

Lauralee told him, her hands knotting a piece of the quilt and then smoothing it out again. She told about the storm, the cellar doors opening, the bloody versions of Virgil and Jay that had pursued her, one

215

through the windswept yard, the other all the way to this bed.

When the gruesome stories were over, Jay snubbed out the cheroot he'd lit after finishing the first one and clasped Lauralee's chin in his hand, his eyes searching hers, reaching into her depths.

"Did you kill Virgil, Lauralee?"

"No," she said hoarsely, honestly, and without hesitation.

"And my brother?"

"I didn't get along with Tim," she managed to answer. "I didn't want him selling spirits. We argued on more than one occasion, including the day he died. But I didn't murder him, Jay McCallum, and you know it."

He did know; she saw it in his face. He let out a long sigh, released Lauralee, and slumped back against the headboard, his eyes averted. "Why the cellar?" he mused, piecing together the fragments of her dreams. "Why the storm? Was it raining that night, Lauralee?"

"Which night?"

Jay sighed again. "It rained the day after Tim died, I remember that, but not on the night it happened. And Virgil was killed in the wintertime, wasn't he?"

Lauralee nodded, swallowed hard. "It was very cold, but there was no snow on the ground."

"And no rain."

"No. At least I don't think there was. And I don't know what the cellar has to do with anything either."

"I guess we can't expect to make sense of a nightmare." He made no move to draw her close; even after—or maybe especially after—the things he'd said, the way he'd acted, Lauralee wanted Jay to hold her. "I'm sorry," he added, blowing out the lamp, keeping to his side of the bed. "Most of the time I think I can let what happened to Tim remain in the past, where it belongs. But sometimes—"

Lauralee wondered if she dared touch him, lay her hand on his chest, perhaps, or his arm. In the end, she huddled down in the cold blankets, shivering, listening to the sound of Jay's breathing and the rage of the storm.

Jay was awake, she knew that. She was awake. But they were of no comfort to each other, because the ghosts of two dead men stood between them. Because Jay did not love her.

"I love you," she said, driven to say the words rather than daring to say them.

Jay didn't answer.

The mood in the house the next morning was glum, dismal. The rainstorm had subsided, but only temporarily, judging by the dark sky.

Clarie and Kate had gathered the eggs, Joe Little Eagle had milked and tended to the cows, Lauralee had given Alexander a bath and dressed him in overalls and a shirt and gotten out the potty-chair she'd bought once, when she was feeling optimistic. Alexander refused to go near it.

Lauralee washed her hands and set about cranking the separating machine. Milk flowed out one pipe, cream out the other. Most of the cream went in to the huge crockery churn, to be made into butter.

"If you add salt to that, it will set up faster," Jay remarked. He'd been sitting by the window since coming back from helping Joe with the cows, and until now, he hadn't said a single word to Lauralee.

Lauralee felt as testy and uneasy as everyone else, and she was tired of always being the strong one, putting a bright face on everything. "That's the lazy way," she said tightly. "Besides, it's bad for the butter."

Jay shrugged, gazed out the window again. "Are you going to Washington with me, Lauralee? I have to know."

So now it was "Are you going with me?" Only the day before, it had been, "I can't go without you." "Aren't you afraid I'll murder you in your bed?" she asked sweetly, the violence she felt going into her churning rather than her voice. "I'm another Lizzie Borden, you know."

Jay's chair scraped against the linoleum as he stood up. "Damnit, don't ever say a thing like that again!"

Lauralee went right on churning. She was going to leave this farm, perhaps forever, in just a few days—if Jay still wanted her. And yet here she was churning butter and making plans to go out and inspect the apple trees. She wondered why she couldn't let those things go.

Jay went out into the drizzling pall of the day, slamming the door behind him, making Lauralee flinch and then churn even harder. She let go of the thick wooden handle, near tears, and moved to the window to look out.

Jay was opening the cellar doors.

For some reason, Lauralee's heart clamored into her throat. She raced outside, full of the same sick fear that had been a part of her nightmare, and hovered at the top of the cellar steps. The wind was blowing and there was a fine, chilly mist in the air, settling on her skin, making her shiver.

"Jay?"

The dank darkness of the cellar was illuminated, at least a little, by the flare of one match. "Don't you use this place?" Jay called back.

Lauralee wanted to go down there and keep him

safe, but from what? She couldn't move, not to go into the house, not to descend the cellar steps. She clasped her arms around herself. "We store potatoes and pumpkins and onions there through the winter," she answered. Why was she so frightened? How could she speak in her normal voice when she was so very scared?

She had to break her inertia somehow. Standing there at the mouth of that cellar was like standing at the edge of hell. Lauralee clasped one hand to her mouth, used the force of her will to turn away, and ran into the house, snatching her woolen cloak from the peg inside the door.

She ventured as far as the parlor doorway and peered into that room, where a cheery fire snapped in the small potbellied stove and lamps burned. Clarie and Kate were playing checkers, laughing because Alexander kept stealing both the red and black game pieces from the board.

"I'm off to look at the trees," Lauralee said, hoping that either Kate or Clarie would volunteer to go along. Asking Jay to go did not even occur to her.

It was as though she hadn't spoken, as though they couldn't see or hear her. Lauralee had a creepy feeling, as if she were a person in a dream, invisible to the people around her. She turned away as Clarie grasped Alexander's plump little arm and began prying a checker piece out of his fingers.

"Sander play, too!" he wailed, furious.

"Sander play, too," Kate said gently.

Lauralee crossed the kitcken, raised the hood of her cloak, and stepped out the back door, nearly falling because she had forgotten about the high threshold. How could she have forgotten that? She was going to have to put a step there—even a wooden box would do—before someone was hurt.

And what point would there be in that if she was going to Washington with Jay? For that matter, did she want to go across country, leave everything familiar behind, for a man who didn't love her?

She reached the first orchard, where the trees were bigger, old enough to bear fruit. They shifted uneasily in the light wind, it seemed to Lauralee, like fitful children teetering upon the left foot and then the right.

Lauralee smiled—my, but she was becoming fanciful, wasn't she, ascribing human attributes to rooted things—and went on to look over the younger, more vulnerable trees. Some of them had been broken in the wind the night before; they lay, leaves battered, on the muddy ground.

Despairing, Lauralee cleared away the branches of those that had not survived the storm, trying to comfort herself with the farmer's knowledge that nature always extracts a price for her gifts of rain and sunshine. There were still almost a hundred trees; in another year or two, they would bear fruit.

The wind was cold, blowing harder than before. Lauralee looked up at the iron-gray sky, and a feeling of hopeless foreboding came over her.

Jay didn't know what he'd hoped to find in that damnable cellar besides spiders and the occasional rotten potato. He was dusting his hands off on the sides of his trousers when he came out, looked up at the brooding sky, and felt a shiver that ran soul deep. It was the same feeling, exactly, that had possessed him just before he'd stepped into that shabby room in the Mud Bucket Saloon, an eon ago, and found his brother dead.

He hurried into the house and the kitchen seemed cold, the abandoned churn forlorn. He strode on to the parlor, wondering at the urgency that drove him there.

Kate, Alexander, and Clarie were playing checkers, after a fashion, their faces happy in the cozy, inside-and-warm-on-a-stormy-day atmosphere.

"Where's Lauralee?"

Kate looked up, Alexander squirming on her lap, her eyes puzzled.

The hailstorm broke at that moment; stones the size of chicken eggs hammered at the roof and the sills of the windows.

Kate's face changed in an instant. "The trees!" she cried. "Jay, she's out there, in the open—"

Jay was already turning away, running through the house, flinging open the door, leaving it to clatter on its hinges behind him. The hailstones pummeled him, stinging his shoulders and his back, pounding his head. The ground passing beneath his feet was covered with them, dented by them, and instead of relenting, they came down harder.

He raced toward the orchards, oblivious to the pain, slid down the embankment beside the creek, splashed through the water, which seemed to chatter under the assault of the hail.

Lauralee stood in the open, watching the white stones flung from heaven batter her cherished trees to the ground. Jay lunged at her and grasped her by one arm. She gave a startled cry, her eyes wide and surprised, as he half dragged and half threw her into the nearby stand of Douglas fir and pine trees. He flung her against the trunk of a giant pine and sheltered her with his body, gasping for breath. The hail beat at the ground now, as if enraged that it could not reach them.

"Are you all right?" Jay managed to ask after several moments.

Lauralee was trembling. "They're dead now. All my trees are dead," she said.

Jay wanted to weep. He dared not hold Lauralee

close; she was small and fragile, and the hailstones had probably bruised her. "No," he said. "The bigger ones are all right."

"Those were Virgil's," she said in a faraway voice. "Mine are dead."

Jay let his forehead fall against hers, stood that way until he heard the hail stop. Then he lifted Lauralee into his arms and carried her back toward the house. Huge balls of white ice lay everywhere, and there was a peculiar silence about the world, as though it had just been punished and was now reflecting upon its sin.

Kate was waiting fitfully in the kitchen, her eyes wide and frightened. Clarie made a clatter at the stove, though she was obviously just as scared as anybody. Only Alexander seemed calm; he was perched on a chair in front of a window, probably eager to go outside and touch those strange balls that had fallen from the sky.

"My trees are gone," Lauralee said, and then she buried her face in Jay's neck and fell into a despondent silence.

Jay took her into Kate's room, knowing somehow that she did not want to go to their own. Together, he and Kate removed her cloak, her dress, her stockings and shoes.

There were red welts all over Lauralee where the hailstones had struck her, but she did not seem to be in pain. She allowed them to put her into one of Kate's nightgowns, a warm flannel thing, and tuck her in like a docile child.

"Lauralee will be all right, Jay," Kate said firmly, softly, from the other side of the narrow bed. "She's the strongest person I've ever known, and she'll be all right."

"She looks like a broken doll," observed Clarie from the doorway.

Alexander was clutching at the bedding, trying to reach his mother. "Sander up," he complained, glaring up at Jay. "Sander up!"

"Sander out," Jay countered, taking the little boy into his arms. Lauralee's eyes were closed, the lashes wet with tears. He bent, kissed her forehead, and left the room.

Kate followed. Clarie was already on her way back to the kitchen.

"That was an odd thing to say," Jay mused, still holding Alexander.

"What?" Kate asked, going to stand near the small stove, extending trembling hands to its warmth.

"What Clarie said, about Lauralee looking like a broken doll."

Kate shrugged. She seemed tired and sad, and Jay wished that Chance would come and get her. If he was half a man, he would. "Clarie is really just a child."

Jay wondered. But he had Lauralee to think about, and Alexander, and the welts hidden beneath his shirt and his trousers stung like hell. He put Clarie's remark out of his mind and took his stepson outside, into a wonderland of melting white balls.

Alexander was overjoyed, grasping the hailstones in his plump little hands, flinging them, crowing as though he'd invented them. Within minutes, however, he was exhausted.

Jay carried the child into the house, divested him of his overalls, and placed him firmly on the potty-chair that sat, challenging, within the warm radius of the parlor stove.

"Sander up," the child fretted, trying to rise, lower lip protruding.

Jay pressed on the top of the gossamer-tufted head. "Sander down," he replied.

And though the little boy couldn't hear him, it was

soon clear that he'd gotten the message. He would rebel against it for a time, no doubt, but he knew what was expected of him and that was a triumph, however minor.

Lauralee awakened to a tremendous clatter in the yard. Were the hailstones falling again?

She closed her eyes. Who cared? Her trees were gone. What damage could any storm do now?

"Kate!" a masculine voice bellowed.

Lauralee sat up in the bed, tossed back the covers, padded to the small window, which was only a few steps away. Every inch of her was covered with stinging bruises, and it hurt to move.

Chance McCallum was there in the yard, mounted on a dancing sorrel stallion and looking for all the world like a storybook knight come to claim his lady.

Despite all that had happened, despite the burning pain that covered her body, despite her ruined trees, Lauralee smiled. She hoped Kate would not make things too easy for Chance.

She saw Jay cross the yard and greet his brother. Chance flushed and said something inaudible as he dismounted, then Jay held the horse's bridle, threw back his head, and laughed.

Lauralee was reminded of the hailstorm. Jay had come through it to find her, to take her to safety, to shield her. Tears sparkled in her eyes as she hurried to get out of the nightgown and into her clothes. She winced as they touched her welted skin.

By the time Lauralee reached the kitchen, the men were coming through the door, having already taken Chance's horse into the barn and settled it there. Kate was cowering in a corner, her eyes wide.

Chance glared at her, but there was an expression of overwhelming relief in his dark eyes, too. Jay took

Lauralee's arm, cleared his throat, and ushered her away into the parlor.

"Were—were you caught in the storm?" Lauralee heard Kate ask in a timorous voice.

"I took a hell of a beating, thank you very much. And so did my horse!"

Both Lauralee and Jay bit down on their lower lips, to keep from laughing. "Let's go for a walk," Jay said as the drama in the kitchen began to grow in intensity.

"What about Clarie and Alexander?" Lauralee asked as her husband took her arm again and urged her toward the seldom used front door.

"Clarie is off wandering somewhere, and Alexander is asleep. We won't be gone long."

They went out, arm in arm. Hailstones lay everywhere, shriveling in the green grass, littering the road. But the sky was clearing and the breeze was warm.

Lauralee and Jay went through the gate, it was still latched when they reached it, and they laughed, sharing the same thought.

"Chance must have urged his sturdy and valiant steed to jump over," Jay said, opening the gate and then relatching it after they had passed through. "I can't picture him bothering to open a paltry gate in the state he was in. Or close it, either."

They crossed the road and stood looking at what would have been the Rumsucker Saloon. The sign swung in the breeze, triumphant, unmarked by the storm.

"I'm at peace about going to Washington, Jay," Lauralee said softly, all the love she felt showing in her eyes. "If you still want me, that is."

"If I still want you? Lady, if you hadn't just been caught in a hailstorm and stoned half to death, I'd pick you up and swing you around!" Jay's face was alight with tenderness, with joy. She waited for him to say he loved her, but he didn't. "I want that sign," he said instead, turning to assess the gilt-trimmed board dangling from the unshingled overhang of the roof.

"What for?" Lauralee asked. It was a long way up to that porch roof to reach the sign, and there wasn't a ladder handy as far as she could tell.

"I want to hang it in our house in Washington," Jay answered. "How many senators have a sign that says Rumsucker Saloon?"

Lauralee had to stay herself from grasping at his sleeve in an attempt to hold him back. She was afraid again, and her misgivings had nothing to do with her belief in the cause of temperance. "We'll send Joe over to get it," she offered lamely.

Jay was already leaving her, walking toward the building. "I'll get it myself," he called back, and then he was climbing agilely up the framework at one side of the structure.

"Be careful." Lauralee closed her eyes, forced herself to open them again.

Jay was moving out onto the storm-slickened, bare-lumber slant of that roof. His being there made the building seem so much higher than before.

Lauralee held her breath as he grinned at her like a cocky little boy and started down over the roof to get the sign.

The accident seemed to happen in sleepy, nightmare stages; in truth, it was over in seconds. Jay lost his footing and tumbled down the steep slant of the roof and over the side.

Lauralee screamed—for a terrible moment she was held inert by her fear—and then broke free of it to bolt forward, stumbled to the place where Jay lay, so still, on the wet, hard-trodden ground.

"Jay!"

He didn't move, didn't open his eyes. There was a cut on his head, bleeding, and his right leg lay at an angle that wrenched at Lauralee's stomach like a fist.

She whirled and ran across the road, screaming for Chance, for Kate, for Joe Little Eagle.

They all came at a run, Chance and Kate from the house, Joe Little Eagle from the barn. Even so, none of them ran as fast as Lauralee. In seconds, she was kneeling beside Jay on the ground, her hands clasping the sides of his head. "He fell. He fell."

"My God," Chance breathed, crouching beside his brother, laying three fingers to the pulsepoint at the base of Jay's neck.

Kate drew Lauralee gently to her feet. "Is—is he dead?"

Chance shook his head. "No, thank God. But there's no telling how badly he's hurt." He exchanged a look with Joe Little Eagle, who said nothing.

Memories of another tragedy welled up in Lauralee's mind, and she dashed at the useless tears gathering in her eyes. "A door," she said. "Joe, we need a door or something, to carry him—"

Joe went inside the unfinished Rumsucker Saloon and found what Lauralee wanted.

Carefully, he and Chance maneuvered Jay onto the hard flat surface. Jay was unconscious, but he kept muttering. Lauralee despaired because she knew that the pain was reaching him.

Chance spoke gently, reasonably, to his brother. "Everything is going to be all right, Jay. You have my word. Everything is going to be all right."

Lauralee took Jay's inert hand, stumbling alongside as the men carried him across the road, while Kate ran ahead to unlatch the gate and swing it wide.

They moved slowly toward the house, and Clarie, back from her wanderings, came out to watch their progress, holding a sleep-flushed Alexander on one hip. "Just like before," she said in an odd tone of voice. "Just like the night Papa died, except there isn't any blood."

Lauralee was in shock, but she released Jay's hand at Clarie's words and turned to face her squarely. Drawing back her own hand, she slapped Virgil's daughter as hard as she could.

Clarie's eyes widened and Alexander wailed as though he'd been slapped himself, squirming until his half-sister was forced to set him down. Her face chalk-white beneath its smattering of freckles, Clarie spat out, "Adrienne Burch wasn't the only one. Papa had lots of women!"

Trembling, Lauralee ignored Clarie's outburst and turned to follow the others into the house, pulling Alexander along by one hand. Jay was important now. Only Jay.

CHAPTER
FOURTEEN

People were moving all around Lauralee, part of a hazy fog; she heard their voices but was conscious only of Jay. He groaned as Chance and Joe Little Eagle gently transferred him from the old door onto the kitchen table.

"Is there a doctor in this godforsaken place?" Chance demanded, his voice at once taut and quiet.

"I'll find him," Joe answered, and then he was gone. Lauralee felt his absence in the small, tight circle of people.

"How did this happen, Lauralee?"

For the first time, Lauralee was able to look away from Jay. She met Chance's bold brown eyes and saw that they were bleak; his helplessness in the face of his brother's pain obviously went against the grain. "He—he wanted the sign. The one that says R-Rum-sucker Saloon. He climbed up to get it and—and then"—Lauralee squeezed her eyes shut tight—"he fell."

"I think his leg is broken," Kate put in. She had taken charge of Alexander without being asked and was holding him in her arms.

Chance flung an ironic look at his wife, but then his countenance softened. "If that's the worst, he'll be lucky." The brown eyes dropped, incredibly gentle, to Jay's waxen face. "Jay? Can you hear me?"

Jay stirred and made a low, moaning sound, but there was no reason to believe he was responding to his brother's question.

"The doctor is on his way," Chance persisted quietly, and Lauralee had a new understanding of him. There was more to Chance McCallum than the affable scoundrel, far more.

A short, miserable silence fell. Then, at a nod from Chance, Kate took Alexander into the parlor and remained there with him. The squeak of the rocking chair mingled with the ragged sound of Jay's breathing.

He was beginning to writhe on the table—the table where Virgil had lain. And died. Lauralee wrenched her thoughts back to the here and now.

"He's coming around," Chance said quickly. "The pain is going to be bad. Lauralee, do you have any whiskey?"

Lauralee's heart was doing a trapeze act in the back of her throat. Did she, the queen of temperance, have whiskey? God in heaven, how she wished she did! "No," she managed to say, her eyes filling with tears.

"Laudanum, then?" persisted Chance. "Lauralee, stop crying and think!"

There was no laudanum, she could be sure of that, but other images were suddenly rising in her mind: Virgil coming out of the toolshed, the barn, the cellar, his eyes red-rimmed, his smile slightly silly, his breath smelling of liquor.

Were there still bottles of whiskey or rum hidden about the place, bottles that Virgil had never gotten back to because someone had killed him? "I'll find

230

something," Lauralee said, snatching a lighted kerosene lamp from the sideboard.

Jay had begun to thrash on the table; she hesitated in the doorway and looked back to see Chance grasp his brother's shoulders and settle him gently.

"Easy," she heard Chance say as she went out. "Just take it easy."

Outside, Lauralee paused, trying to think coherently. There was no point in searching the toolshed or the barn; Joe Little Eagle would have found any liquor hidden in those places and either consumed it himself or handed it over to Lauralee for ceremonial disposal.

Lauralee's nightmares were the farthest thing from her mind as she set the lamp down on the ground and pulled open the cellar doors. They were stubborn, due to their rusted hinges.

She caught the lamp just as it would have toppled over into the grass, and started down the steps, the light spilling before her. The cellar was dark and drafty. Lauralee shivered a little as she stood in the center of the small, cavernlike room, trying to think with Virgil's sodden mind.

There were metal bins, very dusty now, meant to hold potatoes and apples, pumpkins and acorn squash. She looked into their depths and saw nothing, tried to move them to search behind, but they resisted.

The few shelves holding dusty jars of cinnamon pears, cling peaches, and sweet peas could afford no hiding place for a bottle. They simply weren't deep enough. That left only the ancient, chipped crock of water glass, where Lauralee had once stored surplus eggs, before coming to the conclusion that it was more practical to sell those she didn't need to Mr. Wallerman for his store.

She lifted the lid of the crock. It still brimmed with water glass; normally a clear, thick liquid, the stuff was now murky, like swamp water, a layer of dust gathered on top. Lauralee couldn't tip the thing over to see what came out with the water glass, the mess would be dreadful. The crock itself was too heavy for her to lift and carry upstairs, where she might scoop out the gummy liquid inside and dispose of it properly.

Lauralee reminded herself that Jay was hurt, that he was or would be in terrible pain. She set the lamp down on the floor, drew a deep breath, rolled up the right sleeve of her dress, and, with a grimace, reached into the slimy mess.

She felt the shape of a forgotten egg and shuddered to think what condition it would be in after all this time. She found and passed over what might have been a stick. And then her search was rewarded. Her fingers closed around the rounded side of a bottle. She drew her find up and out; it was a pint container of some amber liquor, half full.

Hastily, Lauralee wiped away what she could of the old water glass, shamelessly using her skirt for the purpose, took up her lamp again, and hurried out of the cellar. Through the windswept yard. Into the kitchen, to Jay.

Chance grasped the slimy bottle from her outstretched hand, pulled the cork, sniffed at the contents.

Lauralee was standing beside the table, one of her hands smoothing Jay's bloodied hair back from his forehead. He was awake, the Lord be praised, but his eyes were glazed with pain and his skin was parchment-pale.

"That is liquor, isn't it?" she asked anxiously, her eyes rising to meet Chance's.

He allowed himself a slow, tired grin. "Yes. Where did you find it, in a bucket of cow spit?"

Jay laughed hoarsely at this, the sound underlaid with a moan. Lauralee couldn't understand why he thought such a crudity was amusing. "It was in the cellar, in a crock of water glass," she said tightly. "I would hardly keep buckets of cow saliva about, now would I?"

Both brothers laughed then; if Lauralee hadn't been so frightened for Jay, she would have been furious. She stomped over to a cupboard, took down a jelly glass, and brought it back to the table.

"Fill this," she said to Chance, holding the small glass out.

Chance poured out several ounces of golden ruination, his eyes dancing as he watched Lauralee slide one arm under Jay's shoulders and try to lift him high enough to drink.

"This is ironic, isn't it?" Jay said with some difficulty after he'd consumed the first dose. "She of the hatchets and hymnals pouring firewater down her husband's throat."

"Do you want more?" Lauralee asked evenly.

"Oh yes," Jay replied.

This time, Chance filled the glass nearly to its brim. Lauralee's hand trembled as she held it to Jay's mouth, his brother's much stronger arm supporting him now.

They gave Jay whiskey until the slippery bottle was empty. By that time, the patient was blatantly drunk, but Lauralee didn't care. His pain was greatly reduced, and he was able to bear having Chance cut away his right trouser leg and examine the broken limb beneath.

Chance whistled through his teeth and took the Lord's name in vain.

A bone was visible, jabbing through Jay's flesh. Lauralee swayed and grasped the table to keep from falling. Bile rushed into her throat, and she had to let go of the table edge to clasp a hand over her mouth. She ran outside, past her hail-beaten garden, past the privy veiled in lilacs, and vomited into the hazelnut bushes. When the spate of sickness was over, Lauralee went all the way to the creek to rinse the vile taste from her mouth and splash cold water on her face.

Doc Jameson's buggy was just coming to a stop in the dooryard when she reached the house. She ran to greet him.

"What's this about your brand-new bridegroom falling off a saloon roof?" the doctor demanded with a mock sternness that was meant to comfort. Somehow, it did. Maladies as deadly as measles might have been beyond this country doctor's simple powers, but broken bones were not. The farmers and lumberjacks and millworkers around Halpern's Ferry had given him plenty of practice at setting them.

Lauralee linked her arm through the doctor's and all but dragged him into the house. He saw Jay lying prone on the kitchen table, saw the bone protruding, white and gruesome, below his knee. "Sweet Lord," he said, elbowing Lauralee and Chance aside to get a closer look. "I can fix it, but it's going to hurt like Holy B. Hell."

"He's had whiskey," Lauralee put in, hoping to be helpful.

Doc Jameson gave her an indulgent look, set down his bag with a thump, and shrugged out of his coat. He rolled up his sleeves, almost to the old-fashioned garters above his elbows.

"Any hot water?" he asked of Lauralee. "I'll need to wash my hands."

Lauralee didn't remember setting a kettle on to heat, but there was one there on the stove all the same, lid clattering, steam curling from the spout. She rinsed the washbasin and then filled it, and the doctor cleaned his hands with strong yellow soap.

"Young fella," Doc Jameson said to a quiet, pensive Chance as he took the towel Lauralee offered. "You go and cut me some straight pieces of wood for splints. And don't be dallying around about it, either—I'll be needing you to hold Mr. McCallum here down when the pain gets nasty."

Chance hurried outside, eager to do whatever he could to help.

Lauralee felt the color drain from her face. So the whiskey hadn't been such a help after all. Why had she expected that it would? "Isn't there anything you can do—"

"I've got morphine," the doctor said, coming back to the table and gently straightening Jay's twisted leg. "That sometimes stops a man's heart, so I try not to use it."

Jay was gasping at the pain resulting from the doctor's touch, sweat beading on his forehead and his upper lip. Lauralee found a clean cloth, dipped it in cool water, and bathed his face with it.

"I'll be right here with you," she promised.

His eyes caressed her, but his words were harsh, grating past colorless lips. "No. I don't want anybody here besides the doctor and Chance. Take the others and go away. Please."

Lauralee was wounded. A wife's place was beside her husband, especially at times like this. "Why?"

Jay gasped and squeezed his eyes closed as the doctor began working his boot off. "Damnit, woman, for once don't argue with me. Just get out of here!"

"This is my house, Jay McCallum!"

Doc Jameson caught Lauralee's eye; he, too, was urging her to go. She went out into the yard—it was almost dark now and the first stars were in place, winking against the sky—and lifted her apron to her face to dry away tears of anger and fright.

Chance had made short work of his mission; he came out of the woodshed with two thin, dirty boards he'd found there. He stopped and bent to peer into Lauralee's face.

"Exiled to the yard, are you?" he asked gently.

"I don't understand why I can't be in my own house, with my own husband—"

"What Jay's about to go through is bad enough, Lauralee," Chance answered in reasonable tones, "without his having to worry about what you're seeing. And hearing."

Lauralee shivered. Of course. When Doc Jameson set Jay's broken limb, the pain would be excruciating. He was afraid of crying out in her hearing.

Chance must have seen that she understood; he went into the house without saying more. A few moments later Kate came out, carrying Alexander. She was biting her lower lip and her eyes were averted.

The two women walked in silence toward the barn. Lauralee ached to go back into the house, but she knew that she mustn't. A man had a right to his pride, foolish as it might be.

Inside the barn, lamps were flickering. Joe Little Eagle was milking a cow, and Clarie was standing beside him, telling him that her mother would come back and fetch her one day, for a certainty.

Lauralee felt a surge of sympathy and remorse; she should not have slapped Clarie.

"Things bad inside?" Joe asked from the stool beside Flossie's heaving, rounded belly. The milk made a sharp, rhythmic sound as it struck the side of the bucket.

Lauralee nodded. "I think they might need you,

Joe." She took his place smoothly as he rose from the stool and immediately began to milk Flossie, taking comfort from the routine nature of the task.

Flossie's long tail slapped at Lauralee's sore back as she worked, her fingers strong and practiced. Kate stood nearby, watching, her face tense.

"Has there ever been such a day?" she mused.

Lauralee could smile, as incredible as it seemed, and remembering Chance's dramatic arrival on the stallion that was now comfortably ensconced in a nearby stall, she did smile. "I'm sorry, Kate. About your reunion with Chance, I mean."

Kate shrugged. "He's here, that's the important thing. And it didn't take as long as I thought it would."

Lauralee set the full bucket of milk aside, patted Flossie, found another bucket, and went on to attend the second cow, Lavinia, her long-time friend. Kate stood nearby, her hands caught together behind her back. Clarie had reclaimed Alexander, with a lift of her chin and a defiant toss of her head, and they were a fair distance away, examining Chance's stallion through the gate of his stall.

"You be careful of that horse," Lauralee warned. "He's not like the ones we used to have for plowing." She lowered her voice, looking up at Kate. "Did you and Chance get an opportunity to talk at all?"

Kate sighed. "Not much of one. He had just finished yelling at me for worrying him, making him ride all the way up here from Spokane, when you came back to tell us Jay had fallen."

Lauralee swallowed, thinking of the pain Jay must be enduring now, thinking of the way he had shielded her from the hailstones. Why couldn't she protect him somehow?

"It will be over soon, Lauralee," Kate promised softly.

"I'm hungry," complained Clarie. "Aren't we even going to have supper?"

"Supper," said Lauralee with a sigh. "How that child could think of supper—"

Kate smiled. "She's young."

Lauralee needed to talk, to keep her mind diverted from what was going on inside the house. "Are you going back to Spokane with Chance?"

Kate's smile faltered and then faded away entirely. "I'm not sure. I want more from him than a dramatic scenario, Lauralee. I want to know that things are going to be different."

Lauralee continued milking Lavinia, her forehead resting against the cow's side. "Have you made any plans?"

"I expect I'll take Jenny to Brice and Lucy's. That will give me more time to think."

Lauralee paused in her work and turned to look at Kate. "That sounds ominous."

Kate nodded sadly, her arms folded across her chest. "I've been so pampered and useless all my life, Lauralee. Since I've been here with you, I've seen that a woman can make her own way."

"But you love Chance—"

"Yes. But I'm no longer willing to live for those rare moments he condescends to share with me. I want to be a real woman, a real person, not just a dress-up doll that only has substance when a man chooses to give it."

Chance isn't going to thank me for this, Lauralee thought. "I'll miss you very much, Kate," she said softly.

Nearly an hour later, Chance came into the barn, looking harried and exhausted. Lauralee wondered whether Kate would have the strength to look past the hurt in his eyes and follow through with her plans.

There was no time to pursue the thought, however; she wanted to know about Jay.

"He'll be all right," Chance said in the voice of a man. But when Kate silently held out her arms, he went into them like a little boy.

They remained in the barn, Kate and Chance, while Lauralee lifted her skirt and ran toward the house, Clarie and Alexander following.

Doc Jameson was putting on his coat, and the table was bare. "We put Jay in the spare room, Lauralee," the old man said, speaking to the wild look she knew had arisen in her eyes. "He's going to have a limp—probably permanent—but he'll recover nicely. I want you to keep an eye out for infection, though. If there's any sign of it, you send for me."

Lauralee was dying to go to Jay, but she had something else to do first. "Thank you, Doc." She paused and drew a deep breath. "I wasn't very kind to you that day when Alexander—"

"Can a man get a cup of coffee in this place?" the doctor broke in gruffly.

Clarie was bustling about near the stove, busy and efficient. "Coffee and supper, too," she said, answering for Lauralee. "There'll be a meal ready as quick as I can see to it."

Impulsively, Lauralee went to Clarie and kissed her on the cheek. Later, there would be time to talk, time for Lauralee to apologize to the girl for what had happened earlier. "When you get a moment, will you please pay the doc? There's money in the cocoa tin."

"The young fella already settled up with me," Doc Jameson said.

Lauralee had waited as long as she could. She rushed through the darkened parlor and into the small room that had been Kate's.

Jay lay atop the covers, his leg neatly splinted and

bandaged, his flesh gray and glistening with perspiration, his eyes closed. Lauralee went to him, touched his chest with a gentle hand.

"Lauralee," he said without opening his eyes or moving.

She saw the welts and bruises then, where he had been struck by the hailstones. She imagined that there were more marks, worse, on his back. "You've had a hard day," she said, to keep from crying.

"I have had better," he agreed, sounding rummy. But his eyelids, with their thick black lashes, rose.

Lauralee glanced at his bandaged limb. A thin blanket covered Jay's other leg, his lower torso, and part of his chest. "Did it hurt very much?"

"I screamed like a banshee," he answered. Apparently, there was no shame in admitting that he had cried out, only in letting a woman hear. Lauralee was annoyed, but she loved Jay too much to point out the fallacy in his logic just then. She brushed his hair back from his forehead.

He said, "Where's Chance? I have to talk to him. It's important."

"Talk to Chance in the morning," Lauralee whispered. "You need to rest now."

Jay's lashes lowered again, but he lifted them with an obvious effort. "No. Important—"

"All right," Lauralee agreed with a smile. "But he and Kate are alone in the barn at this very minute—"

Incredibly, Jay managed a lopsided grin. "Not—that important," he said. "Leave them alone."

Lauralee bent and kissed his mouth. "Thank you," she answered. "I will."

Jay chuckled and then promptly fell into a deep, healing sleep. There was a laudanum bottle on the bedside table, the lid sitting beside it.

Lauralee frowned, closed the bottle tightly, and put

it on the top of the window frame, out of Alexander's reach. Then she kissed Jay again, arranged his covers, and left the room.

Kate and Chance did not come to supper.

Clarie took Alexander upstairs to put him to bed. She looked exhausted herself.

Lauralee cleared away the plates and utensils on the table, surprised when Doc Jameson insisted on helping.

"That Clarie's a good little cook," he said. "Long time since I've tasted corned beef hash like that."

Lauralee felt a certain sadness, realizing how lonely the doctor's life must be. His wife had passed away years before and he had no other family, no home except for a little room above Wallerman's Mercantile in town. "Clarie is such a help to me. I don't know what I'd do without her, frankly."

"She'll marry one day, I suppose."

Lauralee was beginning to wash dishes now. Doc Jameson scooped them from the scalding hot rinse water and dried them. "Yes. But not for a while, I hope. Clarie's hardly had a chance to be a child, what with all the work around here. I'd like to see her have a little—well—fun before she marries."

Doc smiled, his hands deft and busy at the task of drying dishes, stacking them neatly on the counter. "What about you, Lauralee McCallum? When was the last time you had fun?"

Lauralee blushed. Modesty would not allow her to answer that question honestly. "If you mean dancing or seeing a play or something like that, I can't remember when. Virgil and I had to work very hard. Then, after he died—"

"You're not married to Virgil anymore, Lauralee. You're married to that fine young fella in there. Even with his leg in splints, he's twice the man Parker ever was. Don't you fight McCallum if he wants to take you away from this farm and give you a look at the world!"

At another time Lauralee might have been angry and defensive. For now, she was too grateful to Doc Jameson to point out that the way she and Jay lived their lives was their business, not his. She sighed. "I don't see how we can leave now, with Jay hurt that way," she reflected.

There was a knock at the door, and at Lauralee's call, Joe Little Eagle came in, looking sheepish. The poor man, he still couldn't go back to his room in the barn.

"Sit down, Joe," Lauralee said with a smile. "Have some coffee."

Joe Little Eagle had never taken a meal at Lauralee's table. It wasn't that she wouldn't have allowed him to; he simply refused, coming to the door for his plate, carrying it to his room in the barn. Even tonight, with all that had happened, he had sat on the back step to eat rather than join the others.

He compromised, taking the cup of coffee, but drinking it standing up. When Doc Jameson finally left, Joe remained.

"I'm sorry that your husband fell that way, Mrs. McCallum."

Lauralee looked at Joe in weary gratitude. "Thank you. He was trying to get that silly sign down—"

"Sign?"

"Across the road, at the saloon."

Joe changed the subject. "You've lost the seedling trees," he said.

Lauralee didn't ask where he'd been during the day; she was too tired to pursue things that didn't matter. She poured herself a cup of coffee and sat down at the table. "I know."

"There are forty acres on this place. You got timber. Why don't you sell timber to Mrs. Burch for her mill?"

The idea of selling so much as a pine cone or a fir branch to Adrienne Burch didn't set well with Lauralee, but she had to admit, now at least, that it made good sense. "The money would pay off the loan I took out for those new trees," she speculated, frowning. "They're not good for anything but kindling now."

Considering his reserve, it must have been very hard for Joe Little Eagle to say what he said then. "Your husband is rich, Mrs. McCallum. You won't lose this place, one way or the other."

Lauralee was still frowning. "I don't know if this will make sense to you or not, Joe, but I've got to hold this farm through my own doing, if I hold it at all."

Joe was silent for a few moments, considering. "Would you sell it?"

Even when she'd been planning to go to Washington and be a senator's wife—they couldn't very well go now, of course, with Jay's leg in that shape—Lauralee had not thought about selling. From the moment of Alexander's birth, in fact, she'd dreamed of passing the orchards and the pastures and the timber on to him someday. But Alexander was deaf and there was no guarantee, even if he should regain his hearing, that he would ever want to live as a farmer.

"I don't know," Lauralee answered belatedly.

"I have saved my money," Joe said evenly and with dignity. "Ever since I have worked here, I have saved my money. I can pay for this land."

Of course. These forty acres had been Joe's in the first place; it was natural enough that he would want to buy them back. Lauralee was ashamed that she'd never considered how he must have felt, working for Virgil and then for her, tending land that, except for a twist of fate, would have belonged to him still.

"I'll need to think, Joe—on selling, I mean. If I decide to, I promise that I'll speak with you first."

Joe nodded.

Just then, Chance and Kate came in. Their clothes were askew, their smiles shy, their eyes averted. Kate had bits of straw caught in her hair, and Chance was carrying the two buckets of milk Lauralee had left behind in the barn.

Joe Little Eagle slipped out just as they were attempting to assemble the awkward metal pieces of the separator. Kate was boasting that she knew how to part cream from milk and that, furthermore, she knew how to make butter.

Chance was gently scornful, challenging her to prove her assertion.

Personally, Lauralee couldn't have cared less if they'd poured the milk out on the ground. After the day she'd had, she didn't give a fig whether the milk and cream were ever separated, the eggs ever gathered, the butter ever churned.

She went upstairs, looked in on Alexander and then on Clarie. In her room, in Jay's room, she stripped the sheets and pillowcases away and remade the bed with fresh linens. Chance and Kate could sleep here tonight.

As if they would sleep, Lauralee thought with a sad and slightly envious smile. It seemed apparent that Chance had managed to change Kate's mind about going on to Brice and Lucy's to visit and gather her thoughts. In view of the McCallum charm, Lauralee was not surprised. One way or the other, she supposed, things would work out and her brother- and sister-in-law would come to some kind of understanding.

Jay's satchel sat near the wardrobe, forgotten, and Lauralee picked it up by its handle, resolved to carry it downstairs to the spare room. Tomorrow, she would give her husband a bath of sorts, and though he wouldn't be able to wear trousers, of course, there might be a nightshirt in there that he could put on.

Jay in a nightshirt! She giggled at the image as she struggled down the stairs with that heavy valise.

In the kitchen, Kate was bent over the separator, industriously turning the crank. Chance sat at the table, his legs propped on another chair, watching her calico-draped bottom with an appreciative grin.

Lauralee chuckled and shook her head. "I've made up our bed for you two," she said. "Kate, don't bother about that separating. It really—"

Chance held up one finger to his lips, and his brown eyes danced. Lauralee sighed and then went on to the spare room.

She put on the nightgown she had worn earlier, took down her hair and brushed it, washed her face, and rinsed her mouth. Then, very carefully, she stretched out on the narrow bed beside Jay and immediately fell asleep.

CHAPTER
FIFTEEN

The sign was lying on the kitchen table, big as you please, its gilt lettering catching the morning sunlight.

RUMSUCKER SALOON.

Knowing that this was Joe's doing—sometime during the night he'd gone and fetched the sign for her—Lauralee smiled through a yawn and went out into the dewy morning, the grass cool beneath her bare feet, her wrapper held tightly around her.

Purple and white lilacs nodded at her; a robin chirped on the privy's ramshackle roof. Lauralee smiled again and opened the creaky door.

She was on her way back to the house, bathed in bright sunlight, thinking that she might have dreamed the disasters of yesterday for all the evidence this polished morning gave of them, when Adrienne Burch's surrey turned in at the gate and clattered up into the dooryard.

How was it that Adrienne always managed to catch her coming from the privy or wearing mosquito paste on her face and dressed in Virgil's clothes?

"I came as soon as I heard!" Adrienne sang out, wrapping the surrey's reins around the brake lever with efficient hands. Today she was wearing a lemon-yellow dress with a matching jacket. Her hat was exactly the same color, and so was the elegant little whisper of a veil that fell from its brim.

"How is Jenny?" Lauralee asked, determined to be polite this time. Joe's idea about selling timber rights to Adrienne was a good one, and she didn't want to jeopardize it by giving in to the rancor she felt toward this woman.

Adrienne pouted prettily. "She's a love, dusting everything, helping Cook. I don't know what we did without her."

Lauralee resisted an urge to roll her eyes. "Won't you come in, Adrienne?" she asked sweetly. *Never mind that it's practically the crack of dawn and we both know that you want to fuss over my injured husband and annoy me as much as possible in the process.* "Clarie must have the coffee on by now, and I'd like to discuss a business proposition."

Adrienne arched one perfect brown eyebrow and took her parasol and handbag—both lemon-yellow, of course—from the surrey's seat. "You must forgive me for coming to call so early," she said, as though they had been the dearest of friends for all their lives. "I was so terribly concerned when I heard about poor Jay. Is it very bad?"

Jay had bitten at Lauralee like a bear when she'd greeted him that morning; he was clearly not going to be a winsome patient. Still, what point was there in admitting that to Adrienne? "He's in a lot of pain," she said as they walked toward the kitchen door, arm in arm like school chums. "Doc Jameson says he'll need a cane even after the break has healed, but of course it could have been much, much worse. Jay might have lost his leg, you know."

Lauralee would have sworn that nothing could

247

throw Adrienne off balance, but it seemed that her kindly, talkative reception had done just that. The beautiful visitor looked as though she would like to get back into her fancy surrey and drive away.

The kitchen was bedlam, with Kate and Chance and Clarie all there tripping over each other, the women cooking breakfast, Chance trying valiantly to set the table. He slid his laughing eyes over Adrienne's lemon-yellow personage and a spark danced in their depths—Lauralee supposed a person couldn't change entirely in a matter of a few days, and decided to take a charitable attitude toward her brother-in-law. Of course, if he betrayed Kate, she would personally horsewhip him.

"Have you looked in on Jay?" Lauralee asked, beaming upon Chance but letting the warning shine in her blue-green eyes. "Mrs. Burch has come to call on him, but we don't want to catch the poor dear unawares, do we?"

Chance grinned. The warning had registered with him, and Lauralee had the feeling that he liked her for it. "I'll make sure my brother is presentable," he offered, promptly disappearing into the parlor.

While they waited, Adrienne tugged nervously at her lemon-yellow gloves, her parasol caught under one slender arm, her handbag dangling from her wrist. Clarie glared at her, her hostility palpable, and as she broke eggs into a skillet, she looked as though she might enjoy breaking Adrienne's head in much the same manner.

Lauralee saw that Kate had not missed the exchange between Mrs. Burch and Chance, but she smiled politely and offered not only coffee, but breakfast, too. Adrienne declined the meal but accepted the coffee, sinking gratefully into a chair at the table to drink it.

Presently, her eyes fell on the sign from the saloon, which someone had propped up on the broad window-sill. "How quaint," she said.

Lauralee was more comfortable with this Adrienne than with the politer one she had encountered moments before. "Isn't it?" she chimed in sunny tones. And then she excused herself to go upstairs.

When she came down again, she was wearing one of her new dresses, her hair neatly bound into a single braid, her hands and face scrubbed clean. And all for naught, because Adrienne was not in the kitchen waiting to be impressed.

Chance, sitting at the table beside Kate, read the question in her eyes as ably as he had read the warning minutes before, and he gave her an insolent wink. "Jay was eager to see Mrs. Burch," he said.

"Chance!" Kate hissed; from the way he flinched, it appeared that she had kicked him.

Lauralee drew a deep breath and forced herself to smile. What did Chance think she was going to do, bolt into that spare room and do battle for her husband? It galled her that she wanted to. "Where is Alexander?" she asked.

"Parlor," said Clarie through a mouthful of toasted bread.

It was a perfectly reasonable excuse to go within earshot of the spare room, and Lauralee took it. The door was closed and Alexander was sitting on his potty-chair, near the stove, his face red with effort.

Lauralee cringed to think that Adrienne had seen this homely tableau on her way through the parlor. Feminine laughter chimed from behind the spare room door, and Lauralee's face turned as red as Alexander's. With the greatest of effort, she went back to the kitchen, poured herself a cup of coffee, and sat down at the table. She hoped no one would notice her lack of appetite.

Jay was glad when Adrienne Burch left; the glaring color of her dress hurt his eyes, and his broken leg was throbbing as though it had just been stung by a hundred wasps.

Lauralee came into the room, her eyes averted, the sunlight from the window glistening along the heavy braid of saffron hair falling over one shoulder. Her mouth was taut, and patches of pink outrage mottled her cheekbones. "Are you ready for your breakfast?" she asked.

She was jealous. Irritably, Jay wondered why she'd let Adrienne Burch come in here in the first place, feeling the way she did. What was he supposed to have done—jumped up and run away?

"Where the hell is the laudanum?" he countered.

Lauralee went to the window, stretched on tiptoe to reach the brown bottle. Jay saw a tremor in her shoulders and regretted speaking so sharply.

She came to the bed, took up the spoon that was still lying on the table beside it, and poured a dose of the bitter medicine into it. "You mustn't leave this open on the table," she said distantly, her eyes still skirting his. "Alexander could get into it."

"Lauralee—"

She jammed the spoon into his open mouth, refilled it while he was still grimacing and sputtering over the taste, and crammed it in again before he had the wits to close his mouth.

"There," she said, sealing the bottle and taking it back to the window. He saw the curve of her left breast lift as she reached and yearned to catch its plump fullness in his hand.

"Lauralee."

She turned and stared through him as though he were transparent. "Yes?"

"You're jealous."

Blue-green defiance sparked in her eyes. "Did you have your chest uncovered like that when Adrienne was in here?" she demanded.

Jay laughed. "No. I pulled the covers up to my nose and peered at her over clenched knuckles."

An appealing flush flooded up Lauralee's neck and into her face; Jay wished he could see the rest of her, see if her perfect breasts and satiny stomach were blushing, too. "I'll be gone all morning," she said. "So if you need anything, you'll have to depend on Kate or Chance or Clarie."

The pain in Jay's leg was easing; he knew the laudanum would not assuage that completely, but only make it bearable. In place of the gnawing discomfort was a sharp wariness that made him sit up straighter against the pillows propped behind him. "What do you mean, you'll be gone all morning?"

"I have business with Adrienne, at her house."

"What kind of business?"

"Nothing that concerns you, Jay McCallum."

"Everything you do concerns me. You hate that woman and I want to know what the hell kind of business could be important enough that you would pay a call on her!"

Slim shoulders lifted in a shrug. "We all wonder about things that simply aren't ours to know, don't we?" she responded with a biting sort of pleasantry. "Do you want breakfast or not?"

She wasn't going to tell him, and there wasn't a damn thing he could do about it. Jay clenched the covers in his fists. "I want a chamberpot," he said.

Unruffled, Lauralee brought a clean one from beneath the bed, removed the lid, and held it out to him. This was an aspect of his injury Jay had not considered, and for all his sophistication, he was wildly embarrassed. He also felt as though his bladder would burst.

Lauralee smirked, reading his dilemma well, but she did at least have the decency to leave the room. When she came back minutes later, she brought warm water, soap, and a washcloth.

She gave Jay a sponge bath, taking pains to arouse him, and when she left the room again, she took the chamberpot with her. She returned with it several minutes later, set it on the side table within reach, and took up the basin of soap-skimmed water, the cloth floating in it.

"Kate will bring your breakfast in a few minutes," she said.

Did she actually think she was going to get off that easily? Jay grasped her wrist and held it, and some of the water spilled over the edge of the basin. "Lauralee."

She met his eyes, her own bright with challenge. "Let go of me, Jay. I'll be late."

"There's a book in my satchel. Would you get it for me, please?"

Lauralee knew that he was stalling; it was evident in the way she bit down on her lower lip. But she did set aside the basin and hoist the satchel onto the foot of the bed—Jay winced at the pain caused by the motion of the mattress—and rummage through until she found the book.

Her cheeks glowed a transparent pink as she read the title while offering him the heavy tome. "You're studying sign language?"

Jay gave a long-suffering sigh and opened the book. "Alexander will be taught to communicate this way, when he goes to school. I, for one, would like to be able to converse with him."

She drew nearer, her beautiful eyes curious as they took in the symbols demonstrated in the book. "This is—this is the book you were reading in Spokane, isn't it?"

Jay nodded, suppressing a grin of triumph. "I bought it the day the doctor told us that Alexander might always be deaf," he said, frowning with pretended concentration.

Lauralee peered over his arm, scanning the page he was reading, obviously fascinated. He smiled when he saw, out of the corner of his eye, her small hand tentatively mimicking some of the symbols.

Then she ruined it all with a resigned sigh and, "I have to leave now or I'll surely be late."

Jay was undone. He slammed the book shut and Lauralee jumped back, startled by the sharp sound.

"Damnit, Lauralee, if you're borrowing money from that woman, I'll blister you! I have enough money—"

She smoothed a lock of hair back from his forehead, her lips twitching with tenderness and amusement. "I would never borrow money from Adrienne Burch," she said. "I do have some pride, you know."

"Then why are you going there?"

"I'd like to make sure that Jenny is all right," she said.

It was only a partial truth, and Jay knew it. But short of strong-arming Lauralee and holding her prisoner, how could he stop her from going about whatever scheme she had in mind? "Tell me the rest, Lauralee."

She shook her head and wisely stepped back out of range. She had set the basin down due to her interest in the book, and she was not foolish enough to reach for it. "I'll tell you everything when I get home."

"Lauralee!"

She crossed the room, opened the door, and went out. Jay bellowed her name again, but she didn't come back. No, damnit all to hell, Chance came in her place, grinning, cocky as a banty rooster.

Sure, he'd be grinning, the bastard. His leg wasn't broken. He'd probably been making love to his wife half the night—

"You'll be up and around in a few weeks, Jay," Chance assured him perceptively. "Try to be patient, will you?"

Jay scowled. "Coming from you, that is ironic advice indeed!"

Chance laughed and leaned back against the door, his arms folded across his chest. He was wearing tight breeches, one of those stupid flowing shirts he was so fond of, and muddy riding boots. "Life is full of little ironies," he said.

Jay settled into his pillows, feeling dismal. "Dad and Mother have already left Spokane, I suppose?"

Chance nodded, his expression sober now. "By now they're probably at sea. They were about to board a train for Seattle when Dad finally broke down and told me that Kate was here with Lauralee. I think he enjoyed seeing me out of my mind."

"Where's the novelty in that?" Jay snapped. "You've been out of your mind ever since I can remember."

Chance came to the foot of the bed, removed the satchel Lauralee had forgotten there, and sat down very carefully, so as not to jar Jay's injured leg. "If you're through reminding me what a waster I've been, we'd better talk."

"I can't go to Washington," Jay said. And that, to him, was a disappointment so bitter that he very nearly couldn't tolerate it. "You'll have to do it, Chance."

There was a short silence, then Chance cleared his throat diplomatically and said, "I'll take over the Senate seat, Jay—but only until you're better."

Jay was surprised. He'd thought Chance would leap at the opportunity to become a senator.

Chance grinned, but there was an element of sadness in his manner. "I see you're rendered speechless by my noble generosity," he observed.

"It never occurred to me that you would be willing to give up a Senate seat once you'd managed to land one."

Chance's gaze shifted to the window and some far distance beyond it. "I'll need something to do for the next couple of months to keep myself from going mad. Kate's leaving me."

"What? But Lauralee said—"

"That Kate and I slept together last night?" Chance was looking at Jay now, and the sadness in his eyes was deep. "We did. But my dear wife isn't willing to live under the same roof with me, on a permanent basis at least, until I've made a few promises and proven that I can keep them."

"I'm sorry, Chance."

"Why don't you say what you're really thinking? That I deserve this, that you warned me—"

Jay sighed heavily. "Can you do what Kate wants, Chance?"

His brother shrugged. "I don't know. I guess I'll find out soon enough." There was a brief, reflective pause. "In any case, I can handle the Senate seat for a couple of months, Jay. You don't need to worry that I'll undermine democracy as we know it."

Jay chuckled. "Just promise me one thing."

"What?"

"That you'll buy some decent shirts!"

Chance threw back his head and laughed.

CHAPTER
SIXTEEN

Lucy was sick. Lucy! Brice McCallum, filled with consternation and fear, paced the broad hallway outside their bedroom, his hands clasped behind his back. How could Lucy be sick? She had always been so strong, so brave, so full of laughter and competence and mischief.

The door opened just when Brice would have flung himself at the thing and broken it down, and the doctor he had summoned from Spokane came out, bag in hand, the expression on his face ominous.

Brice moved to brush past him, bent on seeing Lucy, and was stopped with a crisp, "She's resting, Mr. McCallum. It's important to let her rest."

Brice was thirty-seven years old, strong as the proverbial bull, and used to giving orders, not taking them. This was his house and that was his wife lying in there. He flung the doctor's hand away.

"I only want to look at Lucy—see that she's all right!"

"She isn't all right," Dr. Summers said gravely. "I

warned Lucy about keeping this from you." The older man paused, shook his head. "I warned her."

The hallway seemed to dip and sway and undulate beneath Brice's dirty boots. "Keeping what from me?" he demanded in a hoarse whisper.

"My God, man, don't you have eyes in your head? The woman's been in constant pain for weeks, and she must have lost a good twenty pounds in that time!"

Brice had noticed the weight loss, and it was true that Lucy had often seemed wistful, but she'd never once complained of so much as a headache. An anguish of guilt welled up within him, rendering him speechless.

The doctor took pity on him and spoke gently. "Come downstairs with me. Please. We'll talk."

Brice cast an agonized look at the open doorway. Just a glimpse of Lucy would give him strength for anything—he had to see her once. He grasped the doorframe in both hands to steady himself, to keep from storming into that room and demanding that his wife stop all this nonsense and get up out of that bed.

She looked so small, lying there asleep, her hands pale against the blankets. Was that his strong, sturdy Lucy? His Lucy, always complaining that she was as big as a man? Brice felt tears claw at the inside of his throat and burn in his eyes. "Oh God," he muttered. "God in heaven."

The doctor's voice was still kindly, but it had taken on a note of insistence. "Brice, please. Come with me."

Brice turned with the greatest of effort and followed the physician down the hallway and the stairs into the parlor. He needed a drink, and he made a lot of noise opening the liquor cabinet, taking out two glasses, and uncorking a bottle.

Dr. Summers sank into a chair with a weary sigh. "I

know it won't mean much to you now, Mr. McCallum, but I am sorry."

Brice was jolted out of his daze. Sorry? "What the hell do you mean, you're sorry? You sound like she's dead or something!"

"She will die, Mr. McCallum. And if the good Lord is mercifully inclined, it will be soon."

Both the glasses clattered to the floor, spilling their contents onto a rug that Lucy had hooked with her own capable, unerring hands. "What!"

"I'm sorry. Mrs. McCallum has a cancer. She's had it for some considerable time, I'd say. Her passing will be a blessing—"

"A blessing?" Brice bellowed senselessly, clasping the doctor's lapels in his farmer's hands, hauling him up out of the chair, shaking him like a rag doll. He heard the kitchen girl Janet cry out—she must have come in to clean up the broken glass and spilled liquor—and then there were arms restraining Brice, forcing him to release the doctor.

Somehow, Brice managed to regain his dignity. He dismissed the girl and the farmhands she had summoned from the kitchen with her scream.

"Isn't there anything you can do to save my wife?" he asked when he and the ruffled, nervous little doctor were alone again.

"Short of giving Lucy laudanum for the pain and praying that she goes quickly, Mr. McCallum," said Dr. Summers, "there is little any of us can do."

Brice went back to the liquor cabinet and poured himself a double shot, tossed it back, poured another. The heat of the whiskey coursed through his system; he couldn't be sure whether it was strengthening him or making him weak, but it did help him deal with the shocks that were still echoing through his soul.

The doctor left bottles behind, half a dozen brown

bottles. He wrote prescriptions for more. And then, without another word, he left, driving away in his hired buggy.

Brice stood at the window, drink in hand—damn those little glasses; he had the whole bottle now—watching the cloud of dust left behind by the doctor's buggy, watching the wheat waving in the dry breeze, hating the world.

"Can I get you something, Mr. McCallum?" the kitchen girl asked from behind him, her voice small and timorous.

So she knew. Even she, with her empty brain and her work-reddened hands, knew that Lucy was going away. Brice hated her for knowing when he hadn't. "Leave me alone," he growled.

"I could send for your kinfolk, Mr. McCallum—"

"I said get out!"

Brice drank until noon, when that pesky wretch of a girl came back with a bowl of stew and a plate of fresh-baked biscuits. He hurled the biscuits at her, rapid-fire, and even though she fled in tears, he threw the bowl of stew, too.

And then he sank into his chair and covered his face with his hands. "Lucy," he said. "Lucy."

He looked like a ghost, Lucy's gentleman farmer, towering in the doorway of their bedroom, his face wan and broken, his eyes reddened.

The pain was bad indeed and just lifting her hand was an effort of startling magnitude, but Lucy McCallum managed it.

Brice stumbled toward her, sank to his knees beside the bed, and buried his face in her bosom. His great shoulders moved spasmodically as he wept, and the sound was hoarse and convulsive and terrible to hear. Lucy's heart broke within her.

"Mary will come," she said, for that was all she had to offer, besides her love.

"I don't want Mary!" he sobbed raggedly.

Tears slipped down Lucy's cheeks. How she hated going. How she hated the suddenness, the viciousness, of her sickness. Why, only weeks before, she'd been strong enough to help with the planting. Now the new wheat was knee-high and she was dying. "Promise me you won't send my sister away, Brice."

He could not promise, he could only weep. Lucy understood that, and she held Brice in her arms, her fingers playing, for perhaps the last time, in his coarse, dense hair.

The wire was waiting on a table in the entryway, seemingly innocuous in its yellow envelope. Assuming that it was a bon voyage message meant for his parents, aching because he'd soon be parting from Kate when he'd just learned that he loved her, Chance glanced at it and passed it by.

Kate, coming in behind him because she had been fussing over an awe-stricken Jenny French, lingered to pick up the envelope and open it. Her gasp stopped Chance on the stairway and made him turn to look at her.

"What is it?"

Tears were rolling down Kate's sunburned cheeks, and her hands were trembling. "Oh, dear God—" she cried. "Dear God, no!"

Jenny French stepped back, looking as though she might bolt outside and run down the sidewalk.

Chance sprinted back down the stairs and snatched the telegram from Kate's fingers. The words printed on it had the impact of a two-by-four striking his middle full force.

Lucy was dead.

Kate was wailing in her grief. Chance reached out, held her close with one arm, propping his chin in her soft hair. His vision blurred, the familiar entryway went out of focus, came in again, and went out.

"What are we going to do?" Kate sobbed, her face buried in his shoulder. "What are we going to do without our Lucy?"

What was Brice going to do without Lucy? Chance wondered. What could he say to his eldest brother; what could he do to help?

Chance sighed, let the telegram waft to the floor, and held Kate in both arms. He'd wanted the responsibilities due a man, and now he would have to meet them. The senator was already at sea, Jay was a hundred miles away, laid up with a broken leg. He caught his hand under Kate's quivering chin and forced her to look at him.

"Tell the housekeeper to see that our things are packed and shipped to Washington," he said hoarsely, unashamed of the tears on his face.

"But—"

"We'll see Brice before we leave, Kate. Just do as I tell you." She gave him a beleaguered look and started toward the back of the house. He caught her and pulled her back. "I love you," he said.

She threw her arms around him and held on tightly.

It was getting dark by the time they reached Brice's farm, but no welcoming lights burned in the windows. The fact that Lucy did not run outside to greet them, as had been her exuberant habit, made Chance's throat tighten.

He drew back on the reins of the buggy he'd rented after leaving the train in town and a shudder trickled down his spine. Good God, what help could he be to Brice? There were four years and a great many differences between the two of them.

262

Two barefooted boys came from the barn, their faces filthy, their eyes wary. One of them took charge of the surrey the moment Chance had climbed down from the seat and lifted Kate after him.

The other one stood, shifting from one foot to the other and sniffling. "Big Mister's bad off," he said.

Big Mister. Chance might have smiled under other circumstances. The name fit Brice like a supple, well-worn boot. "Where is my brother?" he asked, one arm curved around Kate's waist.

"He's in the barn. Mr. McCallum, he done tore apart the whole house, and now he's set to out there—"

Leaving Kate to go into the house with Jenny, Chance strode toward the barn, and as he neared it, he could hear the hoarse, broken sound of his brother's grief and the accompanying destruction.

He paused in the open doorway and drew a deep breath. After a moment, his eyes adjusted to the dim light inside. Brice, bull-strong in his sorrow, caught both hands under one side of a buckboard and, with a throaty bellow of rage, overturned it completely.

CHAPTER
SEVENTEEN

Lauralee crept into the spare room as quietly as she could and propped the saloon sign on top of the bureau for Jay to see when he awakened. Perhaps that would brighten his nasty mood; certainly, nothing else had.

She sighed as she pulled the door closed behind her again. The house seemed huge and empty without Chance and Kate, and Lauralee was very much at loose ends. It had been a full week since Jay's accident and almost that long since her meeting with Adrienne.

Mrs. Burch had agreed to buy the timber rights to Lauralee's property and for a price that the banker had approved of as fair. The papers were being drawn up by Adrienne's attorneys in Spokane, and once they were signed, there would be sawyers on the land, felling the great pines and Douglas firs.

For the time being, there was no point in going to the orchards; only the older trees remained, and what pruning and spraying they needed was being done by Joe Little Eagle. The small trees, regarded by Lauralee as her own, had all been destroyed in the hailstorm.

She touched one finger to a melodeon key; the

sound it made was doleful, deepening her loneliness. Alexander, like Jay, was asleep; Clarie was off somewhere, wandering; and Jenny, of course, had gone to Brice McCallum's farm with Kate and Chance.

Lauralee considered awakening one or both of her men, just for company, but she couldn't bring herself to do it. Jay and Alexander needed their rest, and besides, they probably wouldn't be good company anyway.

Wistfully, she glanced toward the closed door of the spare room. Jay wasn't past the stage of rebelling against his confinement, and his disappointment at sending Chance to serve out even a part of his father's Senate term in his place was fathomless. Furthermore, he was furious with Lauralee for selling Adrienne Burch the right to take timber from the land, not because there was any danger of depleting the supply of trees—at Joe Little Eagle's suggestion, Lauralee had gotten Adrienne to agree that a seedling would be planted for every tree that was felled—but because Lauralee had not come to her own husband for the money she needed.

She had tried to explain that paying off the loan she had taken out to buy those ill-fated apple seedlings was a way of tying up the strands of her old life so that she could step with a clear mind into the new one, but Jay didn't understand that. Sometimes, Lauralee wasn't sure she understood it herself, but something within her demanded that she meet her own responsibilities.

The sound of a wagon made her hurry to the window—merciful heavens, she would even be glad of a chat with Adrienne Burch, she was so restless and bored—but the battered vehicle making its way up from the gate belonged to the peddler, Mr. Neggers. The pots and kettles he sold thumped and jangled against the sides of the somber black wagon—it had once, he loved to say, belonged to an undertaker—and Lauralee was overjoyed at the clamor.

Lauralee ran outside, skirt in hand, beaming.

Mr. Neggers, a plain man with a narrow, weathered face and wise blue eyes, greeted her with a rotted grin and a tip of his dusty bowler hat. "Hear tell you're married again," he crowed, pulling his two-horse team to a stop. "High time, too!"

Lauralee laughed. She was always glad to see Mr. Neggers; he told funny stories and played a ferocious game of checkers, and he carried a fascinating stock-in-trade in the bargain, everything from serviceable calico to Chinese finger puzzles and the latest sheets of parlor music. "High time, is it? I wanted to marry you, Mr. Neggers, but you never declared yourself."

The peddler beamed, sliding his hat to a rakish angle on the back of his almost hairless head. "Day late, dollar short. That's me." The broad grin faded. "Your husband don't mind you takin' in boarders, now, does he? Wouldn't set well with some men, you know."

Lauralee was petting one of his two shabby, swaybacked horses; the poor weary creatures needed water and feed and a night's shelter in a sturdy barn. "You'll have the best room in the house, Mr. Neggers, and don't be concerned about my husband. He's got a broken leg."

Neggers climbed down from the wagon seat with a grateful sigh and began unhitching his team. He would, as always, leave the wagon at the side of the house until he was ready to move on. "Good," he teased as he worked. "Won't be up to chasing me around the house if I pull a shenanigan or two."

Lauralee chuckled and shook her head before turning back to the house. The peddler loved to joke, but he was a true gentleman for all his lack of education and polish.

266

She had set coffee on to perk and cut a slice of cherry pie by the time Mr. Neggers got back from the barn. He paused just outside the door, at the wash bench, to splash his face and hands clean and thump his ancient hat against one thigh until the dust flew in every direction.

"Nigh forgot," he said as he sat down to his pie and coffee with a look of weary appreciation. "Cy Wallerman stopped me when I was passin' through town and gave me these here. . . ." Mr. Neggers reached into the inside pocket of his vest and brought out a yellow envelope with Jay's name written across the front and a letter addressed to Clarie.

Clarie's letter was thick, the address penned in a neat, feminine hand. Some sixth sense told Lauralee that the time the girl had awaited so long had finally come. With a sigh, she set the missive aside, to rest unopened until Clarie returned, and frowned at the yellow envelope.

Knowing that Clarie would probably be going away had given her a sense of sweet sadness, but the telegram filled Lauralee with alarm.

She tried to put down the feeling of unease to the fitfulness of being all but confined to the house for the better part of a week. "Did Mr. Wallerman say what this was about?" she asked, wishing she dared read the message.

Mr. Neggers shook his head and tucked into his pie. "Me and Wallerman ain't chummy, you know," he observed. "He don't like me sellin' goods that could be bought in his store for twice the price, and since he's had that telegraph gadget in his store, on top of installin' his telephone and bein' appointed postmaster, he's been a mite above the rest of us."

Lauralee looked at the envelope once more, sighed, and slipped it into her apron pocket. When Jay awakened, she would give it to him and hope that he cared to share its contents. If he didn't, that was his right, for letters and messages were private things, no matter how intriguing they might be to others.

After two pieces of pie and a second cup of coffee, Mr. Neggers went out to his wagon to bring in the things he wanted to show Lauralee. There were books, including one by Charles Dickens, along with colorful threads for crocheting, small toys that would delight Alexander, an array of hair ribbons that would set Clarie's eyes alight. Lauralee let her gaze rest for one wistful moment on the letter addressed to her step-daughter and sighed. Things were happening so fast. Everything was changing.

Normally, Lauralee could afford to buy little or nothing, though she often let Mr. Neggers pay for his room and board and the feed for his horses in goods instead of coin. Now, however, she was going to have the money to meet her mortgage, due to the timber agreement with Adrienne, plus a respectable sum to set aside for Alexander. It wouldn't hurt, then, to spend a few pennies.

She had chosen a toy horse for Alexander and was puzzling over ribbons representing every hue of the rainbow—these would be Clarie's going-away present should the letter contain what she suspected it did—when Jay awakened and thundered out, "Laura-lee!"

Lauralee gave Mr. Neggers a long-suffering look and went into the spare room. Jay was sitting up, but his face was gray with pain. "Who's out there?" he demanded.

His wife went to the window, brought down the bottle of laudanum, and gave him the prescribed two spoonfuls before answering. "Mr. Neggers, the peddler. He boards here when he passes through."

Scowling, Jay reached for the box of cheroots he kept on the bedside table. "Send him in here, will you?" He stopped and, in spite of himself, grinned sheepishly. "Please."

Lauralee smiled. Grumpy as he was, she was delighted that Jay was awake. "Maybe he has crutches to sell. I didn't think to ask."

"God, it would be good to get out of this bed, even if I did have to hobble around with a couple of sticks holding me up."

Lauralee kissed him gently on the forehead. "I'll ask. And if Mr. Neggers doesn't have crutches, Mr. Wallerman might sell them in his store. Or Joe could make a pair."

The mention of the storekeeper reminded Lauralee of the message in her pocket. She took it out and offered it in silence as Jay struck a match to light his cheroot.

When Lauralee returned to the little bedroom off the parlor, she found her husband paler than before, the yellow paper of the telegraph message crumpled in one hand, his eyes staring sightlessly at the sign that said RUMSUCKER SALOON.

"What is it?" she whispered, afraid.

Without looking at her, Jay extended the paper. Lauralee took the hand-copied telegram and read it with disbelief. The wire was from Chance. LUCY HAS PASSED AWAY. BRICE BEYOND REASON. I TRIED, BUT THERE IS NO CONSOLING HIM. ON MY WAY EAST BY THE TIME THIS REACHES YOU. KATE IS WITH ME. SORRY YOU HAD TO FIND OUT THIS WAY. CHANCE.

Lauralee had never met Lucy, but she had heard a great deal about Brice's wife from Kate, who had adored the woman. She was devastated for Brice and for her own husband, who could do nothing to help his brother now, when he needed it most.

"I knew it," Jay rasped, still staring disconsolately ahead. "I knew it."

"If you'll tell me what to say, Jay, I'll go right into town and send our condolences—"

"Condolences!" The word exploded, harsh and sharp, from the depths of Jay's chest. "Condolences, hell. I'm going over there!"

Lauralee took his hand, speaking softly, reasonably. "How can you do that, Jay? You can't even walk across the room."

Jay wrenched his hand free, glaring at Lauralee as though she were a stranger, and a callous one at that. "I'm going, damnit, if I have to crawl!" he bellowed. "Get me my clothes!"

"I will not. If you try to walk on that leg, you'll be a cripple for the rest of your life."

He hurled back his covers and edged toward the side of the bed, sending Lauralee into a tizzy.

"All right!" she cried wildly. "At least let me get you crutches first!"

Mr. Neggers, as luck would have it, sold everything but crutches. He did, however, have the knowledge for fitting them, and he measured Jay with a tailor's tape, from his armpits to his feet.

Lauralee hastened out to the orchard and prevailed upon Joe to stop his pruning and make crutches, and soon he was in the woodshed, fashioning them from boards he'd found across the road on Jay's abandoned building site.

Alexander had awakened from his nap, but Clarie was back from wherever she'd been, and she took over the child's care without question.

"There's a letter for you," Lauralee informed her softly, her heart pressing into her throat.

The leaping light in Clarie's face was touching to see. She snatched the letter from the table and went outside to read it, Alexander perched comfortably on her hip.

By late evening, the crutches had been finished and Jay was ready to try them out.

With Mr. Neggers on one side of him and Joe Little Eagle on the other, Lauralee looking on nervously from a small distance, he worked his way out of bed and stood up, the crutches supporting him. He cursed, and what little color there had been in his face faded completely away, but he was able to remain standing and, after a few faltering attempts, to thump his way across the room and back.

"Pack what we'll need," he said to Lauralee as he sat down on the edge of the bed again, perspiring from the effort and the pain. "We're taking tomorrow's stagecoach as far as Colville."

By then, Lauralee knew the grinding itinerary. The stagecoach to Colville, the train from there. Just the thought of it filled her with despair. "Do you really think you can endure a trip like that, Jay? Have you forgotten what it's like to travel miles and miles in a cramped stagecoach, even when you're well?"

His gray eyes were fierce. "You don't have to go if you don't want to, lady," he said.

Lauralee's heart shriveled. She tried to remember that Jay had lost someone dear to him, that he was wild with worry for his brother, that he was in dreadful physical pain as well. "If you're going, Jay McCallum," she said, with dignity, "I'm going, too. What about Clarie and Alexander?"

Joe and Mr. Neggers maneuvered Jay back into bed, left the room.

"We'll take them with us, of course." Jay spoke more gently now. "The servants can look after them in Spokane while we're with Brice."

Lauralee swallowed, still hurting over words that

271

echoed in her mind and heart. *You don't have to go if you don't want to, lady.* "I'm so sorry," she managed to say, "about Lucy."

Jay nodded, closed his eyes, and mourned alone, shutting Lauralee away from his grief.

If Lauralee Parker McCallum had gotten up that morning and made a list of the things she wanted to do, hitching up her seldom-used buggy to Jay's horse, driving to town, and knocking on Adrienne Burch's front door would not have been on it. Yet here she was, twilight falling all around her, lifting the brass lion's head and thumping it resolutely against the wood.

Adrienne herself answered the door, pretending to be surprised at finding Lauralee there on her step. In truth, she had probably watched her making her wary course up the steep, curving driveway, struggling to control Jay's headstrong gelding all the way. The beast obviously thought itself too good to pull a buggy.

"Lauralee!" Adrienne cried, swinging open her door. "What a pleasant surprise! I didn't know you drove!"

Lauralee bit back a tart response. She was here as a supplicant, and she couldn't afford to forget that. "I've come to ask a favor," she said, keeping her shoulders straight and her chin high as she got out of the buggy, leaving the reins to rest on the dusty seat. "It's—it's for Jay."

Adrienne's face lost some of its hard brightness. She took Lauralee's arm, squired her into an overdecorated parlor. Seeing this room for the second time, Lauralee was again struck by the fact that pictures of the late Mr. Burch graced every surface—the mantel, the top of the piano, the elegant little ivory inlaid tables within reach of twin brocade sofas. And again

272

she thought what an irony it was that Adrienne had probably entertained Virgil and who knew how many other lovers in this shrinelike place.

"Tell me how I can help."

Lauralee kept her composure somehow. She'd come this far, there was no turning back. She explained the death in Jay's family and his determination to reach his brother's farm as soon as possible, even if he had to suffer a day-long stagecoach journey over rough roads to do it.

"When I have boats!" Adrienne cried in magnanimous triumph. "Why, I wouldn't hear of it!"

Lauralee sighed, relieved, still standing before Adrienne with her hands entwined and her pride in her throat. "Thank you," she said.

"Of course, the boats are full when they make the trip upriver, you know. Positively loaded down with lumber. I'm afraid there wouldn't be room for any extra passengers besides Jay."

Lauralee was in no position to quibble and felt no inclination to remind Adrienne that there had been room for herself, Jay, Brice, and Alexander on that other trip. She cared only about sparing Jay the pain and the brutal exhaustion that would result from a long stagecoach ride. "I understand," she said.

"I'll look after Jay during the trip, of course," Adrienne promised brightly. Smugly. "Don't you worry, Lauralee."

Lauralee met Adrienne's eyes directly. "I won't worry at all," she replied, and that was all she dared allow herself to say. Behind the simply stated words, a dangerous rage pounded and surged, straining to be free.

Going back outside and finding that Jay's dratted horse had left without her did not improve her mood.

Adrienne's lips quivered as she tried to suppress

laughter. "Let me get the surrey and see you home," she pleaded, and her warmth was a brittle thing, hollow and cold at the core. "It's so very dark—"

"I'll walk, Adrienne. I've presumed upon your kindness enough as it is." Lauralee lifted her drooping shoulders and marched down the brick walk. At the head of the driveway, she paused, looked back over her shoulder at the woman who had taken Virgil from her and now wanted Jay, as well. "Thank you," she said.

It was already getting dark, and Lauralee wished she'd thought to bring a lantern to light her way. Of course she hadn't expected that fool horse to abscond with the buggy and leave her afoot, but it would have been wise to carry a lamp just in case. She hadn't been thinking clearly. Her entire mind had been occupied with the necessity of making travel arrangements for Jay.

Halpern's Ferry lay behind her, beyond the mill and Adrienne's house, and Lauralee considered going there, asking Ellery or Pete Townsend for a ride home, but in the end, she chose not to. Her brother was probably away on business, as usual, and even if Pete were back from fetching the gambler suspected of killing Virgil, which seemed unlikely, in view of the distance involved, he would surely be disinclined to go to so much trouble for a woman who had allowed him to hope and then had married another man.

Lauralee trudged on, trying to avoid the ditch and the rocks and ruts in the road, wishing that the sliver of a moon riding above the dark treetops would give more than a hint of light.

She fell once, skinning her right knee. Tears completely unrelated to that small injury slipped down her cheeks. She might just as well stay right here at Halpern's Ferry, pruning trees and enduring hailstorms for the rest of her life, as follow Jay McCallum all over the state! He might have resisted Adrienne's appeal so far, but how long would that last once they were on that lumber boat? Adrienne would fuss over Jay, pamper him, charm him. And broken leg or no, that kind of temptation was hard for any man to ignore.

In despair, Lauralee stumbled on, barely able to see for the darkness and the tears shimmering in her eyes. It was only a mile from town to the door of her house, but tonight it seemed like ten.

Finally, she reached her gate, opened it just far enough to squeeze through, closed and latched it again. Mr. Neggers and Clarie were sitting at the kitchen table, talking earnestly, but at the sight of Lauralee, they both fell silent and stared at her.

"Is Alexander in bed?" she asked.

"He's with Jay," Clarie said. "Lauralee, the letter—it's from my mother. . . ."

Mr. Neggers got up and left the kitchen by way of the back door, and Lauralee sat down in a chair facing Clarie's. "I know," she said gently.

The glow in Clarie's face made Lauralee's heart swell. "She's married a gentleman, Lauralee," the child rushed on in a breathless whisper. "They want me to come to Denver and live with them. They sent a railroad ticket and money."

Lauralee closed her eyes for a moment. She mustn't think of her own feelings now, but of Clarie's. "And you want to go."

"Yes." Impulsively, Clarie threw her arms around Lauralee's neck. "Oh, yes!"

"Then you shall. We'll miss you very much, though, Alexander and Mr. McCallum and I."

"I promise that I'll write as often as I can, and I'll tell you all about everything. . . ."

Lauralee drew back far enough to look into Clarie's eyes, then laid one hand to the child's cheek. "If you aren't happy with your mother and her new husband for any reason, you must write and tell me, Clarie. Jay and I will be in Washington, but if you need us—"

One tear streaked down Clarie's luminous face. "Sometimes I thought Mama would never want me back. Oh, Lauralee, I prayed and prayed and God answered, even after all those mean things I said about Him when I found out Alexander couldn't hear—"

"Shh." Lauralee touched the child's trembling lips. "God didn't stop loving you when you lost faith, and I won't stop loving you either, Clarie. Not ever. You remember that, won't you?"

A cloud seemed to form in the girl's round brown eyes. "Lauralee—what I said to you about Papa's other women—"

Lauralee remembered the telegram, the death in Jay's family. "Not now, Clarie," she said.

"But, Lauralee, it was—"

"Not now," Lauralee repeated firmly, and Clarie fell silent.

A moment later, though, as Lauralee was lifting her skirt to examine her skinned knee and silently cursing Jay's horse—God knew where it was by now, and pulling her buggy behind it, too—Clarie spoke again.

"Lauralee, I think you're in trouble."

What else was new? "Oh?" Lauralee echoed, unconcerned. There was always something going wrong, and in view of the events of the last few days, how important could one more thing be?

"Pete Townsend is here. He's out in the barn right now, talking with Joe."

Lauralee turned, alert and vaguely uneasy. "What kind of trouble could I be in?"

Clarie's face was white, every freckle standing out,

and her eyes were wide. "That gambler told Pete that he saw you arguing with Papa that night he was killed. You never said you went over to the Mud Bucket that night, Lauralee. How come you never said you went over there?"

Lauralee was trembling. She groped her way back to the table and sank into a chair. "That gambler couldn't have seen me with Virgil. I was right here, in this house."

"I don't know why Pete would believe anything that lying poker sharp has to say, anyway," grumbled Mr. Neggers as he came through the door.

Lauralee sighed, weary. Was she never to have a moment's peace? Why, she suffered more disasters in the last two years than in all the rest of her life put together. "Clarie, you go out and get Pete, please. Tell him I want to talk to him right now."

Clarie scraped back her chair and dashed to obey, leaving Lauralee and Mr. Neggers alone in the shadowy kitchen.

"Does my husband know about any of this?" Lauralee asked, folding her hands together on the tabletop to stop their trembling.

"Don't believe so," replied the kindly peddler. "He's been asleep ever since he tried out them crutches."

"I don't want him to hear about it, Mr. Neggers," Lauralee fretted, her voice low. "There has been a death in Jay's family and then there's his leg—I won't have him worrying about me, too."

"Man's wife ought to come before anything else, it seems to me," reflected Mr. Neggers.

Lauralee didn't answer. She saw the light of a lantern swinging across the stretch between the barn and the house and she jumped up and ran outside. Clarie went on past her into the house, but Pete

Townsend stopped, holding the lantern high, visibly bracing himself.

"What do you mean, Pete Townsend," Lauralee hissed, "by coming out here and upsetting my family this way?! You know very well that I didn't kill Virgil or anybody else no matter what that no-account gambler says! How could you?!"

Pete cleared his throat. "Now, Lauralee, I didn't say anything of the sort—"

"Yes you did!" Lauralee broke in, furious and wounded to the soul. "Clarie told me that you believe I was over at the Mud Bucket the night of the murder—"

"Did she?" Pete scoffed quietly. "Well, that's right interesting, since all I said was that my witness saw Virgil arguing with a woman!"

"Your witness! Since when can the word of a suspected murderer be trusted?"

"We don't know that Will Enright is a murderer, Lauralee. The man can't be convicted for grousing over a hand of cards or even for leaving the Mud Bucket right after Virgil did. In fact, unless I find some evidence that Mr. Enright did kill your husband, I'll have to let him go."

"I'd like to talk to Mr. Enright. Right now, tonight."

Even in the darkness, Pete's blush of annoyance was plainly visible. "No lady goes into a jailhouse in the middle of the night!"

"No lady gets arrested either, but I did. Remember?"

Pete spat a swear word. "I'll never forget it!" he hissed. "But you're not going near the place, and that's final!"

"We'll see about that, Pete Townsend. I have a right to face my accuser!"

"You haven't been accused of anything!"

"Haven't I? I want to talk to this witness of yours, and I want to talk to him now. He says he saw a woman with Virgil that night—well, I want to know what she looked like!"

Pete sighed. "So do I, Lauralee, but Enright says it was dark and he couldn't see her. He says she was wearing a cloak with a hood and he only knew she was a woman by what she said."

"And what was that?"

Pete hesitated. In the light of the lantern, he looked forlorn. Reluctant. "She was telling Virgil that she loved him, that she couldn't stand to see him ruin himself with drink."

"So you naturally assumed that that woman was me."

"Damn you, Lauralee, I didn't assume anything! It's just that some folks are going to hear that and—"

"And believe that I went over there and tried to reason with Virgil, and when I couldn't, I killed him."

"Did you?"

"No! And I have no idea who did, but I do know who the woman was, and you should, too!"

"Adrienne?"

"Adrienne," confirmed Lauralee briskly. "I know all about her love affair with Virgil, Pete—she was kind enough to describe it in detail. And if you're going to question me and question Joe Little Eagle, you'd damn well better question Mrs. Burch, too!"

"I will."

"You'd better be quick about it. She's taking my husband on a boat trip to Colville tomorrow morning, and heaven only knows when she'll be back."

Pete's mouth fell open as Lauralee swirled and stomped back into the house.

Alexander, sound asleep, was curled up next to a wakeful, brooding Jay. Without a word to her husband, Lauralee gathered up her son and carried him to his own bed. When she came back, she had several of the dresses Kate had bought for her along with her sewing basket. She sat down in a chair in the corner of the little room and set about finishing the alterations.

"I wish you'd known Lucy," Jay said quietly after a long time.

Lauralee continued to sew, though she ached for her husband. "Kate thought Lucy was the most wonderful woman in the world," she commented gently. If Jay needed to talk, she would listen.

"That's a distinction that belongs to you, Mrs. McCallum," Jay replied, surprising his wife. "But Lucy was a fine woman, always laughing and making things with her hands. Whenever any of us came to visit, she wasn't content to wait sedately in the parlor—she had to come running out to meet the buggy. I don't know what Brice is going to do without her."

"He's going to hurt, Jay. He's going to cry. But he'll go right on living—he doesn't have any other choice."

"He has one choice," Jay answered. "And that's what worries me."

Lauralee's needle stopped in midair. "You don't mean he'd kill himself? Brice? He didn't strike me as that sort of man at all!"

"What sort of man does it take, Lauralee?"

She went back to her stitching, the needle poking through the fabric with little angry stabs. The thought of anyone taking his own life, for any reason, infuriated her. "It's a weak, cowardly thing to do," she muttered. "No man who cared for his friends and his family could possibly—"

Suddenly, one of Jay's crutches crashed to the floor. Lauralee jumped, startled, and stared at him.

"You don't know what you're talking about, Laura-lee," Jay half whispered, half snarled. "We're not discussing cowards and weaklings here, we're discussing my brother! So keep your uneducated opinions to yourself!"

Lauralee's eyes filled with tears. She rose out of the rocking chair and flung the dress she had been working on to the floor, where it made a cloud of emerald-green lawn. "I know your leg hurts, Jay McCallum! I know your heart hurts, too! But I won't have you taking your troubles out on me, not anymore!"

With that, Lauralee left the room, and she did not return until she was certain that Jay was asleep.

*CHAPTER
EIGHTEEN*

It soon became apparent that Jay was not sleeping at all; he had only been pretending. He reached out, closed one strong hand over Lauralee's breast, and chuckled at the moan and shiver the gesture brought from her.

"I thought you would be too angry to sleep in here tonight," he said quietly.

Lauralee's cheeks throbbed in the darkness because her breast was throbbing beneath Jay's hand, warming to it, the nipple reaching. Reluctant desire was flowing into every part of her body, swirling like a river eddy in her middle, dissolving the bones and muscles in her legs. "Where else would I sleep?" she demanded tartly. "Mr. Neggers is in my room."

Jay chuckled again; nothing in her tone could have fooled him when the response of her body was so very obvious. He moved her nightgown upward and slipped his hand between her legs, stroking her inner thighs until she groaned and parted them for him. "Where were you tonight?"

Lauralee shuddered with grudging pleasure as he began to toy with her, his fingers brazen. "I met my lover," she said, hoping to anger Jay, hoping that he would release her.

He did not. He laughed, apparently at the idea that anyone would want Lauralee for a lover, and continued his delicious torment, intensified it. "Did your lover do this?" he asked, and the sound was low and gruff and challenging.

Lauralee arched at the thrust of his hand, unable to help the whimpering gasps his attentions wrought. "Yes!" she whispered fiercely.

Jay released her to open the buttons of her nightgown, baring her breasts to the cool night air. The brief respite ended when his hand went back to the junction of her thighs and his mouth closed over one protruding, eager nipple. "This?" he persisted, between tender forays of his tongue.

Lauralee was distraught with pleasure; she could play the game no longer. "Jay—how will you—your leg—"

He took leisurely suckle at each breast before answering, his hand busy all the while. "Don't worry," he said. "I can. But you'll have to do most of the work. Oh, Lord, Lauralee, how I need you—"

Lauralee was already near explosion. When he urged her, with his hands, to sit astraddle of him, she went readily. His steely length was sheathed within her in a gliding motion that wrung a cry from her and wrought moisture from her flesh. This joining, denied to both of them for a full week, was shatteringly sweet.

Jay's hands were frantic and strong as they caught at her waist, where the flannel of her nightgown was bunched, lifting her, pressing her downward again. Already well primed for passion, Lauralee whimpered as the fierce convulsions began, her hands stroking the broad warmth of his chest, her fingers tangling in the coarse sworls of hair that covered it.

Jay was merciless, filling her, stroking her from within, intensifying his own need as he fulfilled hers. When she collapsed, gasping, onto his chest, he combed her flowing hair with his fingers.

Lauralee sat up again, and this time the motion of her body was slow and rhythmic. Up and down she moved, the velvet walls of her womanhood rippling along the length of his shaft.

Finally, with a strangled gasp and an involuntary upward thrust of his body, Jay surrendered to her fully, beautifully, and then sank, shuddering, into the hollow of the mattress. The loving had broken something brittle and cold within him; in his satisfaction, he wept for Lucy, for his brother.

Lauralee snuggled close beside her husband, holding him in her arms, speaking softly, comforting. And when he slept, she held him still.

For all their communion in the night, Jay was an absolute beast come the morning.

Lauralee got out of bed, fetched the laudanum, and cajoled him until he swallowed two spoonfuls.

"My God," he spat. "How do people manage to get addicted to that stuff?"

Lauralee shrugged, her rumpled nightgown falling from her shoulders, her hair a wild tangle flowing down her back. She fetched the chamberpot and went out to the kitchen to heat water for Jay's morning ablutions and her own.

She was bathing him as best she could when he once again demanded to know where she had been the night before. "And don't tell me you were with your lover, either!" he snapped.

Lauralee deliberately circled one of his nipples with soft strokes of the warm, soapy cloth. "But I was," she insisted sweetly. "I was with you."

"Lauralee!"

"All right. I went to see Adrienne Burch. Are you satisfied?"

"Why?"

"Why would you be satisfied?"

"Why did you go to see that woman, damnit!" He caught her wrist in an iron grip and stopped the washing of his nipple.

Lauralee lowered her eyes and swallowed. It was time to be honest, and that wasn't going to be easy, considering his mood. "I asked her to take you to Colville on her boat. So you wouldn't have to ride the stagecoach."

The hand released her wrist, caught firmly under her chin, the thumb crossing back and forth beneath her mouth, stirring needs that were all too similar to the ones that had possessed her in the night. There was a long, discomforting silence, which Jay finally broke with a hoarse, "After all Adrienne has done to you, you went to her—you humbled yourself like that?"

There was no accusation in Jay's words or in his tone. Only a stricken sort of surprise and something that might be regret. "You're so stubborn, Jay McCallum!" Lauralee blurted through a threatening shimmer of tears. "What else could I do? You would have ridden that stupid stagecoach, and believe me, the train will be bad enough—"

He gave her chin a gentle shake to silence her. "I love you very much," he said.

Lauralee blinked, stared at him, but she could not speak. She had waited so long to hear those words; now that they had been spoken, she needed all her faculties just to absorb them.

Jay pulled her closer, kissed her, and finally let go of her chin. She could still feel the warmth of his hand where he had touched her. "Adrienne agreed to your request, I assume?"

Lauralee swallowed miserably. Jay was going to be angry when he heard Adrienne's terms, and while that was a good and comforting thing, it was also going to complicate matters. "Partly," she admitted.

"What do you mean, partly?"

She closed her eyes, sought strength within herself, found enough to say, "She hasn't room for anyone but you."

Jay rasped a word Lauralee had not heard since before Virgil's death. Once, in a glorious rage, she'd poured all her late husband's Christmas rum down the privy, and he'd bellowed that word.

For a time, Jay simply lay there seething, his chest rising and falling at a furious rate, the nasty word echoing off the walls. Finally, he said, "We're taking the stagecoach."

"Jay, your leg—"

"Damn my leg! We're taking the stagecoach, and that's final!"

Lauralee backed away from the bed and dashed out of the room. In the kitchen, Clarie was busy preparing breakfast for Mr. Neggers and Alexander, who was sitting on the floor, happily playing with the toy horse Lauralee had purchased for him the day before. He was the only one in the room who didn't have to pretend that he hadn't heard the row in the spare room.

To compound Lauralee's embarrassment, she remembered that she was still wearing her wrapper. Furthermore, her feet were bare and her hair, although brushed, was unpinned. She blushed and, having no other choice, scurried back into the little den where the dark lion brooded.

Avoiding Jay's eyes as best she could—and that was difficult in such a tiny room—Lauralee donned one of the dresses she had finished altering the night before, braided her hair, put on her stockings and her shoes.

"Send that peddler in here, will you please?" Jay surprised her by asking politely. It was as though he hadn't shouted at her at all.

Lauralee was feeling petulant and she said nothing in response. When she reached the kitchen again, however, she relayed Jay's request to Mr. Neggers, who immediately abandoned his breakfast to fulfill it.

"Did you tell Mr. McCallum about my mother?" Clarie ventured when she and Lauralee and Alexander were alone in the warm kitchen.

"Not yet, Clarie. There's been a death in Jay's family—his brother's wife has passed away. Right now, he's concerned with going there as soon as possible."

"But I need to get to Spokane to catch the train," Clarie protested, taking the letter from her apron pocket and waving it in Lauralee's face. "See? I'm supposed to leave the day after tomorrow!"

Lauralee accepted the letter—indeed, as Clarie had said, a railroad ticket was enclosed, along with a bank draft for a respectable sum of money. "You'll be on your train, Clarie," she promised as she began to read.

Louise Maitland's handwriting was loopy and difficult to read, but the message came through with a touching clarity. She loved her daughter, this woman, there was no doubting that. She wrote about her marriage to a Mr. Paul Maitland, a mining engineer, and about their white frame house, where a room had already been set aside for Clarie.

"I don't like the idea of your traveling so far alone," Lauralee mused after finishing the letter, folding it carefully, and handing it back to Clarie. "Perhaps someone could go along as a companion. Maybe Jenny would like—"

"I don't want Jenny going!" Clarie burst out with such spirit that Lauralee jumped in her chair. "I don't want her anywhere around, do you hear me?"

Lauralee sighed. "So it was Jenny you were trying to tell me about last night. Clarie, did you see your father with Jenny?"

Clarie swallowed visibly and nodded. "She used to take him water when he was working in the orchards, remember? And they'd kiss sometimes, right here in this kitchen, when they thought nobody was around. Once, I came inside in the middle of the day, because you'd sent me back to fetch your sunbonnet, and I heard a funny sound. I thought somebody was hurting Jenny, the way she was carrying on, so I went upstairs to help her. I walked real quiet, so maybe I could get the jump on whoever was after her, and they were in y—your room, Lauralee, on the bed."

Lauralee closed her eyes. "Oh Lord," she breathed. "Clarie, I'm so sorry."

"I didn't plan to ever tell you," Clarie said. "Papa said he'd beat me to within an inch of my life if I did, and I believe he meant it."

Lauralee took Clarie's hands in hers and squeezed them. She would think of Jenny's duplicity later, deal with it when they met again, and Virgil's betrayal, being only one of many, had no real sting. "They surely had me fooled, but I don't want you to be worrying about it anymore. It just doesn't matter. I have Jay now."

"Jenny told me she could get Jay just like she got Papa," Clarie whispered.

Now Lauralee was angry. A heated flush flowed up over her breasts and into her face. "Did she, now? Well, that young lady and I will have a few things to talk about when we meet again, won't we?"

Mr. Neggers dashed comically through the kitchen just then, and outside to his wagon. His haste made both Clarie and Lauralee laugh, and the unpleasant moments were past. The peddler dashed through again, seconds later, carrying two large display cases.

"What do you suppose they're up to?" Lauralee speculated as their boarder disappeared into the spare room again.

"Could be anything," Clarie answered, cupping her chin in her hands and settling herself to dream about Denver and her mother, about schools and pretty dresses and new friends.

Lauralee left her to that.

At ten o'clock, the foreman of one of Adrienne's lumber crews appeared at the door, handing over the papers concerning the timber rights to Lauralee's property, along with a bank draft and a sealed note from his employer.

"We'll be about the sawin' now, ma'am," he said. "Starting near the river, if you don't mind."

Lauralee had been staring at the bank draft, dreaming a few dreams of her own. Even after she had paid up her loan at the bank in town, there would still be money left over. She looked up at the grizzled foreman with distracted eyes.

"What about Papa's grave?" Clarie asked cautiously from behind her.

Lauralee was shamed. She had not even thought about the tree-lined knoll where Virgil was buried. How could she not have considered that? "There—there is a grave," she said evenly. "On that knoll above the river—"

"Won't fell no trees on a grave, ma'am," the foreman assured her gruffly. "Don't you worry about that."

Lauralee knew she could believe the man's promise, and she was relieved. "Thank you. I—I guess it's all right for you to set to work then if you're ready."

The sawyer tipped his hat and strode away, a tall man, sturdy as the trees he felled, clad in homespun trousers, oiled boots, and a plaid shirt that left a pungent pine-tobacco-sweat smell lingering behind.

Lauralee closed the door, went to the table, and sat down. It was several minutes before she opened Adrienne's message. "Lauralee dear," she had written, somehow managing to be as cloying on paper as she was in person. "I hope the papers and the bank draft are in proper order. And I'm afraid I can't accompany Jay on his journey upriver, though he is, of course, welcome to the use of my vessel. I wish you all the best. Adrienne."

Pensively, Lauralee reread the note, wondering what could possibly have prevented Adrienne from traveling with Jay. Could it involve Pete Townsend's intention to question Adrienne about the night Virgil had been murdered? Surely, on the word of an itinerant gambler, he wouldn't actually suspect Adrienne . . .

"Lauralee!" The shout, coming from the spare room, was a good-natured, if impatient, one.

She met and passed a pleased Mr. Neggers in the parlor.

"Yes?" she asked, reaching the spare room. Jay had just finished shaving himself, and his dark hair was brushed, but it was his smile that pleased her most.

"Come here." Jay patted the covers beside him. "I have something for you."

Lauralee went to the bed, sat down carefully and just a bit primly, in case he had any untoward ideas brewing behind those mischievous gray eyes. "What?" she asked.

His left hand was in a loose fist; he held it out to her and opened his fingers to reveal a golden wedding band. "Until I can buy you a real ring, will you wear this?"

Lauralee was overcome. As far as she was concerned, this *was* a real ring. Real enough to assure her and the rest of the world that Jay McCallum had indeed married her. Her hand trembled a bit as Jay took it and slid the band onto the proper finger.

There were, as it turned out, more presents. Jay had them all hidden beneath his covers, some of them in places where it was not quite proper to reach. He had bought Lauralee French perfume, a set of tortoiseshell combs for her hair, a leather-bound book of days, a gaily painted tin of chocolates.

She stared at him in amazement. Never, even on Christmas, had she received so many things. "Why—"

Jay laughed and touched her nose with one index finger. "Don't look so wonderstruck. When we finally get out of this place, Lauralee, I mean to buy you the world."

Lauralee's treasures were all in her lap, in a colorful little mound. It seemed to her that he had already given her the world, even without these lovely gifts and the gold ring. She tried to speak and couldn't, not even to say thank you.

"Spoiling you is going to be a hell of a lot of fun," he said tenderly.

Lauralee found her voice, though it did come out as a croaking sound at first, when she tried to thank him.

Did he know that she was thanking him for far more than chocolates and combs, journals and perfume and gold wedding bands?

He kissed her.

It was all Lauralee could do not to cry. She sniffled and made herself show him the note from Adrienne, the papers concerning the timber rights—these he read with the concentration and skeptical arch of an eyebrow one would expect of a lawyer—and the bank draft.

"We don't have to take the stagecoach, at least," Lauralee said brightly when he had read everything. She drew a deep breath and presented Clarie's letter, the railroad ticket and bank draft still inside, and waited while Jay scanned the contents.

"I don't like the idea of her riding all the way to Denver by herself," he said flatly when he'd handed the letter back. "She's so young, and a lot of things can happen—"

"I know, but she's dying to go, Jay. She's been waiting so long." Lauralee's throat tightened; she was going to miss Clarie so much, and Alexander was going to be bereft without her.

"We'll send someone along to act as a companion. Jenny French is probably getting in the way over at Brice's—"

Lauralee thought of all she'd done for Jenny, and was stung. "Not Jenny. It has to be someone else." At Jay's curious look, Lauralee explained, relating what Clarie had told her earlier.

When she had finished, Jay drew her close and held her. "If it's any comfort, my love, you have my promise that I'll never betray you. Not for any reason."

Lauralee permitted herself a few tears and then recovered herself. "Jay, are we coming back here? Ever?"

Jay sighed, watching her. What Lauralee wanted mattered to him; she saw that and loved him the more for caring about things that simply did not concern the average husband. "Do you want to come back, Lauralee?"

"Joe Little Eagle offered to buy back the property, Jay." Lauralee's hands were knotted in her lap, resting upon her treasures.

"Do you want to sell?"

Lauralee sighed. "I don't know."

"Then don't do it. Not until you're ready. For now, we'll just take things a minute at a time." He sighed, as Lauralee had, and his eyes were haunted. Distant. "I've got to go to Brice. It isn't going to be easy, Lauralee. If you want to stay in Spokane with Alexander, I'll understand."

Lauralee lifted her hands to his freshly shaven face and caressed him. "I'll put Clarie on the train and Alexander can stay in Spokane, but I'm going with you."

Jay looked so grateful, so relieved, that Lauralee came near to weeping again. "Thank you," he said.

The rest of the morning was busy. There were trunks and satchels to pack, instructions to be left with Joe, and Mr. Neggers needed a warm meal before he set out with his team and wagon on his selling rounds.

In the end, he took them all, Lauralee and Jay, Clarie and Alexander, to town. Lauralee, who had been sitting in the back of the cluttered vehicle with her husband, climbed out with as much decorum as she could manage, marched into the bank, and paid off a mortgage she knew the banker had been hoping to foreclose on. She smiled as she left with cash in her handbag and a new entry inked into her savings book.

Getting Jay aboard Adrienne's boat, with his

crutches and his stiff, splinted leg, took help from Lauralee and several crewmen, but soon enough he was settled in the wheelhouse, the other three members of his family hovering over him. He was red in the face, being most self-conscious about the way his trouser leg had had to be slit to the middle of his thigh to accommodate the splint. "Good God," he finally boomed, much to the amusement of the captain, who stood at the wheel. "All of you go out on deck! You're driving me mad!"

Clarie went immediately, carrying Alexander in her arms, but Lauralee remained, though she did call out to Clarie to be careful and stay out of the crew's way.

Jay was grim with pain, his splinted leg supported by packing crates that the captain had provided. "Didn't I tell you—"

Lauralee took a laudanum bottle from her bag and held it out. "Take this," she ordered. "You'll just have to do without the spoon."

Jay scowled at her, but he took the bottle, uncorked it, and took a gulp of the stuff. He usually complained of its taste, like a little boy forced to swallow tonic, but this time he made no faces, muttered no curse words. In fact, he smiled sheepishly up at Lauralee as he handed the bottle back.

"You were right," he conceded. "I couldn't have made this trip on a stagecoach."

"Of course I was right," Lauralee said, bending to kiss his forehead as she tucked the medicine bottle back into her bag. "I'm going out on deck now to check on Clarie and Alexander. You be good."

"Be good?" Jay echoed, looking angry again. "I'm not a child!"

Lauralee patted the top of his head and swept out of the wheelhouse.

*   *   *

Adrienne Burch wouldn't have admitted it, but she was very worried. She sat upright in the chair that had been her husband's favorite, but it was the memory of Virgil Parker that she drew her strength from as she faced Pete Townsend for the second time in twenty-four hours.

This time, he'd brought Will Enright, his prisoner, along with him.

Hesitantly, feeling out of place in Adrienne's parlor as well he might, the waster Enright told his story. He'd argued with Virgil in the Mud Bucket that night; he admitted that. He'd even followed him outside. And he'd seen Virgil, heard him arguing with a woman.

"What does any of this have to do with me?" Adrienne demanded afterward, just as she had the night before, when Pete had related the whole thing.

"I think you might have been the woman Virgil was—er—talking to," Pete told her. He'd said the same thing the night before, too. "Were you, Adrienne?"

"No," Adrienne replied.

"You're lying," Pete countered blandly. "You were waiting for Virgil when he came out of the saloon that night, weren't you?"

Adrienne sighed. The whole scene replayed itself in her mind; she felt the cold of the weather, the deeper cold of Virgil's response to her pleas. He wasn't going to see her anymore, he'd said. He loved Lauralee, and he'd been a fool to risk losing her.

Adrienne had wept, begged, preached, and threatened. The memory of that stole the color from her cheeks and betrayed her to Pete. "I was there," she admitted. "Virgil and I—had words." She looked directly at Pete, her gaze unwavering. "I didn't kill him. I wanted to die myself, but I didn't kill Virgil."

She could see that Pete believed her. That he pitied her. "Did you see Mr. Enright go near Virgil?"

Adrienne looked at the gambler as she spoke. "No. But I did see Tim McCallum—he was mad because Virgil planned to go back inside and get into another game. He was going to bet his land, since he was out of money."

"And then?"

Adrienne shrugged, though she felt broken on the inside. She'd cried and thrown herself into Virgil's arms and he'd thrust her away, so hard that she had fallen onto the frosty winter ground. She'd gotten up, run away, stumbling back to town in the darkness. In some ways, she'd been stumbling in that same darkness ever since. "I didn't see anyone else besides Tim. It was dark and cold and I was upset. As far as I knew, Virgil went home to his lovely, pregnant little wife."

"But you didn't see Lauralee?" Pete asked.

"No," Adrienne said. It probably would have been sweet vengeance to lie, but she couldn't. Not about something like this. Lauralee had not killed Virgil, no more than she had.

"So we're right back to nowhere," Pete sighed, discouraged. "Damnit all to hell, we're right back to nowhere."

Lauralee had packed all the gifts Jay had given her, except for the ring on her finger and the box of elegant little chocolates. This she carried in the pocket of her skirt.

She stepped out on deck, drawing in the fresh scent of pine trees reaching all the way from shore, half blinded by the glare of the sinking sun on the river. She shaded her eyes with one hand, looking for Clarie and Alexander on the port side. How they would love these chocolates, though Lauralee meant to be parsimonious in passing them out. Such things were to be savored, not gobbled.

She moved to the starboard side, saw only crewmen, then tossed a glance forward, toward the bow. Perhaps she'd missed them, in the glare—but they weren't there, either.

Exasperated, Lauralee rounded the wheelhouse, then stopped cold. The tin of chocolates clattered to the deck.

Isaiah French was standing near the aft railing, holding Alexander far out over the water while Clarie grabbed at his arm, frantically trying to catch hold of the child.

CHAPTER
NINETEEN

"Mr. French," Lauralee said with quiet firmness, lest Isaiah be startled and drop Alexander into the churning waters behind the steamer.

Slowly, the bearlike man turned, surrendering Alexander to Clarie with a gruff chuckle. The girl immediately scrambled to Lauralee's side, clutching Alexander close.

"Go inside the wheelhouse, Clarinda," Lauralee said, with a calmness that surprised her in view of the fright she'd just suffered. "Take Alexander and go inside."

Isaiah leaned back against the aft rail, his burly arms folded across his chest, a self-satisfied smirk on his face. "Reckon you thought you could hide my Jenny forever, didn't you, Missus Parker?"

Lauralee did not bother to correct him on the matter of her name. Given what Jenny had done to her, there was a part of Lauralee that would have willingly turned the girl over to her monstrous father. But that part lost out to decency. "I have no idea what you're talking about. I haven't seen Jenny in days."

"You could go to hell for lying, missus," Isaiah answered, that obnoxious smirk still twisting his features.

Lauralee squared her shoulders. "If I do go to hell, Mr. French, I'll surely see you there. I would imagine that your sins are many, and if the world's laws can't be brought to bear against you, surely God's can."

Surprisingly, Isaiah paled. Lauralee had a suspicion that she'd struck too close to the truth for Mr. French's comfort, but she didn't linger on the deck to pursue her advantage. Clarie would surely tell Jay what had happened, and Jay would feel called upon, in the way of men, to limp out here on his crutches and challenge Isaiah, who would, no doubt, best him easily.

She turned, with a swirl of her skirt, and went into the wheelhouse.

Clarie had indeed told Jay about the incident on deck, and he was furious, struggling up onto his crutches. Lauralee braced both hands against his chest to stop him.

"Let me by, Lauralee," he said coldly.

The captain interceded before Lauralee could refuse. "I'll tend to that stowaway myself," the old man muttered. "Take the wheel a moment, Mr. Mc-Callum, while I go out and give a few orders."

Jay scowled at the mischievous sparkle in Lauralee's eyes, but he did stump over and take the wheel, however grudgingly, and that left the way clear for the captain to go out on deck. He returned a few minutes later, taking over for Jay, steering the boat toward shore.

"Mr. French is disembarkin'," the grizzled old seaman announced with a twinkle in his blue eyes. "And the bilge rat who let him aboard is joinin' him."

Two splashes, audible even over the roar of the

craft's steam-powered engine, proved that the captain's orders had been carried out.

Lauralee waited a while and then went out on deck, meaning to gather her composure, but Clarie followed her, leading Alexander by the hand, and Jay made his laborious way after them.

Towering trees, rocky hillsides, and green, green meadows slipped by. The mist from the river was cool on Lauralee's face, and Alexander crooned at her side, delighted by the chocolate he was consuming so messily, but she was not really aware of any of those things. She was remembering her terror at seeing Isaiah French holding her son out over the water that way. Was the man really mean enough to drop a baby into a river?

In Colville, they left Adrienne's lumber boat, Lauralee taking the initiative this time and hiring a wagon to take them to the hotel.

The strain of the trip made deep lines in Jay's face; his jaw was set with determination as he struggled up the steps of the hotel and arranged for rooms. Getting him up the stairs, with his crutches, was an enterprise that wore Lauralee out as well.

"Why did you stop me from going after Isaiah French today?" he demanded with a raspy sigh as he sank onto the edge of the bed in the room they would share that night, setting his crutches aside with a hateful thrust of one hand.

Lauralee was trying to settle a whimpering Alexander; in the adjoining room, Clarie was settling herself with noisy delight. She sang, pleased at the glorious prospects of the days to come. She would finally be with her mother again; perhaps that would heal some of the emotional wounds she'd suffered over the past few years.

"The captain dealt with Mr. French quite ably,

didn't he?" Lauralee answered. Her head was aching and she wondered what she would say to Jenny when she saw her again, what she would do about the problems involved. She simply could not see that girl given over to her father, no matter what.

Jay hoisted his gauze-wrapped, splinted leg onto the bed, his gaze dark with biting annoyance as he did so. Lauralee felt sorry for him, knowing that he was not used to being immobilized. "I suppose you thought he'd trounce me or something," he muttered.

Lauralee smiled as Alexander toddled into the adjoining room, looking for Clarie. "Frankly, I didn't want to take the chance."

Jay grimaced as he aligned his injured limb with both hands. "Fine thing, when a man's own wife doesn't believe in him," he muttered.

"Jay McCallum, I do believe in you, and you know it! But you're in no condition to tangle with the likes of that backwoods—"

Jay reached out, pulled one of Lauralee's hands away from her hip, and drew her down to sit beside him on the bed. The look in his eyes was remarkably tender, considering his terseness a moment before. "So you love me, do you, Mrs. McCallum?"

Lauralee laughed. "Of course I love you. Why else would I put up with you?"

"Go and lock that door," he said suddenly, his voice low as he gave Lauralee a little push.

She did so, frowning, thinking that Jay was going to confide something he didn't want Clarie to hear. When she reached the bed again, though, and sat down, he immediately began unbuttoning her dress.

She moved to pull away, but Jay held her by taking a grip on the fabric of her camisole, his warm fingers touching her breasts, making the nipples leap at the contact.

301

Slowly, he drew downward on the thin camisole, baring her to long, delicious moments of perusal. Lauralee's breathing quickened and she gasped as Jay lifted a finger to one taut bud and circled it.

"Not now, Jay!" she whispered testily.

He pulled himself up onto one elbow and grinned. "Oh yes. Right now," he said, and Lauralee could feel his breath on her breast.

Without meaning to at all, she put one hand to the back of his head and pressed him closer. When his mouth closed over her, she moaned and tangled her fingers in his hair. Her head dropped back as he fed greedily, the ceiling blurred above her.

When Jay had finished nursing at that breast, he turned to the other. Lauralee whimpered, helpless in her own pleasure.

Finally, he urged her to stand and she did, stumbling a bit, dazed. Jay sat up, with rather a lot of difficulty, and positioned Lauralee squarely between his legs by grasping her hips in his hands. Reaching up then, he removed her dress, dropping it in a colorful pool at her feet, and untied the ribbons that held her drawers in place. She trembled as he slid them down over her hips and thighs and her knees.

For a long time, Jay stroked her with his hands, delighting in each pleasured ripple that coursed along her bared flesh. He squeezed her plump bottom and weighed each well-suckled breast in his hands, and then he parted her secret place to sample a forbidden sweetness.

Lauralee clapped one hand over her mouth to stifle a wail of delight and clasped Jay's shoulder with the other, to keep from falling. He chuckled and made a sling for her by knitting the fingers of both hands together at the small of his back. She rested against

302

those hands, a certain molten contentment raging through her as the trembling began.

When it was over, Lauralee sank, shuddering, to her knees. After several minutes spent struggling to catch her breath, she took her revenge.

In the aftermath, they slept, stretched out on the narrow hotel bed.

Lauralee dreamed. She was at home, in the cellar, kneeling on the dank earthen floor. The crock of water glass was before her and she was about to reach into it, the sleeve of her dress rolled high enough that it constricted her upper arm. Though she knew she was dreaming, that she was in truth lying beside Jay on a hotel bed in Colville, Lauralee felt squeamish.

She removed the crock's heavy, cracked lid and reached inside, searching for something with her hand. When she pulled it out, her arm was dripping not with water glass, but with blood. A knife she did not remember catching hold of fell from her fingers, and she screamed.

Lauralee awakened to Jay's reasoning, insistent voice, to the strength of his hand on her shoulder. She was trembling, her body damp with perspiration from head to foot, her lungs and throat burning as she gasped for breath.

Jay did not demand to know what she had been dreaming about; he simply held Lauralee close to him, assuring her that everything was all right, that he was there with her. She allowed him to settle her to a degree, but then the terror possessed her again and she bolted from the bed and from his arms, her heart pounding in her throat.

She wrenched open the door between their room and the one Alexander and Clarie were sharing, saw that both children were sleeping peacefully, snuggled together. Feeling foolish and wholly undone, Lauralee quietly closed the door and turned back to Jay.

"I—I was afraid I'd awakened them. . . ."

Jay obviously knew the lie for what it was, but he did not challenge Lauralee. He simply sighed deeply, gave her a look that seemed to reach inside her very soul, and then closed his eyes again.

Lauralee could not go back to sleep, knew that it would be fruitless even to try. She paced, waiting for everyone to awaken again. When they did, the rooms were in an uproar; everyone had to wash and groom themselves, and getting Jay down the stairs was every bit as difficult as getting him up them had been, but Lauralee welcomed the distraction.

All evening—they had dinner in the hotel dining room and then attended an amateur performance of *Ten Nights in a Bar-Room* at the public hall across the street—the dream skulked two steps behind Lauralee, waiting for her to lie down and close her eyes and permit it to attack her mind again.

Clarie was sniffling with emotion as they all trooped up the hotel stairs again; she had been deeply moved by the play. "When that little girl begged her daddy to come home from the saloon and he—"

"Sentimental claptrap!" growled Jay, obviously exhausted.

Lauralee held on to his arm, urging him gently up the stairs, wishing she could suffer the pain and the indignities of his injury for him. He hated going around with one leg of his trousers slit open, hated the looks of curious sympathy strangers invariably threw his way, hated the splints and the crutches and the struggle required to achieve the simplest task. While he often became quietly irascible, Jay never complained, and Lauralee loved him all the more deeply for that.

"We shouldn't have gone to the play," she said

when they were alone in their room again, Clarie and Alexander both washed and tucked safely into bed. "I'm sorry, Jay."

He set aside his crutches and submitted in patience as Lauralee undressed him, removing his suitcoat and his shirt and tie, his one boot, his odd-looking trousers. She took a roll of clean gauze from his satchel, along with a small pair of scissors, and began cutting away the old wrapping that had been grayed by the rigors of the day.

The stitches Doc Jameson had taken in his shin, after putting the protruding bone back into place, made ugly black lines on his flesh, but there was no sign of infection. Gratefully, Lauralee swabbed the area with a carbolic acid solution and checked the wooden splints to make certain that they hadn't slipped out of place. They were still bound tightly with bits of leather cording.

Lauralee was rewrapping Jay's leg with fresh gauze before he made any reply to her earlier comment.

"*Ten Nights in a Bar-Room* is a favorite with temperance people," he ventured, referring to the overly sentimental, message-burdened play they had just seen. "I expected you to be in a state of righteous wrath, to say the very least."

Lauralee smiled at him as she set the scissors aside and tied the gauze in place. "Did you?" she asked lightly.

"I was sure you'd want to rally the troops and raid at least one den of iniquity."

Lauralee chuckled. "In my hurry, I neglected to pack my hatchet," she said.

Jay caught her hand in his own and pulled her down to sit beside him. "You've changed," he said, caressing her fingers with an idle thumb.

She sighed. "I used to think I couldn't rest until

305

every saloon in the country was closed," she confided.

"And now?"

"Now I've come to accept the fact that I can't force other people to abide by my principles. I still believe that liquor destroys people, though, and I still hate it."

Jay lifted his hand, hers still caught inside it, and traced the length of her neck with a gentle index finger. "I've found that just keeping my own life in order takes all I've got. Who has time to whip the rest of the world into shape?"

Lauralee made no answer. She bent and kissed Jay McCallum square on the mouth and after that there was no more philosophy and no more jaded world in need of change: there were only the two of them.

The train ride was not as miserable as Lauralee had expected. Jay was making a valiant effort to keep his discomfort to himself, his fine head bent over the book about sign language, his hands practicing the gestures as he read.

Clarie and Alexander were delighted, gazing out the windows as if they were afraid of missing so much as a twig of the passing countryside. Wheat grew all around Spokane, and it seemed to wave at the children inside the noisy train. Because they were children, they waved back.

It was mid-afternoon when they arrived in Spokane, where whistles blew and bells clanged and wagons and carriages jolted past. Clarie was agape, staring this way and that, frantic to see and hear everything.

Since no one had sent word to Spokane that the McCallums were arriving, the family carriage was not in evidence. Jay hired one and, with the help of the driver, managed to climb inside, after Lauralee and Clarie and Alexander.

Clarie stared out the window, amazed, while Alexander tumbled into a fitful sleep on her lap. She held him with such tender deftness that Lauralee hurt to think of the parting that would soon come. How on earth was she going to make Alexander understand why Clarie had left him?

Lauralee did what she could to make Jay comfortable, though comfort in such a small space was an impossibility under the circumstances, and tried not to think about Clarie's leaving or the problems and grief awaiting them on Brice McCallum's farm. Everything would come right in time, she told herself. She'd look back on this one day soon and smile.

Reaching the massive house was a comfort to Lauralee, partly because she knew that the elder Mrs. McCallum would not be there. The servants treated Jay's wife with pleased deference, hastening to settle Alexander in a room of his own and help Clarie prepare for the longest part of her journey.

Lauralee had expected Jay to find a bed, perhaps on the first floor, and collapse in a stupor of exhaustion. Instead, he went directly to the telephone affixed to the wall in the downstairs hallway.

Lauralee watched in blatant fascination as he turned the handle, causing the polished silver bells on the front of the telephone to clamor softly. "Hello, Central?" he demanded, and Lauralee's eyes widened. The evidence was there, before her, and yet she found it almost impossible to grasp that someone at the other end of a tangle of wires could hear his voice and respond. "Give me Temple 4432," he added brusquely after a short, impatient silence.

Lauralee held her breath; Jay turned away from the jutting, hornlike mouthpiece and grinned at her. She blushed, feeling very much the country bumpkin and yet unable to look elsewhere and pretend disinterest.

"I'm calling my secretary," Jay explained as an aside. "Helene, this is Mr. McCallum. Yes, Jay. How are you?" There was a pause, and then Lauralee could hear a strident sort of chatter coming from the machine, through the earpiece, along with a crackling sound. "Yes," Jay went on presently. "I was sorry to have to change my plans. I'll see Brice tomorrow sometime—yes, I'll be sure to give him your condolences." He stopped, patiently listened, then spoke again. "Helene, my wife and I are in need of a companion for a young lady. The job will entail traveling to Denver by train. I want someone reputable, Helene, and I'll pay well. All expenses included, of course. Thank you—that would be wonderful. Good-bye, Helene."

With that, Jay rang off, a mischievous gleam in his eyes. Lauralee was dying to telephone someone, and he knew it.

He showed her how to ring Central, and she was spellbound to hear an answering voice coming over the wire. She could not think of anyone to ask for, and her cheeks flared with color.

"Ask for the public library," Jay prompted in an amused whisper.

"The public library, please," Lauralee said, and her eyes went round when there was a strange sound on the wire and a human voice said, "Public Library. May I help you?"

Stricken, Lauralee hastened to hang the earphone on its hook at the side of the wooden telephone. "Thunderation!" she muttered.

Jay laughed and balanced himself on one crutch so that he could draw her near. "Never fear, my love," he said into her hair. "Soon enough, you'll be chattering on that contraption day and night. Did you know that all the department stores downtown deliver?"

Lauralee gave him a slight push, not hard enough to risk hurting his injured leg, and then buried her face in his shoulder. But she couldn't resist asking, her voice muffled by the fabric of his suitcoat, "Just because I telephoned, they would bring things to me?"

Jay chuckled, holding her near. "Yes."

Lauralee looked up at him. "How are we going to find a companion in time? Clarie's train leaves tonight."

"We'll find one, Lauralee. If you're not too tired, why don't you take Clarie downtown and buy her some new clothes for the trip?"

Tears of happiness burned in Lauralee's eyes. "You are a most thoughtful man, and I love you, Jay McCallum."

He swatted her bottom with one hand and favored her with a waggish grin. "I'm glad to hear that—naturally, you won't mind affording me the same wifely comforts you favored me with last night."

Lauralee turned crimson, but her smile wouldn't leave her face no matter how she tried to displace it and scowl instead. "Jay!" she gasped, and when he gestured toward the study where she had given herself to him so wantonly the night they were married, she hastened toward it.

More than an hour later, when the first candidates for the companion position began to arrive, sent by an employment agency, Jay was still grinning insufferably. Lauralee wanted to break his good leg.

They interviewed four people, and the last, one Edna Kaminsky, was the one they selected. She was a widow and she not only had references, she had a daughter in a small town near Denver. She could see Clarie safely to Louise's house, make certain that everything was on what she called the up-and-up there, and then go on to enjoy a good long visit with her own dear Capitola.

Lauralee hid her smile. Capitola? she mouthed to

Jay when Mrs. Kaminsky went to examine a potted fern in a far corner of the parlor.

Jay cleared his throat, perhaps trying not to laugh. "What do you think, Mrs. McCallum?" he asked in a whisper. "Will she do?"

Lauralee liked Mrs. Kaminsky even though she had had the bad taste to name an innocent child Capitola. "Oh yes, I think she will."

With that, Mrs. Kaminsky was hired and went hurriedly home to pack her things.

"Why did you have to grin like that the whole time?" Lauralee hissed, embarrassed again. "Anyone would have thought—"

"That I had just been pleasured by my wife," Jay finished for her, laughing at the flush that rose in her face. Almost instantly, he sobered, pulled her close with a roughness that held a touch of desperation.

Lauralee didn't have to ask about the change in his manner; she knew that he was thinking of his brother Brice. "Shhh," she whispered, her fingers gentle in his hair where it curled over the back of his collar. "I'm here."

Jay shuddered in her arms. "My God, Lauralee, what am I going to say to him?"

"You don't need to say anything to Brice. Just be there, just be his brother."

It was time to take Clarie shopping if she was to have some new clothes before the train left, but it was with the greatest reluctance that Lauralee left Jay.

Clarie was wide-eyed at the array of clothing offered in Filbert's Department Store, and so was Lauralee. There were crowds of women gathered around heaping merchandise tables, and little bells rang everywhere while thin cables snaked down from the railed mezzanine. Attached to these cables were small baskets, into which the money from each transaction was carefully placed, and by a pulley system, the baskets were carried upstairs. Moments later, they came careening back down again, containing the proper change.

"Thunderation," Clarie whispered.

"Yes, indeed," agreed Lauralee.

Clarie's eyes were still following the baskets. "Don't they trust the salesladies to make the right change?" she wanted to know.

Lauralee had no answer for that question, so she shrugged and took a deep breath and turned to examine the overwhelming selection of clothing available for purchase.

Clarie had never in her life been on such a spree and seeing her delight at choosing new things eased the ache in Lauralee's heart. It wouldn't be long now, only a few hours, and Clarie would be on her way to Denver. It might be a long time before Lauralee saw her again.

It might be forever.

Tears filled Lauralee's eyes, and she examined the hem of a pink sateen party dress in order to hide them.

Clarie had seen, however, and she caught Lauralee's arm in her hand. "I'll stay if you want me to, Lauralee."

Lauralee took herself in hand and worked up a bright smile. "Why don't you try on this pink sateen? You'd look lovely in it."

Clarie's lower lip was trembling and her eyes were as bright as Lauralee's. "I love you very much, Lauralee," she said softly. "Some women would have been mean, but you were always nice to me. You made me feel like I had as much right to live in your house as Alexander."

Lauralee hugged the girl close for a moment, and

then they finished their shopping and took the waiting carriage back to the enormous house on the hill.

Jay was there and so was Mrs. Kaminsky, who was promptly introduced to Clarie. Instead of being cool to the woman, as Lauralee half expected she would, Clarie seemed relieved that she wouldn't have to make the long trip to Denver alone. Or with Jenny French.

The parting was not an easy one, for Lauralee had come to love Clarie as her own child, and seeing her step onto the train was an emotional wrench she would never forget. It didn't help when Alexander started squirming in Jay's arms and howling Clarie's name as the train pulled out.

Discreetly, Jay ushered his unhappy family into a noisy dining room at the far end of the terminal and settled them at a table. A sympathetic waitress arrived straightaway, beaming on a beleaguered Jay.

"Partin's is hard, ain't they?" she commiserated. "Seems a body's always sayin' good-bye to some'un."

Alexander had recovered himself—his eyes were wide as he took in the peculiarities of a public dining hall—but Lauralee was still sniffling.

"Partin's is hard indeed," Jay remarked in a distant voice, and Lauralee knew that he was thinking of Brice and his lost Lucy.

Immediately, she sat up a little straighter and dried her eyes.

CHAPTER
TWENTY

Mary Cornell stood in the parlor doorway, her eyes dry and burning, like her throat. She had been in this house three full days now, arriving too late to bid her sister farewell or even to attend her funeral, and in those three days Brice McCallum had hardly moved from his chair in the center of this room, except to refill his glass at the liquor table and attend to those physiological necessities that could not be avoided.

He was unshaven and ill-groomed, Brice was, his chestnut hair mussed, his blue eyes rimmed with red, his clothes hopelessly rumpled. Worse still, he smelled.

Lucy would be heartsick if she could see him now. Gone was the strong, self-reliant Brice she had written of in so many proud letters.

A small, dark-haired woman with short curls springing around her face and large brown eyes, Mary drew a deep breath and pushed her shoulders back. "Brice McCallum," she said evenly, bravely, "you stink. Take a bath."

Brice lifted his glass in one hand and took a deep, defiant draught. "I'll tell you the same thing I told

Chance, woman," he replied, his voice thick and raspy. "Mind your own damn business. I didn't ask you to come here and fawn over me!"

"No," answered Mary, her chin rising. "You didn' ask me to come. It was Lucy who did that."

He flinched at the name, reeling under it as though i were a blow. Then a curtain seemed to fall over hi eyes, hiding the naked misery behind a glaze of blear redness. He scowled at Mary and belched.

Mary was as stricken by the loss of Lucy as Brice was—no one in the world had been dearer to her—bu the dead were indeed dead, and the living could no bring them back by despairing and falling into persona sloth. A person had to go on whether he cared to o not, and Lucy would have been the first to say so.

"I have her letter if you'd like to see it," Mar ventured.

Brice tilted his head back and closed his eyes "Leave me be, Mary. I don't want to see any dam letter."

The words injured Mary, though she would neve have allowed Brice to guess that it was so. She won dered what he would think if he knew the whole truth that she had loved him as long and perhaps as deepl as Lucy had, that he was the reason she had neve married. And while she grieved for Lucy, would hav given her own life if that would bring her back, Mar Cornell had no intention of letting the one great love o her life wallow in self-pity until he died of it.

Oh no. She had her plans for Brice McCallum. Sh meant to rally him, marry him, and bear his children and not necessarily in that order.

"That redheaded minx is preparing water for bath," Mary said, comforted by her own resolutions "She and I will carry it in here if that's what you want but you're going to get into that tub, Brice McCallum, if I have to strip you myself!"

That outlandish statement brought Brice far enough out of himself to stare at Mary for a moment in shock. But then, as she had expected, he cloaked himself in surliness again and muttered, "I can't believe you're really a sister to my sweet, gentle Lucy. She would never have made such an indecent remark."

"Indecent or not, Mr. McCallum, I won't have you smelling up this lovely house with your sweat and your liquor. Will you fetch the bathtub from the back pantry, or must I do it myself?"

"Do what you like, you scrawny little autocrat. I don't give a tinker's damn!"

He didn't, and Mary knew that, but she also knew that time had a way of changing a man's attitudes. She turned and marched through the house to the little room behind the kitchen, wrestling the heavy bathtub down from its peg on the wall.

Jenny French sat at the table, gazing off into the hinterlands with a moony expression on her face. Mary hardly knew the girl, and yet something made her want to slap the creature every time she laid eyes on her. She couldn't remember ever taking such an instant and intense dislike to anyone.

"I thought I asked you to put water on to heat," Mary said in measured tones.

Jenny sighed, but her eyes flashed with defiance when they met Mary's gaze. "You're not the mistress of this house," she said.

"Neither are you," Mary pointed out, dragging the tub across the room with an attendant screech that was meant to annoy. "So get off your backside and heat that water."

*   *   *

315

Jay had hired a buggy in town, and using Lauralee's loss of both his horse and her own rig as an excuse for questioning her competence as a driver, he refused to let her drive. This, despite the fact that he was exhausted by the short train ride and in a great deal of pain besides.

Now, as they approached Brice's farm, he was brooding about all that lay ahead.

They turned onto a long, rutted road that wound through acre upon acre of thriving wheat, a water tower and a tall windmill visible in the distance, along with a gracious country house. Aware that Jay was dreading their arrival even as he tried to hurry it, Lauralee was sympathetic.

She patted his knee. "I'm afraid I don't remember much about Brice," she said after a diplomatic clearing of her throat. "I was in a state over Alexander the day I met him. Tell me about your brother, Jay."

After an inner struggle of some sort, Jay glanced at Lauralee and answered somewhat grudgingly, "Brice's workers call him Big Mister, and the name fits. He's intelligent and honorable, and he works as hard or harder than anyone he's ever hired. He has degrees in law and agriculture, but for all his genius, he's naive."

"Naive?"

The wheels of the buggy struck a bump in the road, and the vehicle lurched behind its plodding horse. Jay grimaced in pain, one hand leaving the reins to grope for his splinted leg and then draw back again. "Brice has always believed that things work out for the best."

Lauralee was uneasy. "Don't they?"

"Not necessarily," Jay replied, and that was the end of their conversation.

Moments later, they were drawing to a stop in front of Brice's quietly magnificent house. It was built of red

316

brick, a sprawling place, and its many windows glistened in the afternoon sun. There were flowers growing along the limestone walk, and they conveyed something of Lucy McCallum, a quiet love of beauty and simplicity. Lauralee felt the loss of the woman she had never met as keenly as if they'd been the best of friends.

His jaw set with determination, eyes dark with pain, Jay secured the buggy and got down without waiting for help. Inside the house, a man's voice bellowed curse words that could peel the paint off a barn at fifty paces.

Lauralee was unnerved, but incredibly, Jay allowed himself a grim smile. "At least he's alive," he muttered, extending one hand to his wife and taking her elbow. "Come on. I promise not to let the ogre get you."

The bellowing continued as they made their way up the steps, a slow process because of Jay's crutches. The door was slightly ajar and Jay went in without bothering to knock.

Lauralee was left with no choice but to follow and hope for the best.

"Damn you, woman," roared the monster, from some nearby room. "I can unbutton my own pants!"

Lauralee, not normally prudish, blanched and came to an abrupt halt in the entryway, her eyes rounded. Jay proceeded through an arched doorway to the left, crutches making a bumping sound on the shiny oak floors. "Hello, Brice," he said, as though such carryings-on were entirely normal.

"First Chance, then this infernal woman, and now you!" was the uncordial response. "Good God, can't you people leave a man to mourn in peace?!"

"I'm delighted to see you, too," Jay answered as a diminutive woman with dark, cropped hair dashed into

317

the entryway, the skirt and bodice of her dress soaked
with water.

Harried brown eyes touched on Lauralee and registered a look of relief. "I'll vow that man was schooled
at the devil's knee," she confided in an irritated hiss,
and since she stomped off toward the rear of the
house, Lauralee followed after.

"My name is Mary Cornell," she announced when
they reached the kitchen, leaning back against a
counter and folding her arms across her chest. Mary's
eyes were pert and mischievous, and there was a
slightly nasal quality to her voice that was appealing.
Lauralee liked the woman immediately.

"Lauralee McCallum," she responded, sinking into
a chair at the table without waiting for an invitation. It
had been a long, hard day, and it wasn't over.

Mary stoked up the fire and set a kettle on to boil. "I
was trying to give Brice a bath," she announced
bluntly as she strained to reach a tea tin on a high
shelf.

Lauralee blushed, not quite understanding the situation and not certain that she even wished to understand it. "Oh," she said.

Mary smiled and her gaminelike face did not look so
woebegone. "Brice wouldn't bathe himself, you
know, and he smells like a pig farmer, so I had to take
matters into my own hands, right there in the parlor. I
had almost everything off him by the time you arrived."

Lauralee was glad she didn't have her tea yet, for
she would surely have choked on it. "I see," she said,
to fill the silence.

"Lucy was my sister," Mary imparted next, being,
Lauralee decided, one of those people who careen
recklessly from one subject to another. "I promised

318

her, God rest her soul, that I would take care of Brice, and I mean to do it, so help me. Even if it means—"

Lauralee couldn't help smiling. "Bathing him in the parlor?"

Mary nodded, her eyes bright despite a grief so deep that Lauralee could feel it.

In the distance, a masculine shouting match began, underscored by the sound of wild splashing. Lauralee listened with half an ear, wondering who was bathing whom, and could make out only the occasional word. Most of those would have been better left to obscurity.

"Your husband must be Brice's brother Jay," guessed Mary. "Lucy liked him. What happened to his leg?"

Mary was careening again, but now Lauralee was used to it. "He fell from a roof," she answered, neglecting to mention that the man had risked life and limb for a sign that said RUMSUCKER SALOON.

When the tea was ready, Mary brought it to the table, along with cups and saucers, and then sat down to wholly ignore it, her chip cupped in one hand. She bit her lower lip, listening to the ongoing ruckus in the other room.

"Do you think we dare go in there and find out what's happening?" Her rich brown eyes were wide and quite worried looking.

"Absolutely not," replied Lauralee with conviction.

Mary bit her lower lip, obviously wishing the counsel had been otherwise. When they'd each had a cup of tea, she showed Lauralee to a spacious bedroom on the first floor. Together, the two women put fresh linens and blankets on the bed.

She chattered, did Mary, as she set the room swiftly to rights, opening the window that looked out on a daunting amount of thriving wheat, carrying in a pitcher of fresh water for the washstand, directing the two young boys who had fetched what baggage Jay and Lauralee had brought from the buggy. For all her busywork and her bright attitude, Lauralee knew that Mary was grieving sorely for her sister.

She wasn't really surprised when Mary's lively face suddenly crumpled and she sat down on the edge of the bed and wept into her hands. "I promised Lucy I would look after Brice," she sobbed. "I promised, but the man is determined to perish. . . ."

Lauralee sat down beside Mary and put one arm around her shuddering shoulders. "He's mourning, Mary. That takes time."

Mary sniffled, drying her eyes as best she could with the back of her hands. "I know. I guess I'm just impatient because—because I've always loved Brice McCallum. He was Lucy's beau, and then he was Lucy's husband, but I loved him." Wounded brown eyes searched Lauralee's face for shock or revulsion and found understanding instead. "Lucy knew that I loved Brice. That's why she made me promise long ago that I'd take care of him if anything ever happened to her. I tried not to love him. 'He's your own dear sister's husband, Mary Cornell,' I said to myself, but nothing changed what I felt, so I didn't dare visit. . . ."

Lauralee hugged Mary, smiling through a mist of sympathetic tears. On the other side of his sorrow, Brice would have love waiting for him, and that was something to be grateful for. She just hoped he would have the sense to notice. "It's work, loving the McCallum men," she said, thinking of her own experiences and Kate's. "Though I do believe it's worth the time and trouble. Did you meet Chance and Kate before they left for Washington?"

Mary nodded, her eyes sparkling. "There's a tempest brewing in that teapot!" she said. "But I think they love each other."

"They do."

Mary was frowning again. "I just wish they hadn't left that strumpet here—Jenny French, her name is. She fancies herself the future mistress of this house, I suspect."

The reminder of Jenny was discomforting. Given her new understanding of the girl's nature, Lauralee could well imagine that she might have set her cap for Brice McCallum. "Don't be worrying about Jenny French, Mary. I'll see to her."

"I guess I'm no better, making my plans to marry Brice, but I truly do love him." Having made this statement, Mary went on to outline her plans, which made Lauralee laugh.

Just as her new friend left the room, Jay came *thump-thump*ing down the hallway and into the bedroom, looking exasperated. He was quite as wet as Mary had been earlier, and not nearly so sporting.

"Did Brice get his bath?" Lauralee teased, sitting primly on the edge of the bed, her hands folded in her lap.

Jay looked down at his sodden clothes and grinned ruefully. "Yes, and indirectly, I've had mine, too." When Jay met Lauralee's eyes, she saw within him a tired and distraught little boy. "Brice is in bad shape," he blurted. "And I don't know how to help him."

Lauralee stood up, went to Jay, and ushered him to the bed. She took away his crutches, removed his coat, and settled him with tender efficiency, plumping the pillows beneath his head, covering him with a bright blue and white blanket. "Maybe just being here is helping," she said, bending to kiss her husband's furrowed forehead.

"Or hindering," Jay replied, but his eyes closed, and worn out, he fell asleep almost immediately.

Lauralee kissed him once more and then crept out of the room, easing the door closed behind her. Mary was not in the kitchen, but Lauralee felt no need for company anyway. She opened the screened door and went outside.

Here, as in the front yard, there were flowers. Someone—probably Lucy—had planted them in carefully planned designs. There were beds of tiger lilies that formed star shapes, mums that grew in a wagonwheel pattern, and a row of zinnias and irises set out in such a way that they gave the impression of a colorful braid. The wheat was visible in every direction as far as the eye could see, and even though she was a farmer herself, the sight of it, surrounding her that way, made Lauralee vaguely uncomfortable.

A young girl came toward the house, from the direction of the barn, carrying a bucket of milk in each hand. "Are you some of Big Mister's kin?" she asked forthrightly, pausing to assess Lauralee's fine clothes.

Thinking of all the times she'd carried milk buckets herself, Lauralee smiled. "Yes," she answered. "My husband is Mr. McCallum's brother."

"You'd like to see the grave then, I suppose," answered the girl, setting the buckets down on the back step. "It's 'round that way," she said, pointing.

Lauralee followed the gesture and, after rounding the corner of the house, saw a single willow tree growing beside a small pond. Ducks squawked and splashed on the clear water and somehow their cacophony deepened the peace, rather than spoiling it.

There was no stone to mark Lucy's grave, only a rough-hewn wooden cross. Lauralee touched the cross and felt sad for Lucy, sad for Mary, and saddest of all for Brice.

She sat down in the cool, shaded grass and folded her hands in her lap. Some time had passed when a masculine voice startled Lauralee with a gruff and touchingly bewildered, "I sent for a stone. It's an angel, carved in marble."

Lauralee lifted her eyes to Brice McCallum's handsome, ravaged face and her heart was broken in that instant. She groped for something to say that would ease his dreadful pain.

Brice squatted down on his haunches, wearing a farmer's roughspun trousers and a shirt that gaped open at the neck, and one of his big hands reached out to touch the mound of field stones that covered Lucy's resting place.

"Take Jay away from here," he said after a very long time. "There's no way he can help me."

Lauralee swallowed hard, the wind dancing blithely in her hair and in Brice's. "Jay loves you," she pointed out gently.

"I know." Ice-blue eyes met Lauralee's aquamarine ones. Somewhere within his aching soul, Brice found a fleeting smile and offered it. "He does hate those crutches, doesn't he?"

Lauralee scrounged up a smile of her own, that being the very least she could do. "Oh yes, he despises them."

Brice sighed. "Chance told me how the accident happened, but I don't remember what he said."

"Jay fell from the roof of his saloon. He was trying to get the sign to hang in our—our parlor."

There was a silence; Brice plucked a blade of grass from the loamy ground and tore it between his fingers. Clearly, he was not a man to make small talk. "Take Jay away from here, Lauralee—I can't bear having him see me like this."

Lauralee hesitated, then touched his big, gentle

hand. "I'll try, Brice, if that's what you really want. But Jay is a stubborn man and I'm not at all sure that I can sway him."

Brice rose slowly to his feet, and with remarkable grace for a man of his size. It was no wonder people called this man Big Mister, for there was a quality of quiet nobility in him that was as noticeable as his towering, muscular build. "Try. Please try," he said hoarsely, and then he was striding away, through the tall grasses, toward the fields.

Lauralee saw Jenny appear from nowhere and fall into step beside him, her head upturned, her smile visible even from a distance. Come hither, it said.

But Brice brushed Jenny away as though she were a fly and kept walking, his strides so long that she would have had to run to keep up. Face mottled, shoulders slumped, Miss Jenny French turned toward the house in defeat and saw Lauralee watching her.

She looked uncertain for a moment, as though she sensed that Lauralee knew about her trysts with Virgil, and then approached.

Lauralee stood up, straightening her skirt and dusting away bits of moss and dirt as she did so, but her eyes never left Jenny's face.

"Clarie told you," the girl guessed, and there was no emotion, remorseful or otherwise, in either her voice or her manner.

"Yes."

"Well, I guess that's that, isn't it? The truth's out in the open."

Lauralee nodded, amazed that she'd never noticed Jenny's womanly figure before or her way with men. "I thought you were my friend, Jenny. We studied together, and I helped you get that scholarship so that you could go to Normal School."

Jenny stiffened. "You didn't do so much. I had to

324

scrub floors to make up for what the scholarship didn't pay."

Lauralee was silent, and she was amazingly calm. At one time she would have killed any woman who dared to touch Virgil, but now she felt nothing but a twinge of pity.

"He loved me," Jenny spouted. "We were going away together."

"I do believe he told Adrienne Burch the same thing," Lauralee replied.

Jenny turned crimson. "Virgil was only toying with that woman."

"And what was he doing with you, Jenny? Were you his one true love, the only woman who could save him from himself?"

Jenny's florid color faded to an alarming pallor.

Lauralee saw that she'd struck very near the truth and went quietly on. "That was a line we heard once, you know, in a penny opera. Virgil knew the whole part, and he used to entertain me by reciting it. After a while, when liquor became the most important thing in his life, he not only recited those silly words, he believed them. He fancied himself a lost soul, set upon by an unkind fate."

Jenny trembled, as though she were cold, and hugged herself. "Virgil did love me," she insisted.

"Virgil didn't love anyone, Jenny. He used you, he used Adrienne, and he used me."

"I suppose you hate me now."

Lauralee shook her head. "No. But we can't be friends anymore, Jenny. I could never trust you."

Incredibly, Jenny assumed a smug look, one very reminiscent of her father. "You're worried about your new husband, aren't you, Lauralee? Well, you're right to worry, because there isn't a man on this earth that I can't bed if I set my mind to it."

Lauralee drew in a sharp breath and the heat of challenge on perhaps the most primitive level in the feminine world coursed through her. "Is that so?"

"It's so," Jenny answered blithely.

Lauralee smiled. "I invite you to try seducing Jay," she said. "But know this: Whether you succeed or fail, my dear, I'll tear your hair right out of your head."

Jenny retreated a step, no longer so sure of herself, no longer so smug. "It's Brice I want. I was sweet on Pete Townsend for a while, but he's got nothin' but a badge and a good name, and I want more. I want a place like this. I want to be a lady. You and Kate will have to be nice to me when I'm a lady. I'll be just as much a part of this family as either of you."

"Kate and I tried to help you, Jenny. We were always nice to you."

Almost feverishly, Jenny shook her head. "No. You were better, both of you. No matter how you smiled and talked nice, you were better."

Lauralee sighed. "In any case, Jenny, you'll have to leave. I want you to pack your things and say whatever farewells you think necessary, because you're not going to stay here."

"You're just being spiteful because Virgil took his comfort with me—"

Again, Lauralee sighed. In an effort to keep her composure, she closed her eyes for a moment. "I'm not about to argue with you. Suffice it to say that there is enough trouble and heartache on this farm without your adding to it."

"You expect me to go back to my pa?"

"Of course I don't. There are a thousand places you could go, and I'll see that you have the money you need."

"I'm not going anywhere!"

Lauralee advanced on Jenny, who lost courage and

stumbled backward, nearly falling into the pond. Gathering her skirt, the girl turned and raced toward the house.

For a time, Lauralee paced back and forth beside Lucy McCallum's grave, fretting and stewing. How could she have been such a fool, believing in Jenny all that time, trusting her?

After about fifteen minutes, Lauralee went inside the house again. There was water simmering on the kitchen stove, so she brewed another part of tea and sat down to wait while it steeped, filling the homey room with a comforting, spicy scent.

"It's over," she told herself in a stern whisper, "it's over now. Calm down."

The teapot rattled against Lauralee's cup when she tried to pour. She set the pot down with a thump and covered her face with both hands.

"What on earth—"

Lauralee looked up to see Mary standing on the other side of the table, looking concerned.

"Is everything all right?"

"I don't know. I may have made an utter fool of myself."

Mary sat down, poured tea for herself and Lauralee with a steady hand. "You and the young lady had a row, I take it. She looked mad enough to kill when she came through here."

After several bracing sips of tea, Lauralee confided in Mary, telling her how Jenny and Virgil had betrayed her, how she'd told Jenny she'd have to go away. All the while, and for some hours after, however, part of Mary's statement echoed in her mind.

Mad enough to kill . . .

CHAPTER
TWENTY-ONE

Adrienne was afraid.

One by one, she checked the lock of each door and each window. The house was so big, and so empty, without even Cook there to keep her company, and every shadow threatened to take solid form as man or monster.

She was being silly and fanciful, Adrienne decided. It was all this talk about Virgil's murder. Somehow, it had niggled into her mind and taken root there, like a weed. The quick, shallow meter of her breathing and the creeping sensation along her spine were the fruits that had blossomed from it.

It was very dark outside and the parlor seemed dim, no matter how many lamps were lighted. Adrienne went to the fireplace, considered making a fire on the hearth, and decided against it. The weather was still too warm, and she would swelter.

She turned away from the fireplace and a gasp caught midway between her stomach and her throat. He was there. How had he gotten into the house, a big man like him, without making a sound?

"You hid my girl away here," Isaiah French accused, his voice thick. "Where is she?"

Adrienne swallowed, too frightened to move. "I—how did you get in here?"

"Never you mind how I got in, rich lady. I want to know where my Jenny is."

Adrienne could see no reason whatsoever for keeping her silence; some instinct told her that her life was in peril, that if she did not throw meat to the lion, he would consume her. "S-she took the stagecoach to Spokane. The McCallums are looking after her. That's all I know, I swear it."

French made a hawking sound deep in his throat and spat. "I don't cotton to fancy folks interferin' in my family," he said after an unnerving interval of quiet reflection. "We got our own ways and they do us just fine."

Adrienne could only nod. The stench of liquor and foulness of every other sort was suddenly overpowering.

He took one lumbering, drunken step toward her, his big frame seeming to undulate with suppressed fury. "Everybody interferes. Everybody minds my business."

Adrienne edged backward, just one step, and felt the handle of the fireplace poker touch her upper thigh. "Mr. French, please—if you'll just go now . . ."

He spat again, and pure evil flashed from his small, squinty eyes. "All this trouble started with Virgil Parker," he said. "Afore that, folks left us alone."

Adrienne's heart wedged itself into the back of her throat and thundered there. Memories of that awful night flooded into her mind with stunning clarity, considering her situation. She hadn't seen Isaiah French outside the Mud Bucket, she'd seen only Virgil, the gambler, and Tim McCallum. But there had

329

been a subtle stench, foreign to the crisply clean air of a cold winter night.

"You were there," she said, and though Adrienne instantly regretted the words, it was too late to call them back.

"Parker deserved killin'. He had nothin' to offer my Jenny, him bein' a married man and all, but he broke her heart all the same. He made promises to her, ones he had no mind to keep."

"Dear God," Adrienne breathed. The fireplace poker seemed to burn her flesh, even through the voluminous fabric of her skirt. How could she get hold of it quickly enough to protect herself? French was too close.

"Interferin'. Everybody, interferin'."

Adrienne willed herself not to scream.

"Don't you think Virgil needed killin'? You had reason to hate him, too, Mrs. Burch. Good reason."

"Yes—yes, I had reason—"

" 'Course, if it hadn't been for you, he might have chosen my Jenny. Might have done right by her."

Panic surged up within Adrienne; she could not restrain it. "Virgil used us all! It was Lauralee he loved, the whole time—only Lauralee!"

Sheer hatred contorted French's grizzled face. "It was her that took my Jenny away. I knew it, but couldn't get nobody to listen—"

Save your own skin, counseled Adrienne's practiced survival instincts, all in chorus. "Yes! Yes, it was Lauralee's idea—the whole thing—" Adrienne's hand closed over the handle of the poker; its stand, heavy with the broom and the small brass shovel, toppled noisily to the hearth.

Adrienne's heart was beating so rapidly that the sound seemed to thud against the parlor walls. She eld the poker the way a schoolboy would hold a baseball bat, and she was ready to swing.

French laughed at what must have seemed a puny defense to him, given his great size, and took another unsteady step toward Adrienne.

She swung the poker; it made a whistling sound as it cut through the dense air and made contact with a meaty, immovable shoulder. French made a bellowing sound and lunged at her, his hands clasping her throat, squeezing.

The poker clattered to the stone hearth, and the sound reverberated through Adrienne's mind and soul as she struggled to breathe. The pain was incomprehensible, blinding.

Her knees gave way, and when they did, Isaiah French released her. Her head struck a corner of the fireplace and the pain grew worse, a white-hot light within her, illuminating everything. French cleared his throat and spat again, and she felt his spittle sliding warm and slick along the flesh of her neck like a garden slug.

Her lungs stopped, stilling the rising and falling of her chest, and she stared sightlessly at the ceiling.

Pete Townsend stacked and restacked the papers on his desk. Mostly, they represented busywork.

He sighed and turned up the lamp. The jailhouse was a lonely place, especially when there were no prisoners to jaw with, and since Halpern's Ferry was a quiet town, he seldom had company.

Leaning back in his chair, Pete cupped his hands behind his head and kicked his booted feet up onto the surface of his desk. There was no sense in hanging around here, especially now that he'd released the gambler, Will Enright, to go his way, but if there was one place lonelier than this, it was his room in the boardinghouse down the street.

Pete sighed again. He could sit here and wonder who had killed Virgil Parker as well as there, and he could wonder if that same person had done in Tim McCallum nearly a year later. Though those questions nagged him constantly, they were better than the feelings that overwhelmed him when he thought about losing Lauralee.

Losing her? Had she ever been his?

Pete shook his head in answer to his own question and just then, the door of his office squeaked open and Adrienne Burch all but fell through it.

The air was hot, dense, acrid.

Lauralee stirred in the bed beside Jay, her throat sore and burning, and opened her eyes. Smoke was curling through the open window on the far side of the room, the glass glowing with a hellish red light.

"Fire," she croaked, immobilized for a moment by her terror. When Jay only grumbled in his sleep and then coughed, she screamed the word.

Jay sat bolt upright, looked wildly around him, and his chest moved in a spasm of coughs. "My God—"

"There's a fire!" Lauralee prattled, bounding out of bed, groping for her wrapper and slippers.

Jay reached for his crutches and stumped his way to the window with surprising agility. "The wheat—good God, he's burned the wheat—"

Lauralee had developed a sense of what her husband was thinking at any given time. Now, in her haste, she knew that he believed that Brice himself had set the fire that was raging outside, but she had no time to weigh the matter one way or the other.

Bells were clanging all over the farm, and she could

near the sleepy, disbelieving shouts of the workers as
they came from their bunks to do battle against an old
and vicious enemy.

"What can I do to help?" she choked out, barely
able to breathe now for the smoke, as she struggled to
help Jay into his clothes.

"You stay here inside this house," Jay ordered
sternly, trembling in the effort to endure being dressed
when his every instinct demanded that he go to find his
brother, to stand against the fire as the other men did.
"I mean it, Lauralee. We don't know how bad this
thing is, and I don't want you out there unless it's
absolutely necessary!"

Lauralee had managed to clothe her husband after a
fashion, and she made him sit on the bed so that she
could work his boot onto his good foot. On the other,
he wore a slipperlike affair that would offer little
protection in the midst of a fire. Despairing, she nodded her promise to stay, and prayed that God would
look after them all.

Janet and Mary and a dazed-looking Jenny, the only
one fully dressed, were all in the kitchen. Mary,
obviously in charge, was pumping water onto blankets
and thrusting them at Janet, who promptly lugged the
sodden woolens to the door and passed them into the
hands of someone who waited there.

Outside, there was a great deal of shouting. Lauralee could make no sense of the words because of the
roar of the fire itself. Seeing no other way to help, she
ran back to the room she had shared with Jay and tore
the blanket from the bed.

Jenny was sitting at the kitchen table, her eyes
closed, a smudge of soot on one cheek. "It's horrible," she said. "It's like hell."

"Thank you for clearing that up," said Mary, with

brisk dislike, as she took Lauralee's blanket and
drenched it under the pump. "We were all wondering
about it!"

"H-How bad is the fire?" Lauralee ventured, her
eyes burning from the smoke. "Are we in danger?"

"The wind's moving away from the house," Janet
answered. "Long as it carries the fire that way, we're
all right."

"I tried to make him feel better," Jenny went on
witlessly, "but he wouldn't let me. . . ."

Every eye in the kitchen turned to her then. Mary
was the first to move; she stopped her pumping,
walked over to the table, and wrenched Jenny to her
feet by the hair.

"What are you talking about?"

"Mr. McC—Brice was out walking in the dark, and I
went after him. I tried to make him feel good, but he
threw me down on the ground and walked away. He
started the fire himself—I saw him!" Jenny's lower lip
jutted out as she freed her hair from Mary's knotted
fingers and squared her shoulders.

Lauralee was reflecting stupidly that Jay's guess had
been right when Mary gave a cry and whirled to run
outside, screaming Brice's name, Janet following duti-
fully after her.

"That's a bad fire out there!" observed an eager
male voice, and both Lauralee and Jenny started
turning as one to see a scrawny young man standing
just inside the door leading into the dining room, his
clothes and face covered with soot. Clearly, he wasn't
one of Brice's workers, nor was he a hand from a
neighboring farm, come to help.

"Who are you?" Lauralee found the wit to ask.

"I'm with Western Union, ma'am. Got an important
wire here for a Mrs. Lauralee McCallum—"

It was the height of idiocy. A wire in the middle of a

aging fire! Lauralee crossed the room and snatched the bit of folded yellow paper from the boy's hand.

"We deliver, no matter what," the courier said proudly, lingering in a kitchen bathed in the very light of hell.

"Thank you very much, and please go away," Lauralee replied distractedly as she unfolded the paper and tried to focus her eyes—they burned so badly that she could barely see—on the words scrawled there.

"What is it?" Jenny asked, looking curiously at the paper in Lauralee's hands.

Lauralee was still struggling to make out the message. The shouts of the firefighters, the roar of the blaze, and the slamming of the front door behind the Western Union courier all faded away as she fixed all her attention on the telegram.

Finally, she deciphered the message, and when she did, her knees buckled and she had to grope for a chair.

"My God," she breathed.

"What is it?" Jenny repeated, hovering too close.

Lauralee drew a deep, scoring breath. "The telegram is from Pete Townsend. Adrienne must have told him where to find us." The kitchen swayed and dipped around Lauralee as she tried to absorb the truth. "Y-your father has been arrested, Jenny. He's confessed to killing Virgil."

Jenny gave a strangled cry and snatched the paper from Lauralee's hands. As she read, the high color drained from her face and blue veins stood out on her hands, so tight was her grip. "Oh, God in heaven—it was him—I thought—"

An alarm having nothing to do with the fire in the wheat fields made Lauralee stand up abruptly and retreat a step. "What did you think, Jenny?" she asked in a voice that was at once soft and ragged.

"I found the knife. It was Tim's knife, and I hid it in the water glass, down in the cellar, so that nobody would find it and know why—"

"What are you talking about?" Lauralee pressed reasonably, though she had a horrible sense that she already knew. She was remembering her nightmares, remembering reaching into the water glass in the hope of finding one of Virgil's bottles and feeling something sticklike. She was remembering Jenny prattling that day, in fear of being made to go away with her father. *I'm sorry for all the bad things I did,* she'd said.

Lauralee's heart thundered in her chest as Jenny closed her fist, crumpling the message and dropping it to the floor.

"I thought it was Tim McCallum that killed Virgil," she said in a voice all the more alarming for its calm, quiet meter. "I heard them arguing. That Burch woman came, and so I hid. She was crying and making such a fool of herself, but Virgil sent her away. I couldn't hear what he said, but I know he sent her away because of me. Because we were going away together."

Lauralee lifted one hand to her throat and willed herself to stay calm. She mustn't panic. There were men everywhere; if she needed help, they'd come at a scream from the house.

Would they hear a scream from the house?

Jenny's color was vivid again, and there was a glint in her eyes as she recounted her view of the incident outside the Mud Bucket Saloon. "I was going to tell Virgil that he'd done right when I heard Mr. McCallum again. He called Virgil a no-account and Virgil said something back, and then everything was quiet. I waited for a while, and then I came around the corner of the saloon and Virgil was lying there on the ground. There was a knife in his chest. I knew Mr. McCallum

336

had killed him, so I took the knife and I ran back to your house."

As subtly as she could, Lauralee looked around the kitchen for something to defend herself with should the need arise. "Why did you want the knife, Jenny?" she asked calmly, as though they were discussing a troublesome needlework pattern instead of a murder.

"Don't you see, Lauralee? He who lives by the sword dies by the sword. Tim McCallum had done murder, and he had to die by the same knife he killed Virgil with."

Lauralee kept herself still. Quiet. It was crucial that she keep her head. "I understand," she lied. "You hid the knife in the water glass so nobody would guess what you planned to do."

Jenny nodded, somewhat feverishly, then looked crestfallen. "Only I made a terrible mistake. I didn't know Pa had killed Virgil. I was sure Tim had done it."

Lauralee said nothing. She'd read somewhere that the insane were stronger than normal people. Much stronger. Wasn't there something in this kitchen she could use as a weapon?

She saw the realization of what she'd admitted dawn in Jenny's face, and the sight was horrible.

"You'll tell Brice," she said, glaring at Lauralee, "and he won't want me. He won't make me into a lady."

It was useless for Lauralee to say that she would not tell; even in her madness, Jenny would know that for the lie it was. Lauralee turned and fled through the kitchen doorway, planning to escape by the front door and find the others.

Only Jenny caught up to her in the darkened dining room and knocked her to the floor, forcing the wind from her lungs. Strong hands tangled in Lauralee's hair; a murderess's breath burned in her face. She

337

tried to struggle, but Jenny was kneeling on her upper arms.

"Jenny, please—listen to reason—"

"You! It was all because you wouldn't let go of Virgil, even when he didn't want you anymore! It was all because of you!" A shower of Jenny's spittle rained down in Lauralee's face and she freed her hands from her hair with a painful wrench, only to close them around Lauralee's throat. "How I hated you, you icy, self-righteous bitch! How we both hated you, Virgil and me!"

Lauralee was desperate for a moment's freedom. She knew she could gain the upper hand and save herself if she could just get one arm free, but Jenny's fingers were digging into her throat and soon she wouldn't be able to speak at all. "He laughed about you, Jenny!" she cried. "You were a joke to Virgil! Did you think I didn't know?"

The lie stunned Jenny, just as Lauralee had prayed it would. Her fingers loosened and one of her knees slipped and Lauralee freed her arms, caught her hands in Jenny's hair, and thrust her off. It was so dark, though, and Lauralee could barely see. She crouched under the dining-room table like a hunted animal, trying to catch her breath, to think.

Jenny's voice was pitifully plaintive in the darkness. "Did he really laugh?"

Lauralee wasn't about to answer and give herself away. Lord God in heaven, she prayed, let her think I got out.

"He did laugh!" Jenny screamed in her madness, and Lauralee shuddered to see her skirt brushing past the table, back and forth, within touching distance. "He *did* laugh at me, didn't he, Lauralee?"

Lauralee closed her eyes, holding her breath. She

felt the swish of Jenny's skirt as she whirled away from the table, heard a drawer open, a cylinder click.

"You'd better come out, Lauralee," Jenny wheedled in a singsong voice. "I have a gun here, and I'm going to start shooting. All I have to do is light a lamp, and then I'll be able to see you."

Lauralee gauged her chances of reaching the kitchen door before Jenny could light a lamp and fire the gun, and made a dive. The light flared just as she touched a hand to the door. She pushed as hard as she could and rolled through the opening.

Jenny screamed and fired two shots. Lauralee waited for the pain, but there was none. There was only the warm tile under her cheeks and palms and distant shouting and the glow of the fire.

She got to her feet slowly, silently, like an animal being stalked, but she could not run. She must have stood there, so near freedom, fro. in horror and fear, for fully a minute.

"Jenny?" she whispered when she dared.

There was no answer, only a deep, telling silence that seemed to pulse like a heartbeat.

"Jenny?" she called again.

This time, Lauralee thought she heard a moan. She pressed one palm to the door and pushed, holding her breath. The light of the kitchen lanterns spilled into the dining room, spilled onto Jenny, who lay on the floor in a crimson circle of her own blood. Lauralee would never forget her eyes, open and staring.

She backed away, muttering a prayer, and then she whirled, running blindly out into the red and flickering night. Some instinct drove her to the willow tree and the little pond, and she stumbled, sobbing, as she hurled herself toward it.

Jay was there, safe and strong. She could see him,

his familiar frame outlined by the light of the fire. She tried to cry out, but his name would not pass her parched and swollen throat.

There were other people gathered near the pond, too, Lauralee saw, as she fell and got up again and stumbled on. Janet. The two young boys who worked in the barn.

And Brice.

Seeing him kneeling there, beside Lucy McCallum's grave, his great broad shoulders heaving with grief, Lauralee forgot her own horror, forgot that Jenny was lying, dead or dying, in the house. She reached Jay and squeezed under his arm, displacing his crutch.

The fire had nearly spent itself, but the smoke was still thick and the air was nearly unbreathable for that and the stench of sodden, charred wheat.

Brice was sobbing Lucy's name. Covered with soot, he pounded at the ground with his huge brawny hands as though to rouse his lost love by the noise and fury of his despair.

Quietly, her nightgown torn and blackened, her face a mask of dirt, Mary stepped out of the shadows, dragging a blanket along with her. Gently, so gently that Lauralee's heart rose into her throat at the sight, she covered Brice's shoulders, knelt beside him on the ground, and drew him into her arms.

Excepting those two, everyone drifted away. Jay leaned on Lauralee and Lauralee leaned on Jay and together they reached the back door of the house.

There, on the step, Lauralee remembered and stopped cold in her tracks.

Jay didn't notice her hesitation; he was intent on the difficult task of making his way up the back steps. "It's been one hell of a night," he rasped.

Tears slipped down Lauralee's face. "Jay," she said, "I think Jenny is dead."

He turned to stare at her. "What?"

Lauralee sat down on the bottom step, leaving Jay no choice but to sit beside her. In a remarkably calm, quiet voice, she explained.

Washington, D.C.

The house that would now be Lauralee's home was a quaint structure of brick, tall and narrow and surrounded by other houses just like it. As the carriage rolled to a stop in front, the door burst open and Kate came through the opening, her skirts bunched in her hands, her face shining and eager.

"They're here!" she cried, dashing down the walk to the gate. "Chance, come quickly. They're here!"

Chance strode along behind her, grinning broadly. "Thank God," he said in tones that carried, and before the driver could attend to the duty, he'd opened the carriage door.

He reached inside and took Alexander into the curve of one arm, using his free hand to help Lauralee down. Jay followed somewhat laboriously, and he was clearly tired, but neither his wife nor anyone else failed to notice the light that shone in his eyes.

Jay was in Washington now, and within the week, he would be a senator. All his dreams had come true.

"I want a complete list of everything you've voted on, with full particulars," he informed Chance as the family moved en masse toward the house, but there was warm affection in his voice despite the sternness of his words.

Kate wrested Alexander from her husband's arms and immediately began spoiling him, making him giggle by nuzzling his nose with her own. "I've bought a whole roomful of toys for you," she told him.

Lauralee looked back, and just as she did so, a soft, fluffy snow began to fall. Almost simultaneously, the gas-powered streetlamps flared into brilliance, casting golden shadows into the twilight.

Kate and Chance went inside, leaving a proud Jay to manage the steps with the help of Lauralee and his cane.

"I hate this thing," he muttered, scowling at the ivory-handled walking stick in his hand.

Lauralee slipped her arm through his. "Nonsense. It makes you look distinguished, Senator."

Jay laughed, the snowflakes catching on the brim of his elegant black top hat and melting along his eyelashes. "I love you," he said. "The moment we're alone—"

Lauralee blushed, as much with anticipation as with scandal. "Jay McCallum!"

He drew her close and kissed her. When the kiss ended, he whispered, "The first thing I'm going to do—"

"The first thing you're going to do," Lauralee hissed, "is catch pneumonia!"

The first thing Jay did, as it happened, was hang a sign over the fireplace in the main parlor. It read RUMSUCKER SALOON and was a favorite topic of conversation in Washington for three tempestuous terms.

AUTHOR'S NOTE

Does someone close to you, a relative or a friend, drink too much? They may be suffering from the disease of alcoholism.

This disease affects entire families, but there is help for you that wasn't available to Lauralee: the Al-Anon Family Groups that meet in your area. Al-Anon members understand, and they care. Please, give them a chance to share their experience, strength, and hope with you.

To find times and dates of meetings near you, check the listing in the white pages of your telephone directory or write:

Al-Anon Family Groups, Inc.
P.O. Box 862
Midtown Station
New York, New York 10018-0862